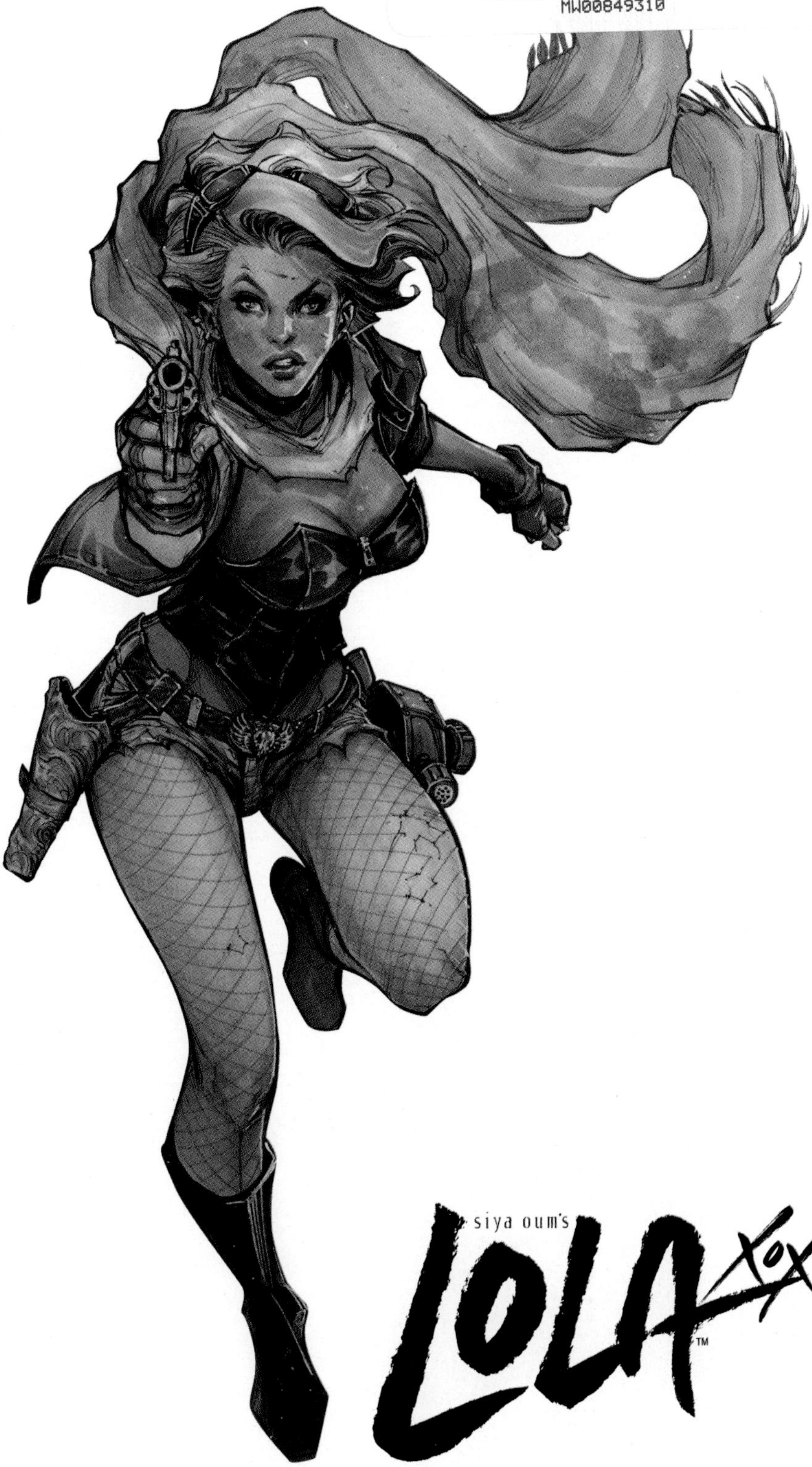

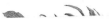

siya oum's

LOLA XOXO™

Siva Oum

story and illustrations

Josh Reed

lettering

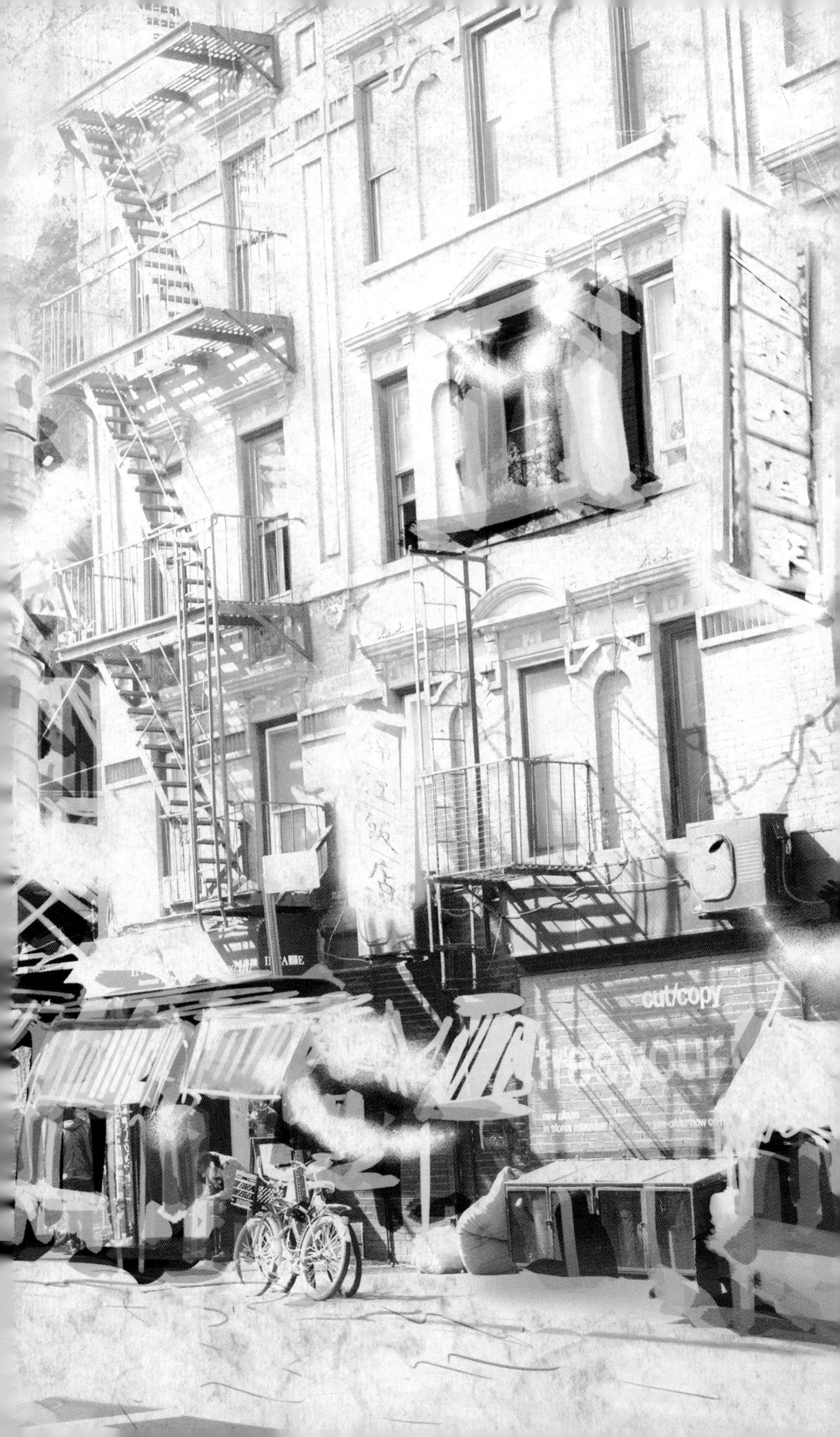
cut/copy
new album

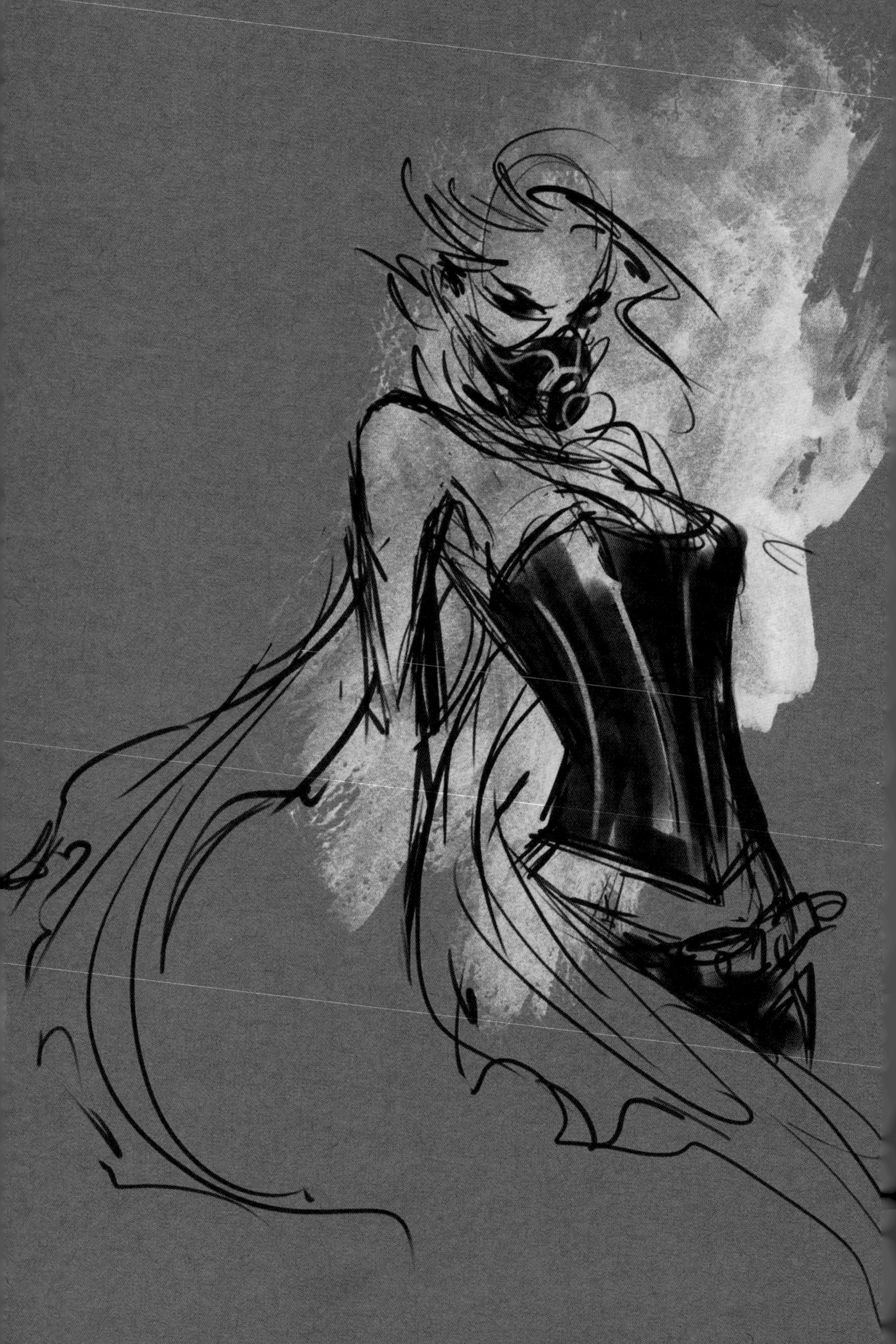

esiya oum's

LOLA xoxo™

LOLA XOXO™ VOLUME 1
Collects material originally published as LOLA XOXO™ vol. 1 Issues 1-6

PUBLISHED BY ASPEN MLT, INC.
Office of Publication: 5701 W. Slauson Ave Suite. 120, Culver City, CA 90230.
The Aspen MLT, Inc. logo® is a registered trademark of Aspen MLT, Inc. LOLA XOXO™ and the LOLA XOXO logo,
are the trademarks of Siya Oum. The entire contents of this book, all artwork, characters and their likenesses are © 2015 Siya
Oum and Aspen MLT, Inc. All Rights Reserved. Any similarities between names, characters, persons, and/or institutions in this
publication with persons living or dead or institutions is unintended and is purely coincidental. With the exception of artwork
used for review purposes, none of the contents of this book may be reprinted, reproduced or transmitted by any means or in
any form without the express written consent of Aspen MLT, Inc. PRINTED IN THE UNITED STATES OF AMERICA

Address correspondence to:
ASPEN COMICS *c/o*
Aspen MLT Inc.
5701 W. Slauson Ave. Suite. 120
Culver City, CA. 90230-6946
or fanmail@aspencomics.com

Visit us on the web at:
www.aspencomics.com
www.aspenstore.com
www.facebook.com/aspencomics
www.twitter.com/aspencomics

COLLECTED EDITION EDITORS: GABE CARASCO, MARK ROSLAN AND FRANK MASTROMAURO
ORIGINAL SERIES EDITORS: VINCE HERNANDEZ AND FRANK MASTROMAURO
BOOK DESIGN: MARK ROSLAN, CHAZ RIGGS AND PETER STEIGERWALD
COVER DESIGN: CHAZ RIGGS
COVER ILLUSTRATION: SIYA OUM

For Aspen:

FOUNDER: MICHAEL TURNER
CO-OWNER: PETER STEIGERWALD
CO-OWNER/PRESIDENT: FRANK MASTROMAURO
VICE PRESIDENT/EDITOR IN CHIEF: VINCE HERNANDEZ
VICE PRESIDENT/DESIGN AND PRODUCTION: MARK ROSLAN
EDITORIAL ASSISTANTS: JOSH REED, GABE CARASCO
PRODUCTIONI ASSISANT: CHAZ RIGGS
OFFICE MANAGER: MEGAN MADRIGAL
ASPENSTORE.COM: CHRIS RUPP

To find the Comic Shop
nearest you...

888-COMIC-BOOK
csls.diamondcomics.com
1-888-266-4226

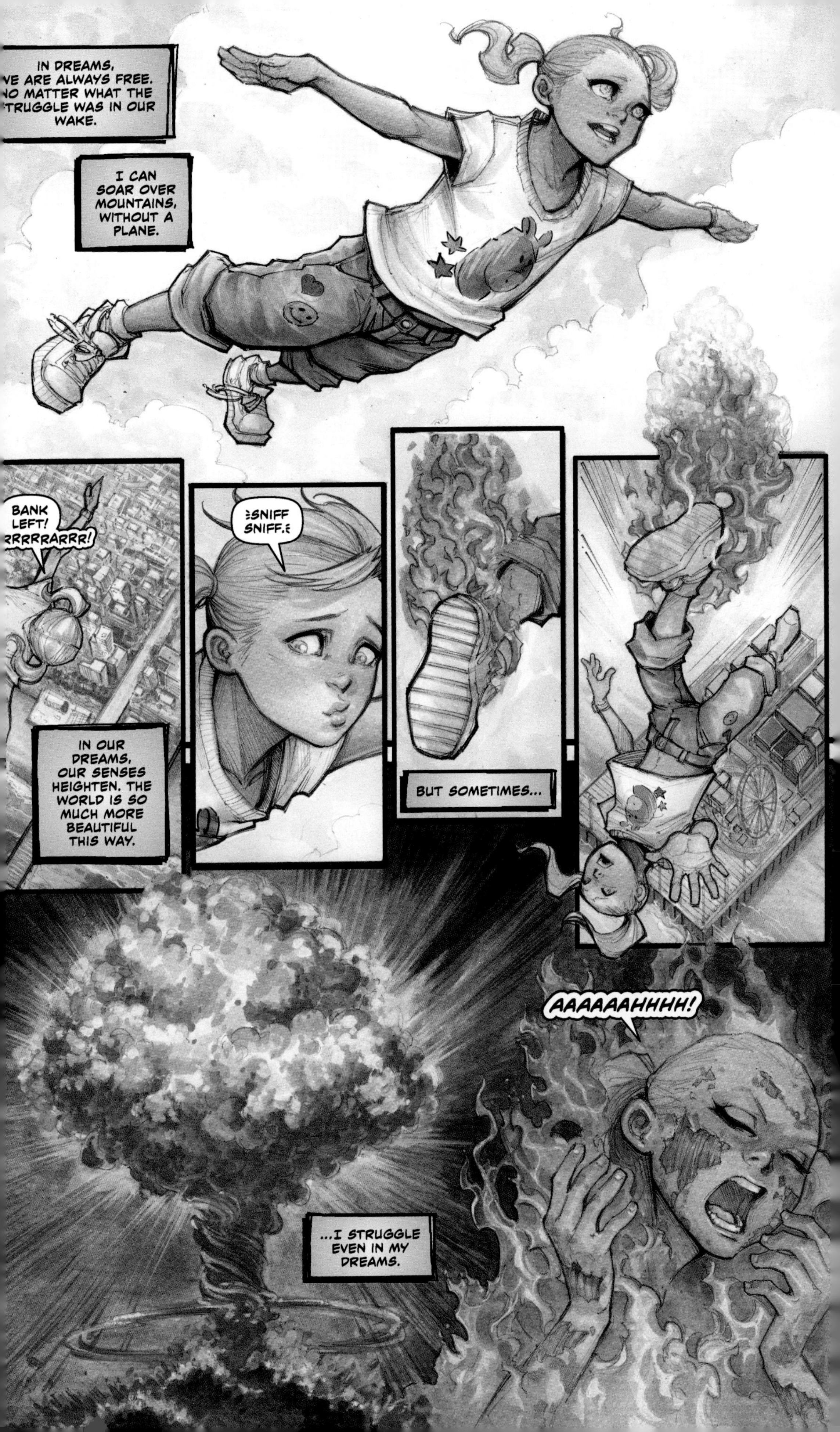
IN DREAMS, WE ARE ALWAYS FREE. NO MATTER WHAT THE STRUGGLE WAS IN OUR WAKE.
I CAN SOAR OVER MOUNTAINS, WITHOUT A PLANE.
BANK LEFT! RRRRRARRR!
IN OUR DREAMS, OUR SENSES HEIGHTEN. THE WORLD IS SO MUCH MORE BEAUTIFUL THIS WAY.
SNIFF SNIFF.
BUT SOMETIMES...
...I STRUGGLE EVEN IN MY DREAMS.
AAAAAAHHHH!

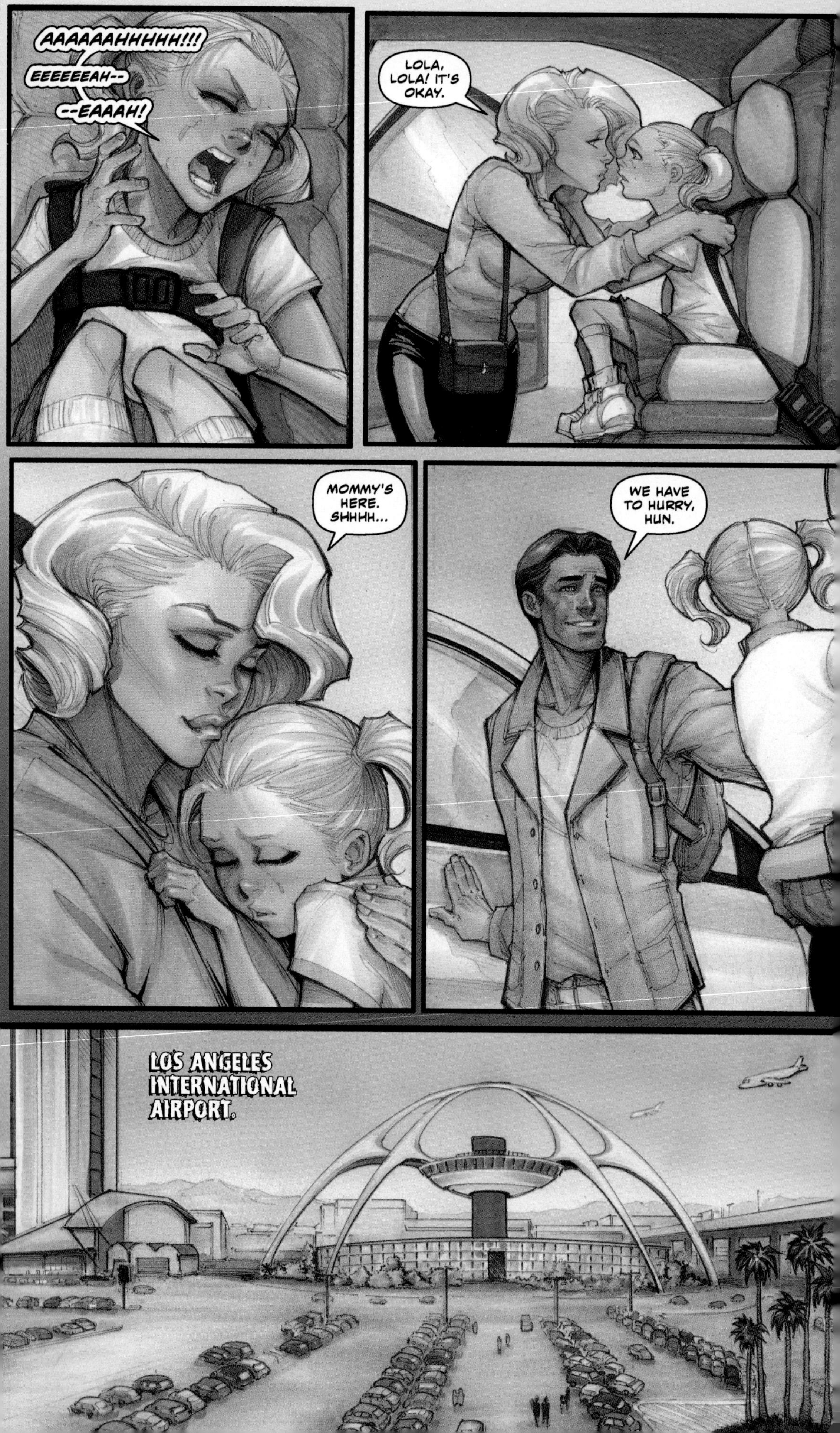
AAAAAAHHHHH!!!
EEEEEEAH--
--EAAAH!
LOLA, LOLA! IT'S OKAY.
MOMMY'S HERE. SHHHH...
WE HAVE TO HURRY, HUN.
LOS ANGELES INTERNATIONAL AIRPORT.

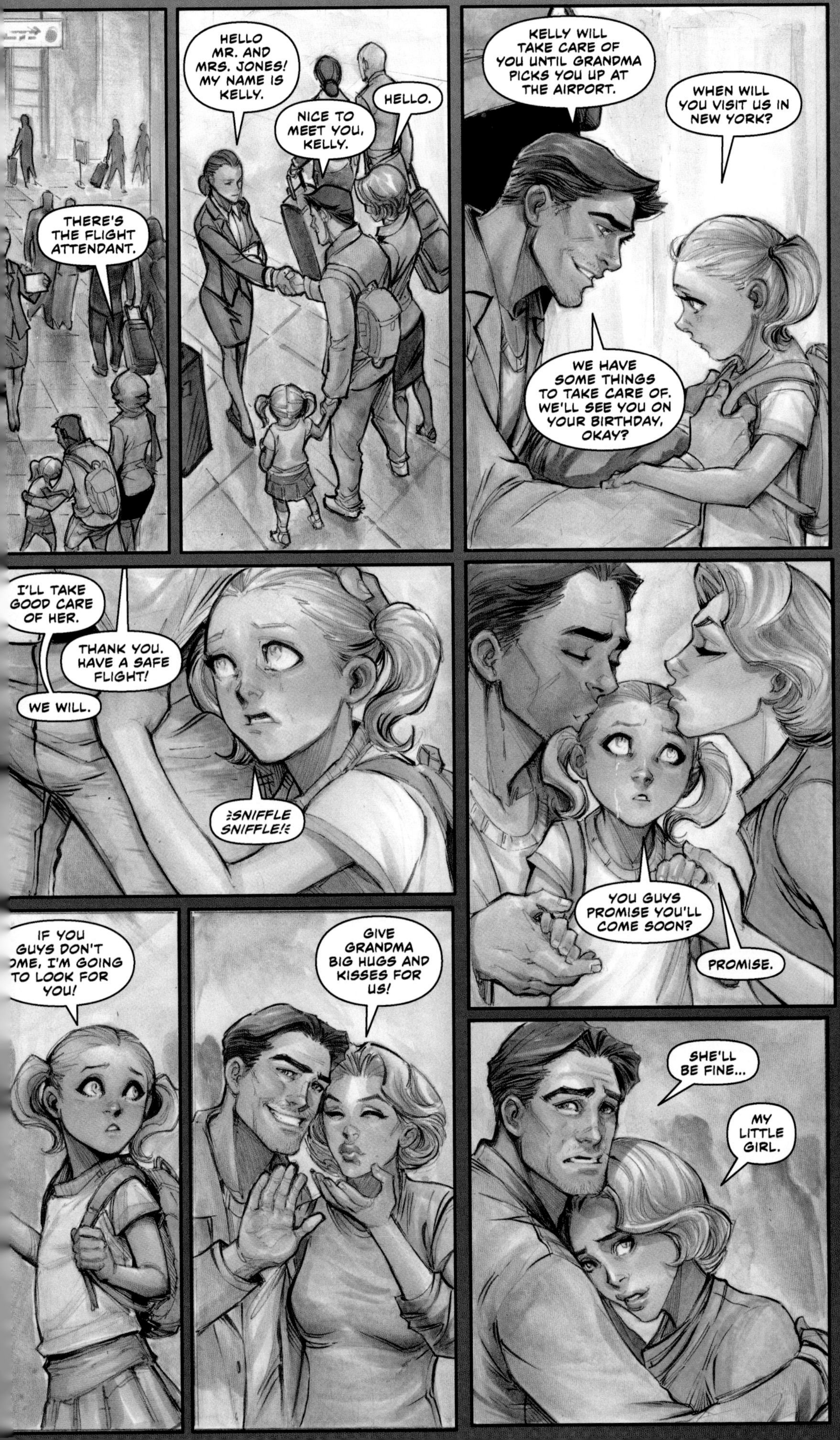
THERE'S THE FLIGHT ATTENDANT.
HELLO MR. AND MRS. JONES! MY NAME IS KELLY.
NICE TO MEET YOU, KELLY.
HELLO.
KELLY WILL TAKE CARE OF YOU UNTIL GRANDMA PICKS YOU UP AT THE AIRPORT.
WHEN WILL YOU VISIT US IN NEW YORK?
WE HAVE SOME THINGS TO TAKE CARE OF. WE'LL SEE YOU ON YOUR BIRTHDAY, OKAY?
I'LL TAKE GOOD CARE OF HER.
THANK YOU. HAVE A SAFE FLIGHT!
WE WILL.
SNIFFLE SNIFFLE!
YOU GUYS PROMISE YOU'LL COME SOON?
PROMISE.
IF YOU GUYS DON'T OME, I'M GOING TO LOOK FOR YOU!
GIVE GRANDMA BIG HUGS AND KISSES FOR US!
SHE'LL BE FINE...
MY LITTLE GIRL.

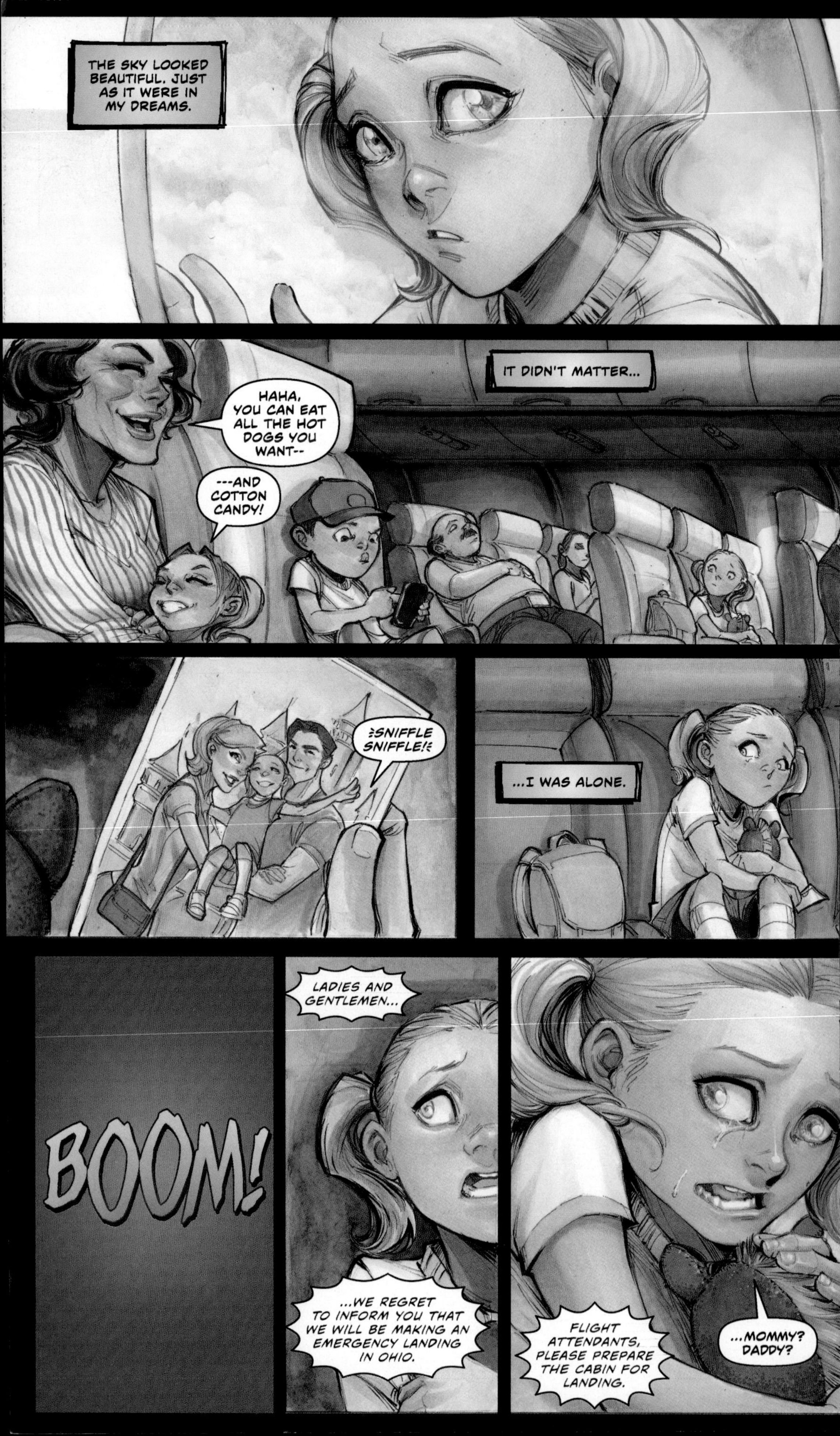
THE SKY LOOKED BEAUTIFUL. JUST AS IT WERE IN MY DREAMS.
IT DIDN'T MATTER...
HAHA, YOU CAN EAT ALL THE HOT DOGS YOU WANT--
---AND COTTON CANDY!
SNIFFLE SNIFFLE!
...I WAS ALONE.
BOOM!
LADIES AND GENTLEMEN...
...WE REGRET TO INFORM YOU THAT WE WILL BE MAKING AN EMERGENCY LANDING IN OHIO.
FLIGHT ATTENDANTS, PLEASE PREPARE THE CABIN FOR LANDING.
...MOMMY? DADDY?

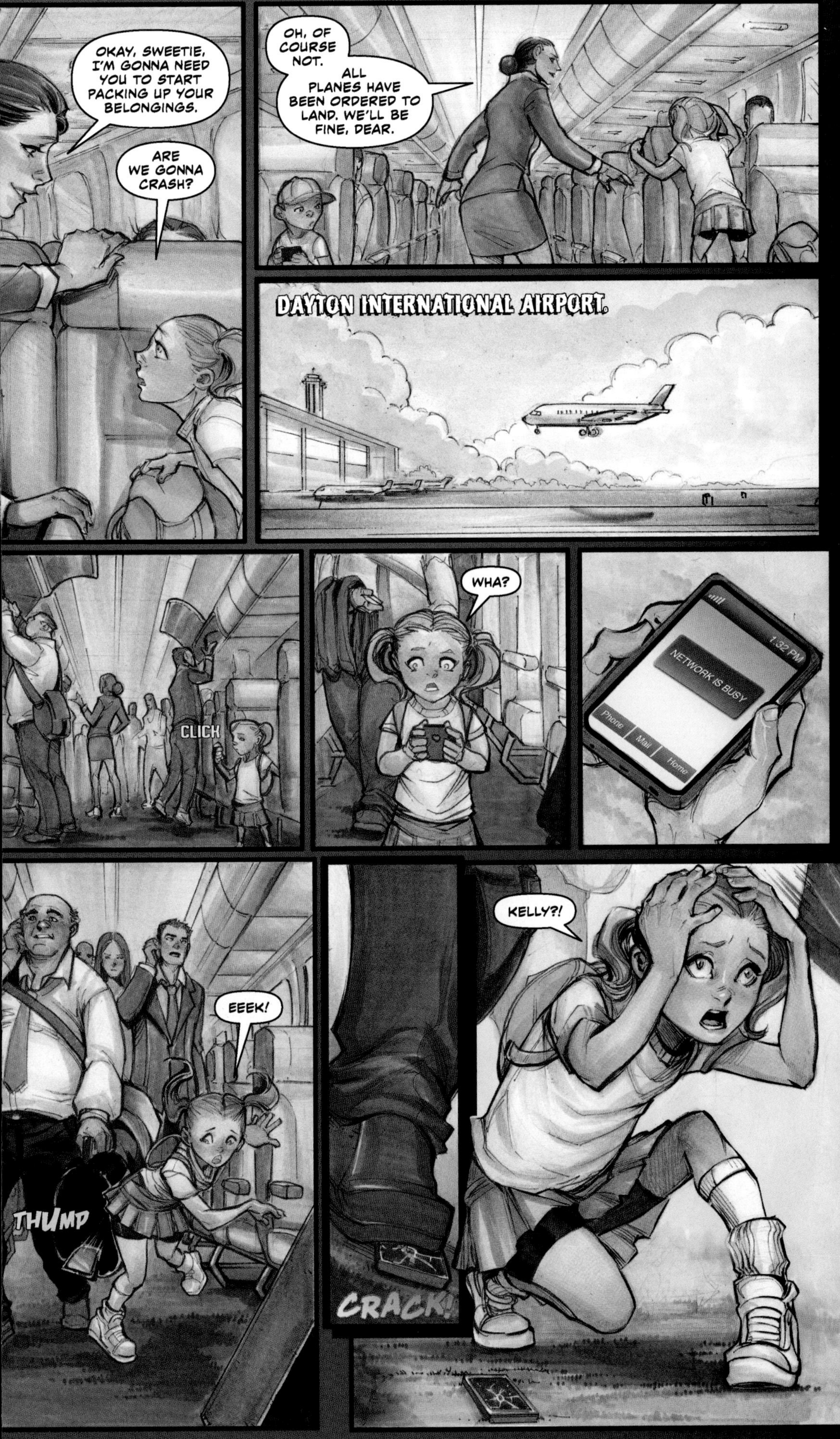
OKAY, SWEETIE, I'M GONNA NEED YOU TO START PACKING UP YOUR BELONGINGS.
ARE WE GONNA CRASH?
OH, OF COURSE NOT.
ALL PLANES HAVE BEEN ORDERED TO LAND. WE'LL BE FINE, DEAR.
DAYTON INTERNATIONAL AIRPORT.
CLICK
WHA?
1:32 PM
NETWORK IS BUSY
Phone
Mail
Home
EEEK!
THUMP
KELLY?!
CRACK!

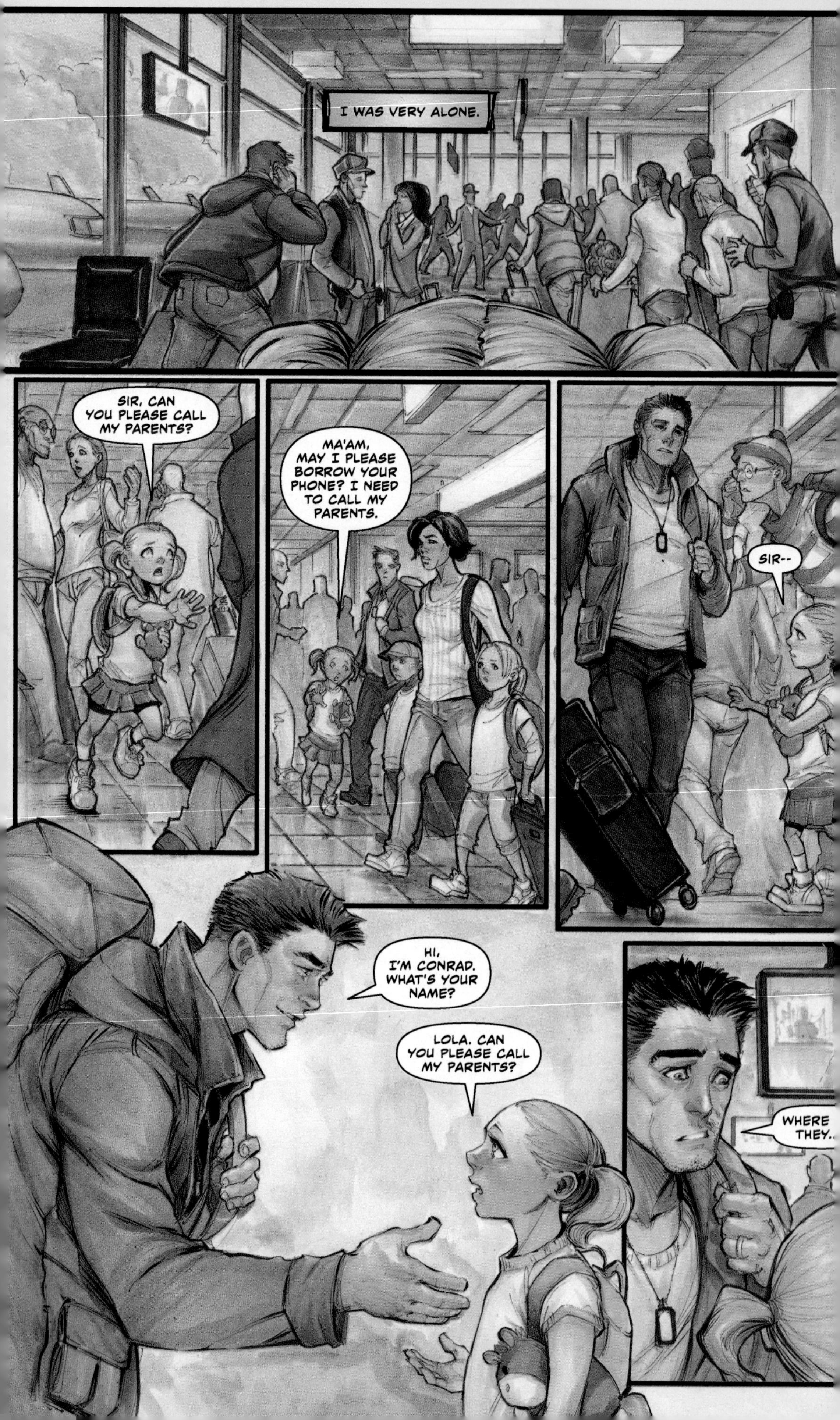

I WAS VERY ALONE.
SIR, CAN YOU PLEASE CALL MY PARENTS?
MA'AM, MAY I PLEASE BORROW YOUR PHONE? I NEED TO CALL MY PARENTS.
SIR--
HI, I'M CONRAD. WHAT'S YOUR NAME?
LOLA. CAN YOU PLEASE CALL MY PARENTS?
WHERE THEY...

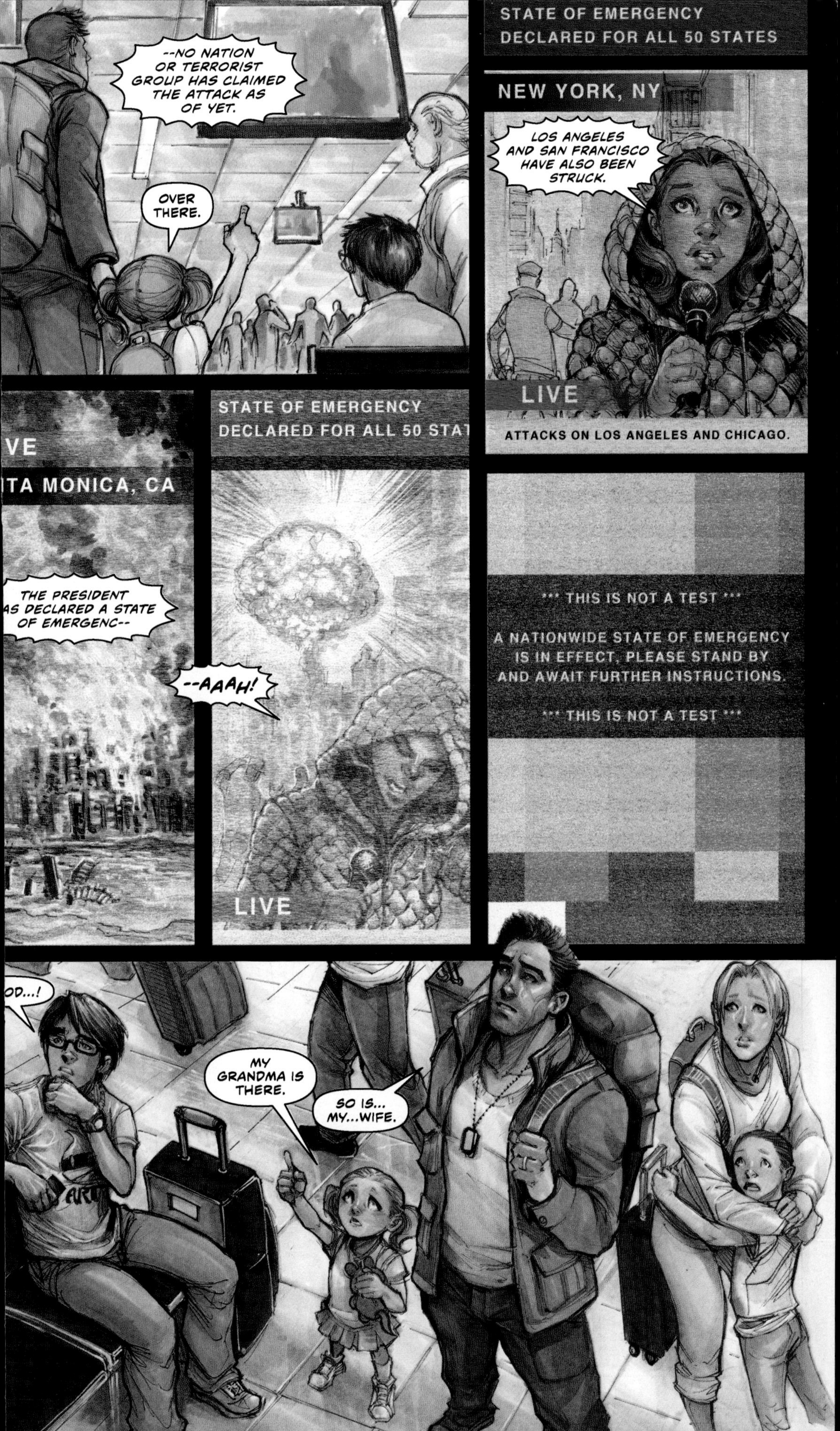
--NO NATION OR TERRORIST GROUP HAS CLAIMED THE ATTACK AS OF YET.
OVER THERE.
STATE OF EMERGENCY DECLARED FOR ALL 50 STATES
NEW YORK, NY
LOS ANGELES AND SAN FRANCISCO HAVE ALSO BEEN STRUCK.
LIVE
ATTACKS ON LOS ANGELES AND CHICAGO.
VE
ITA MONICA, CA
THE PRESIDENT AS DECLARED A STATE OF EMERGENC--
STATE OF EMERGENCY DECLARED FOR ALL 50 STAT
--AAAH!
LIVE
*** THIS IS NOT A TEST ***
A NATIONWIDE STATE OF EMERGENCY IS IN EFFECT, PLEASE STAND BY AND AWAIT FURTHER INSTRUCTIONS.
*** THIS IS NOT A TEST ***
OD...!
MY GRANDMA IS THERE.
SO IS... MY...WIFE.

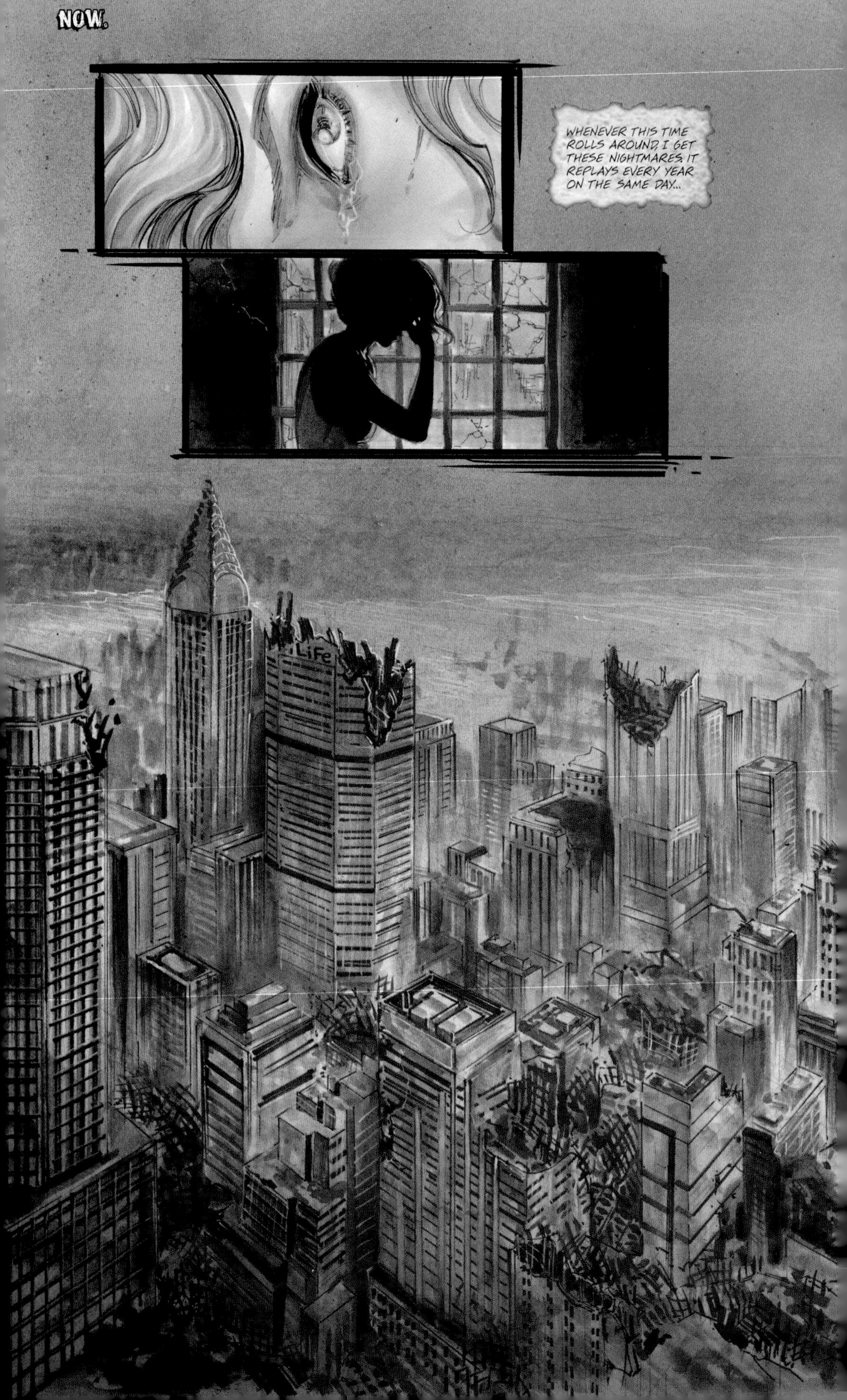
NOW.
WHENEVER THIS TIME ROLLS AROUND, I GET THESE NIGHTMARES. IT REPLAYS EVERY YEAR ON THE SAME DAY...
LiFe

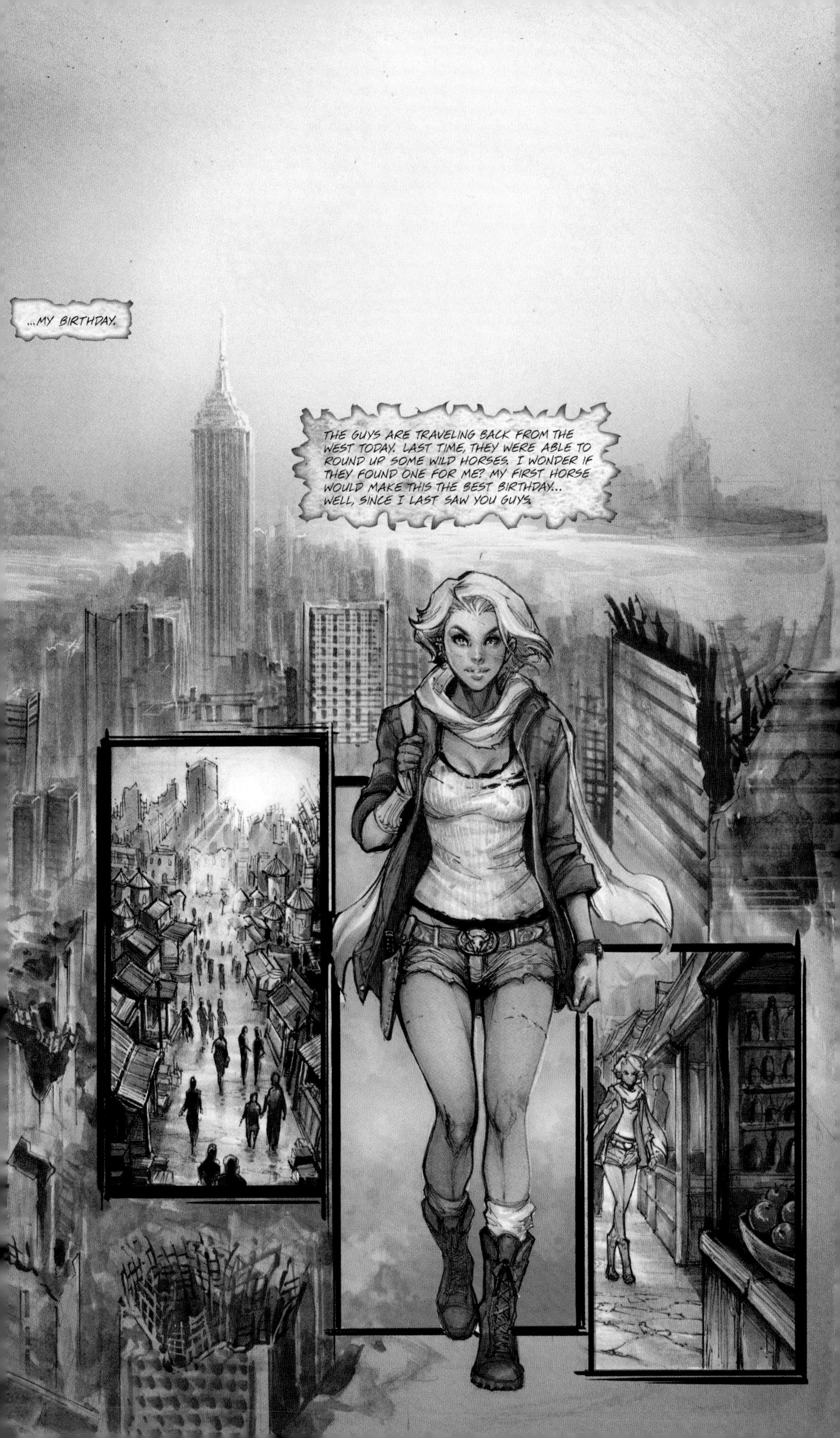
...MY BIRTHDAY.
THE GUYS ARE TRAVELING BACK FROM THE WEST TODAY. LAST TIME, THEY WERE ABLE TO ROUND UP SOME WILD HORSES. I WONDER IF THEY FOUND ONE FOR ME? MY FIRST HORSE WOULD MAKE THIS THE BEST BIRTHDAY... WELL, SINCE I LAST SAW YOU GUYS.

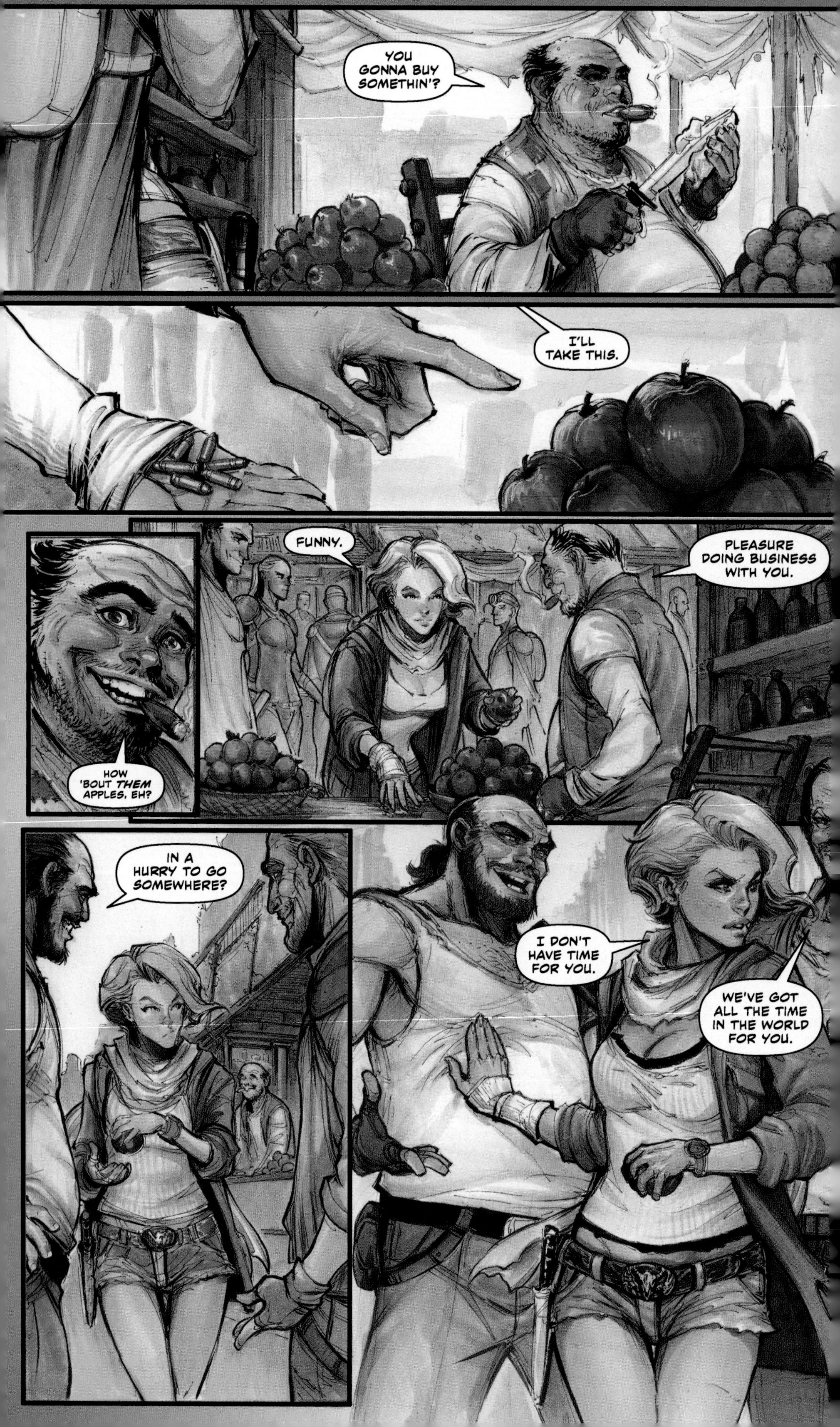
YOU GONNA BUY SOMETHIN'?
I'LL TAKE THIS.
HOW 'BOUT *THEM* APPLES, EH?
FUNNY.
PLEASURE DOING BUSINESS WITH YOU.
IN A HURRY TO GO SOMEWHERE?
I DON'T HAVE TIME FOR YOU.
WE'VE GOT ALL THE TIME IN THE WORLD FOR YOU.

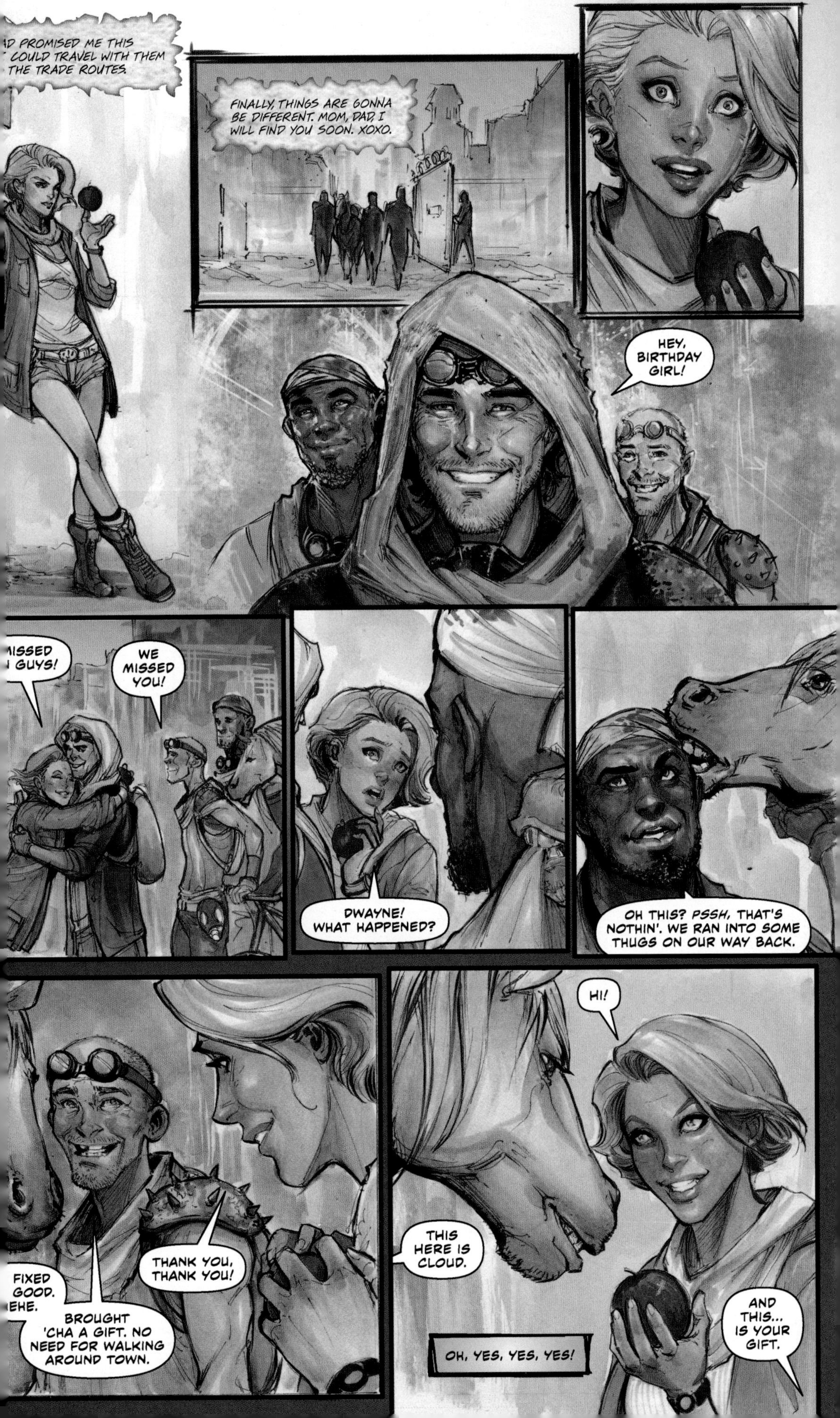

AD PROMISED ME THIS
COULD TRAVEL WITH THEM
THE TRADE ROUTES.
FINALLY, THINGS ARE GONNA BE DIFFERENT. MOM, DAD, I WILL FIND YOU SOON. XOXO.
HEY, BIRTHDAY GIRL!
MISSED GUYS!
WE MISSED YOU!
DWAYNE! WHAT HAPPENED?
OH THIS? PSSH, THAT'S NOTHIN'. WE RAN INTO SOME THUGS ON OUR WAY BACK.
FIXED GOOD. EHE.
BROUGHT 'CHA A GIFT. NO NEED FOR WALKING AROUND TOWN.
THANK YOU, THANK YOU!
HI!
THIS HERE IS CLOUD.
AND THIS... IS YOUR GIFT.
OH, YES, YES, YES!

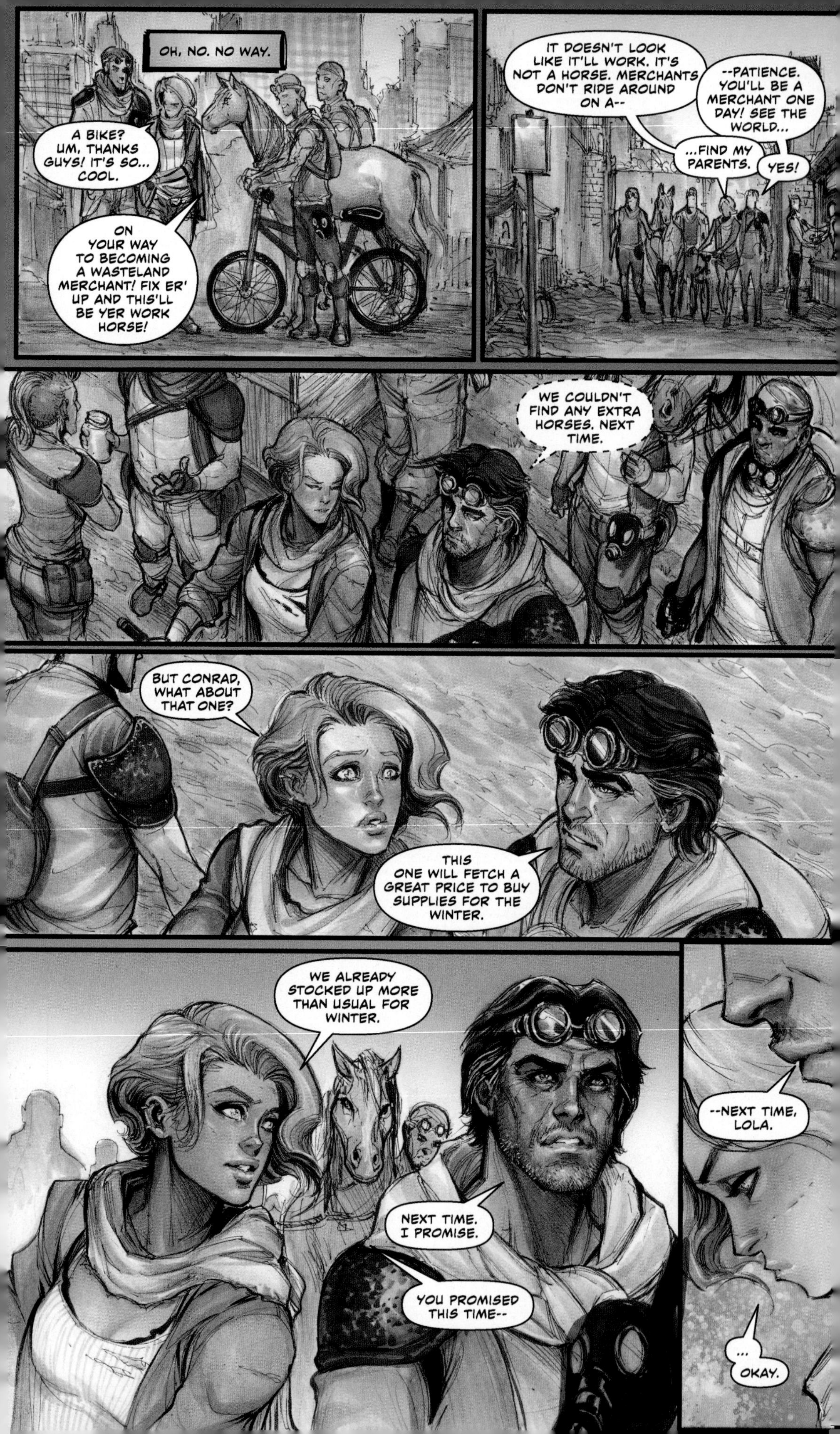
OH, NO. NO WAY.
A BIKE? UM, THANKS GUYS! IT'S SO... COOL.
ON YOUR WAY TO BECOMING A WASTELAND MERCHANT! FIX ER' UP AND THIS'LL BE YER WORK HORSE!
IT DOESN'T LOOK LIKE IT'LL WORK. IT'S NOT A HORSE. MERCHANTS DON'T RIDE AROUND ON A--
--PATIENCE. YOU'LL BE A MERCHANT ONE DAY! SEE THE WORLD...
...FIND MY PARENTS.
YES!
WE COULDN'T FIND ANY EXTRA HORSES. NEXT TIME.
BUT CONRAD, WHAT ABOUT THAT ONE?
THIS ONE WILL FETCH A GREAT PRICE TO BUY SUPPLIES FOR THE WINTER.
WE ALREADY STOCKED UP MORE THAN USUAL FOR WINTER.
NEXT TIME. I PROMISE.
YOU PROMISED THIS TIME--
--NEXT TIME, LOLA.
... OKAY.

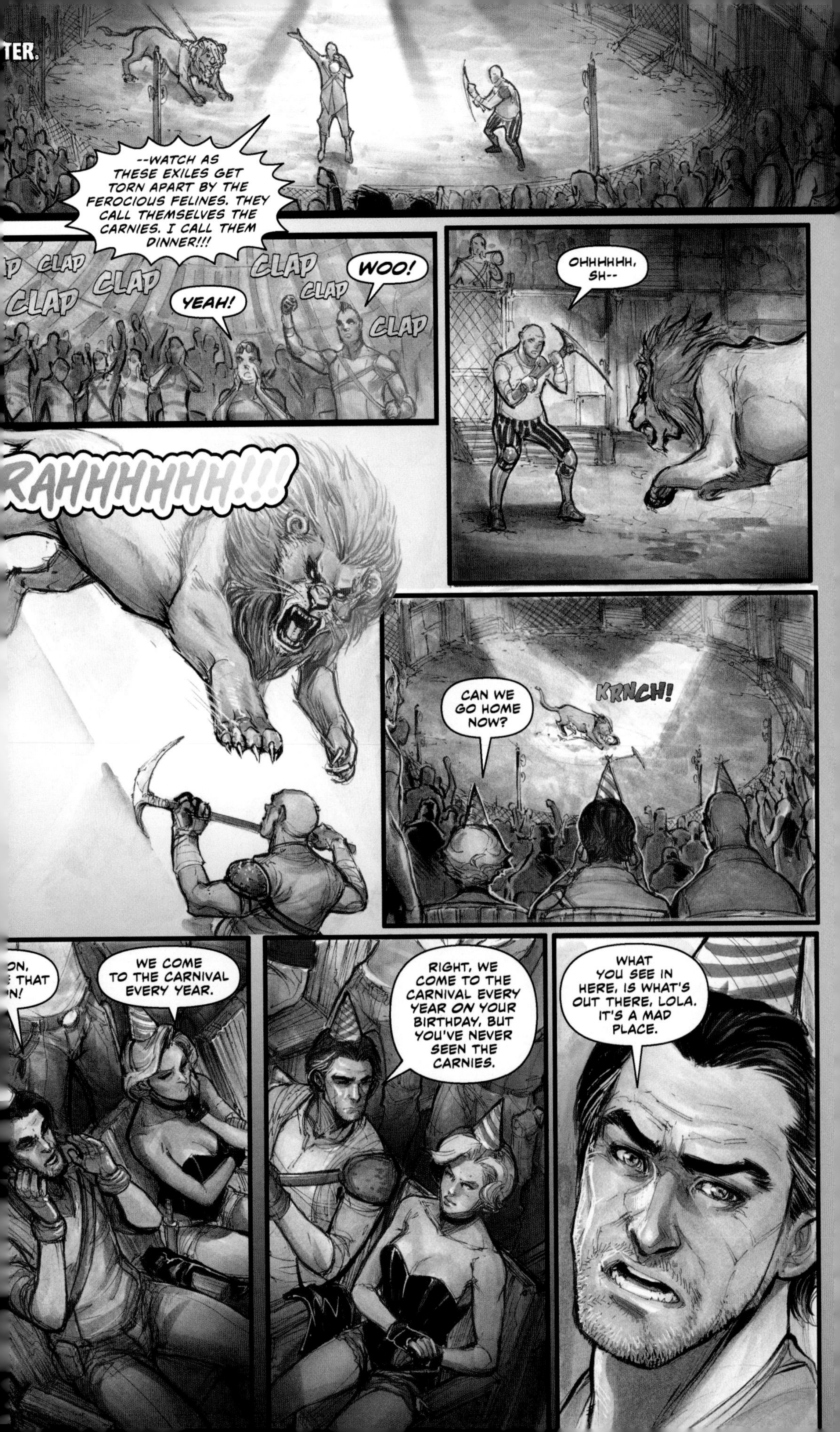
TER.
--WATCH AS THESE EXILES GET TORN APART BY THE FEROCIOUS FELINES. THEY CALL THEMSELVES THE CARNIES. I CALL THEM DINNER!!!
CLAP CLAP CLAP CLAP CLAP CLAP CLAP
YEAH!
WOO!
OHHHHHH, SH--
RAHHHHHH!!!
CAN WE GO HOME NOW?
KRNCH!
WE COME TO THE CARNIVAL EVERY YEAR.
RIGHT, WE COME TO THE CARNIVAL EVERY YEAR ON YOUR BIRTHDAY, BUT YOU'VE NEVER SEEN THE CARNIES.
WHAT YOU SEE IN HERE, IS WHAT'S OUT THERE, LOLA. IT'S A MAD PLACE.

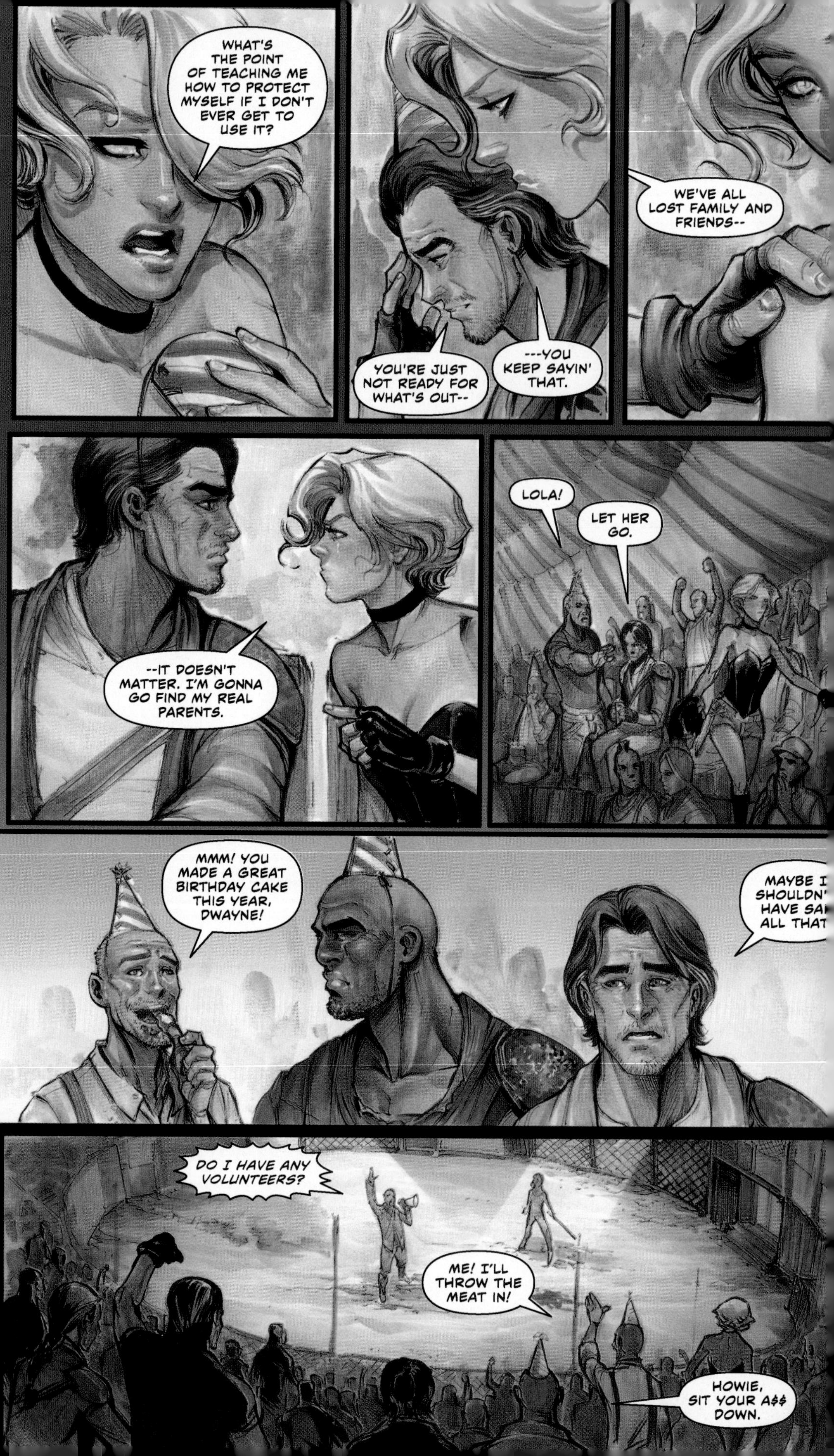
WHAT'S THE POINT OF TEACHING ME HOW TO PROTECT MYSELF IF I DON'T EVER GET TO USE IT?
YOU'RE JUST NOT READY FOR WHAT'S OUT--
---YOU KEEP SAYIN' THAT.
WE'VE ALL LOST FAMILY AND FRIENDS--
--IT DOESN'T MATTER. I'M GONNA GO FIND MY REAL PARENTS.
LOLA!
LET HER GO.
MMM! YOU MADE A GREAT BIRTHDAY CAKE THIS YEAR, DWAYNE!
MAYBE I SHOULDN' HAVE SA ALL THAT
DO I HAVE ANY VOLUNTEERS?
ME! I'LL THROW THE MEAT IN!
HOWIE, SIT YOUR A$$ DOWN.

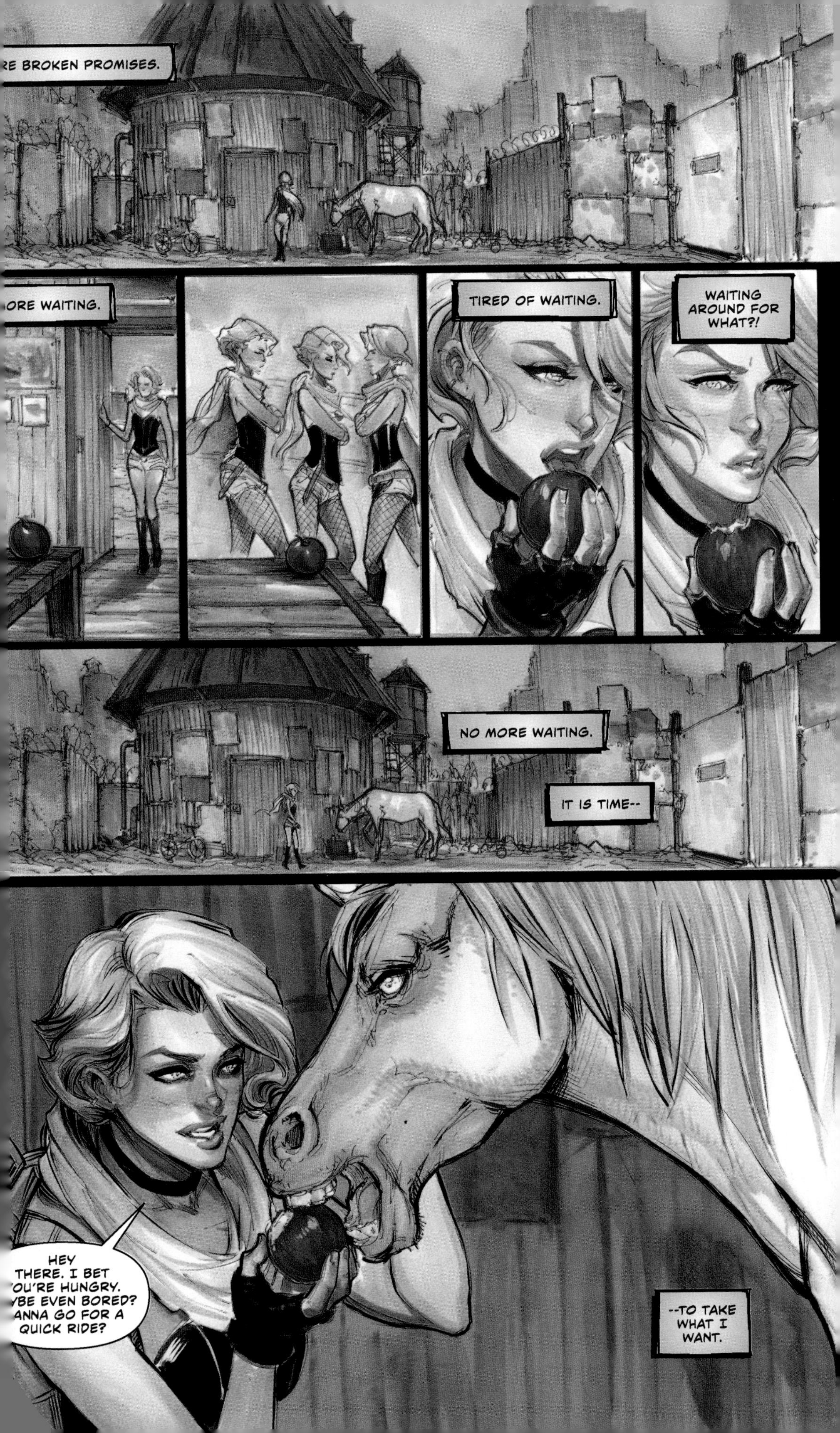
RE BROKEN PROMISES.
ORE WAITING.
TIRED OF WAITING.
WAITING AROUND FOR WHAT?!
NO MORE WAITING.
IT IS TIME--
HEY THERE. I BET OU'RE HUNGRY. YBE EVEN BORED? ANNA GO FOR A QUICK RIDE?
--TO TAKE WHAT I WANT.

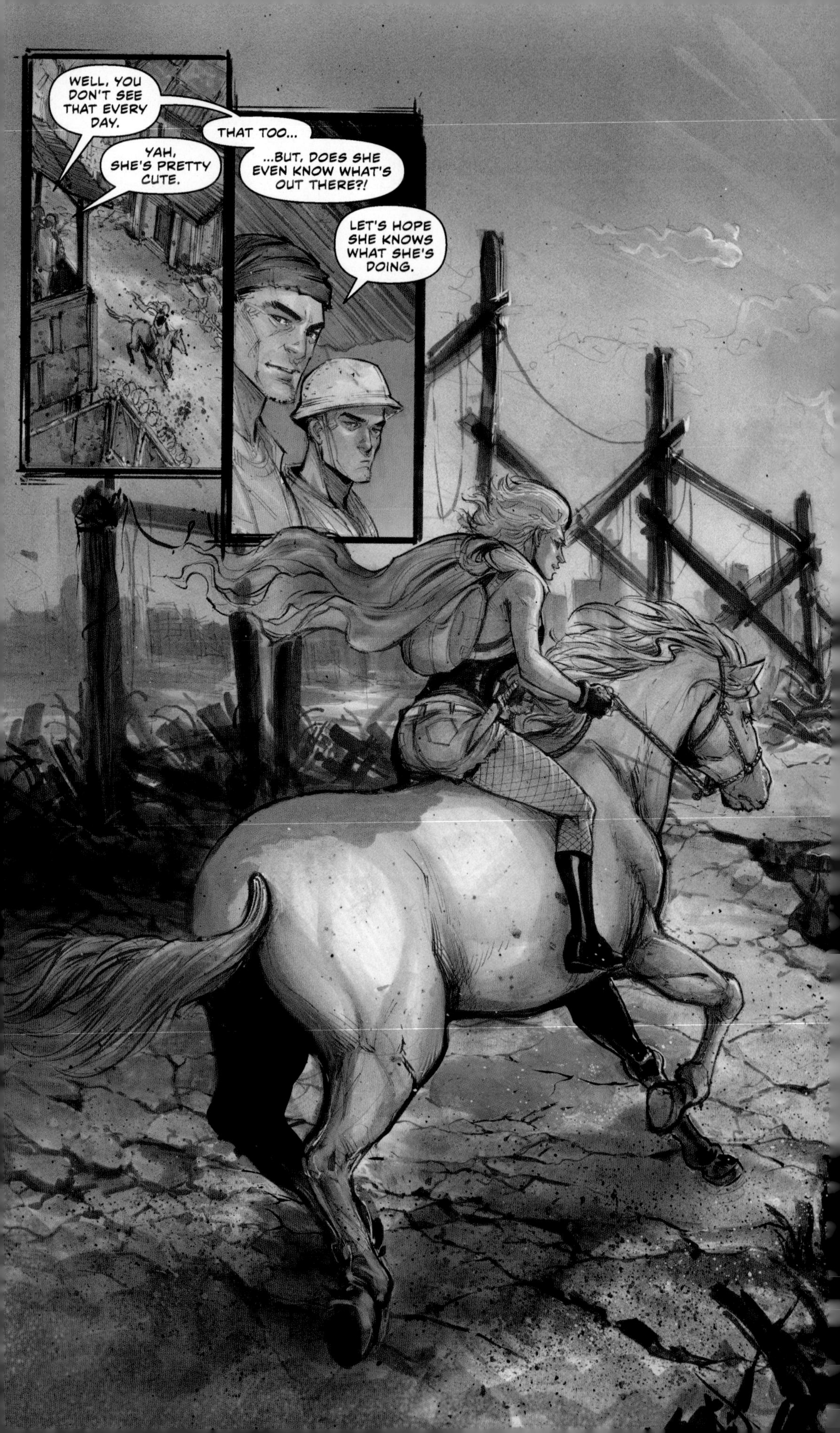
WELL, YOU DON'T SEE THAT EVERY DAY.
YAH, SHE'S PRETTY CUTE.
THAT TOO...
...BUT, DOES SHE EVEN KNOW WHAT'S OUT THERE?!
LET'S HOPE SHE KNOWS WHAT SHE'S DOING.

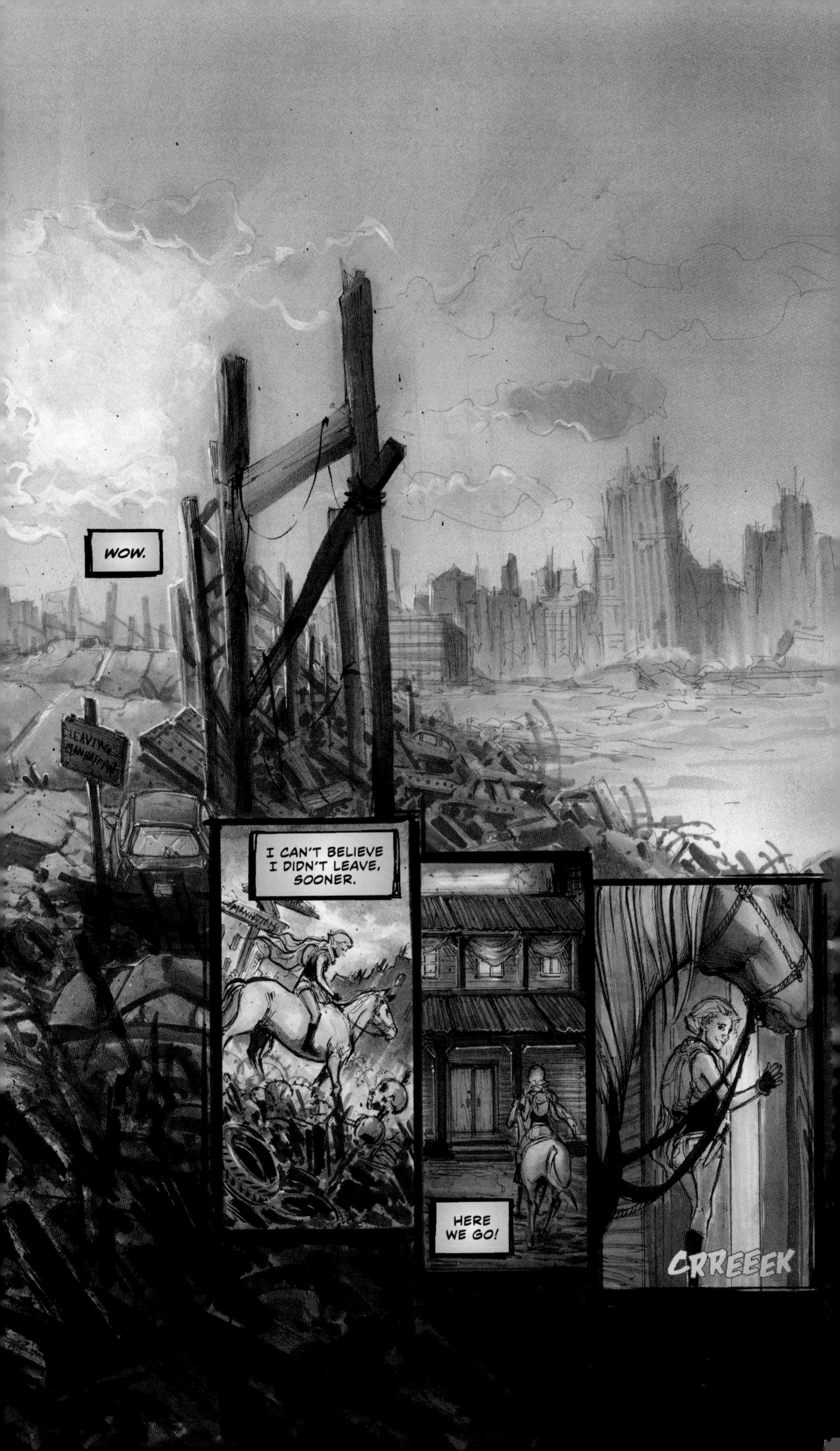
WOW.
I CAN'T BELIEVE I DIDN'T LEAVE, SOONER.
HERE WE GO!
CRREEEK

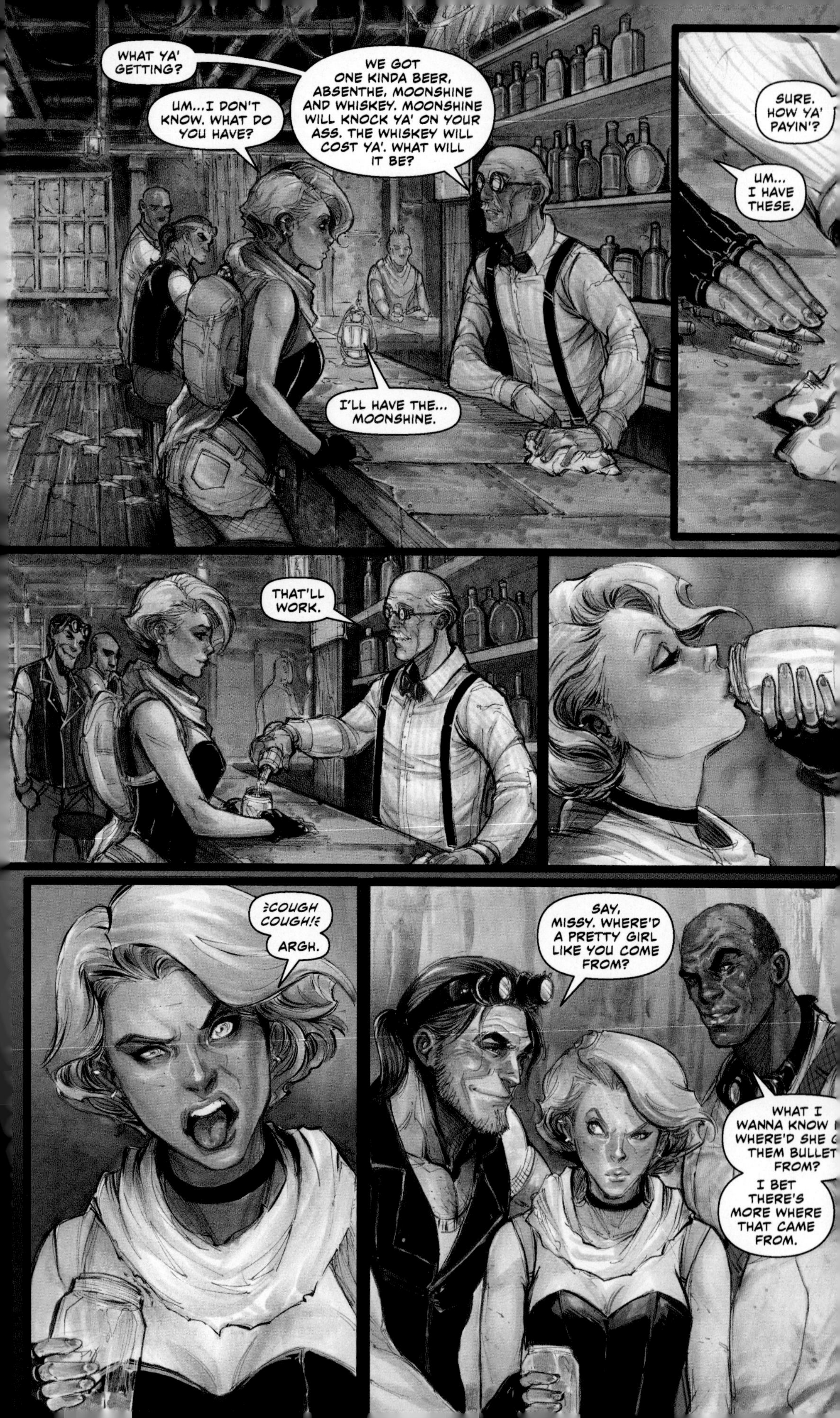
WHAT YA' GETTING?
UM...I DON'T KNOW. WHAT DO YOU HAVE?
WE GOT ONE KINDA BEER, ABSENTHE, MOONSHINE AND WHISKEY. MOONSHINE WILL KNOCK YA' ON YOUR ASS. THE WHISKEY WILL COST YA'. WHAT WILL IT BE?
I'LL HAVE THE... MOONSHINE.
SURE. HOW YA' PAYIN'?
UM... I HAVE THESE.
THAT'LL WORK.
COUGH COUGH!
ARGH.
SAY, MISSY. WHERE'D A PRETTY GIRL LIKE YOU COME FROM?
I BET THERE'S MORE WHERE THAT CAME FROM.

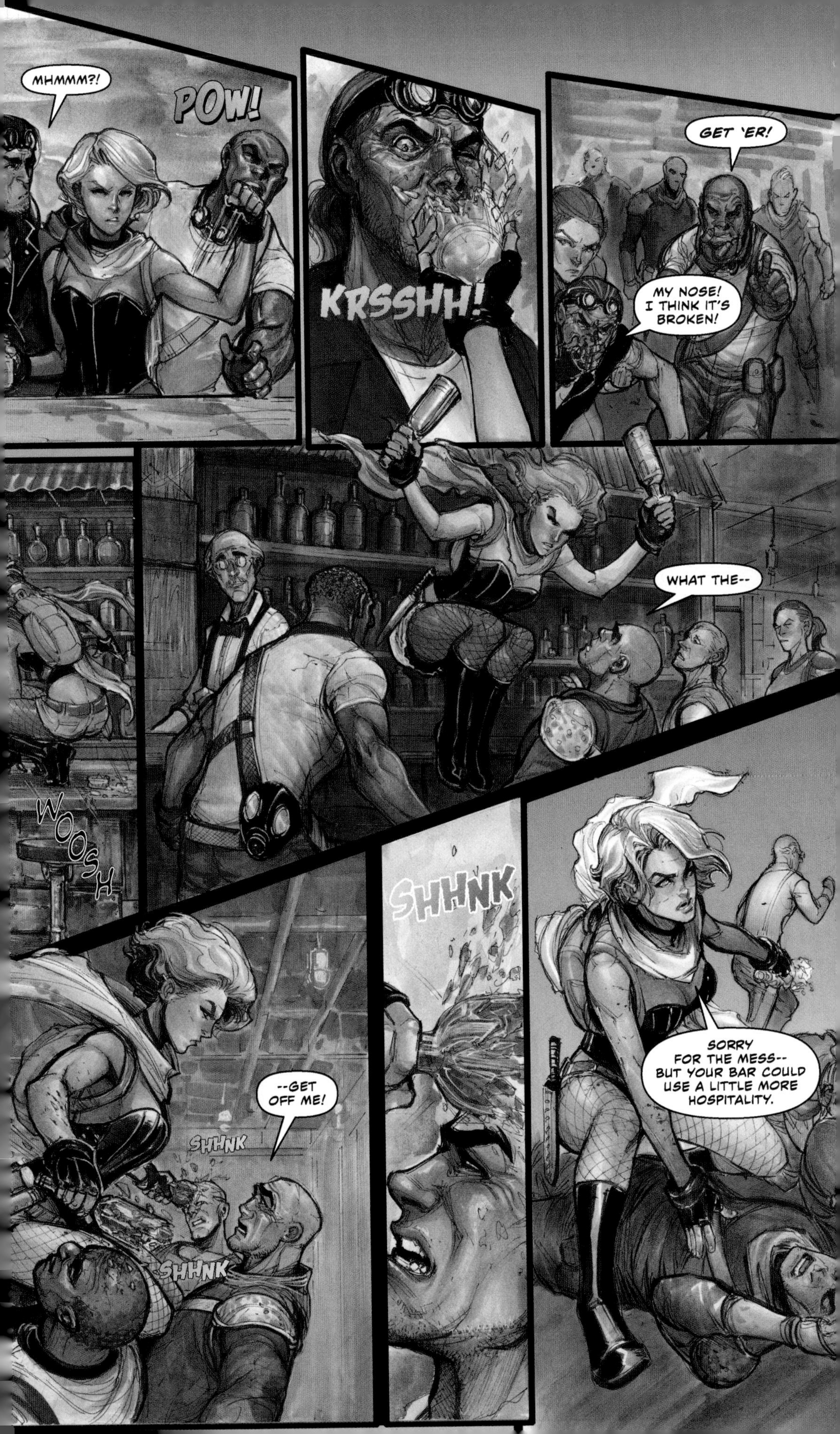
MHMMM?!
POW!
KRSSHH!
GET 'ER!
MY NOSE! I THINK IT'S BROKEN!
WHAT THE--
WOOSH
SHHNK
SHHNK
--GET OFF ME!
SHHNK
SORRY FOR THE MESS-- BUT YOUR BAR COULD USE A LITTLE MORE HOSPITALITY.

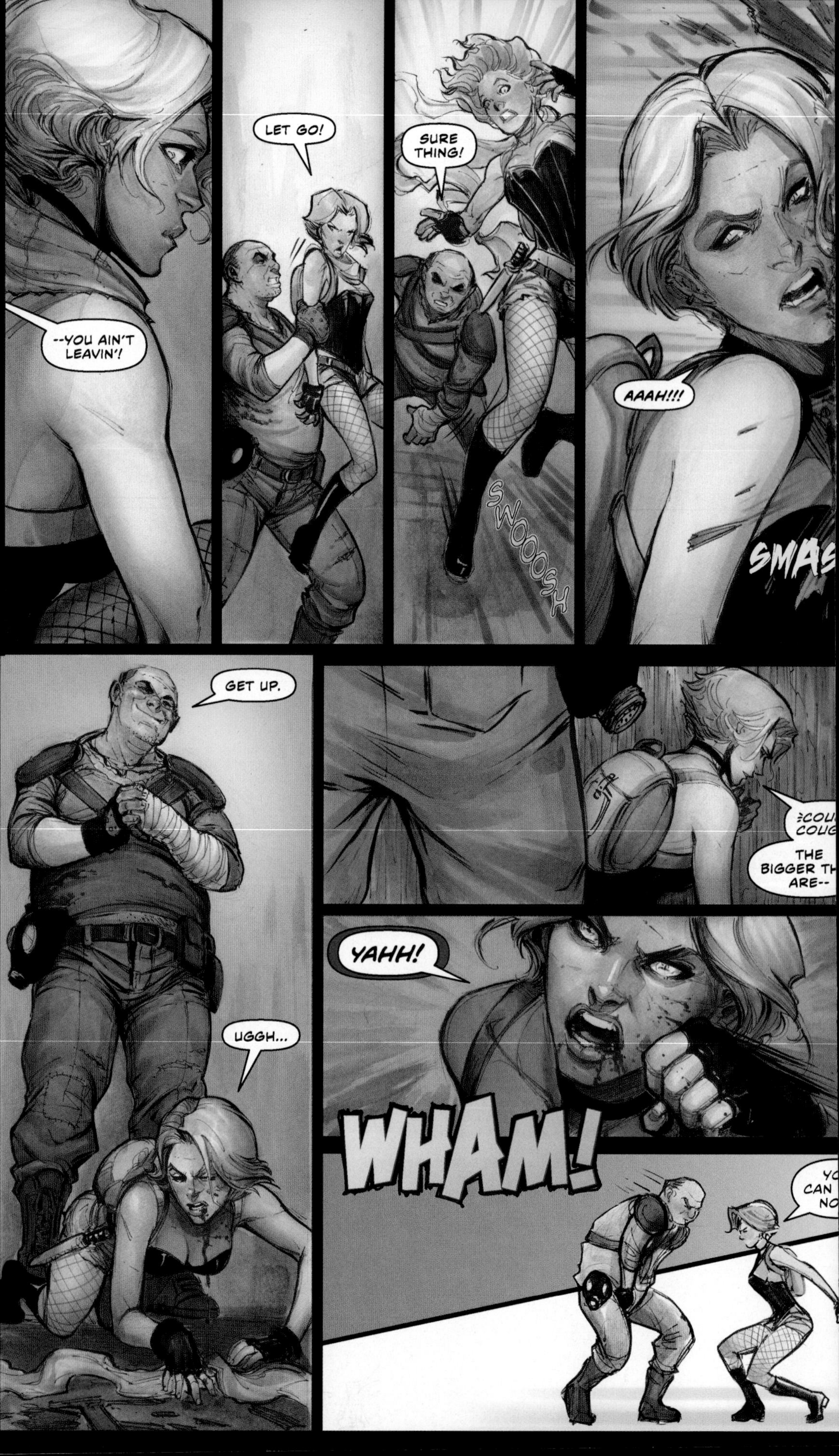
--YOU AIN'T LEAVIN'!
LET GO!
SURE THING!
SWOOOSH
AAAH!!!
SMAS
GET UP.
UGGH...
COU COUG
THE BIGGER TH ARE--
YAHH!
WHAM!
YO CAN NO

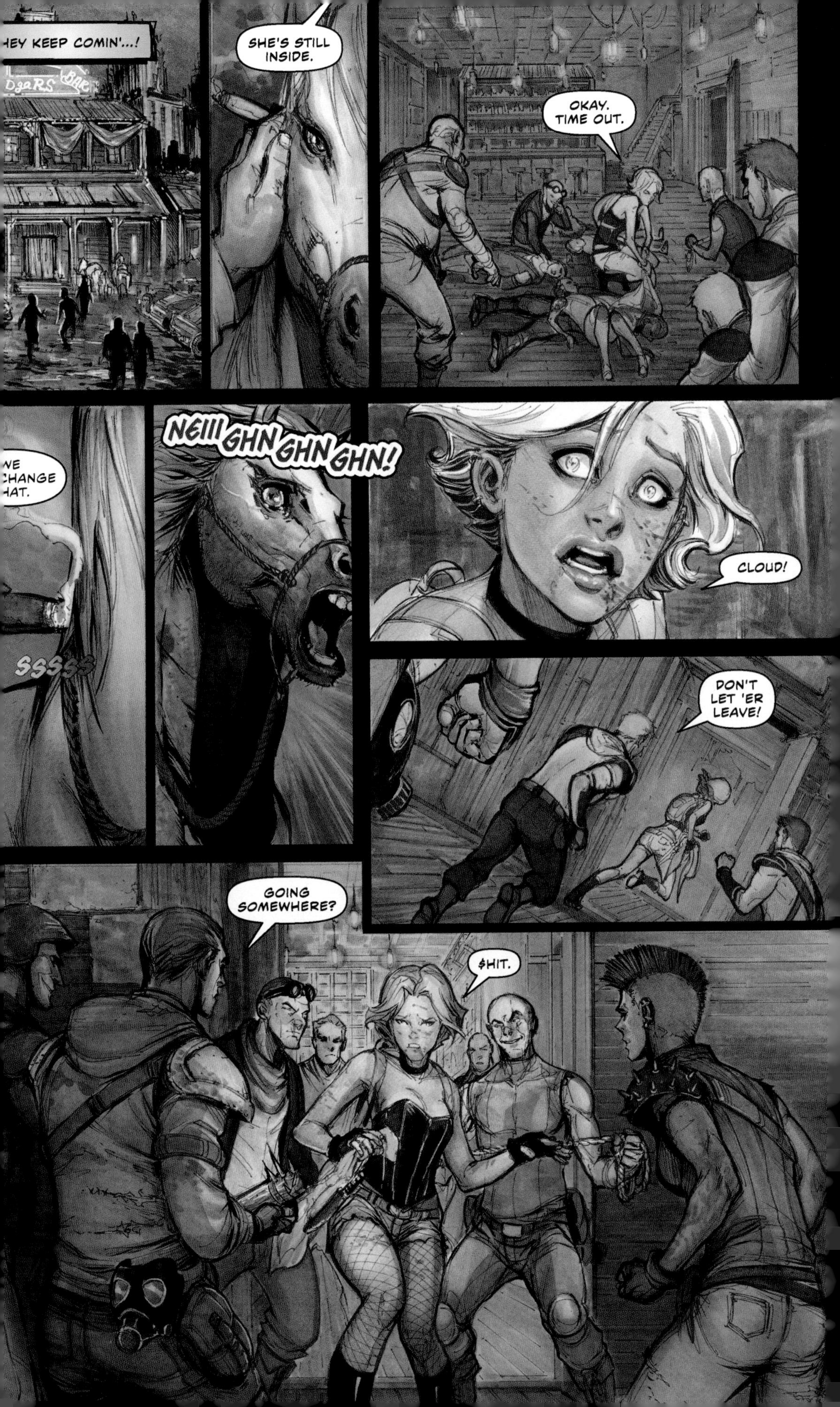
HEY KEEP COMIN'...!
SHE'S STILL INSIDE.
OKAY. TIME OUT.
WE CHANGE HAT.
SSSSS
NEIIIGHNGHNGHN!
CLOUD!
DON'T LET 'ER LEAVE!
GOING SOMEWHERE?
$HIT.

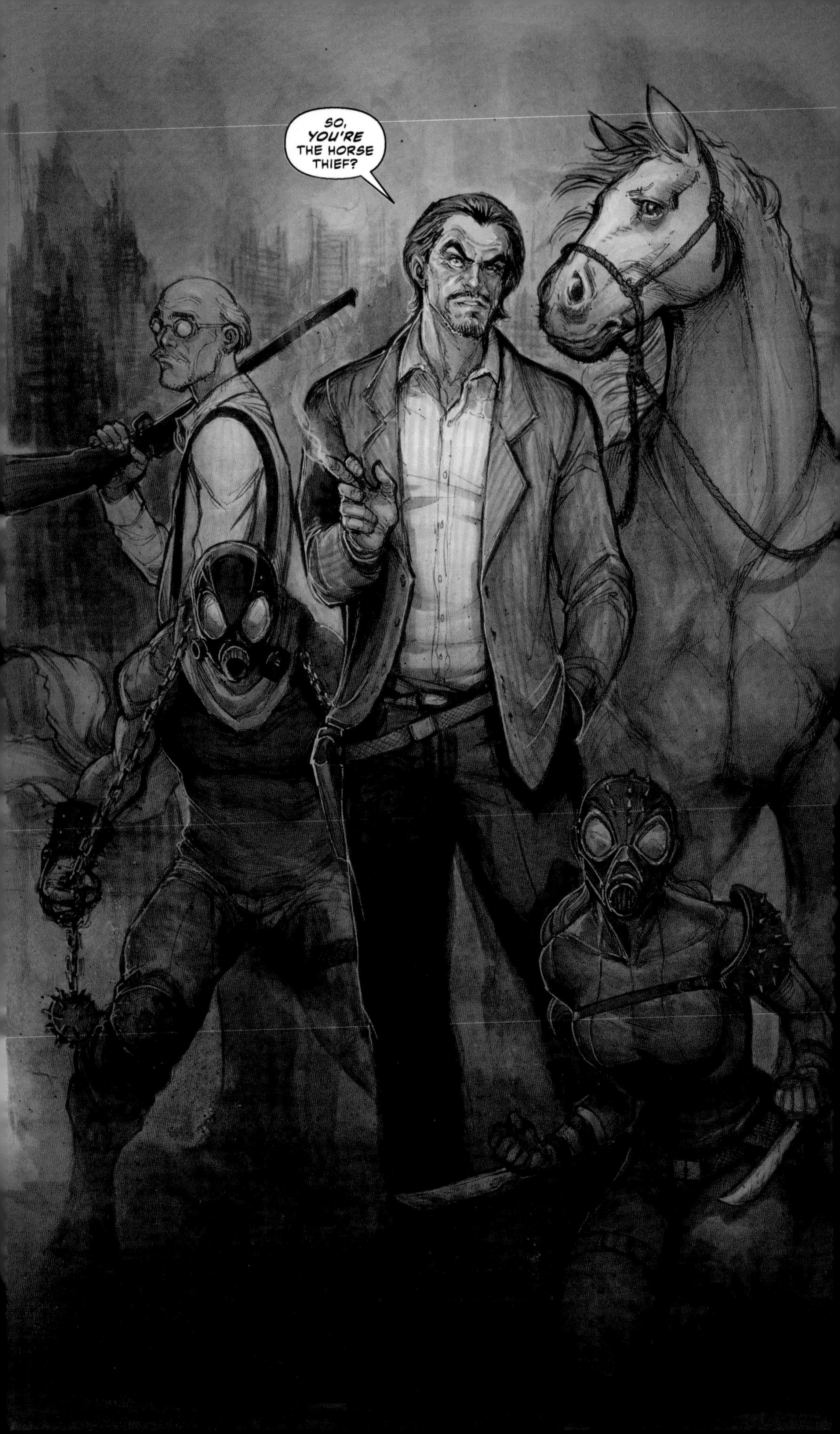
SO, YOU'RE THE HORSE THIEF?

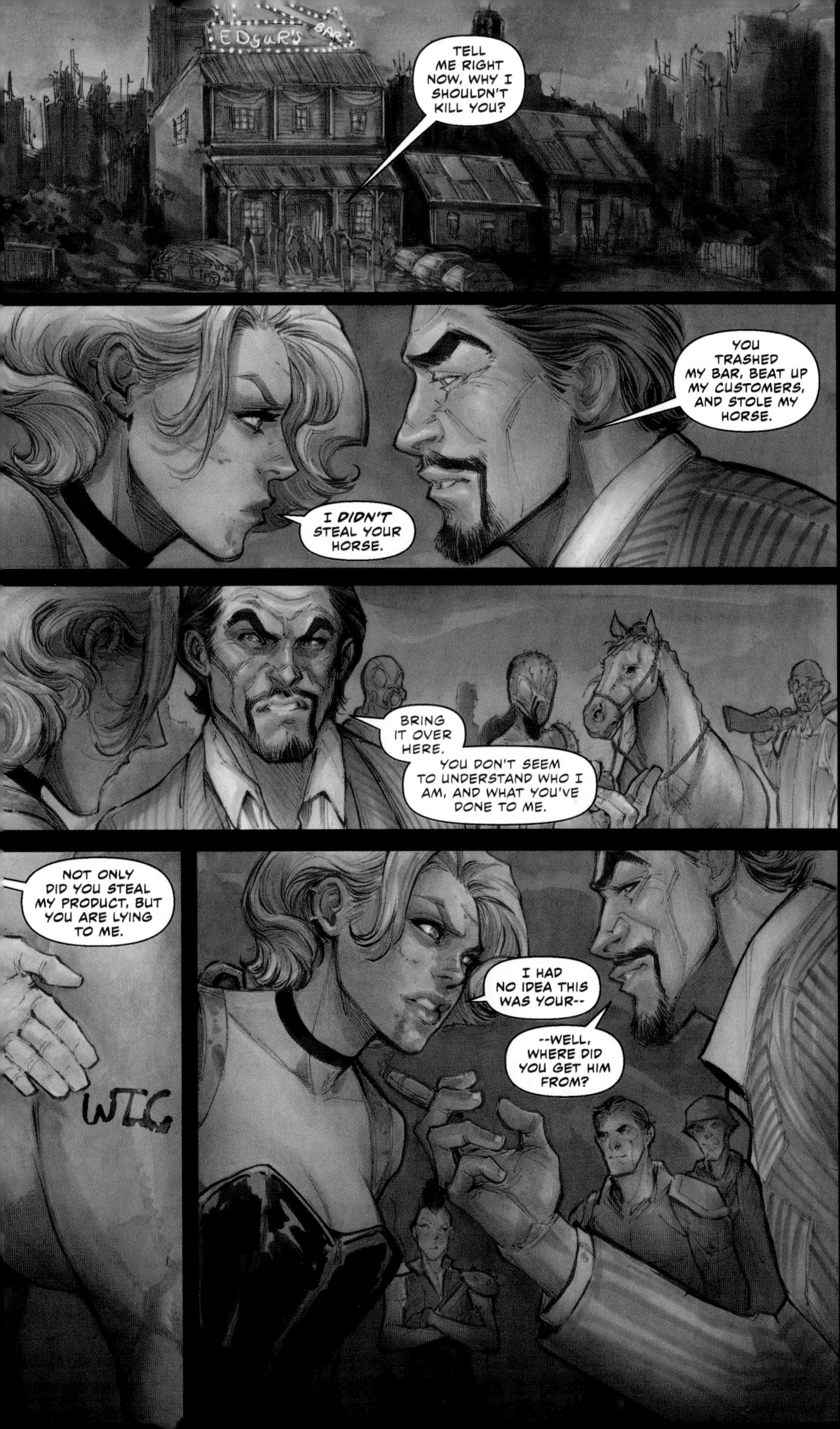
EDgaR'S BAR
TELL ME RIGHT NOW, WHY I SHOULDN'T KILL YOU?
YOU TRASHED MY BAR, BEAT UP MY CUSTOMERS, AND STOLE MY HORSE.
I *DIDN'T* STEAL YOUR HORSE.
BRING IT OVER HERE.
YOU DON'T SEEM TO UNDERSTAND WHO I AM, AND WHAT YOU'VE DONE TO ME.
NOT ONLY DID YOU STEAL MY PRODUCT, BUT YOU ARE LYING TO ME.
I HAD NO IDEA THIS WAS YOUR--
--WELL, WHERE DID YOU GET HIM FROM?
WLG

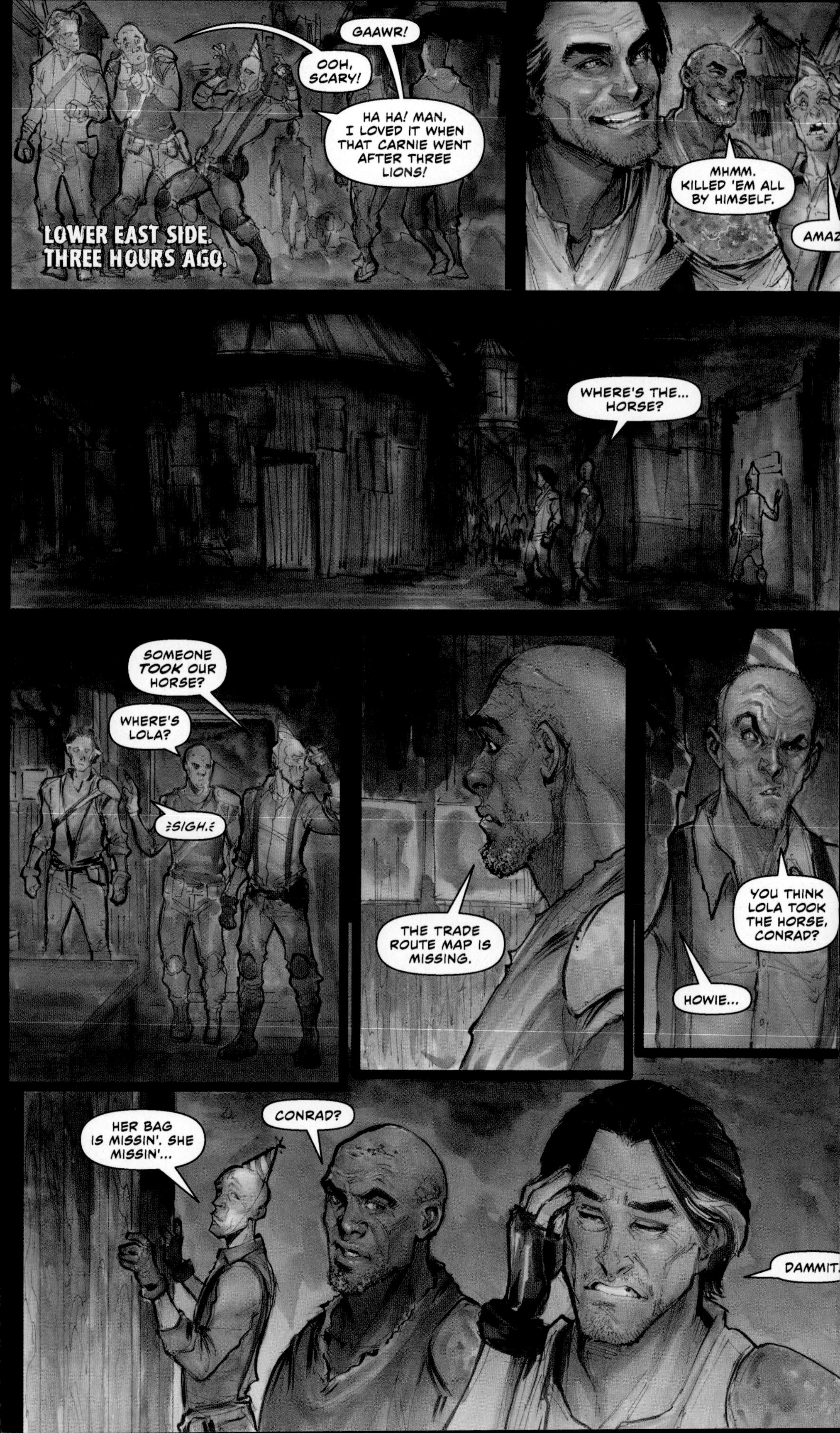
GAAWR!
OOH, SCARY!
HA HA! MAN, I LOVED IT WHEN THAT CARNIE WENT AFTER THREE LIONS!
LOWER EAST SIDE. THREE HOURS AGO.
MHMM. KILLED 'EM ALL BY HIMSELF.
AMAZ
WHERE'S THE... HORSE?
SOMEONE TOOK OUR HORSE?
WHERE'S LOLA?
SIGH.
THE TRADE ROUTE MAP IS MISSING.
YOU THINK LOLA TOOK THE HORSE, CONRAD?
HOWIE...
HER BAG IS MISSIN'. SHE MISSIN'...
CONRAD?
DAMMIT

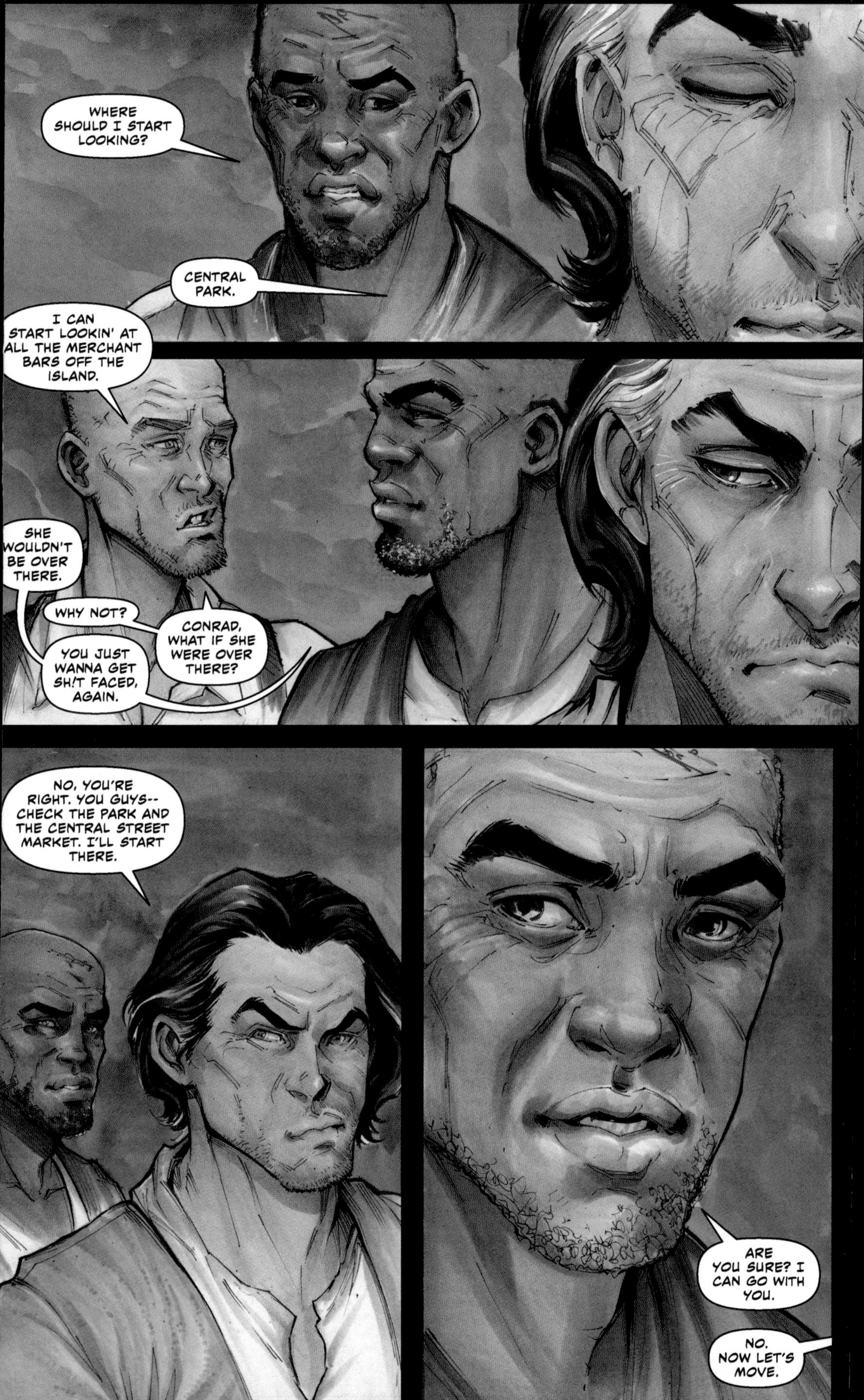
WHERE SHOULD I START LOOKING?
CENTRAL PARK.
I CAN START LOOKIN' AT ALL THE MERCHANT BARS OFF THE ISLAND.
SHE WOULDN'T BE OVER THERE.
WHY NOT?
CONRAD, WHAT IF SHE WERE OVER THERE?
YOU JUST WANNA GET SH!T FACED, AGAIN.
NO, YOU'RE RIGHT. YOU GUYS-- CHECK THE PARK AND THE CENTRAL STREET MARKET. I'LL START THERE.
ARE YOU SURE? I CAN GO WITH YOU.
NO. NOW LET'S MOVE.

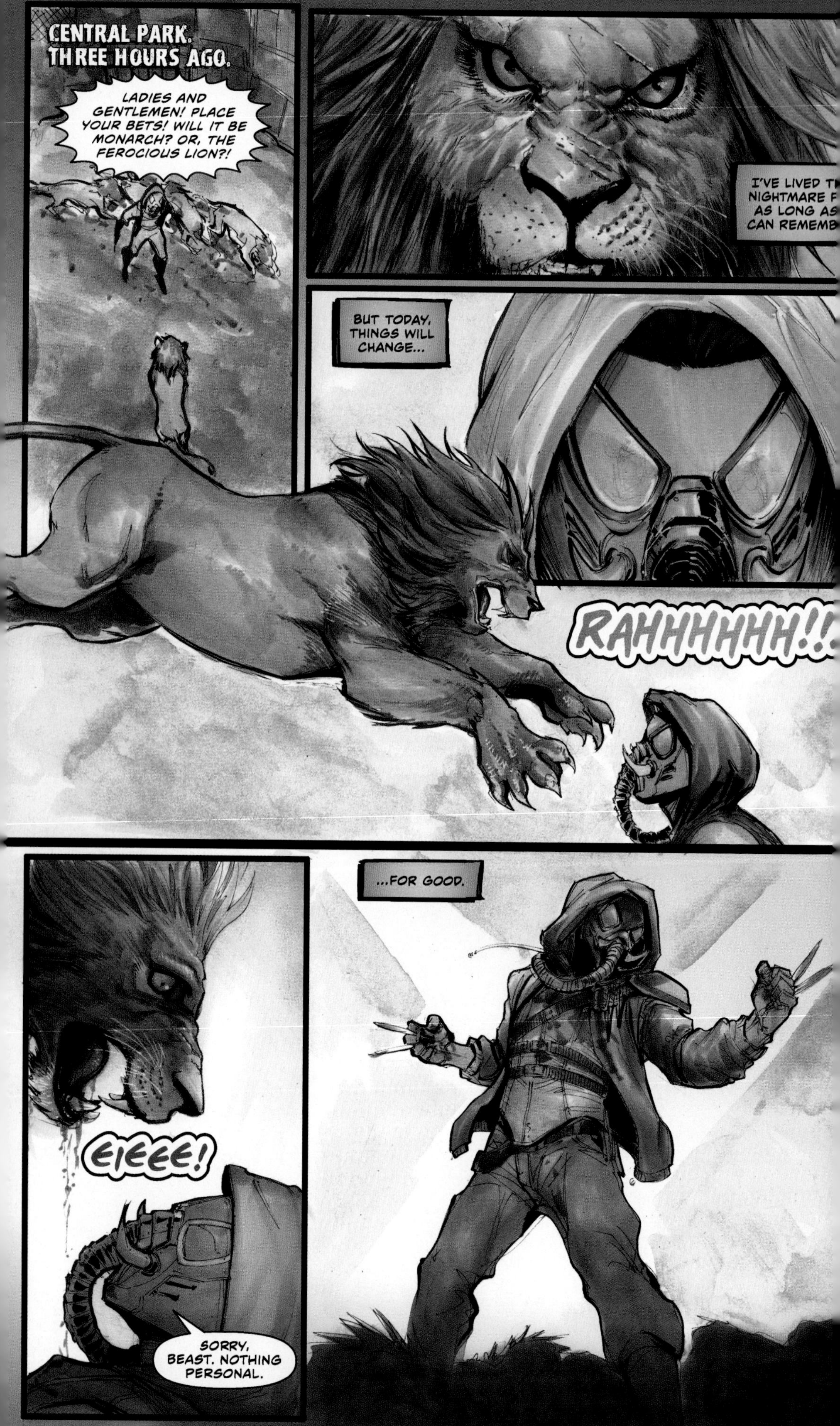
CENTRAL PARK. THREE HOURS AGO.
LADIES AND GENTLEMEN! PLACE YOUR BETS! WILL IT BE MONARCH? OR, THE FEROCIOUS LION?!
I'VE LIVED T NIGHTMARE F AS LONG AS CAN REMEMB
BUT TODAY, THINGS WILL CHANGE...
RAHHHHHH!!
...FOR GOOD.
EIEEE!
SORRY, BEAST. NOTHING PERSONAL.

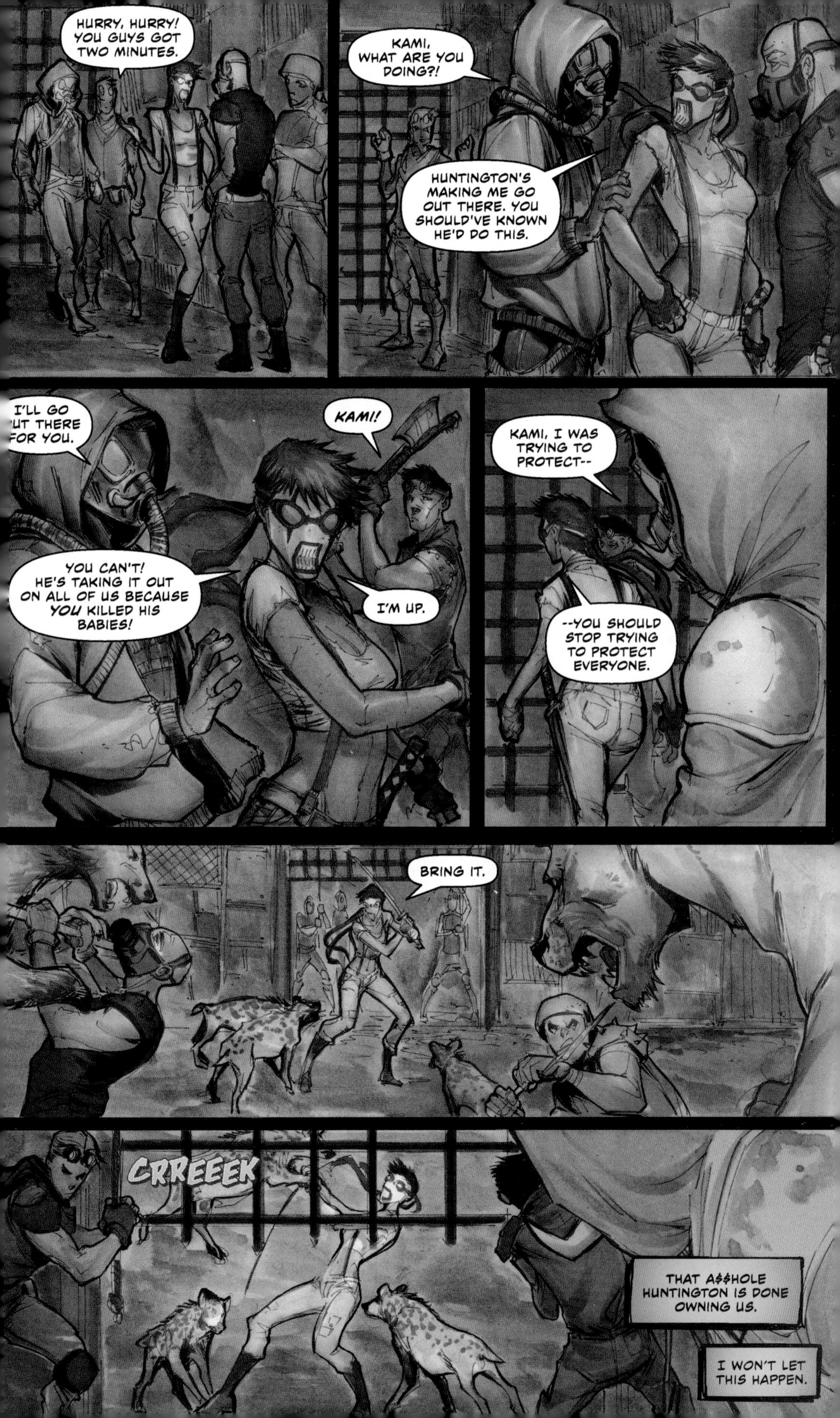

HURRY, HURRY! YOU GUYS GOT TWO MINUTES.
KAMI, WHAT ARE YOU DOING?!
HUNTINGTON'S MAKING ME GO OUT THERE. YOU SHOULD'VE KNOWN HE'D DO THIS.
I'LL GO UT THERE FOR YOU.
KAMI!
YOU CAN'T! HE'S TAKING IT OUT ON ALL OF US BECAUSE YOU KILLED HIS BABIES!
I'M UP.
KAMI, I WAS TRYING TO PROTECT--
--YOU SHOULD STOP TRYING TO PROTECT EVERYONE.
BRING IT.
CRREEEK
THAT A$$HOLE HUNTINGTON IS DONE OWNING US.
I WON'T LET THIS HAPPEN.

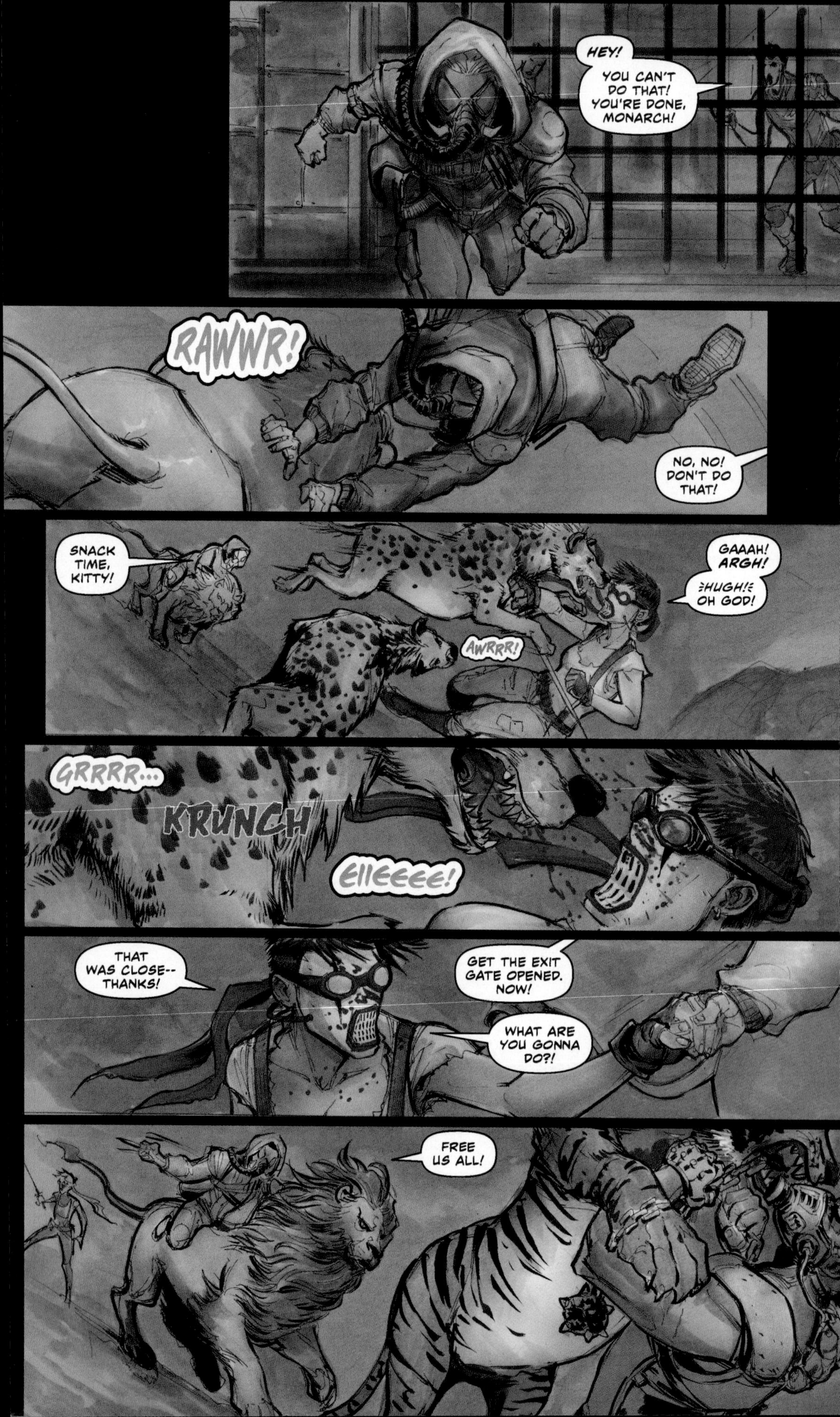
HEY!
YOU CAN'T DO THAT! YOU'RE DONE, MONARCH!
RAWWR!
NO, NO! DON'T DO THAT!
SNACK TIME, KITTY!
GAAAH! ARGH!
HUGH! OH GOD!
AWRRR!
GRRRR...
KRUNCH
EIIEEEE!
THAT WAS CLOSE-- THANKS!
GET THE EXIT GATE OPENED. NOW!
WHAT ARE YOU GONNA DO?!
FREE US ALL!

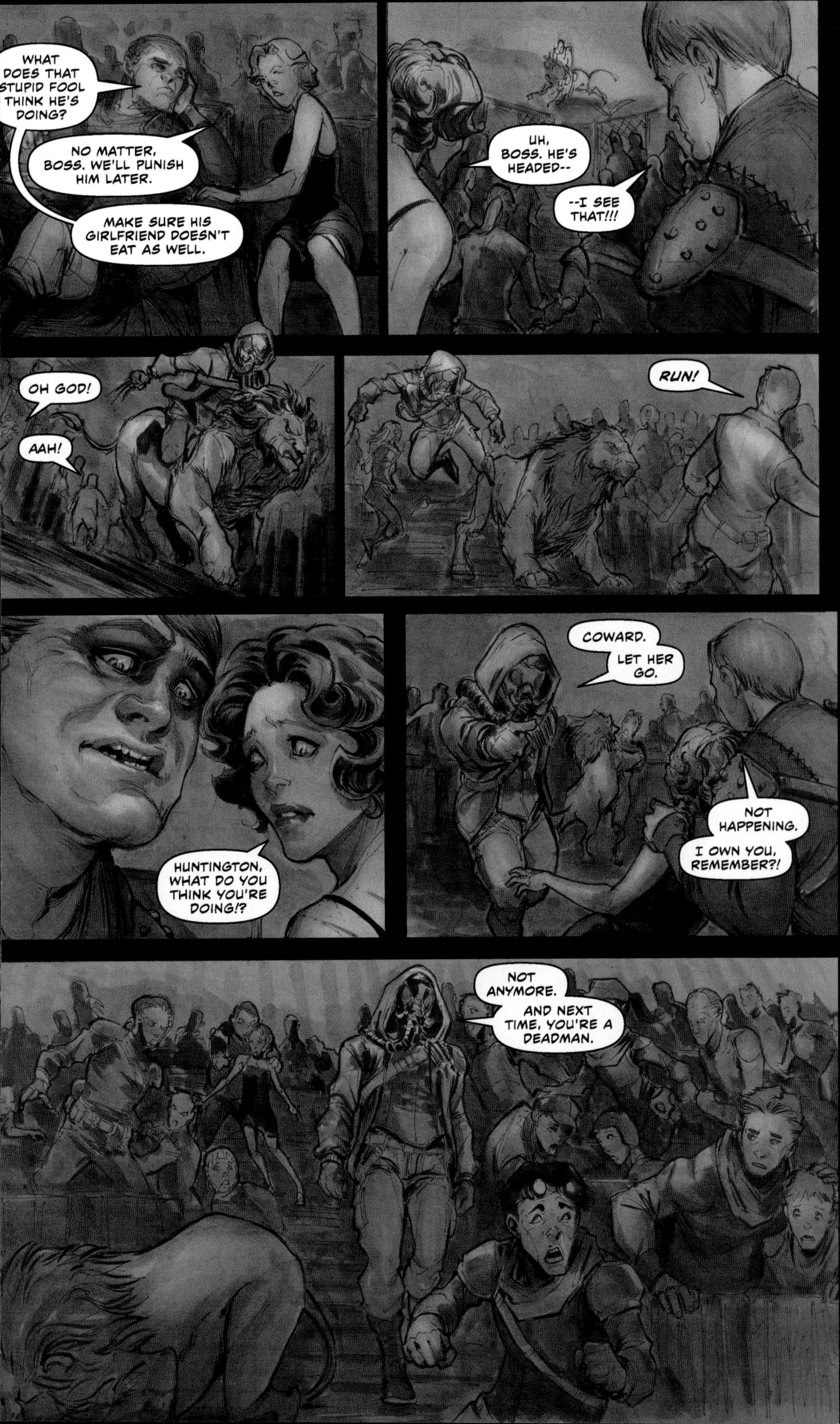
WHAT DOES THAT STUPID FOOL THINK HE'S DOING?
NO MATTER, BOSS. WE'LL PUNISH HIM LATER.
MAKE SURE HIS GIRLFRIEND DOESN'T EAT AS WELL.
UH, BOSS. HE'S HEADED--
--I SEE THAT!!!
OH GOD!
AAH!
RUN!
HUNTINGTON, WHAT DO YOU THINK YOU'RE DOING!?
COWARD.
LET HER GO.
NOT HAPPENING.
I OWN YOU, REMEMBER?!
NOT ANYMORE.
AND NEXT TIME, YOU'RE A DEADMAN.

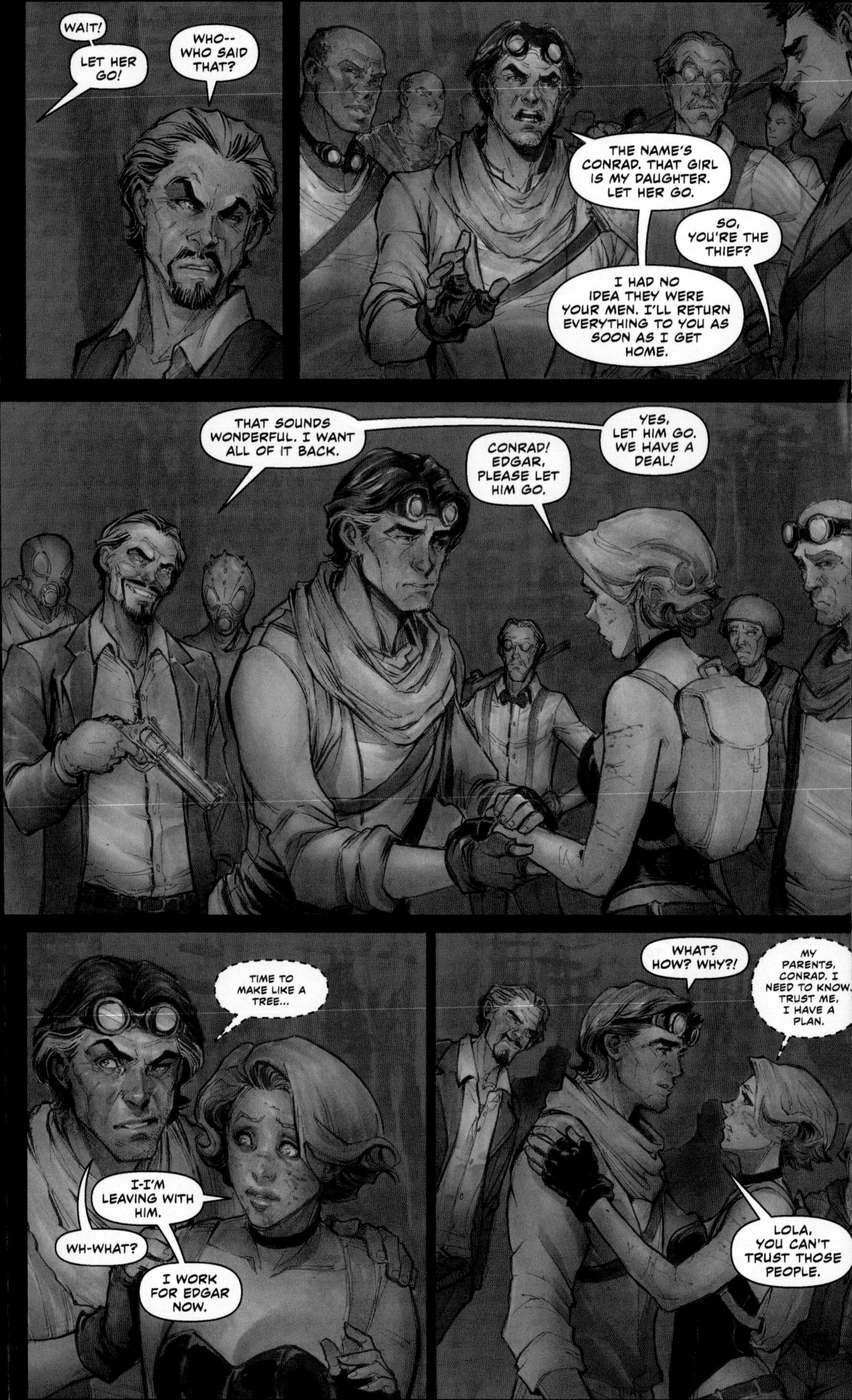
WAIT!
LET HER GO!
WHO-- WHO SAID THAT?
THE NAME'S CONRAD. THAT GIRL IS MY DAUGHTER. LET HER GO.
SO, YOU'RE THE THIEF?
I HAD NO IDEA THEY WERE YOUR MEN. I'LL RETURN EVERYTHING TO YOU AS SOON AS I GET HOME.
THAT SOUNDS WONDERFUL. I WANT ALL OF IT BACK.
YES, LET HIM GO. WE HAVE A DEAL!
CONRAD! EDGAR, PLEASE LET HIM GO.
TIME TO MAKE LIKE A TREE...
I-I'M LEAVING WITH HIM.
WH-WHAT?
I WORK FOR EDGAR NOW.
WHAT? HOW? WHY?!
MY PARENTS, CONRAD. I NEED TO KNOW. TRUST ME, I HAVE A PLAN.
LOLA, YOU CAN'T TRUST THOSE PEOPLE.

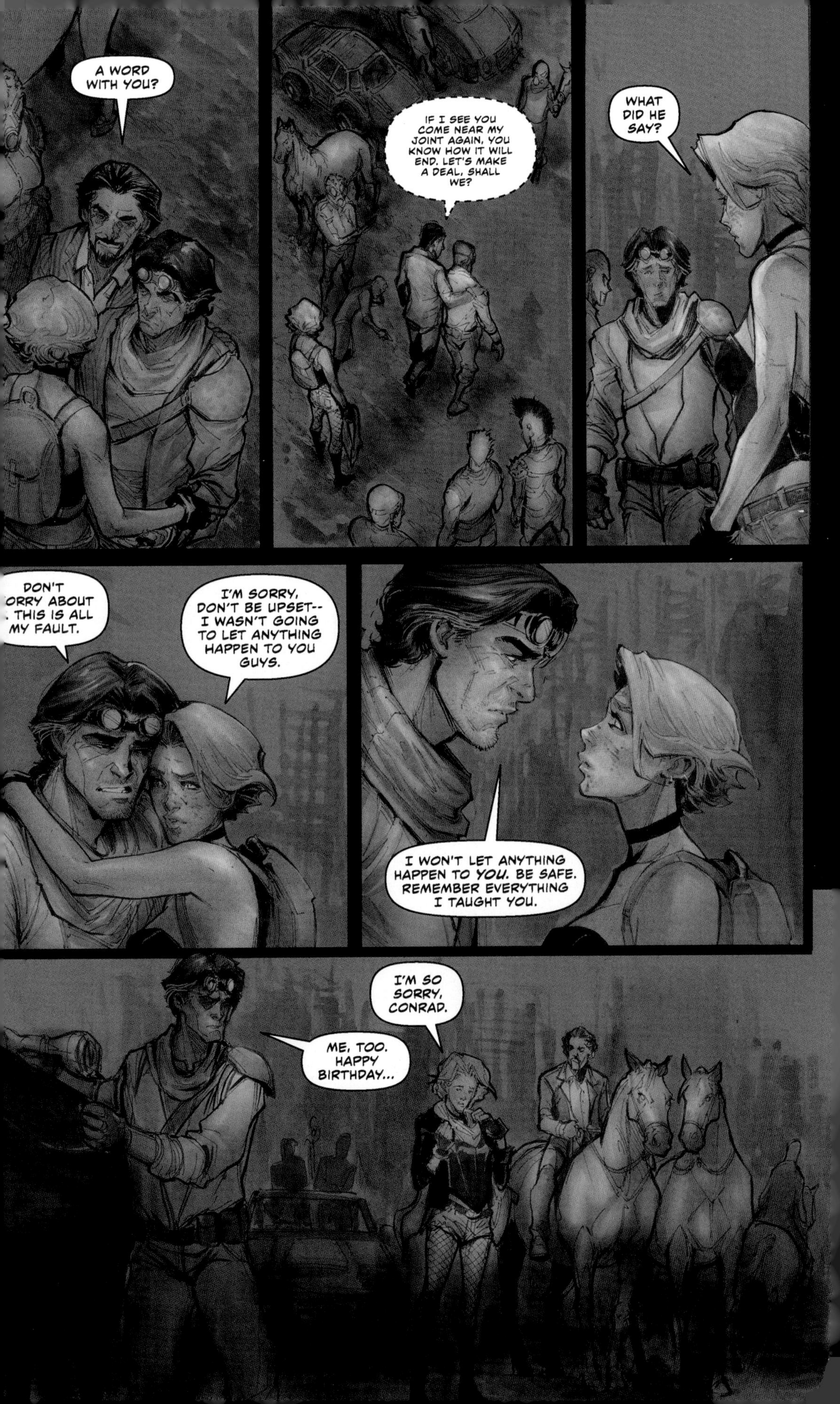
A WORD WITH YOU?
IF I SEE YOU COME NEAR MY JOINT AGAIN, YOU KNOW HOW IT WILL END. LET'S MAKE A DEAL, SHALL WE?
WHAT DID HE SAY?
DON'T ORRY ABOUT . THIS IS ALL MY FAULT.
I'M SORRY, DON'T BE UPSET-- I WASN'T GOING TO LET ANYTHING HAPPEN TO YOU GUYS.
I WON'T LET ANYTHING HAPPEN TO *YOU*. BE SAFE. REMEMBER EVERYTHING I TAUGHT YOU.
I'M SO SORRY, CONRAD.
ME, TOO. HAPPY BIRTHDAY...

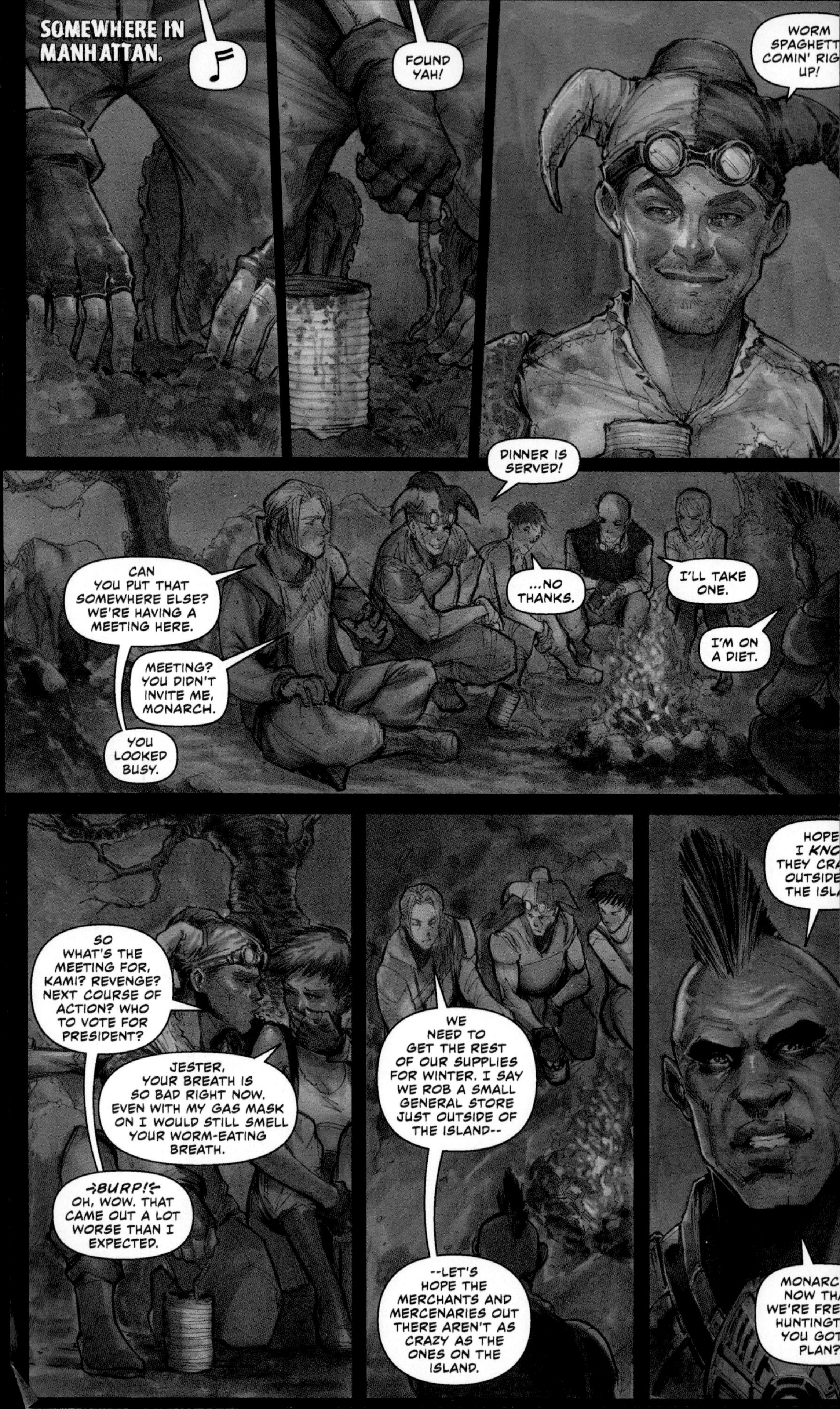

SOMEWHERE IN MANHATTAN.
FOUND YAH!
WORM SPAGHETT COMIN' RIG UP!
DINNER IS SERVED!
CAN YOU PUT THAT SOMEWHERE ELSE? WE'RE HAVING A MEETING HERE.
MEETING? YOU DIDN'T INVITE ME, MONARCH.
YOU LOOKED BUSY.
...NO THANKS.
I'LL TAKE ONE.
I'M ON A DIET.
SO WHAT'S THE MEETING FOR, KAMI? REVENGE? NEXT COURSE OF ACTION? WHO TO VOTE FOR PRESIDENT?
JESTER, YOUR BREATH IS SO BAD RIGHT NOW. EVEN WITH MY GAS MASK ON I WOULD STILL SMELL YOUR WORM-EATING BREATH.
-BURP!- OH, WOW. THAT CAME OUT A LOT WORSE THAN I EXPECTED.
MONARC NOW THA WE'RE FRE HUNTINGT YOU GOT PLAN?
WE NEED TO GET THE REST OF OUR SUPPLIES FOR WINTER. I SAY WE ROB A SMALL GENERAL STORE JUST OUTSIDE OF THE ISLAND--
--LET'S HOPE THE MERCHANTS AND MERCENARIES OUT THERE AREN'T AS CRAZY AS THE ONES ON THE ISLAND.
HOPE I KNO THEY CRA OUTSIDE THE ISLA

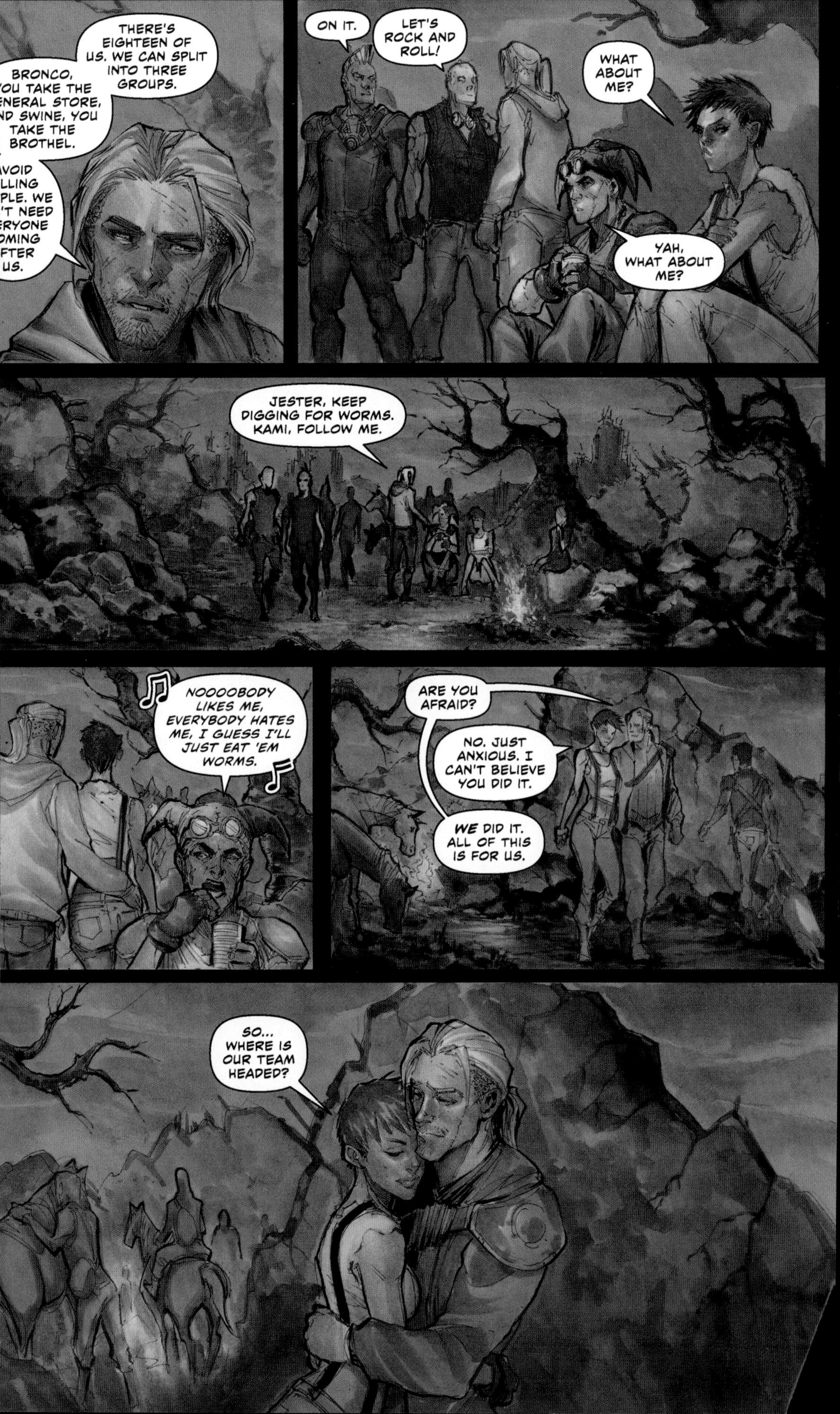
THERE'S EIGHTEEN OF US. WE CAN SPLIT INTO THREE GROUPS.
BRONCO,
OU TAKE THE
ENERAL STORE,
ND SWINE, YOU
TAKE THE
BROTHEL.
VOID
LLING
PLE. WE
'T NEED
RYONE
OMING
FTER
US.
ON IT.
LET'S ROCK AND ROLL!
WHAT ABOUT ME?
YAH, WHAT ABOUT ME?
JESTER, KEEP DIGGING FOR WORMS. KAMI, FOLLOW ME.
NOOOOBODY LIKES ME, EVERYBODY HATES ME, I GUESS I'LL JUST EAT 'EM WORMS.
ARE YOU AFRAID?
NO. JUST ANXIOUS. I CAN'T BELIEVE YOU DID IT.
WE DID IT. ALL OF THIS IS FOR US.
SO... WHERE IS OUR TEAM HEADED?

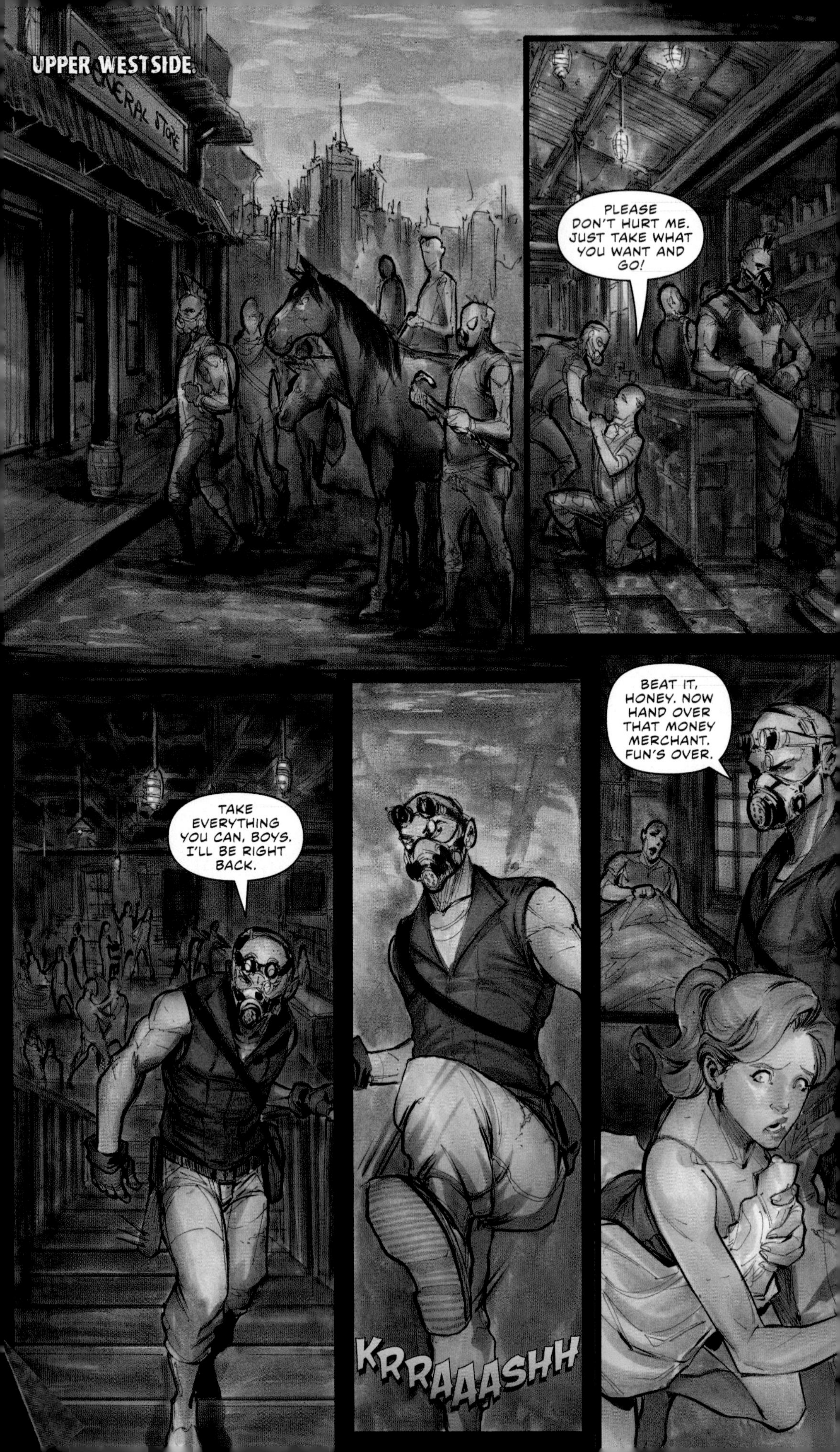
UPPER WESTSIDE.
GENERAL STORE
PLEASE DON'T HURT ME. JUST TAKE WHAT YOU WANT AND GO!
TAKE EVERYTHING YOU CAN, BOYS. I'LL BE RIGHT BACK.
KRRAAASHH
BEAT IT, HONEY. NOW HAND OVER THAT MONEY MERCHANT. FUN'S OVER.

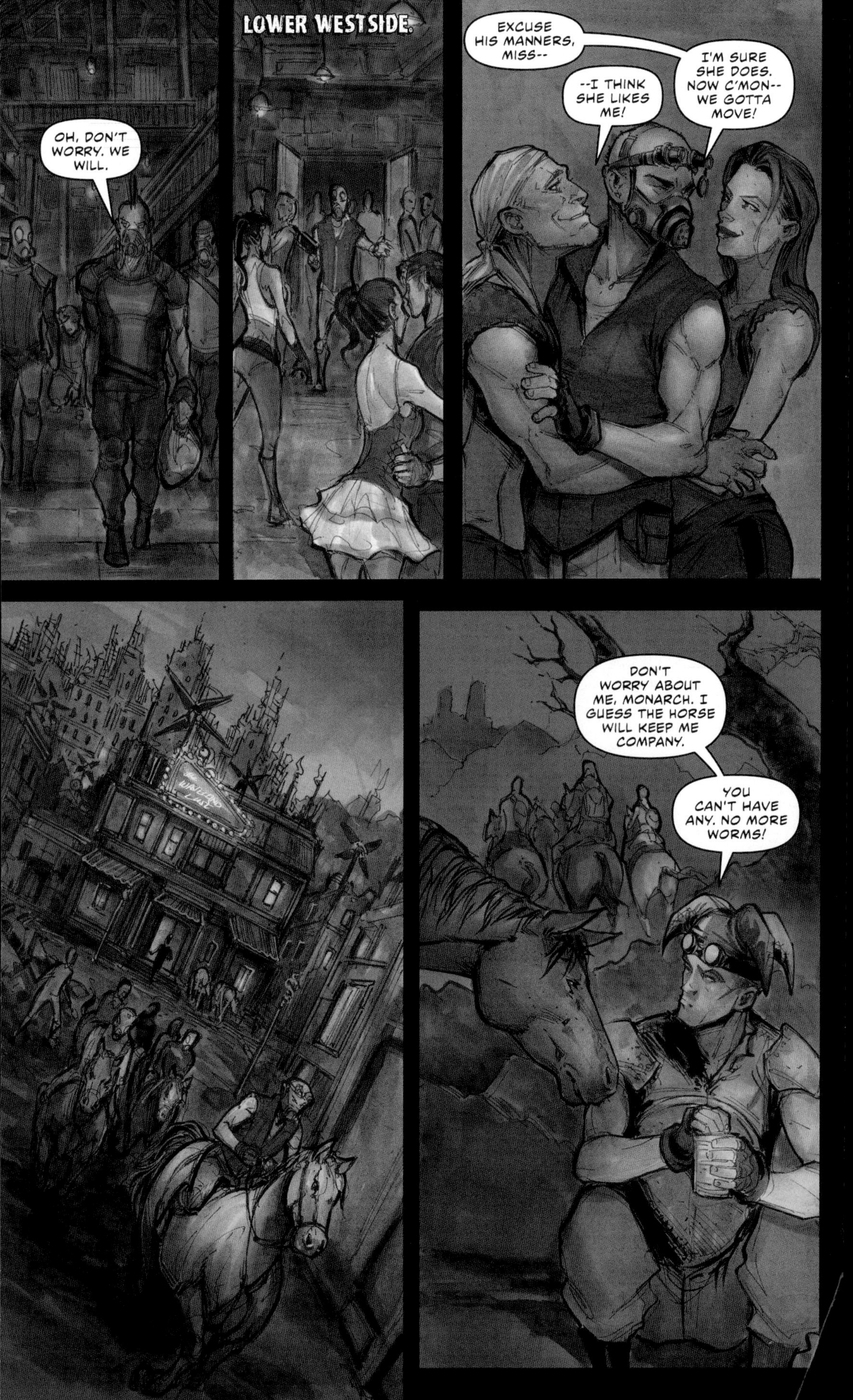
OH, DON'T WORRY. WE WILL.
LOWER WESTSIDE.
EXCUSE HIS MANNERS, MISS--
--I THINK SHE LIKES ME!
I'M SURE SHE DOES. NOW C'MON-- WE GOTTA MOVE!
DON'T WORRY ABOUT ME, MONARCH. I GUESS THE HORSE WILL KEEP ME COMPANY.
YOU CAN'T HAVE ANY. NO MORE WORMS!

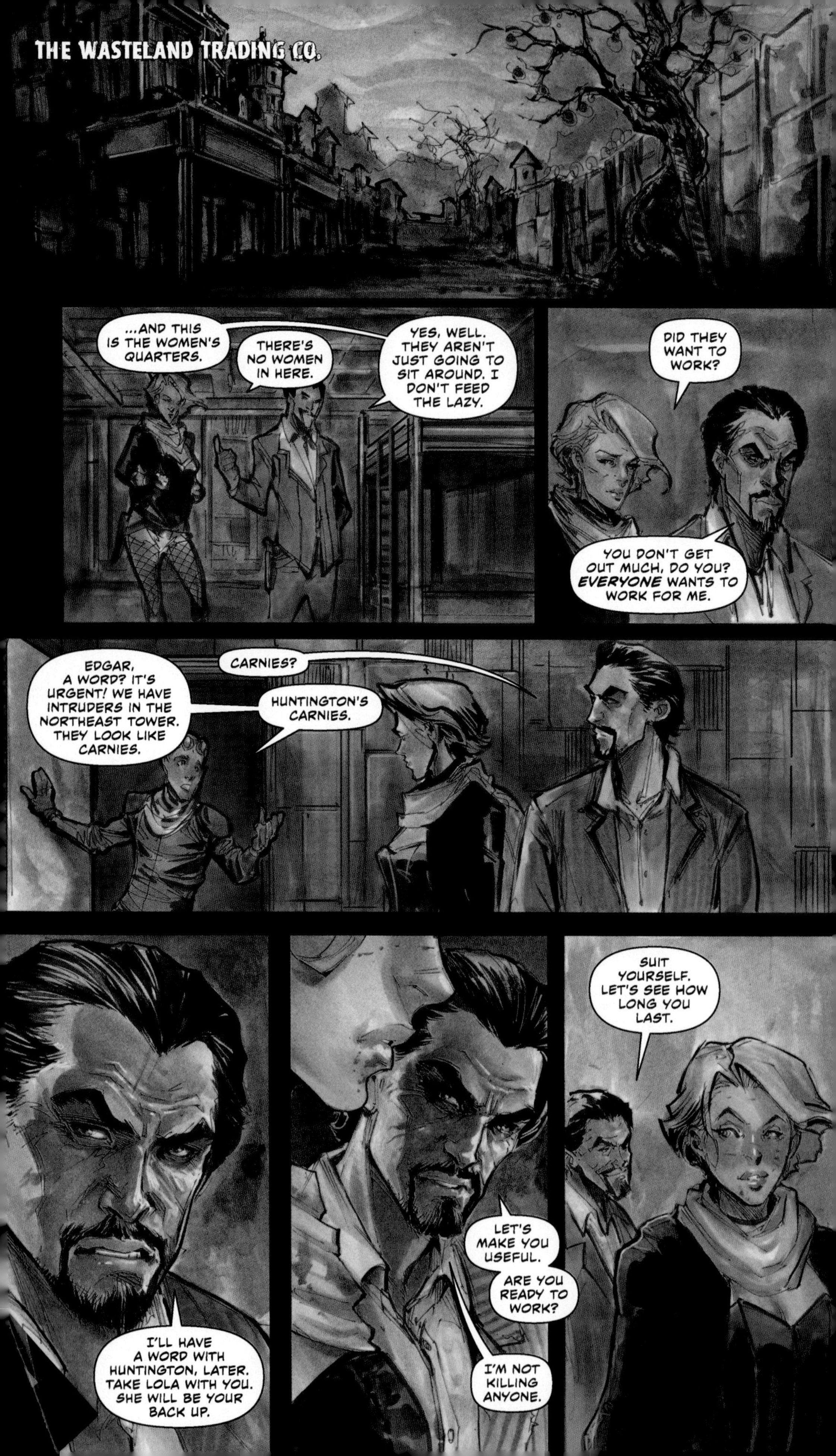
THE WASTELAND TRADING CO.
...AND THIS IS THE WOMEN'S QUARTERS.
THERE'S NO WOMEN IN HERE.
YES, WELL. THEY AREN'T JUST GOING TO SIT AROUND. I DON'T FEED THE LAZY.
DID THEY WANT TO WORK?
YOU DON'T GET OUT MUCH, DO YOU? EVERYONE WANTS TO WORK FOR ME.
EDGAR, A WORD? IT'S URGENT! WE HAVE INTRUDERS IN THE NORTHEAST TOWER. THEY LOOK LIKE CARNIES.
CARNIES?
HUNTINGTON'S CARNIES.
I'LL HAVE A WORD WITH HUNTINGTON, LATER. TAKE LOLA WITH YOU. SHE WILL BE YOUR BACK UP.
LET'S MAKE YOU USEFUL.
ARE YOU READY TO WORK?
I'M NOT KILLING ANYONE.
SUIT YOURSELF. LET'S SEE HOW LONG YOU LAST.

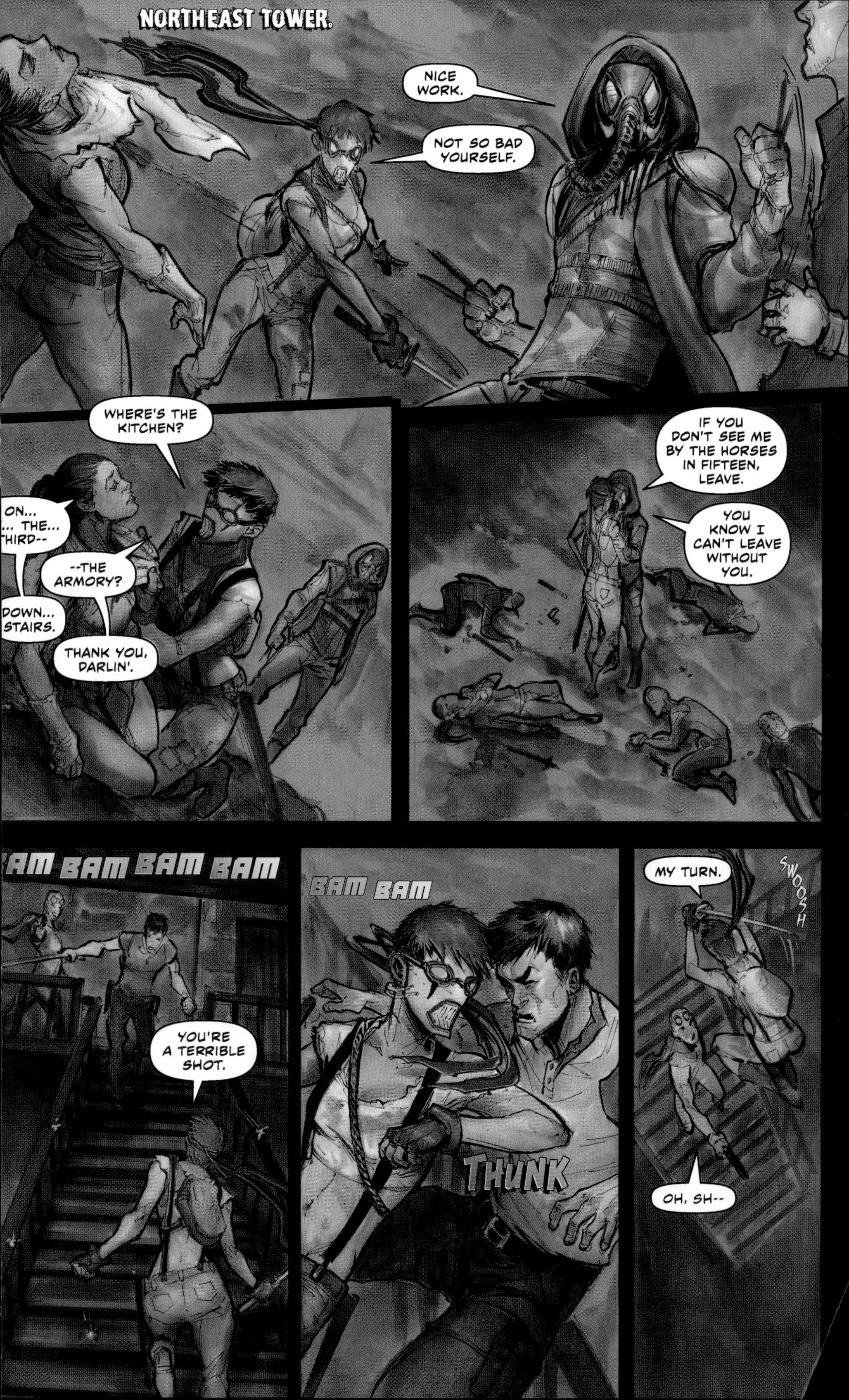
NORTHEAST TOWER.
NICE WORK.
NOT SO BAD YOURSELF.
WHERE'S THE KITCHEN?
ON... ... THE... THIRD--
--THE ARMORY?
DOWN... STAIRS.
THANK YOU, DARLIN'.
IF YOU DON'T SEE ME BY THE HORSES IN FIFTEEN, LEAVE.
YOU KNOW I CAN'T LEAVE WITHOUT YOU.
AM BAM BAM BAM
YOU'RE A TERRIBLE SHOT.
BAM BAM
THUNK
MY TURN.
SWOOSH
OH, SH--

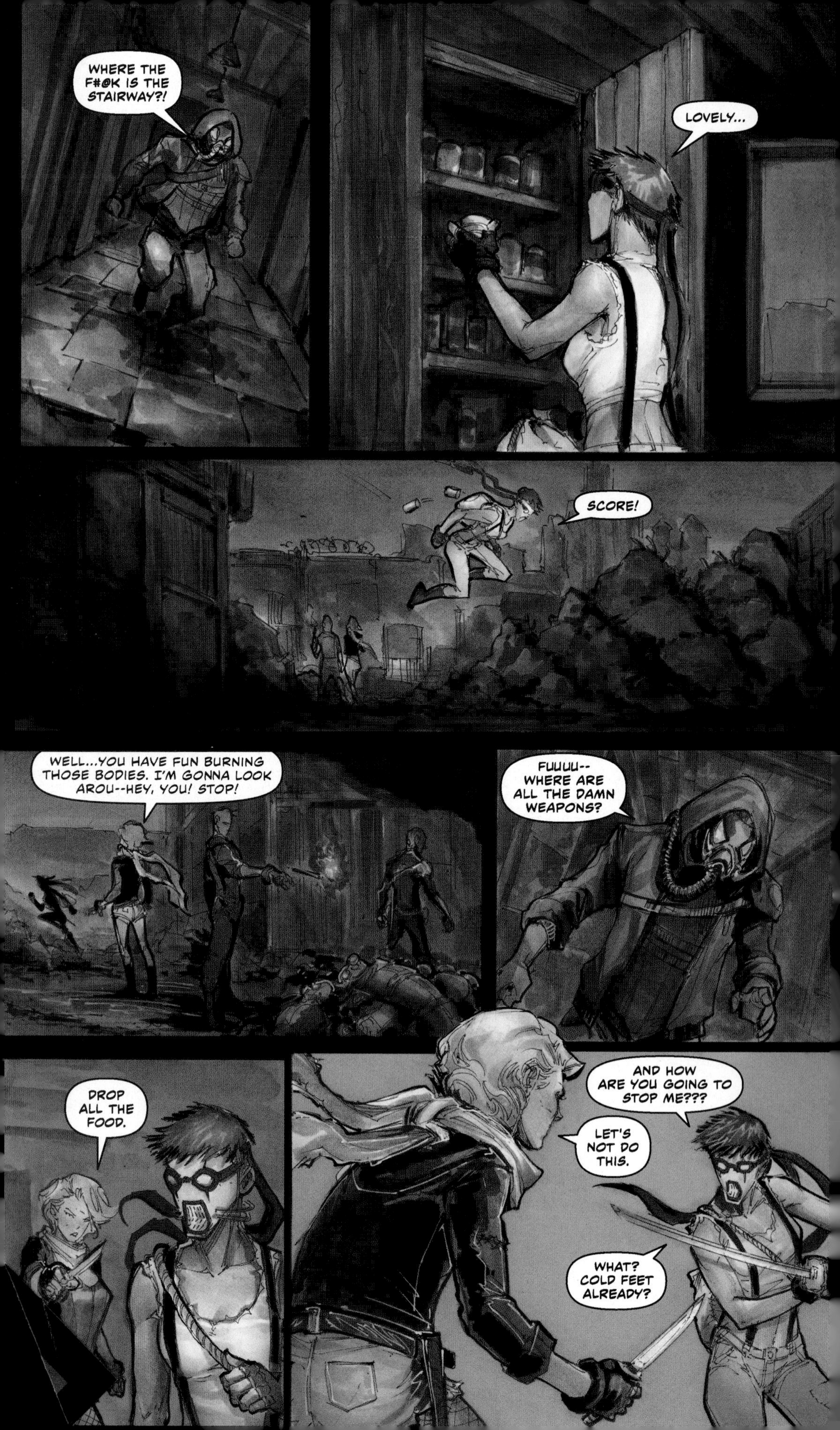
WHERE THE F#@K IS THE STAIRWAY?!
LOVELY...
SCORE!
WELL...YOU HAVE FUN BURNING THOSE BODIES. I'M GONNA LOOK AROU--HEY, YOU! STOP!
FUUUU-- WHERE ARE ALL THE DAMN WEAPONS?
DROP ALL THE FOOD.
AND HOW ARE YOU GOING TO STOP ME???
LET'S NOT DO THIS.
WHAT? COLD FEET ALREADY?

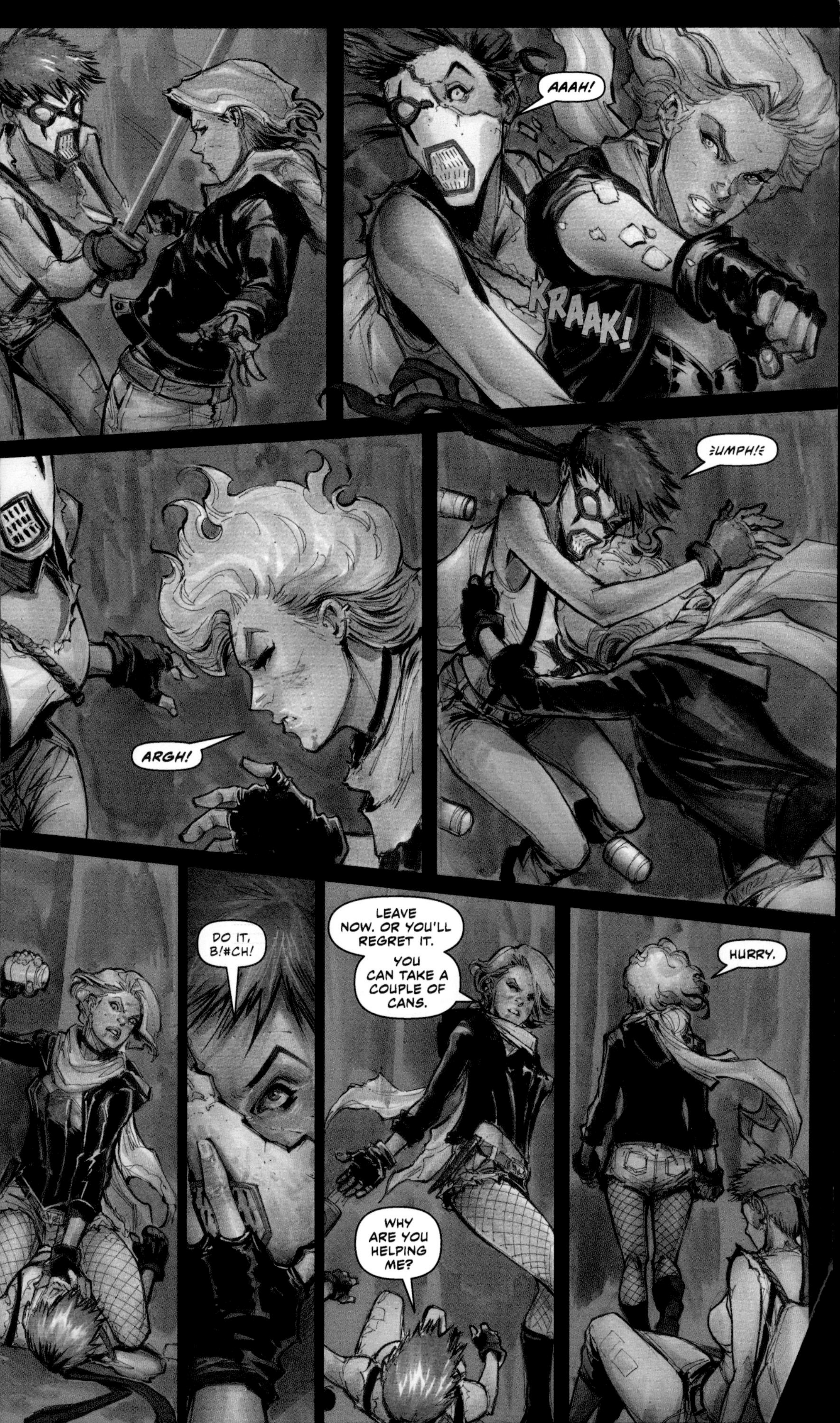
AAAH!
KRAAK!
ARGH!
UMPH!
DO IT, B!#CH!
LEAVE NOW. OR YOU'LL REGRET IT.
YOU CAN TAKE A COUPLE OF CANS.
WHY ARE YOU HELPING ME?
HURRY.

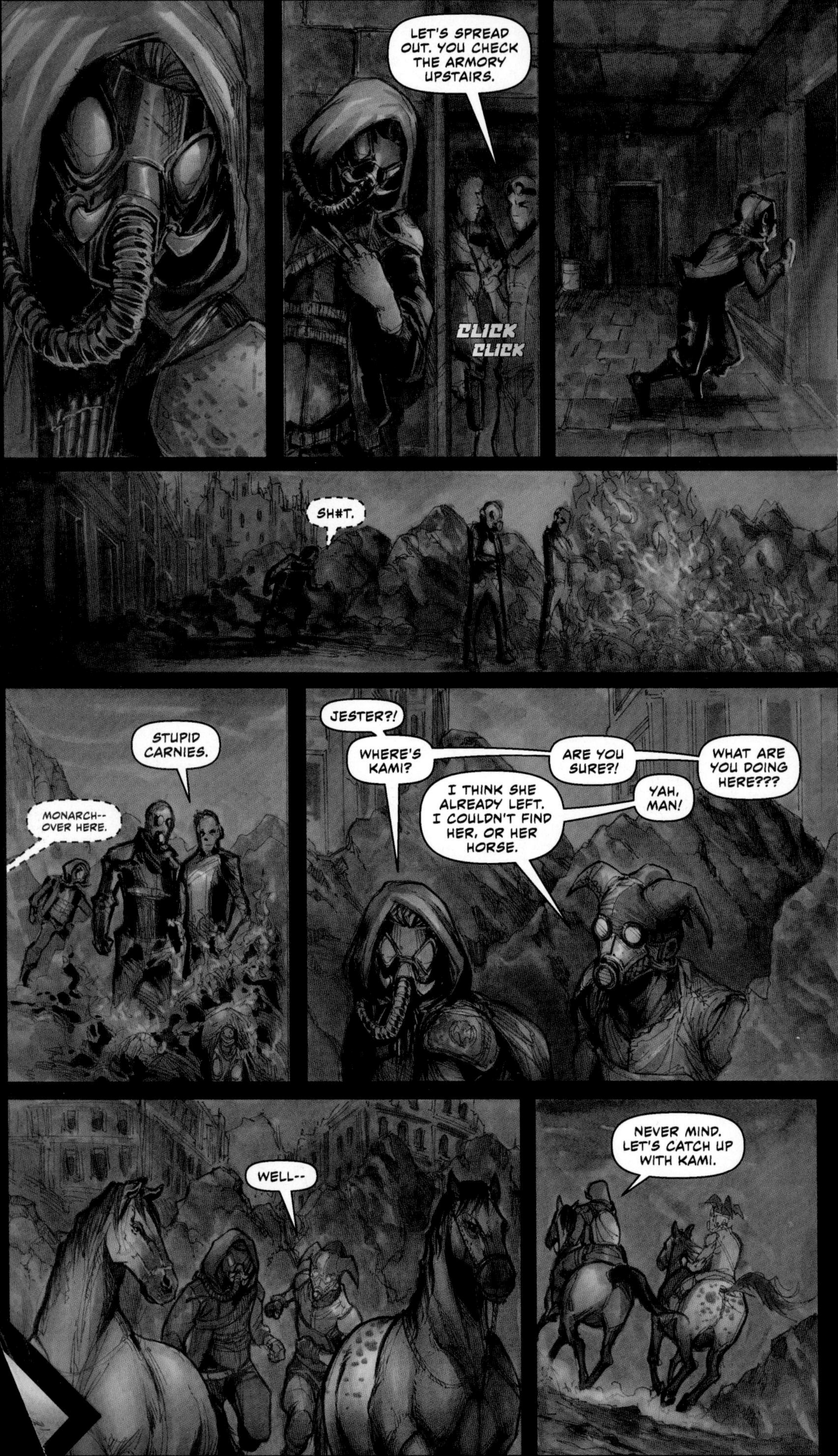
LET'S SPREAD OUT. YOU CHECK THE ARMORY UPSTAIRS.
CLICK CLICK
SH#T.
STUPID CARNIES.
MONARCH-- OVER HERE.
JESTER?!
WHERE'S KAMI?
ARE YOU SURE?!
WHAT ARE YOU DOING HERE???
I THINK SHE ALREADY LEFT. I COULDN'T FIND HER, OR HER HORSE.
YAH, MAN!
WELL--
NEVER MIND. LET'S CATCH UP WITH KAMI.

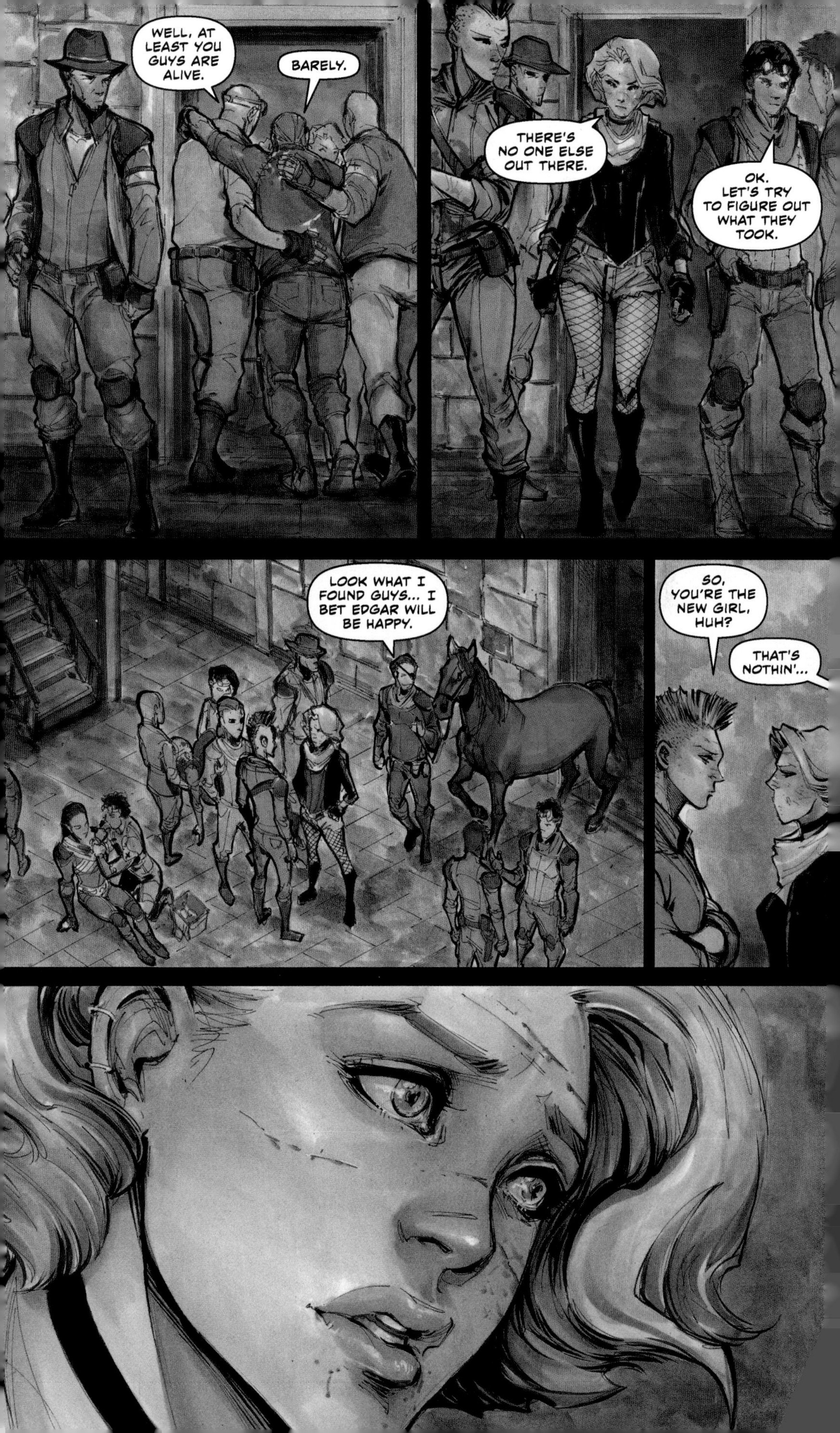
WELL, AT LEAST YOU GUYS ARE ALIVE.
BARELY.
THERE'S NO ONE ELSE OUT THERE.
OK. LET'S TRY TO FIGURE OUT WHAT THEY TOOK.
LOOK WHAT I FOUND GUYS... I BET EDGAR WILL BE HAPPY.
SO, YOU'RE THE NEW GIRL, HUH?
THAT'S NOTHIN'...

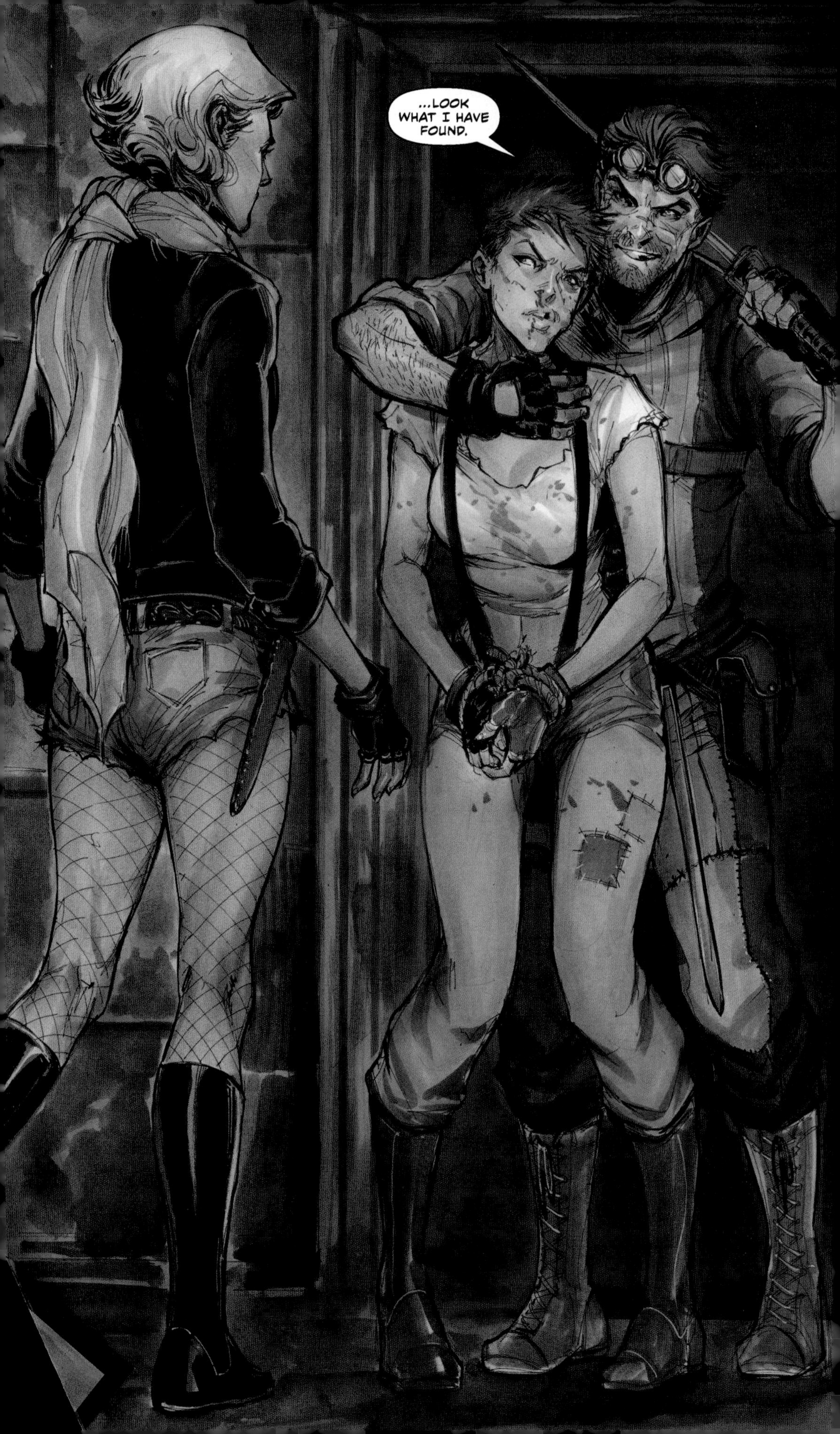
...LOOK WHAT I HAVE FOUND.

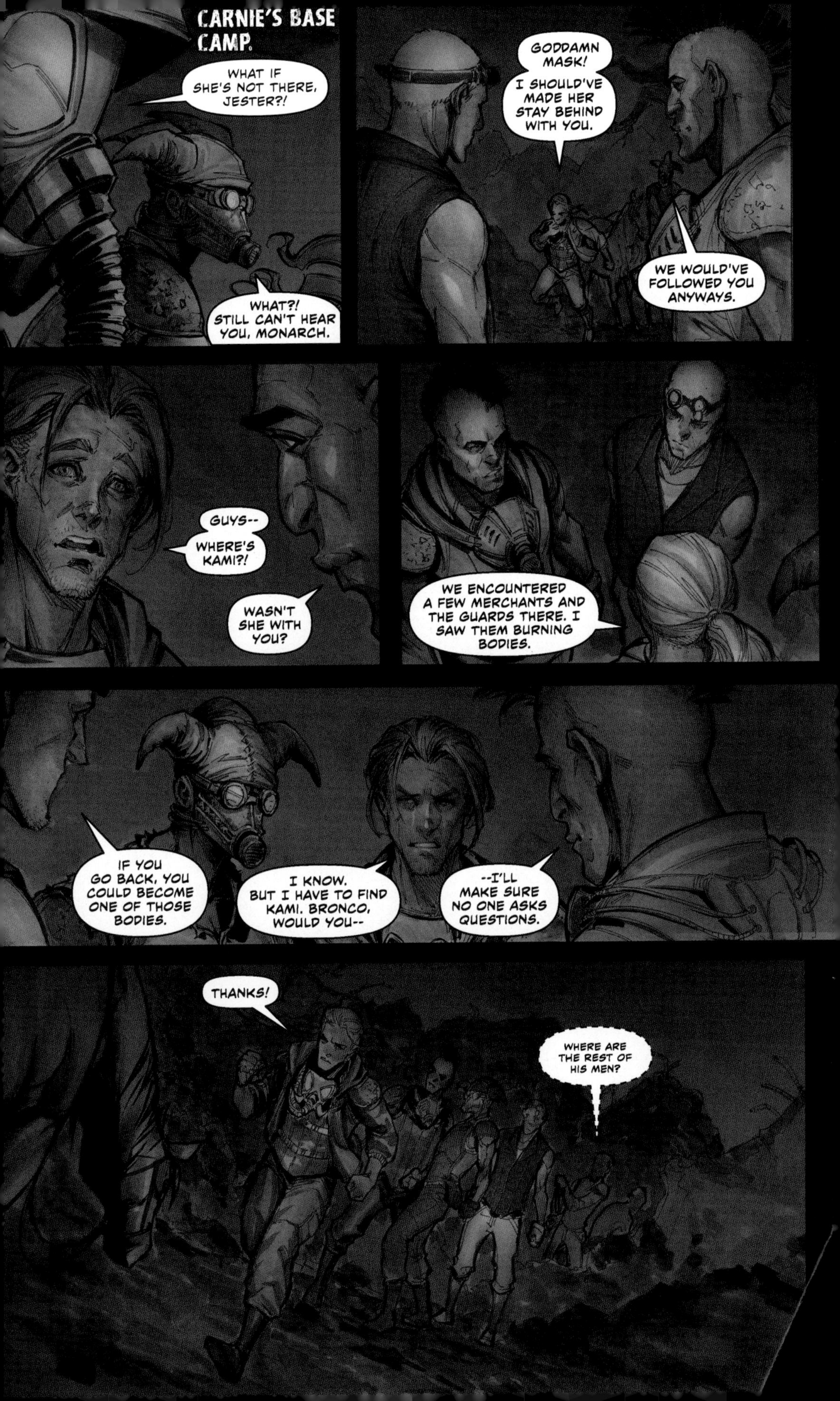
CARNIE'S BASE CAMP.
WHAT IF SHE'S NOT THERE, JESTER?!
WHAT?! STILL CAN'T HEAR YOU, MONARCH.
GODDAMN MASK!
I SHOULD'VE MADE HER STAY BEHIND WITH YOU.
WE WOULD'VE FOLLOWED YOU ANYWAYS.
GUYS--
WHERE'S KAMI?!
WASN'T SHE WITH YOU?
WE ENCOUNTERED A FEW MERCHANTS AND THE GUARDS THERE. I SAW THEM BURNING BODIES.
IF YOU GO BACK, YOU COULD BECOME ONE OF THOSE BODIES.
I KNOW. BUT I HAVE TO FIND KAMI. BRONCO, WOULD YOU--
--I'LL MAKE SURE NO ONE ASKS QUESTIONS.
THANKS!
WHERE ARE THE REST OF HIS MEN?

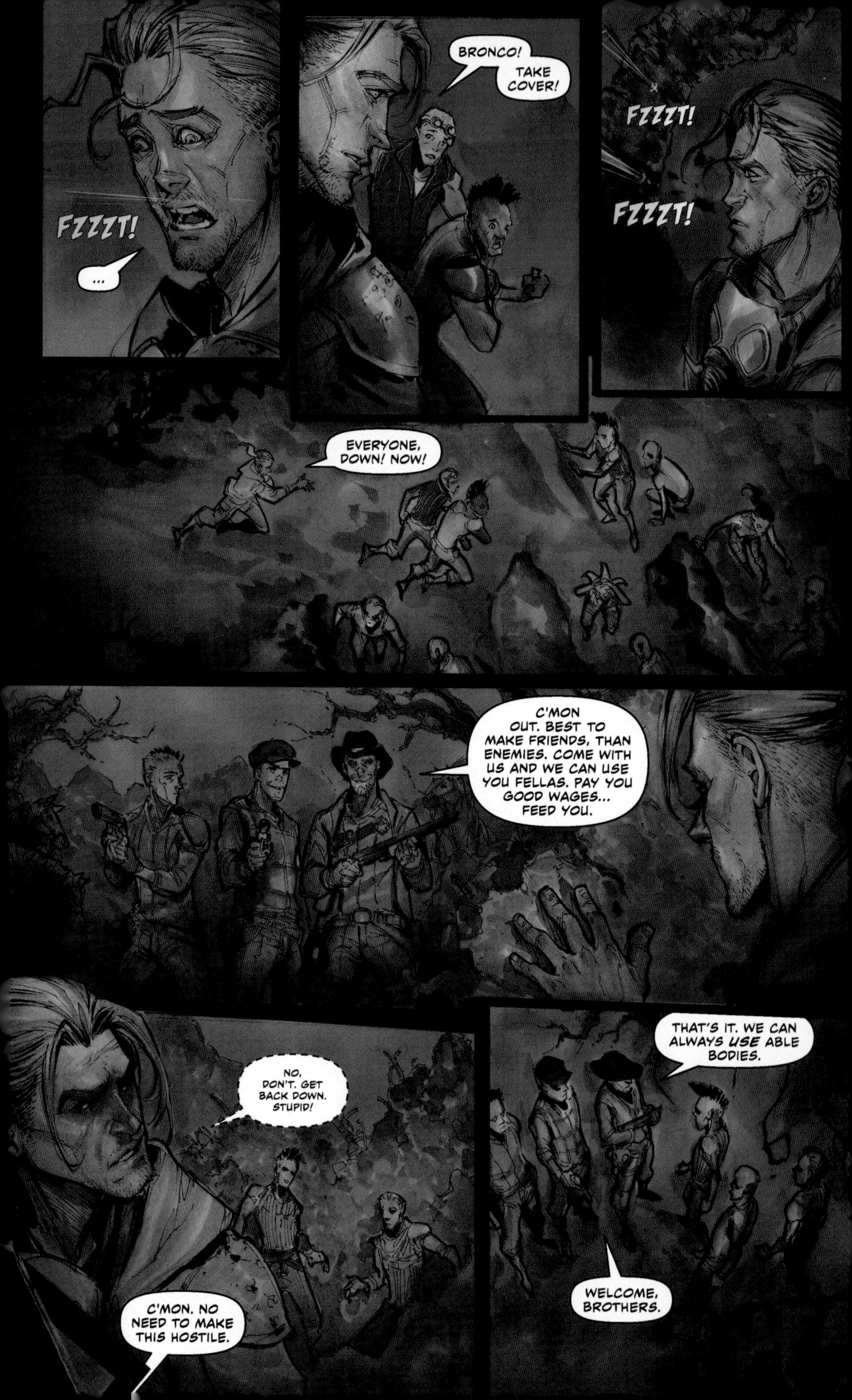
FZZZT!
...
BRONCO!
TAKE COVER!
FZZZT!
FZZZT!
EVERYONE, DOWN! NOW!
C'MON OUT. BEST TO MAKE FRIENDS, THAN ENEMIES. COME WITH US AND WE CAN USE YOU FELLAS. PAY YOU GOOD WAGES... FEED YOU.
NO, DON'T. GET BACK DOWN. STUPID!
C'MON. NO NEED TO MAKE THIS HOSTILE.
THAT'S IT. WE CAN ALWAYS USE ABLE BODIES.
WELCOME, BROTHERS.

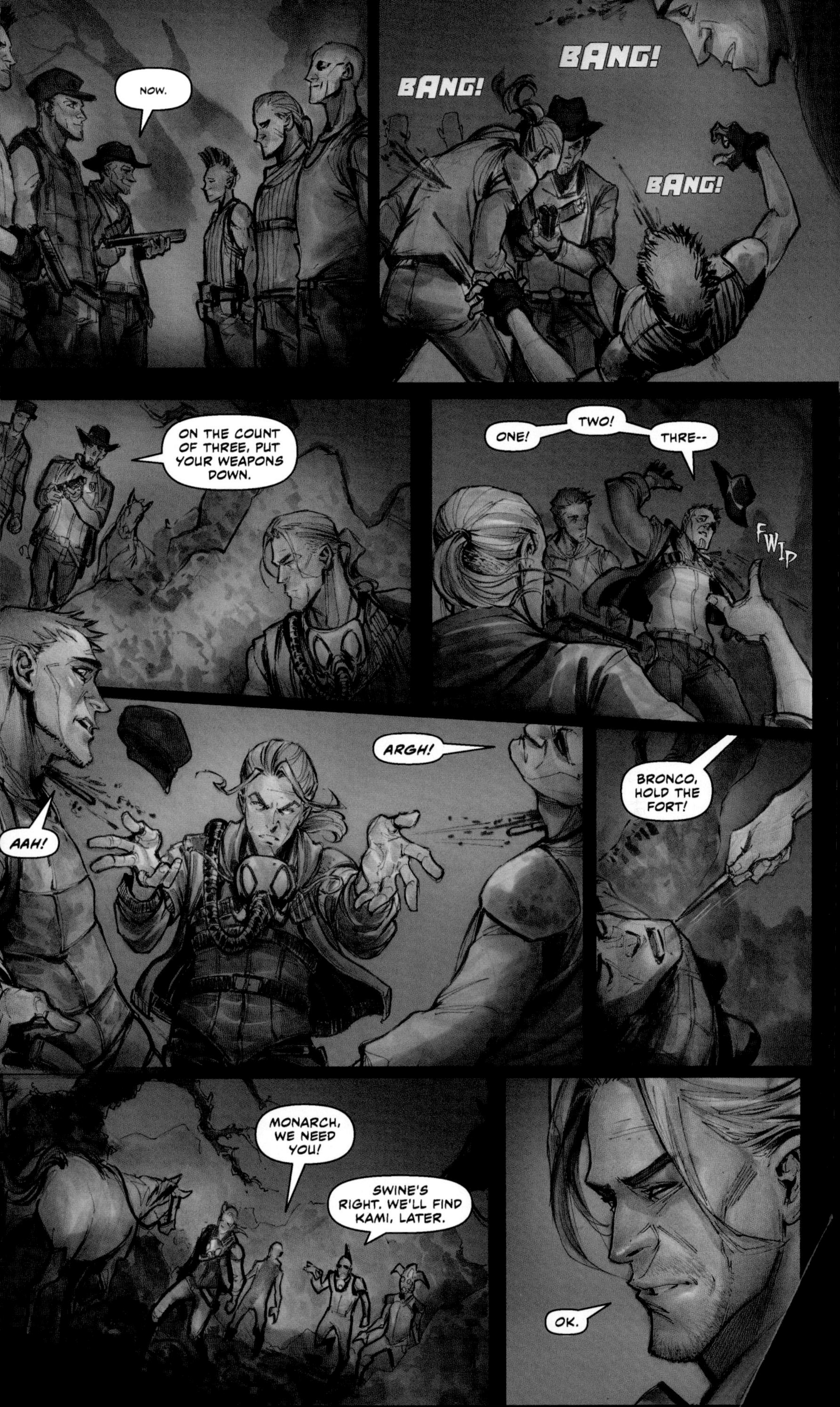
NOW.
BANG!
BANG!
BANG!
ON THE COUNT OF THREE, PUT YOUR WEAPONS DOWN.
ONE!
TWO!
THRE--
FWIP
ARGH!
AAH!
BRONCO, HOLD THE FORT!
MONARCH, WE NEED YOU!
SWINE'S RIGHT. WE'LL FIND KAMI, LATER.
OK.

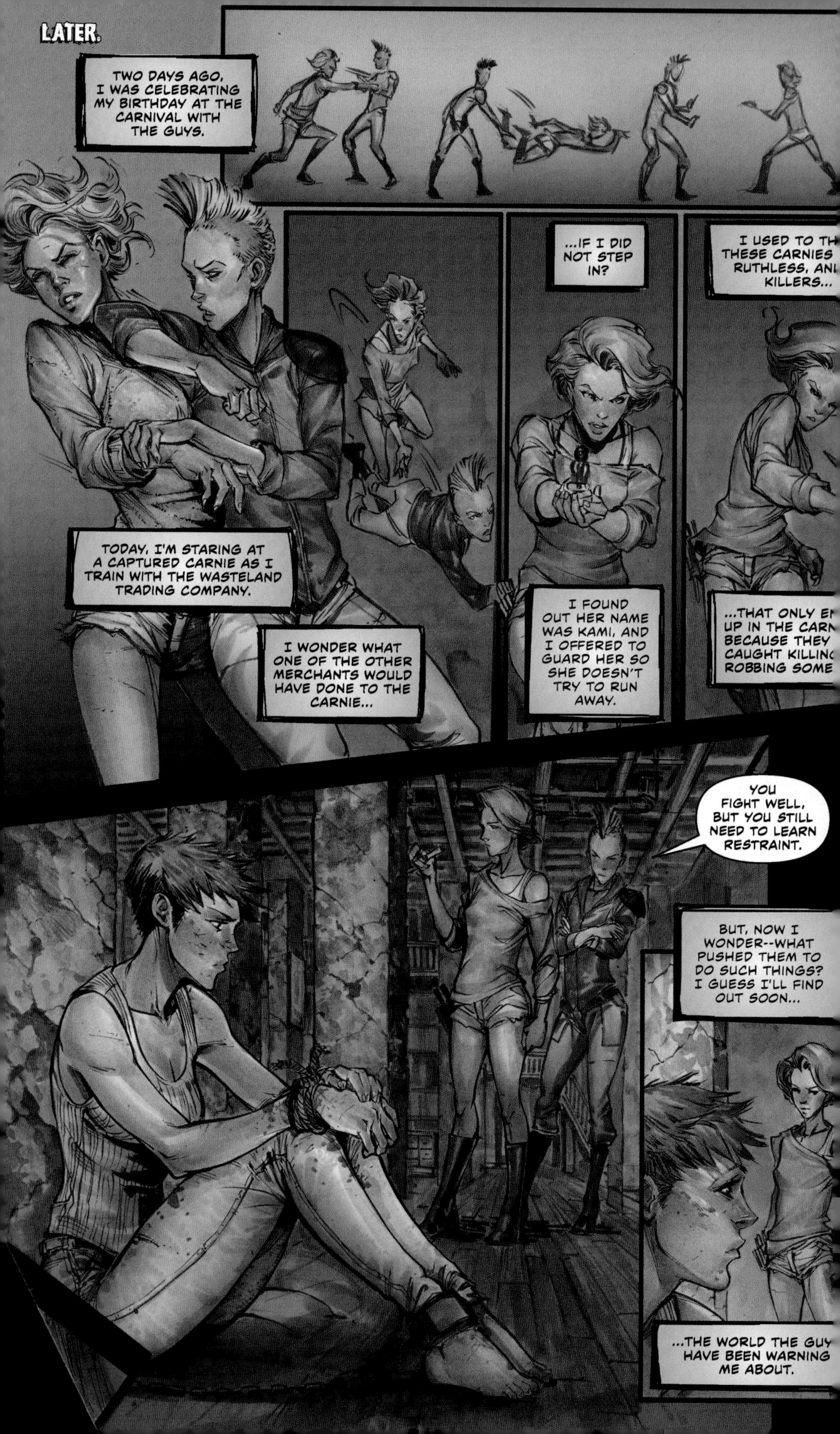
LATER.
TWO DAYS AGO, I WAS CELEBRATING MY BIRTHDAY AT THE CARNIVAL WITH THE GUYS.
TODAY, I'M STARING AT A CAPTURED CARNIE AS I TRAIN WITH THE WASTELAND TRADING COMPANY.
I WONDER WHAT ONE OF THE OTHER MERCHANTS WOULD HAVE DONE TO THE CARNIE...
...IF I DID NOT STEP IN?
I FOUND OUT HER NAME WAS KAMI, AND I OFFERED TO GUARD HER SO SHE DOESN'T TRY TO RUN AWAY.
I USED TO TH
THESE CARNIES
RUTHLESS, AN
KILLERS...
...THAT ONLY EN
UP IN THE CARN
BECAUSE THEY
CAUGHT KILLING
ROBBING SOME
YOU FIGHT WELL, BUT YOU STILL NEED TO LEARN RESTRAINT.
BUT, NOW I WONDER--WHAT PUSHED THEM TO DO SUCH THINGS? I GUESS I'LL FIND OUT SOON...
...THE WORLD THE GUY
HAVE BEEN WARNING ME ABOUT.

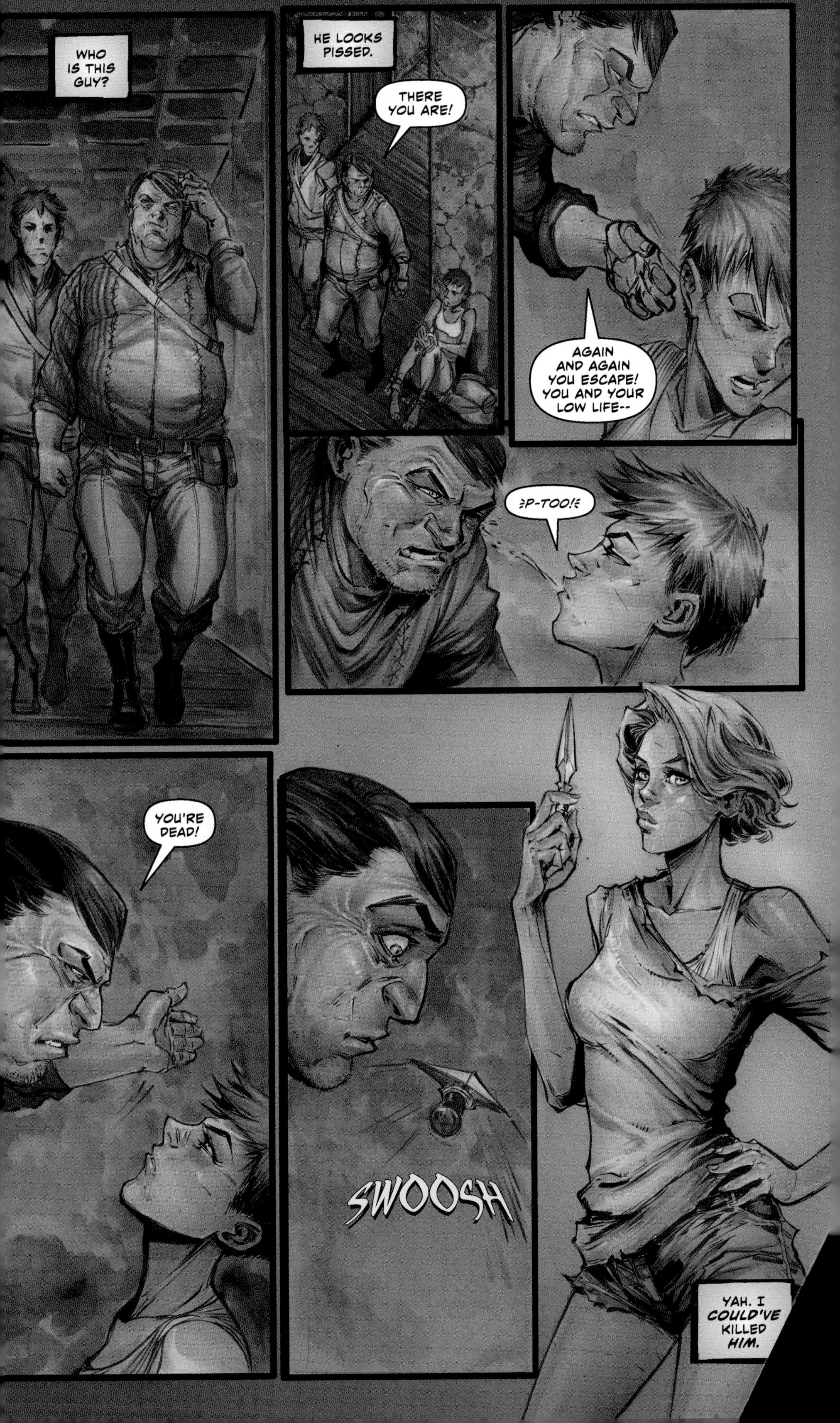
WHO IS THIS GUY?
HE LOOKS PISSED.
THERE YOU ARE!
AGAIN AND AGAIN YOU ESCAPE! YOU AND YOUR LOW LIFE--
P-TOO!
YOU'RE DEAD!
SWOOSH
YAH. I COULD'VE KILLED HIM.

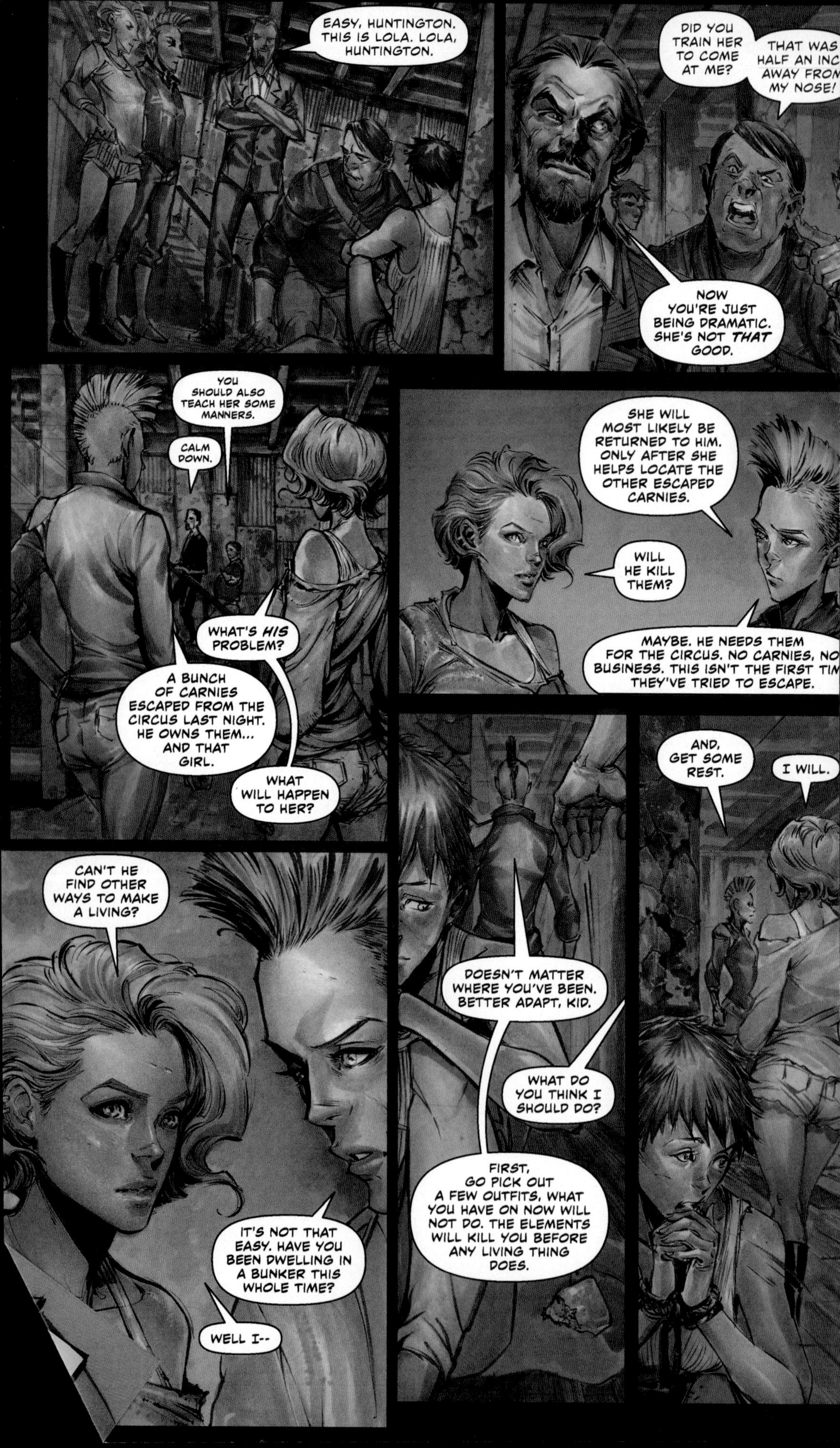
EASY, HUNTINGTON. THIS IS LOLA. LOLA, HUNTINGTON.
DID YOU TRAIN HER TO COME AT ME?
THAT WAS HALF AN INC AWAY FROM MY NOSE!
NOW YOU'RE JUST BEING DRAMATIC. SHE'S NOT THAT GOOD.
YOU SHOULD ALSO TEACH HER SOME MANNERS.
CALM DOWN.
WHAT'S HIS PROBLEM?
A BUNCH OF CARNIES ESCAPED FROM THE CIRCUS LAST NIGHT. HE OWNS THEM... AND THAT GIRL.
WHAT WILL HAPPEN TO HER?
SHE WILL MOST LIKELY BE RETURNED TO HIM. ONLY AFTER SHE HELPS LOCATE THE OTHER ESCAPED CARNIES.
WILL HE KILL THEM?
MAYBE. HE NEEDS THEM FOR THE CIRCUS. NO CARNIES, NO BUSINESS. THIS ISN'T THE FIRST TIM THEY'VE TRIED TO ESCAPE.
CAN'T HE FIND OTHER WAYS TO MAKE A LIVING?
IT'S NOT THAT EASY. HAVE YOU BEEN DWELLING IN A BUNKER THIS WHOLE TIME?
WELL I--
DOESN'T MATTER WHERE YOU'VE BEEN. BETTER ADAPT, KID.
WHAT DO YOU THINK I SHOULD DO?
FIRST, GO PICK OUT A FEW OUTFITS, WHAT YOU HAVE ON NOW WILL NOT DO. THE ELEMENTS WILL KILL YOU BEFORE ANY LIVING THING DOES.
AND, GET SOME REST.
I WILL.

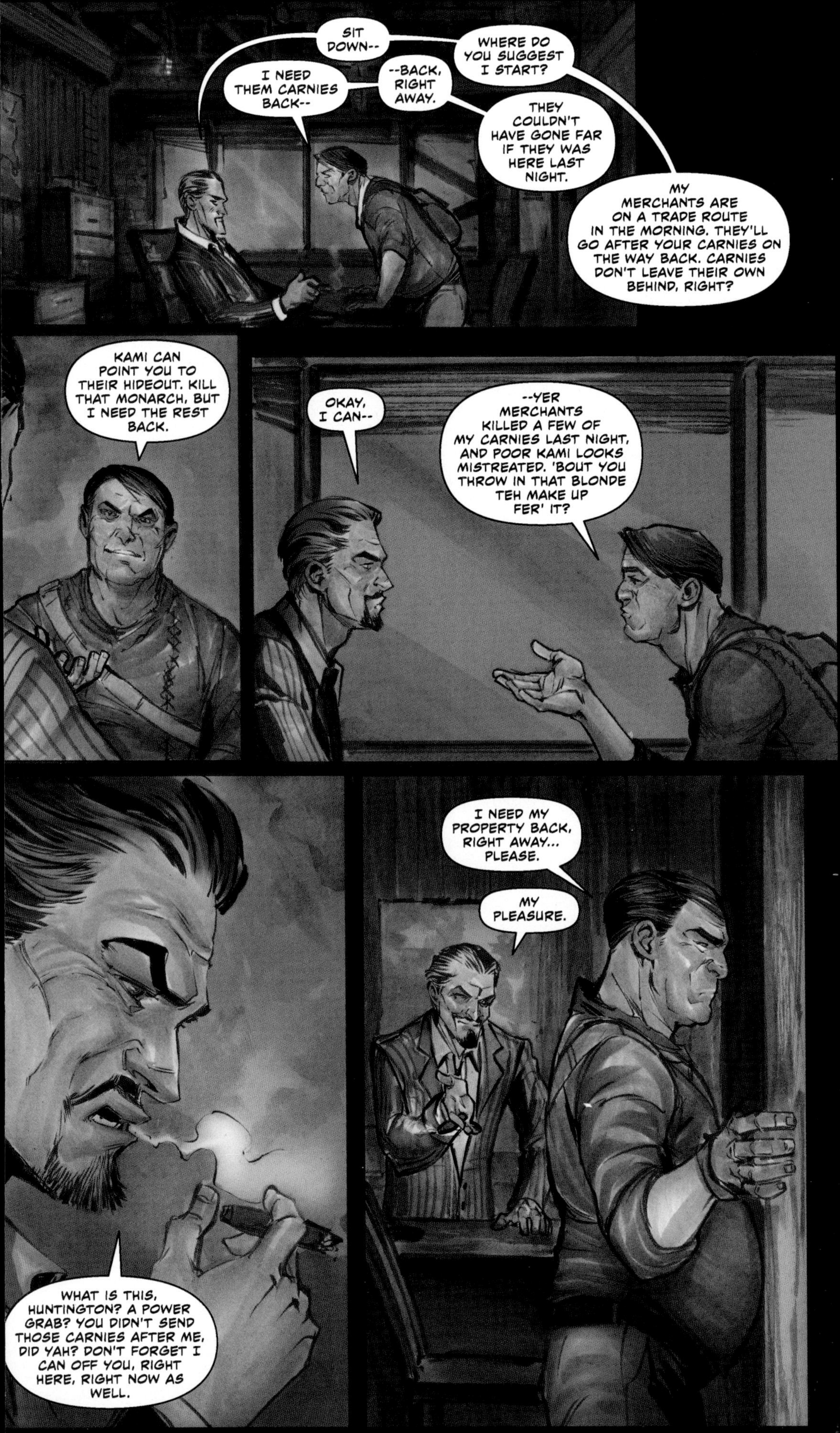
SIT DOWN--
WHERE DO YOU SUGGEST I START?
I NEED THEM CARNIES BACK--
--BACK, RIGHT AWAY.
THEY COULDN'T HAVE GONE FAR IF THEY WAS HERE LAST NIGHT.
MY MERCHANTS ARE ON A TRADE ROUTE IN THE MORNING. THEY'LL GO AFTER YOUR CARNIES ON THE WAY BACK. CARNIES DON'T LEAVE THEIR OWN BEHIND, RIGHT?
KAMI CAN POINT YOU TO THEIR HIDEOUT. KILL THAT MONARCH, BUT I NEED THE REST BACK.
OKAY, I CAN--
--YER MERCHANTS KILLED A FEW OF MY CARNIES LAST NIGHT, AND POOR KAMI LOOKS MISTREATED. 'BOUT YOU THROW IN THAT BLONDE TEH MAKE UP FER' IT?
WHAT IS THIS, HUNTINGTON? A POWER GRAB? YOU DIDN'T SEND THOSE CARNIES AFTER ME, DID YAH? DON'T FORGET I CAN OFF YOU, RIGHT HERE, RIGHT NOW AS WELL.
I NEED MY PROPERTY BACK, RIGHT AWAY... PLEASE.
MY PLEASURE.

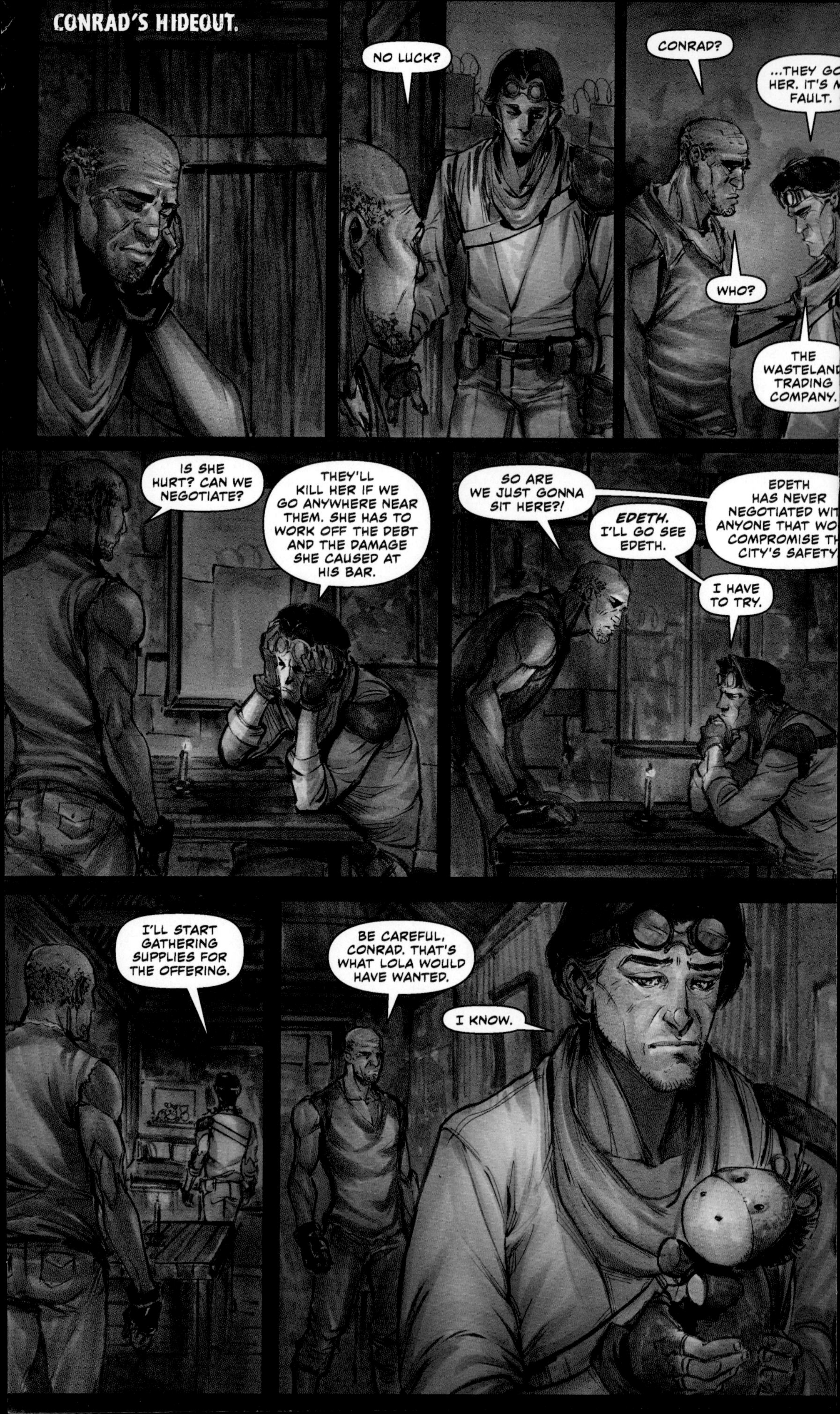
CONRAD'S HIDEOUT.
NO LUCK?
CONRAD?
...THEY GO HER. IT'S M FAULT.
WHO?
THE WASTELAND TRADING COMPANY.
IS SHE HURT? CAN WE NEGOTIATE?
THEY'LL KILL HER IF WE GO ANYWHERE NEAR THEM. SHE HAS TO WORK OFF THE DEBT AND THE DAMAGE SHE CAUSED AT HIS BAR.
SO ARE WE JUST GONNA SIT HERE?!
EDETH HAS NEVER NEGOTIATED WIT ANYONE THAT WO COMPROMISE TH CITY'S SAFETY
EDETH. I'LL GO SEE EDETH.
I HAVE TO TRY.
I'LL START GATHERING SUPPLIES FOR THE OFFERING.
BE CAREFUL, CONRAD. THAT'S WHAT LOLA WOULD HAVE WANTED.
I KNOW.

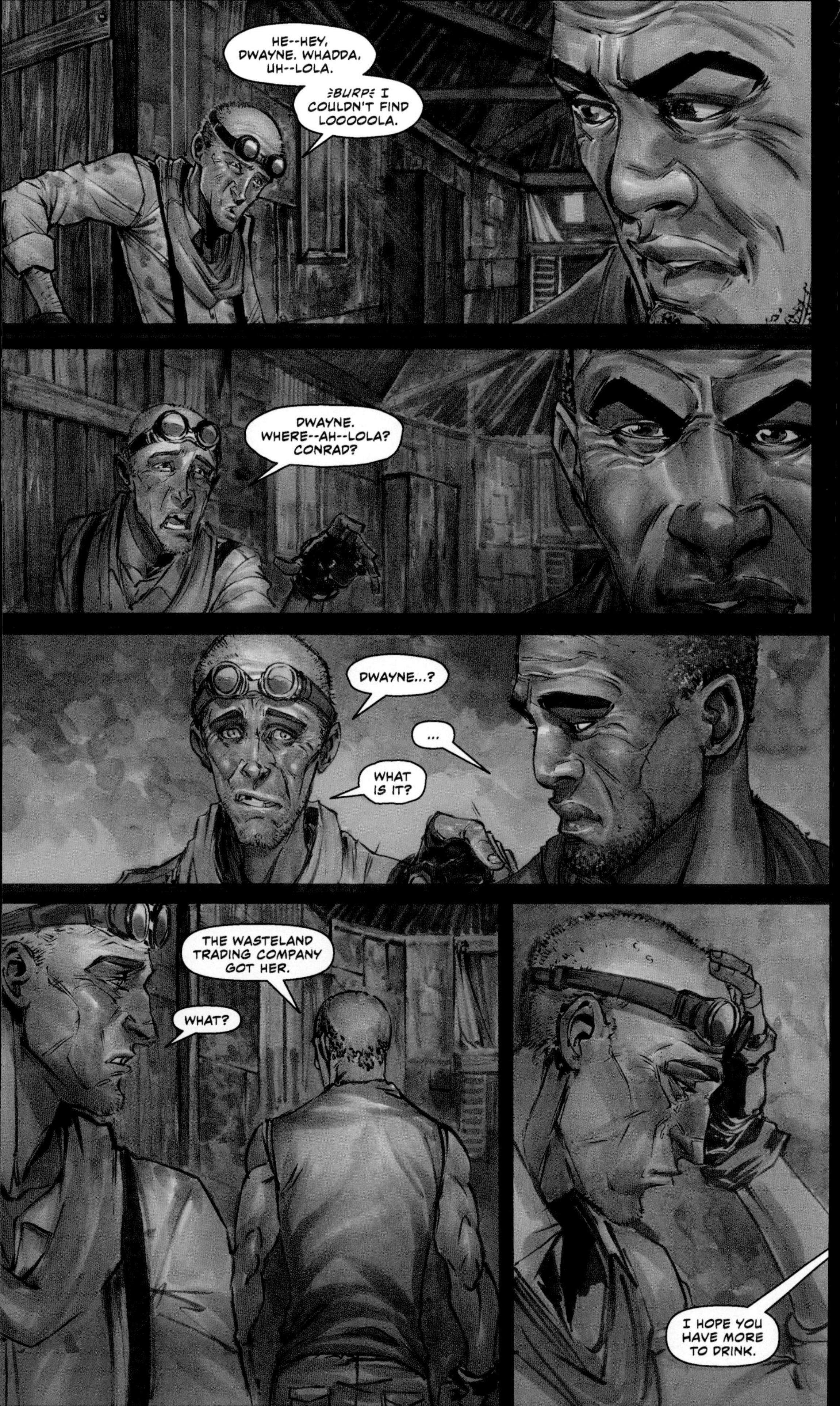
HE--HEY, DWAYNE. WHADDA, UH--LOLA.
≥BURP≤ I COULDN'T FIND LOOOOOLA.
DWAYNE. WHERE--AH--LOLA? CONRAD?
DWAYNE...?
...
WHAT IS IT?
THE WASTELAND TRADING COMPANY GOT HER.
WHAT?
I HOPE YOU HAVE MORE TO DRINK.

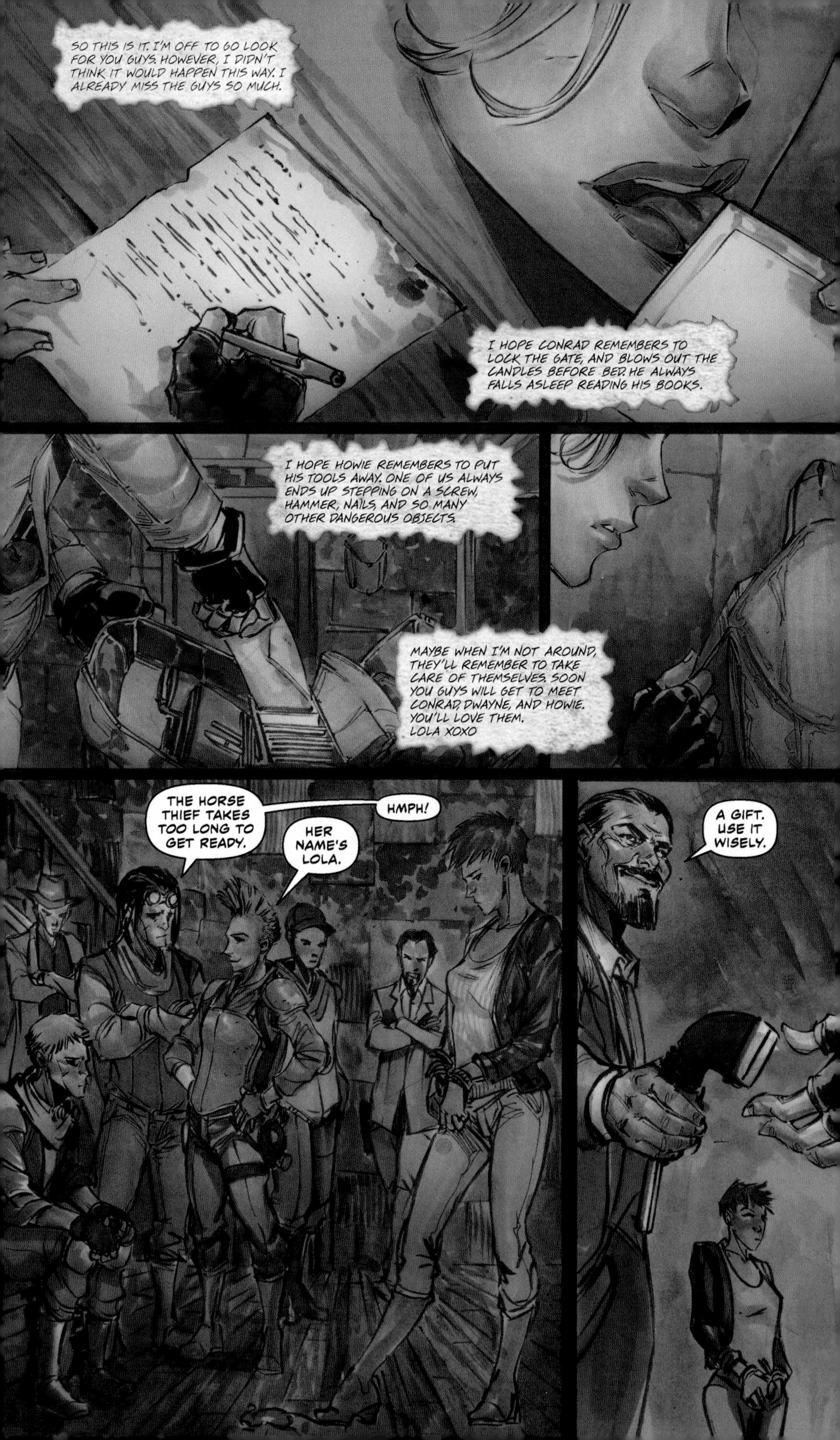
SO THIS IS IT. I'M OFF TO GO LOOK FOR YOU GUYS. HOWEVER, I DIDN'T THINK IT WOULD HAPPEN THIS WAY. I ALREADY MISS THE GUYS SO MUCH.
I HOPE CONRAD REMEMBERS TO LOCK THE GATE, AND BLOWS OUT THE CANDLES BEFORE BED. HE ALWAYS FALLS ASLEEP READING HIS BOOKS.
I HOPE HOWIE REMEMBERS TO PUT HIS TOOLS AWAY. ONE OF US ALWAYS ENDS UP STEPPING ON A SCREW, HAMMER, NAILS, AND SO MANY OTHER DANGEROUS OBJECTS.
MAYBE WHEN I'M NOT AROUND, THEY'LL REMEMBER TO TAKE CARE OF THEMSELVES. SOON YOU GUYS WILL GET TO MEET CONRAD, DWAYNE, AND HOWIE. YOU'LL LOVE THEM. LOLA XOXO
THE HORSE THIEF TAKES TOO LONG TO GET READY.
HMPH!
HER NAME'S LOLA.
A GIFT. USE IT WISELY.

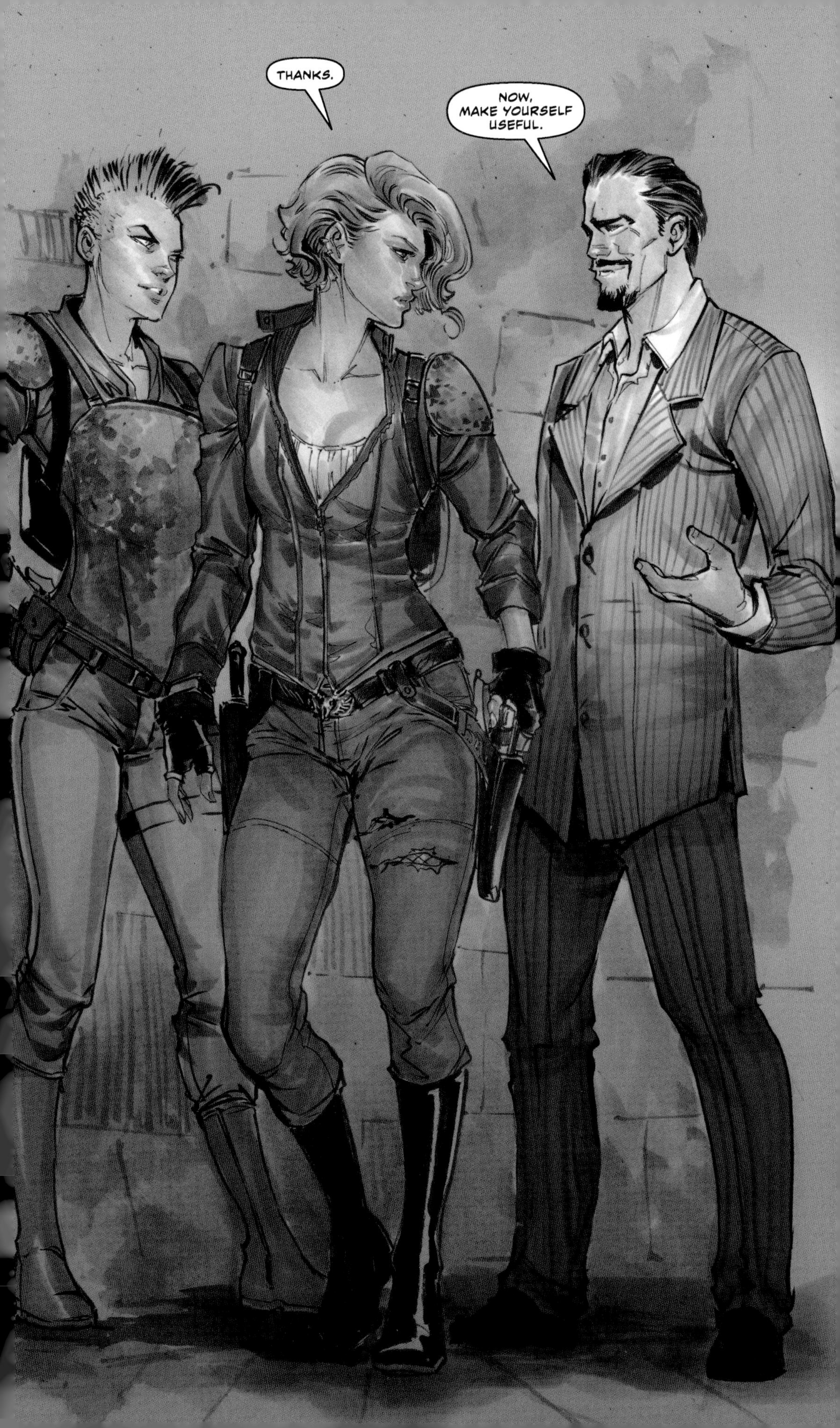
THANKS.
NOW, MAKE YOURSELF USEFUL.

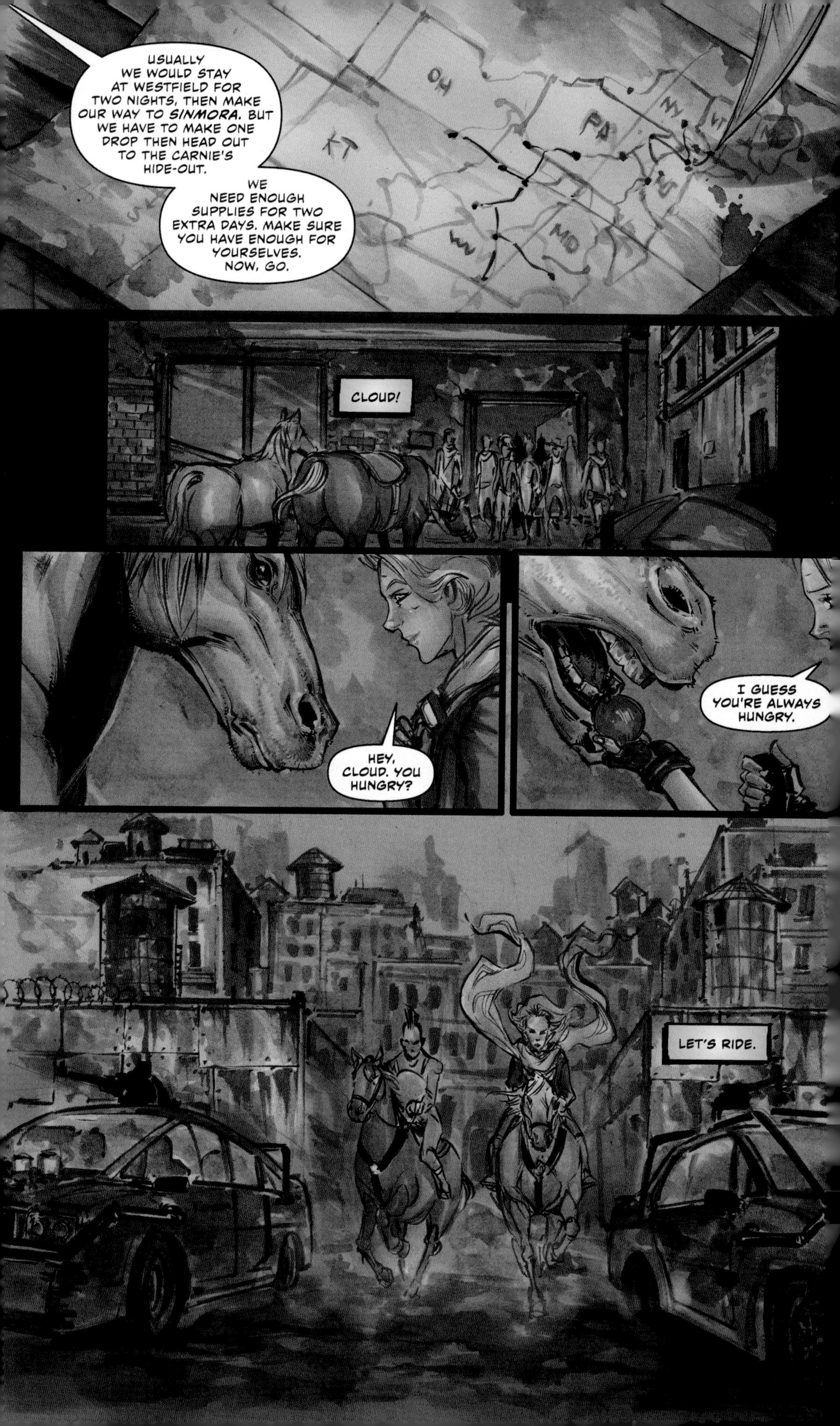
USUALLY WE WOULD STAY AT WESTFIELD FOR TWO NIGHTS, THEN MAKE OUR WAY TO *SINMORA.* BUT WE HAVE TO MAKE ONE DROP THEN HEAD OUT TO THE CARNIE'S HIDE-OUT.
WE NEED ENOUGH SUPPLIES FOR TWO EXTRA DAYS. MAKE SURE YOU HAVE ENOUGH FOR YOURSELVES. NOW, GO.
CLOUD!
HEY, CLOUD. YOU HUNGRY?
I GUESS YOU'RE ALWAYS HUNGRY.
LET'S RIDE.

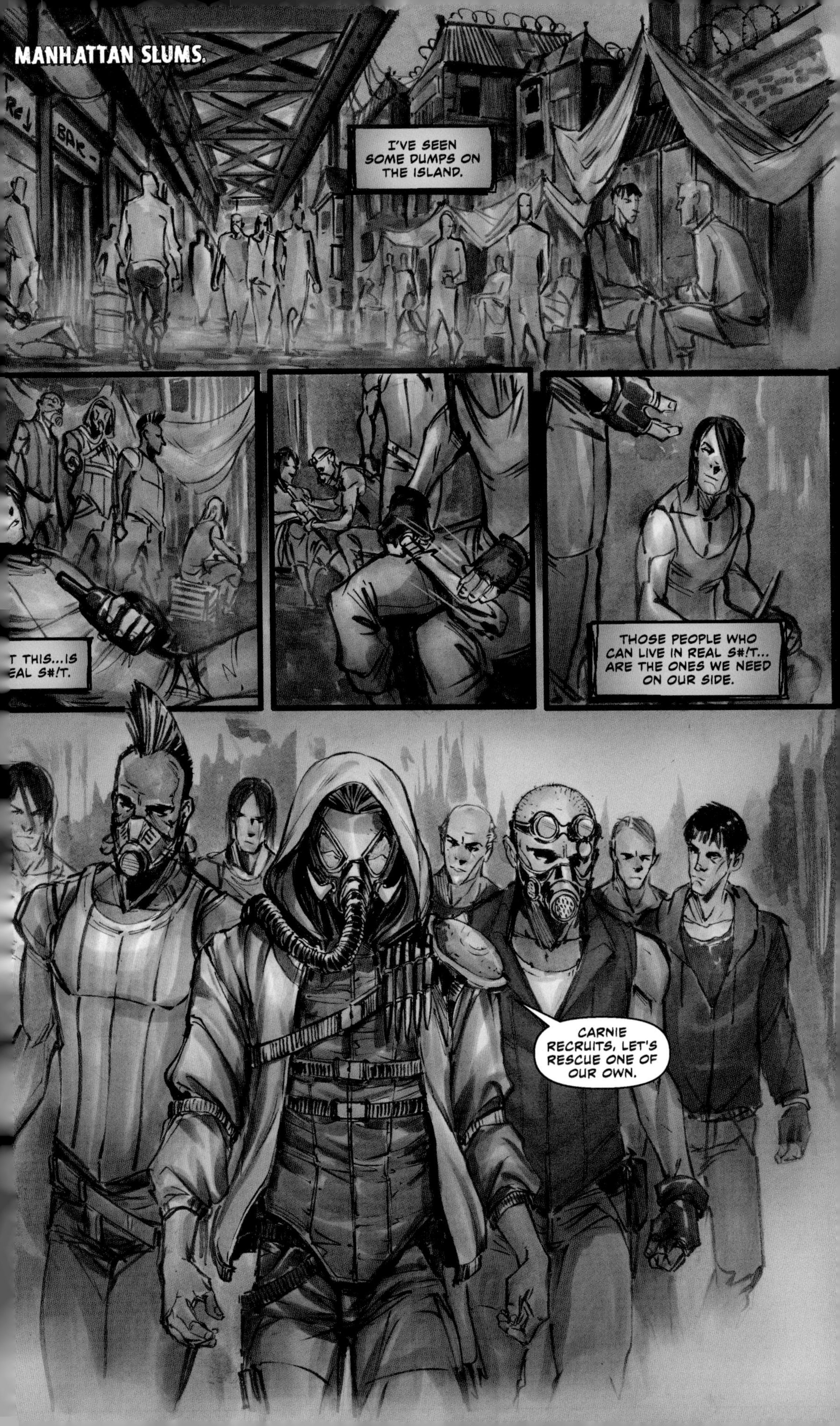
MANHATTAN SLUMS.
I'VE SEEN SOME DUMPS ON THE ISLAND.
T THIS...IS EAL S#!T.
THOSE PEOPLE WHO CAN LIVE IN REAL S#!T... ARE THE ONES WE NEED ON OUR SIDE.
CARNIE RECRUITS, LET'S RESCUE ONE OF OUR OWN.

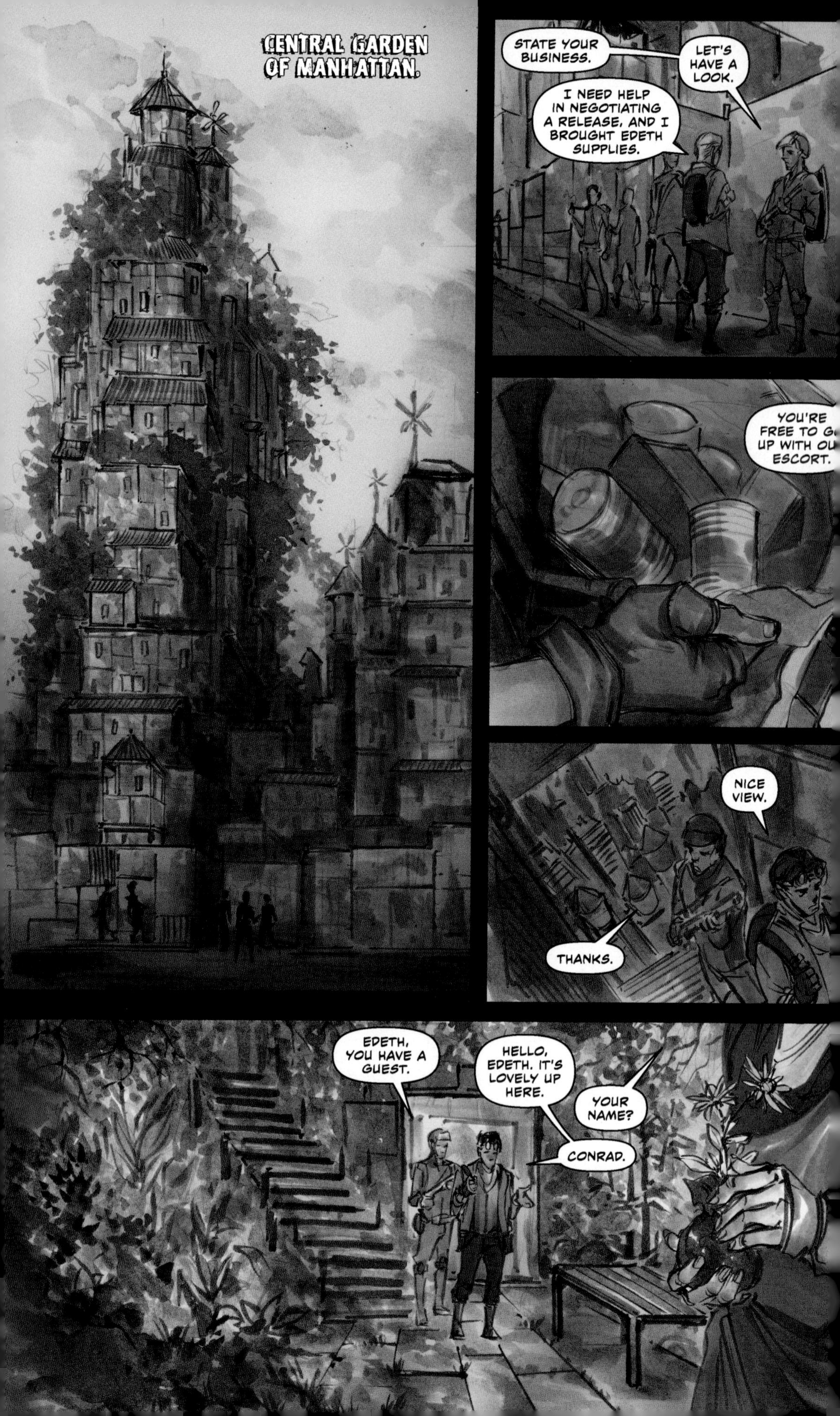
CENTRAL GARDEN OF MANHATTAN.
STATE YOUR BUSINESS.
LET'S HAVE A LOOK.
I NEED HELP IN NEGOTIATING A RELEASE, AND I BROUGHT EDETH SUPPLIES.
YOU'RE FREE TO G UP WITH OU ESCORT.
NICE VIEW.
THANKS.
EDETH, YOU HAVE A GUEST.
HELLO, EDETH. IT'S LOVELY UP HERE.
YOUR NAME?
CONRAD.

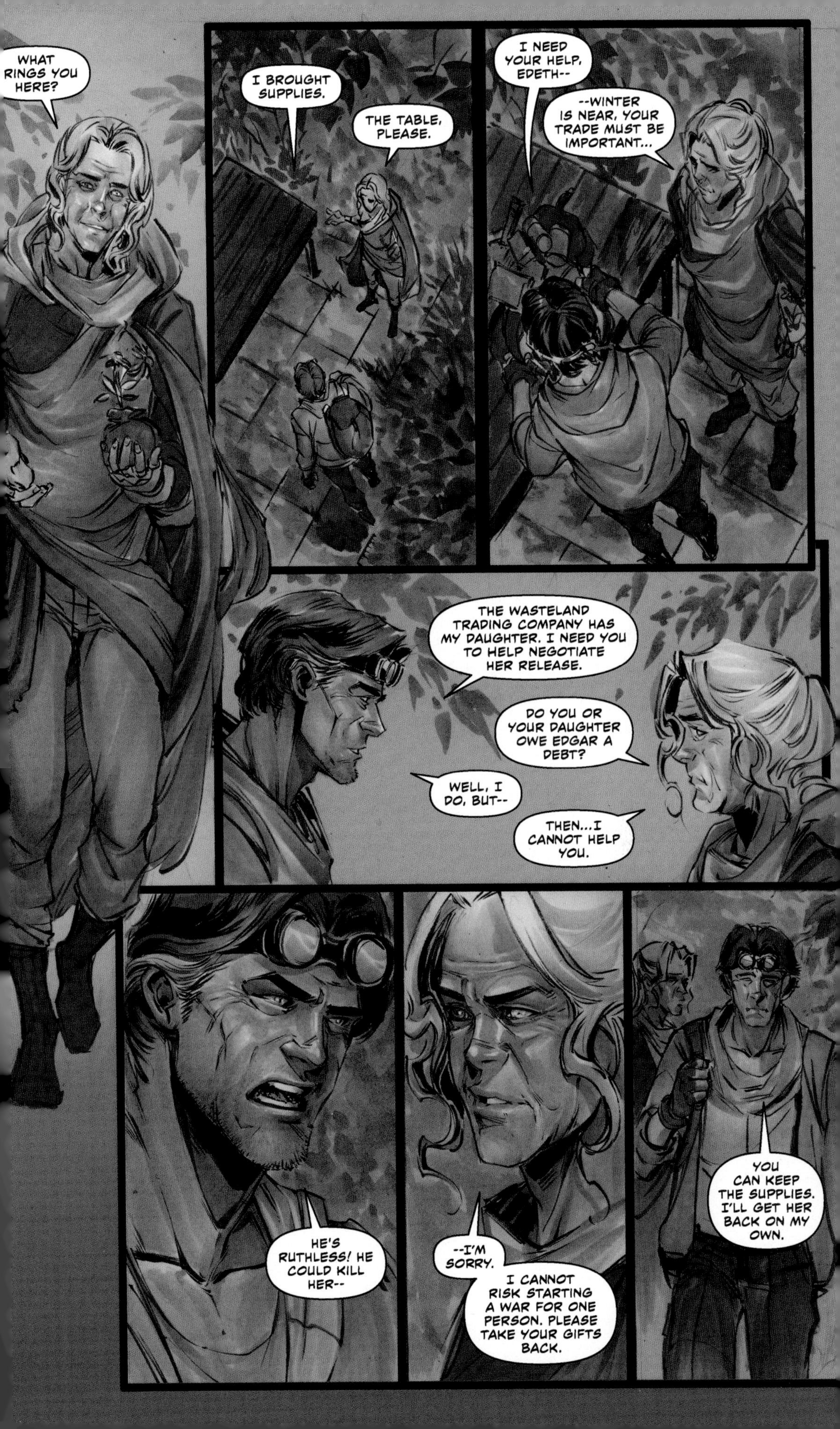
WHAT RINGS YOU HERE?
I BROUGHT SUPPLIES.
THE TABLE, PLEASE.
I NEED YOUR HELP, EDETH--
--WINTER IS NEAR, YOUR TRADE MUST BE IMPORTANT...
THE WASTELAND TRADING COMPANY HAS MY DAUGHTER. I NEED YOU TO HELP NEGOTIATE HER RELEASE.
DO YOU OR YOUR DAUGHTER OWE EDGAR A DEBT?
WELL, I DO, BUT--
THEN...I CANNOT HELP YOU.
HE'S RUTHLESS! HE COULD KILL HER--
--I'M SORRY.
I CANNOT RISK STARTING A WAR FOR ONE PERSON. PLEASE TAKE YOUR GIFTS BACK.
YOU CAN KEEP THE SUPPLIES. I'LL GET HER BACK ON MY OWN.

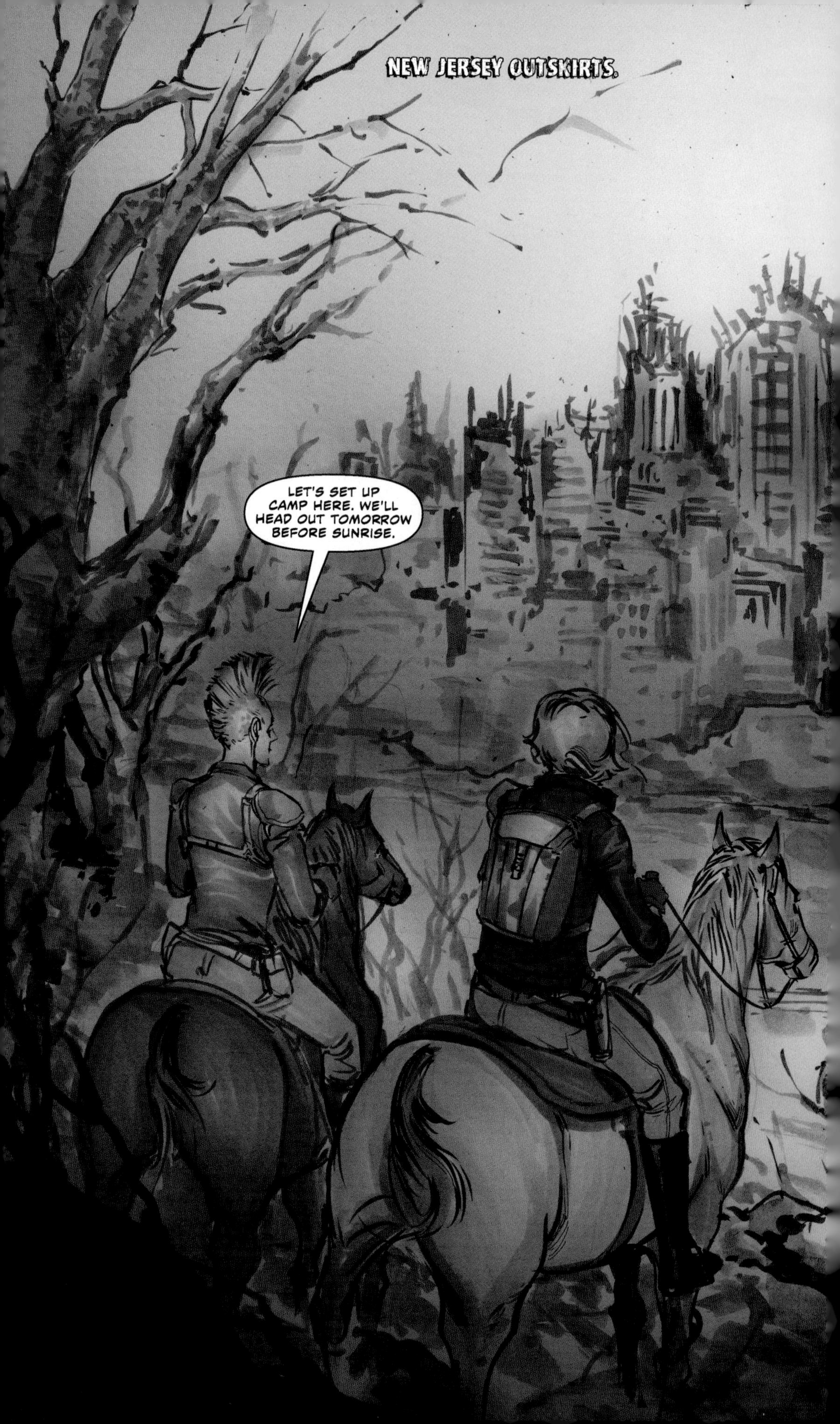
NEW JERSEY OUTSKIRTS.
LET'S SET UP CAMP HERE. WE'LL HEAD OUT TOMORROW BEFORE SUNRISE.

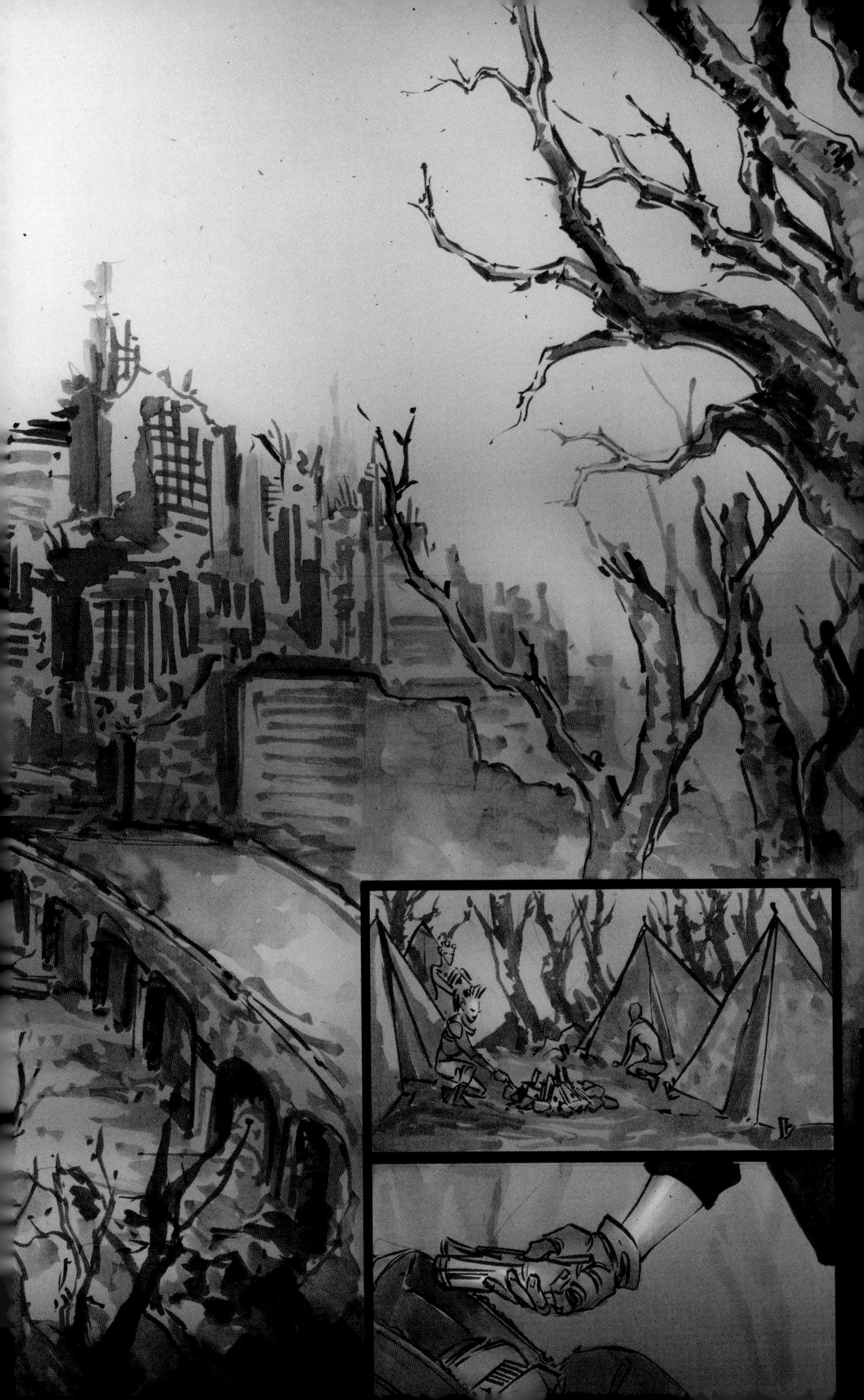

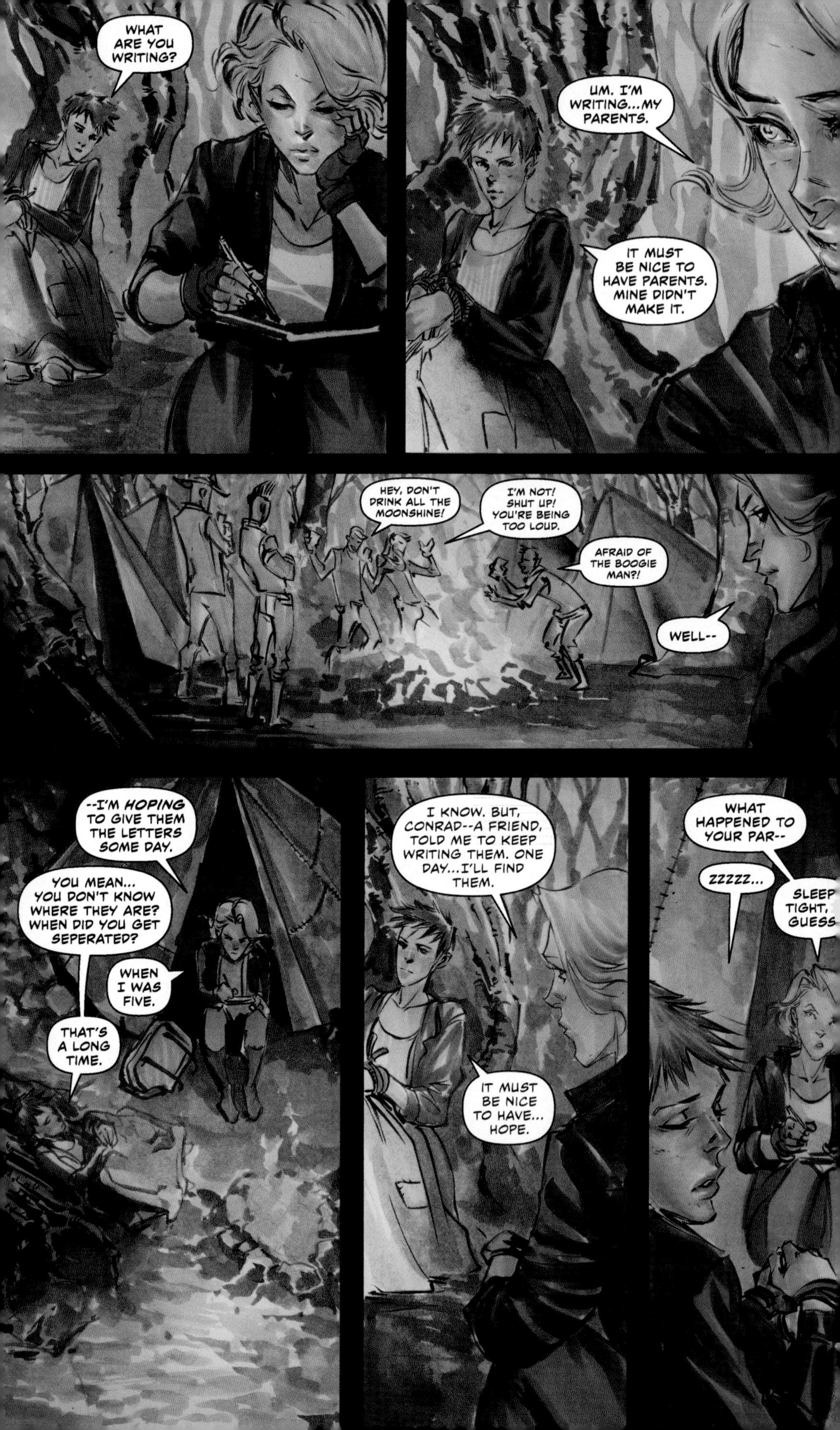

WHAT ARE YOU WRITING?
UM. I'M WRITING...MY PARENTS.
IT MUST BE NICE TO HAVE PARENTS. MINE DIDN'T MAKE IT.
HEY, DON'T DRINK ALL THE MOONSHINE!
I'M NOT! SHUT UP! YOU'RE BEING TOO LOUD.
AFRAID OF THE BOOGIE MAN?!
WELL--
--I'M *HOPING* TO GIVE THEM THE LETTERS SOME DAY.
YOU MEAN... YOU DON'T KNOW WHERE THEY ARE? WHEN DID YOU GET SEPERATED?
WHEN I WAS FIVE.
THAT'S A LONG TIME.
I KNOW. BUT, CONRAD--A FRIEND, TOLD ME TO KEEP WRITING THEM. ONE DAY...I'LL FIND THEM.
IT MUST BE NICE TO HAVE... HOPE.
WHAT HAPPENED TO YOUR PAR--
ZZZZZ...
SLEEP TIGHT, GUESS

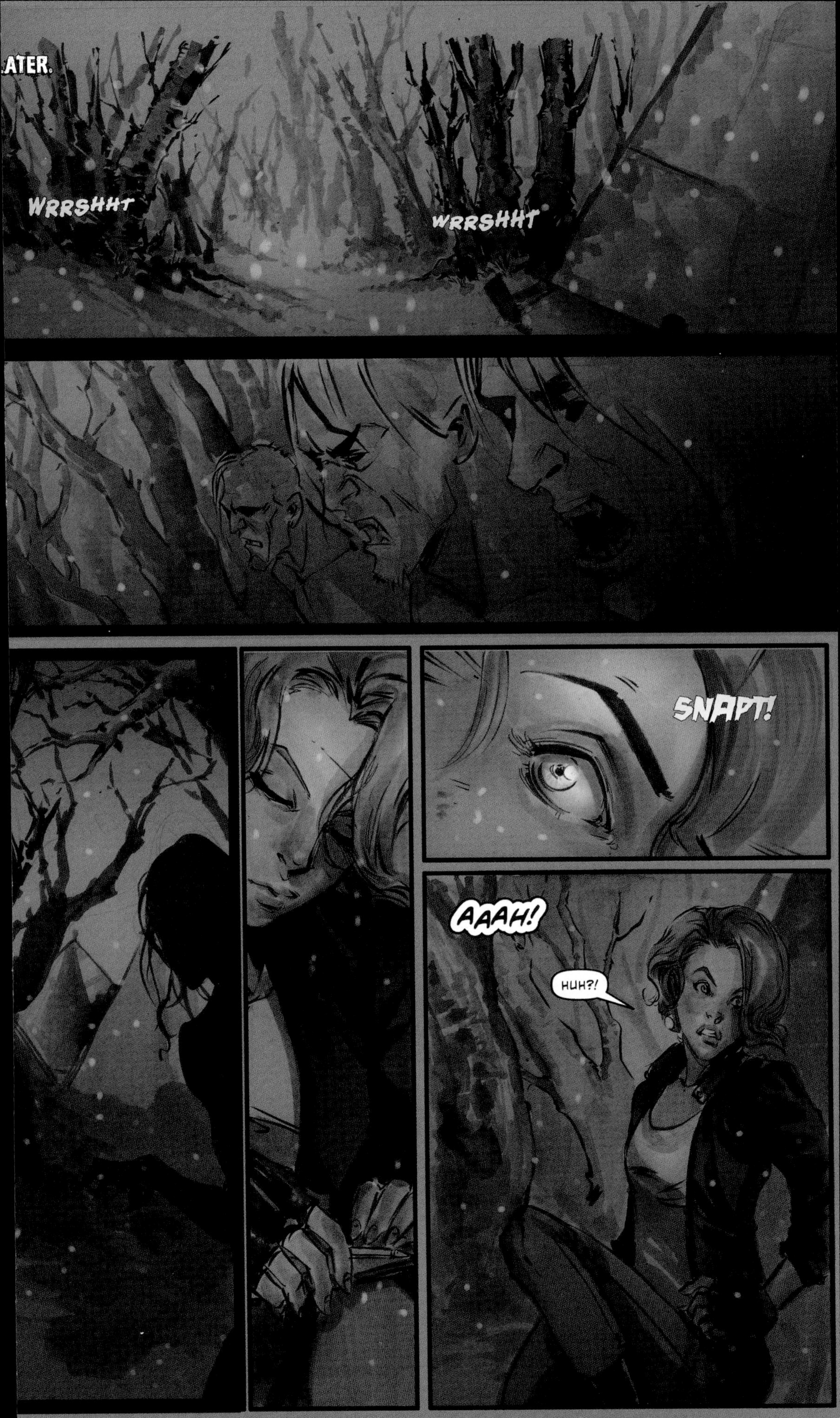

LATER.
WRRSHHT
WRRSHHT
SNAPT!
AAAH!
HUH?!

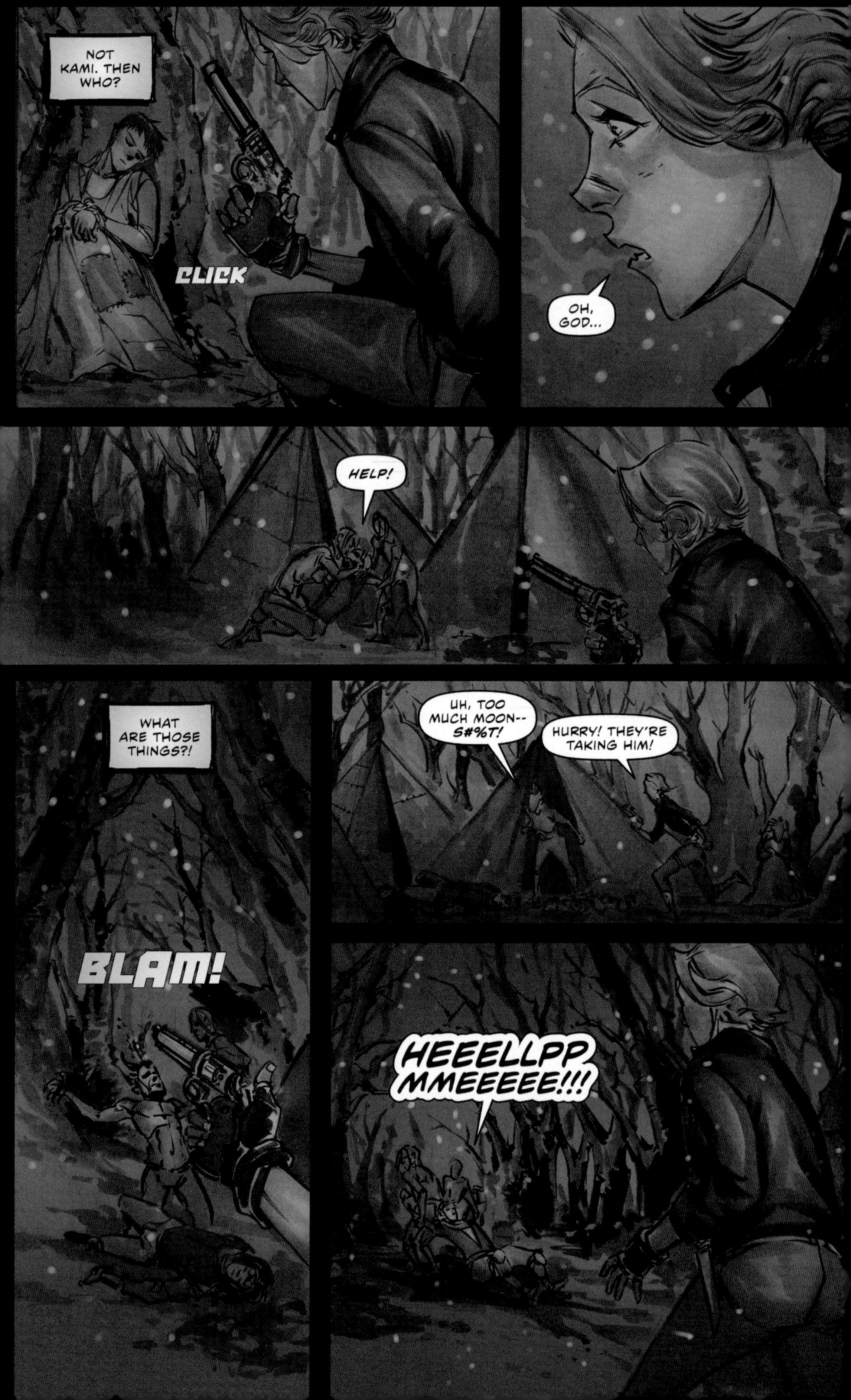
NOT KAMI. THEN WHO?
CLICK
OH, GOD...
HELP!
WHAT ARE THOSE THINGS?!
BLAM!
UH, TOO MUCH MOON-- S#%T!
HURRY! THEY'RE TAKING HIM!
HEEELLPP MMEEEEEE!!!

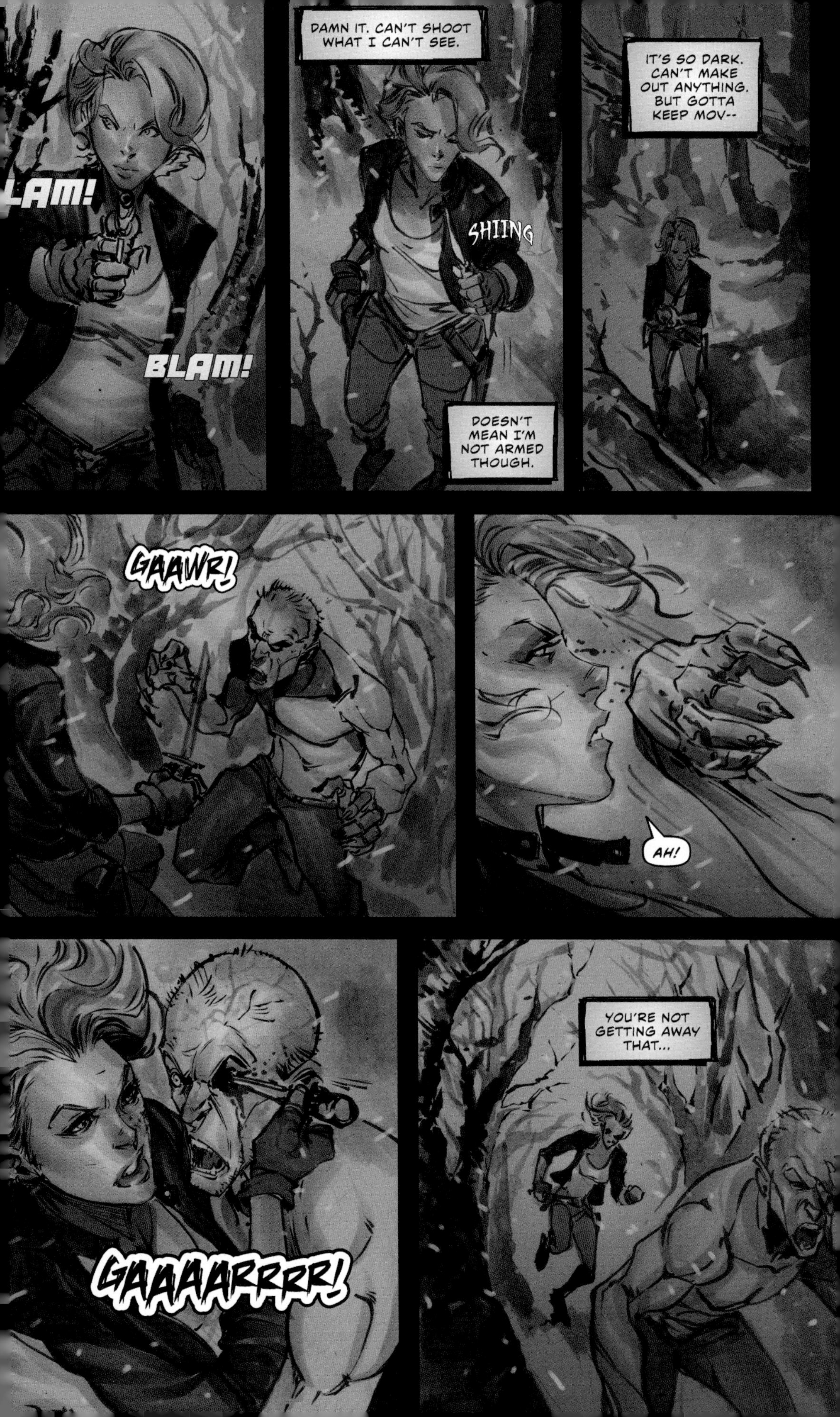
LAM!
BLAM!
DAMN IT. CAN'T SHOOT WHAT I CAN'T SEE.
SHIING
DOESN'T MEAN I'M NOT ARMED THOUGH.
IT'S SO DARK. CAN'T MAKE OUT ANYTHING. BUT GOTTA KEEP MOV--
GAAWR!
AH!
GAAAARRRR!
YOU'RE NOT GETTING AWAY THAT...

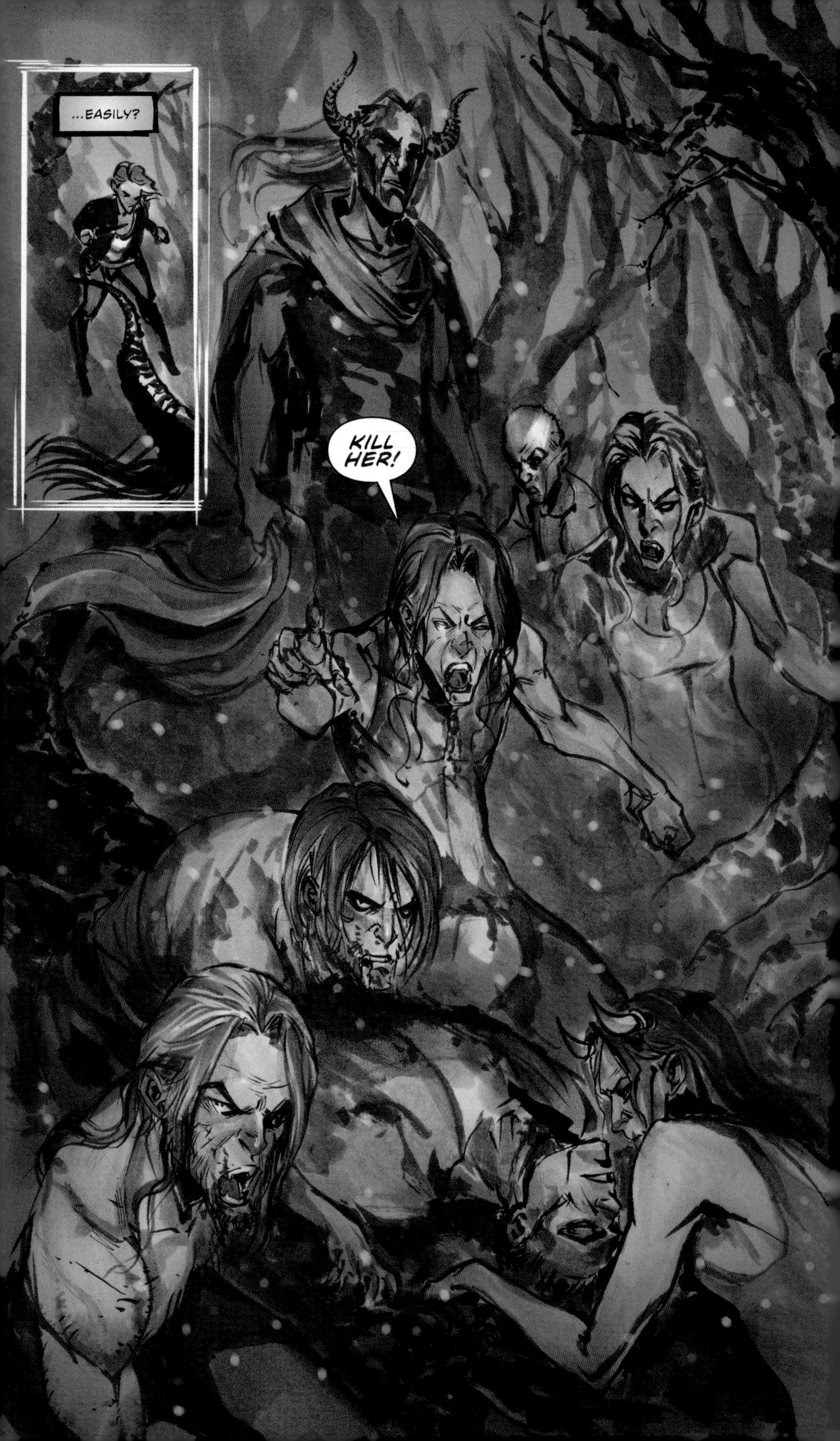
...EASILY?
KILL HER!

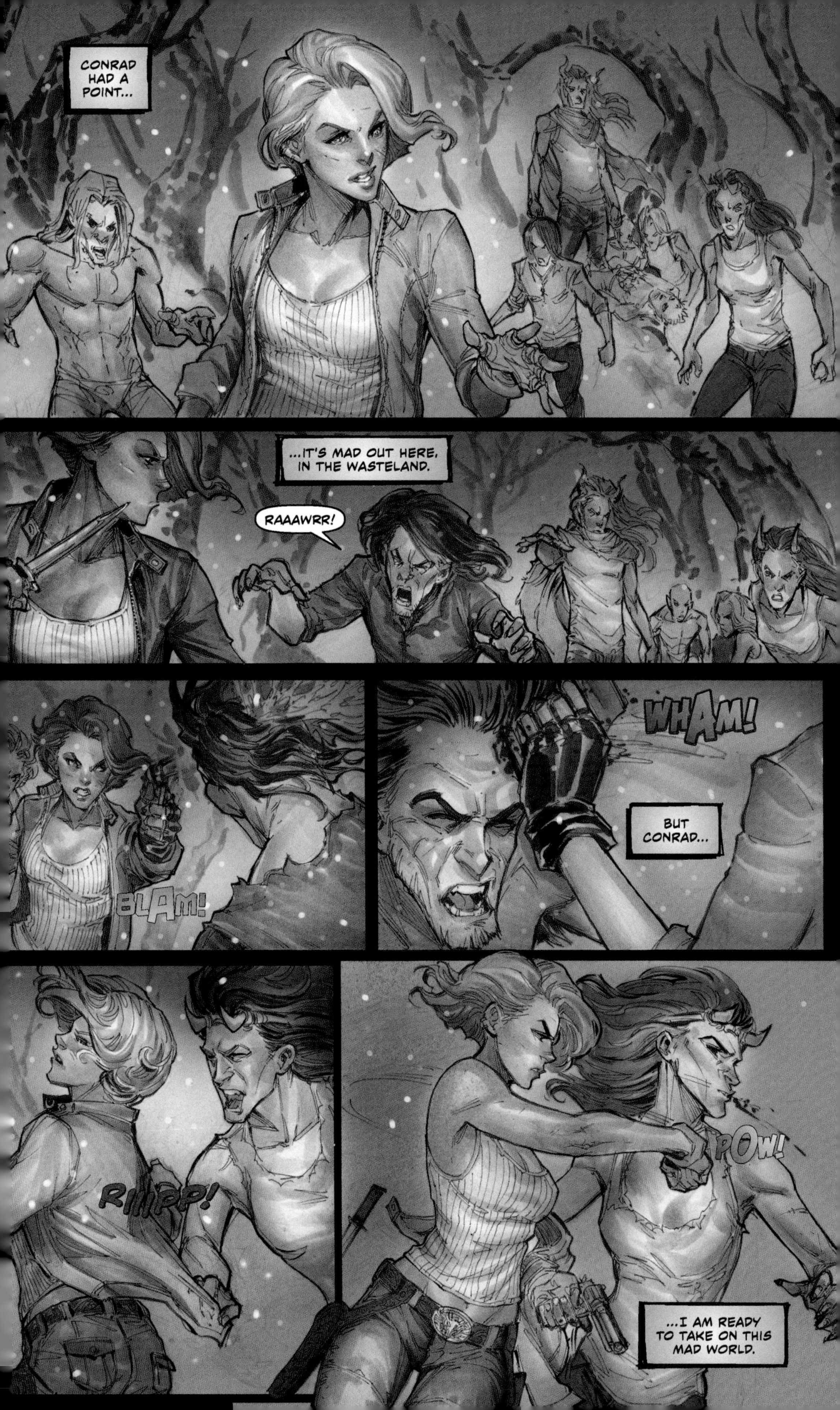

CONRAD HAD A POINT...
...IT'S MAD OUT HERE, IN THE WASTELAND.
RAAAWRR!
BLAM!
WHAM!
BUT CONRAD...
RIIIPP!
POW!
...I AM READY TO TAKE ON THIS MAD WORLD.

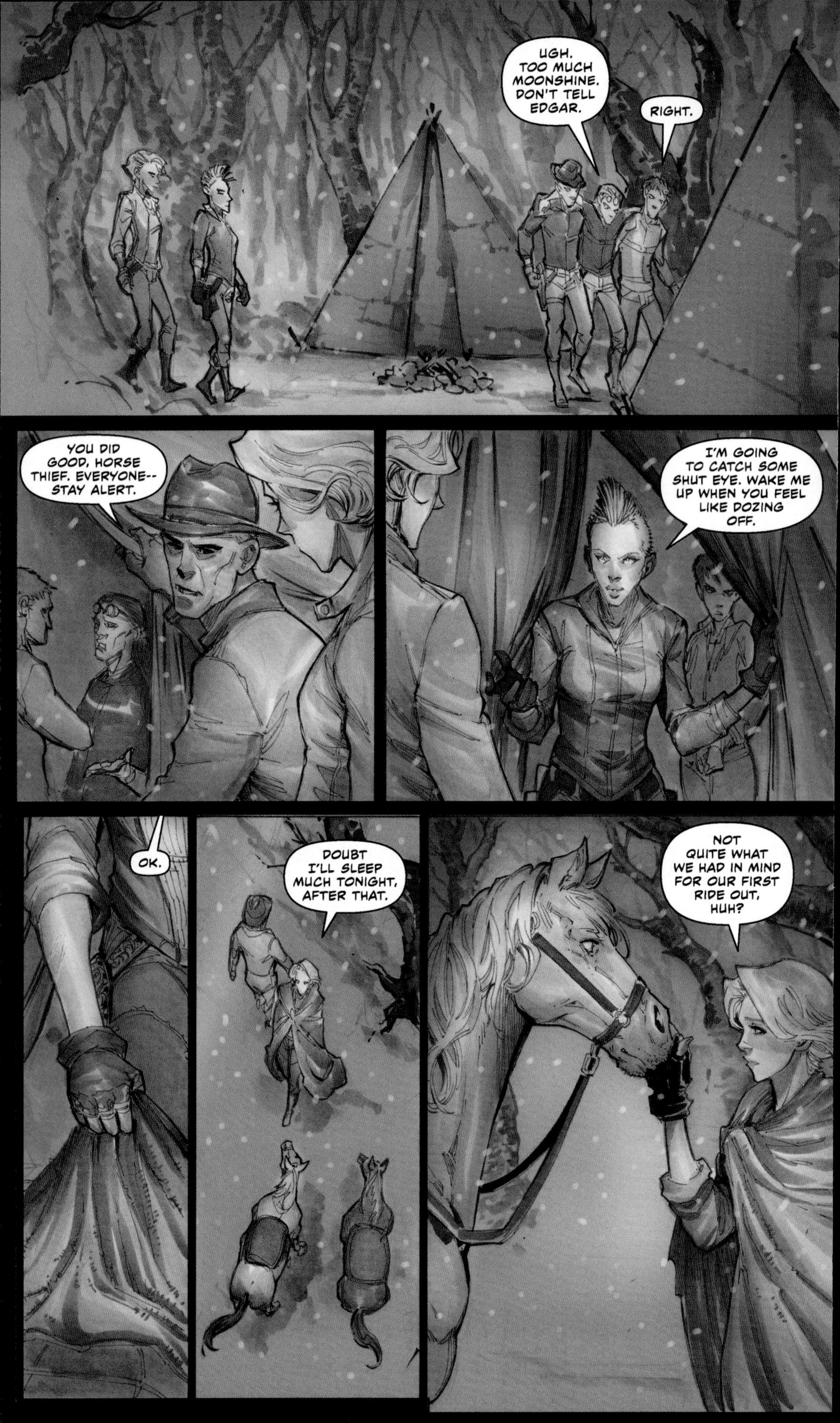
UGH. TOO MUCH MOONSHINE. DON'T TELL EDGAR.
RIGHT.
YOU DID GOOD, HORSE THIEF. EVERYONE-- STAY ALERT.
I'M GOING TO CATCH SOME SHUT EYE. WAKE ME UP WHEN YOU FEEL LIKE DOZING OFF.
OK.
DOUBT I'LL SLEEP MUCH TONIGHT, AFTER THAT.
NOT QUITE WHAT WE HAD IN MIND FOR OUR FIRST RIDE OUT, HUH?

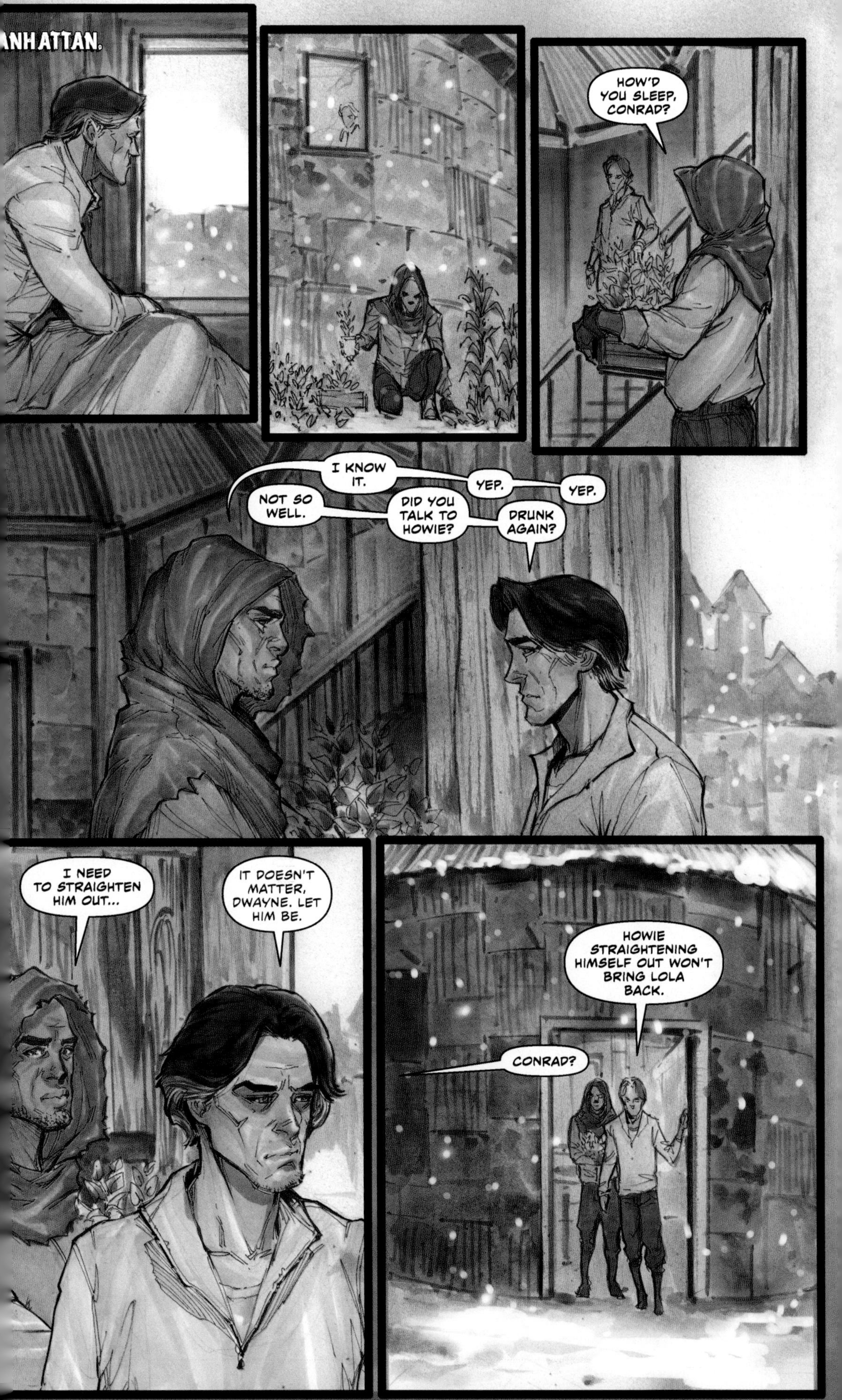
ANHATTAN.
HOW'D YOU SLEEP, CONRAD?
NOT SO WELL.
I KNOW IT.
DID YOU TALK TO HOWIE?
YEP.
DRUNK AGAIN?
YEP.
I NEED TO STRAIGHTEN HIM OUT...
IT DOESN'T MATTER, DWAYNE. LET HIM BE.
HOWIE STRAIGHTENING HIMSELF OUT WON'T BRING LOLA BACK.
CONRAD?

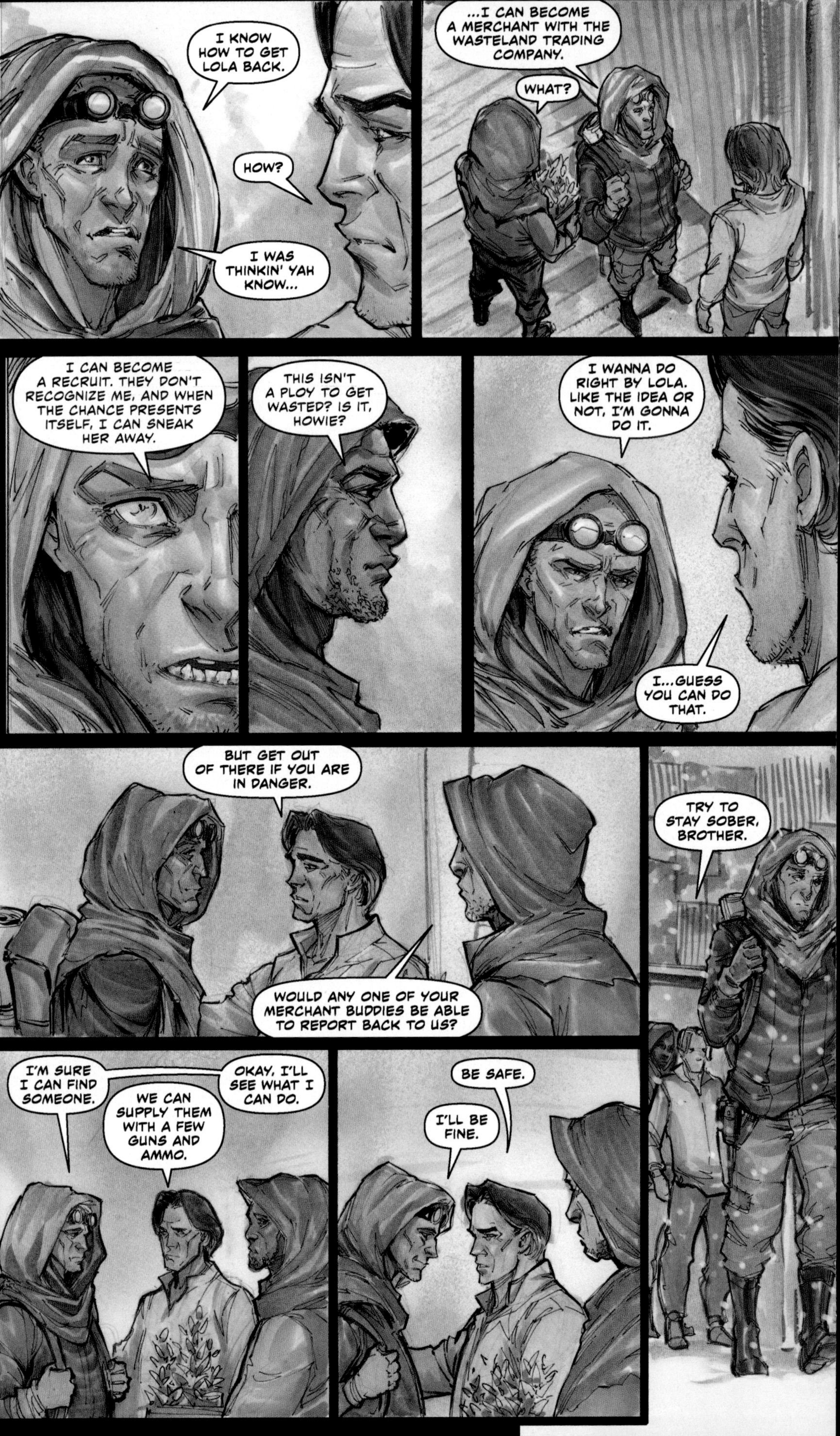
I KNOW HOW TO GET LOLA BACK.
HOW?
I WAS THINKIN' YAH KNOW...
...I CAN BECOME A MERCHANT WITH THE WASTELAND TRADING COMPANY.
WHAT?
I CAN BECOME A RECRUIT. THEY DON'T RECOGNIZE ME, AND WHEN THE CHANCE PRESENTS ITSELF, I CAN SNEAK HER AWAY.
THIS ISN'T A PLOY TO GET WASTED? IS IT, HOWIE?
I WANNA DO RIGHT BY LOLA. LIKE THE IDEA OR NOT, I'M GONNA DO IT.
I...GUESS YOU CAN DO THAT.
BUT GET OUT OF THERE IF YOU ARE IN DANGER.
WOULD ANY ONE OF YOUR MERCHANT BUDDIES BE ABLE TO REPORT BACK TO US?
TRY TO STAY SOBER, BROTHER.
I'M SURE I CAN FIND SOMEONE.
OKAY, I'LL SEE WHAT I CAN DO.
WE CAN SUPPLY THEM WITH A FEW GUNS AND AMMO.
BE SAFE.
I'LL BE FINE.

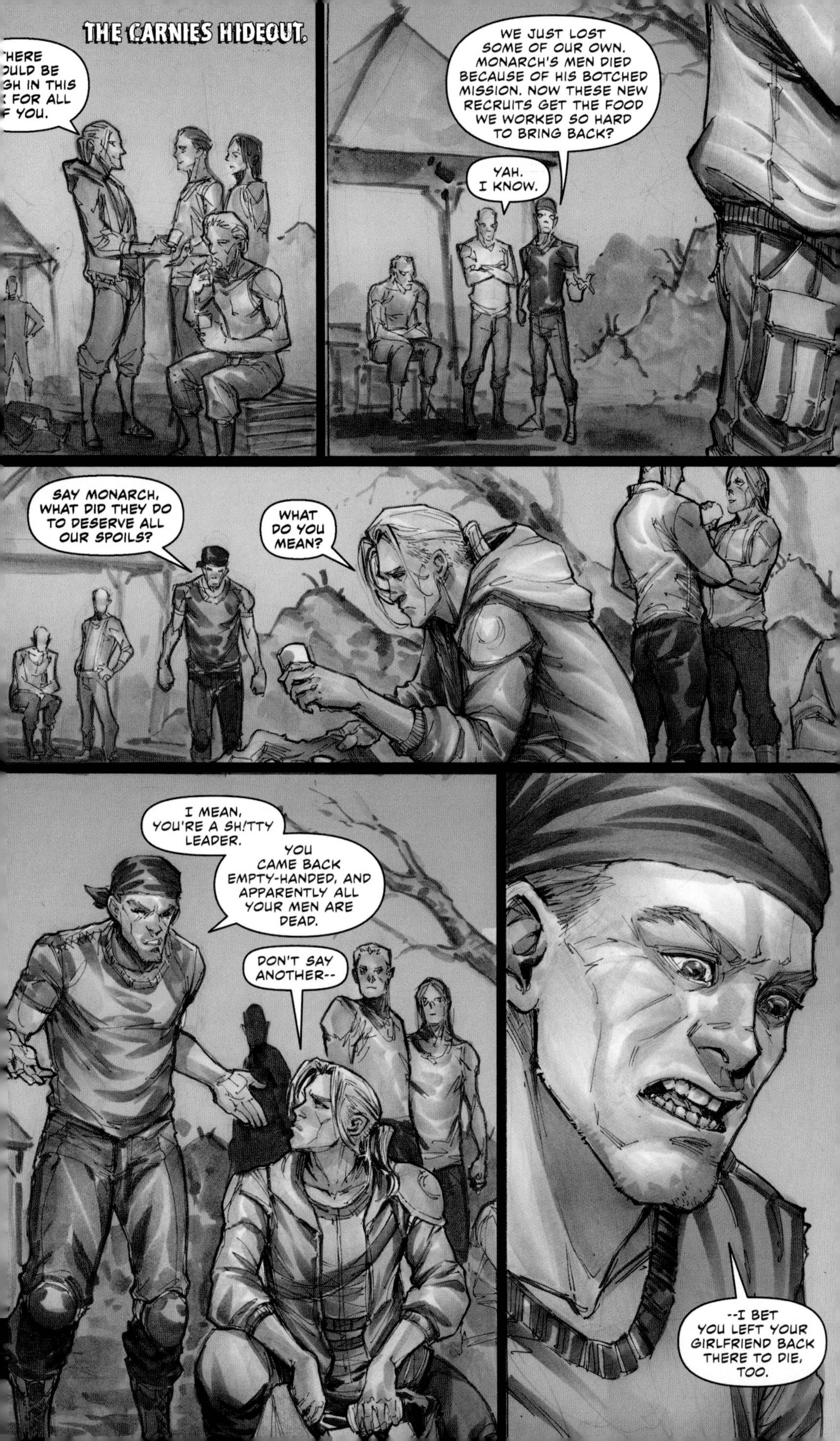
THE CARNIES HIDEOUT.
THERE OULD BE GH IN THIS FOR ALL F YOU.
WE JUST LOST SOME OF OUR OWN. MONARCH'S MEN DIED BECAUSE OF HIS BOTCHED MISSION. NOW THESE NEW RECRUITS GET THE FOOD WE WORKED SO HARD TO BRING BACK?
YAH. I KNOW.
SAY MONARCH, WHAT DID THEY DO TO DESERVE ALL OUR SPOILS?
WHAT DO YOU MEAN?
I MEAN, YOU'RE A SH!TTY LEADER.
YOU CAME BACK EMPTY-HANDED, AND APPARENTLY ALL YOUR MEN ARE DEAD.
DON'T SAY ANOTHER--
--I BET YOU LEFT YOUR GIRLFRIEND BACK THERE TO DIE, TOO.

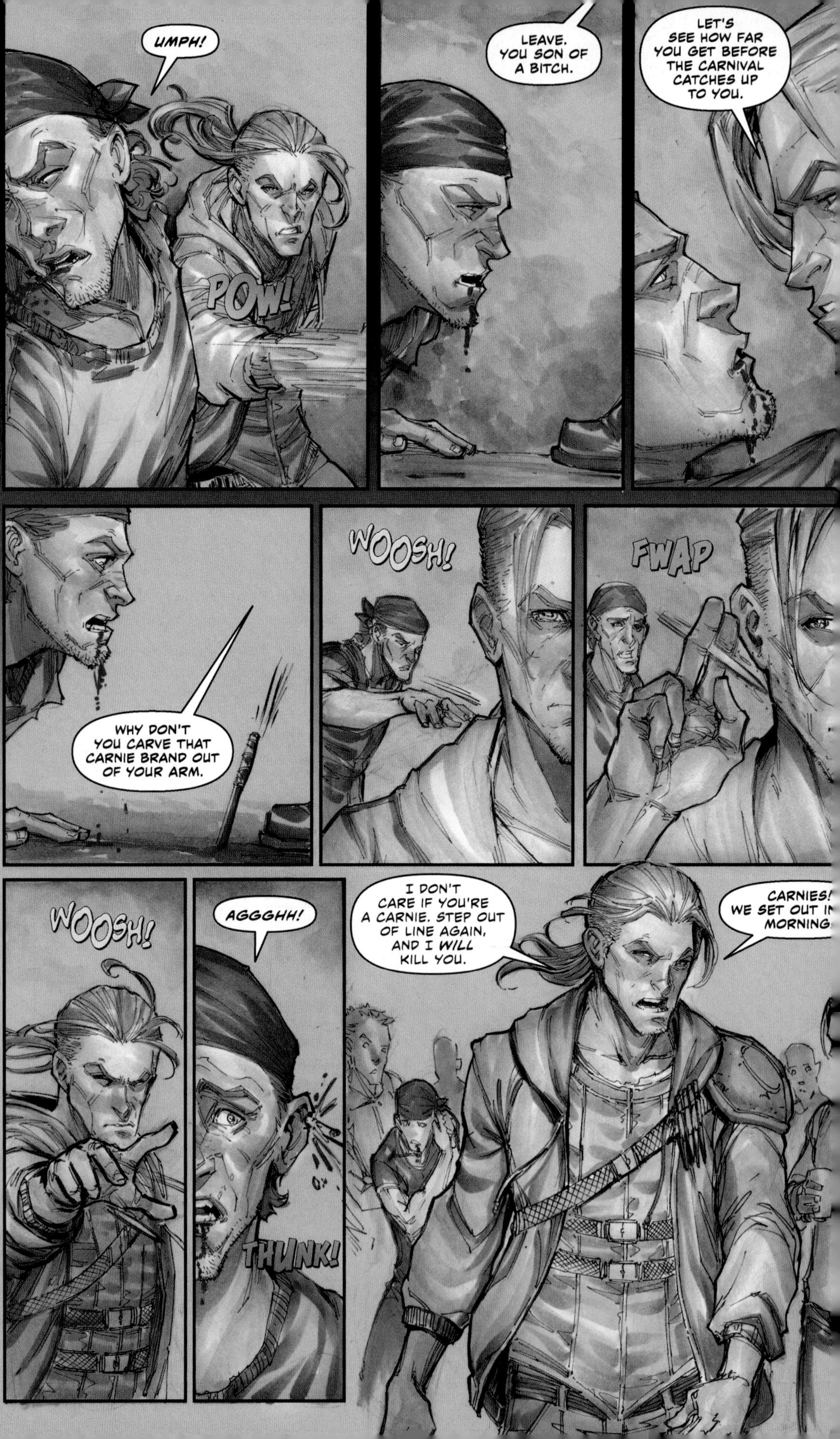
UMPH!
POW!
LEAVE. YOU SON OF A BITCH.
LET'S SEE HOW FAR YOU GET BEFORE THE CARNIVAL CATCHES UP TO YOU.
WHY DON'T YOU CARVE THAT CARNIE BRAND OUT OF YOUR ARM.
WOOSH!
FWAP
WOOSH!
AGGGHH!
THUNK!
I DON'T CARE IF YOU'RE A CARNIE. STEP OUT OF LINE AGAIN, AND I *WILL* KILL YOU.
CARNIES! WE SET OUT IN MORNING.

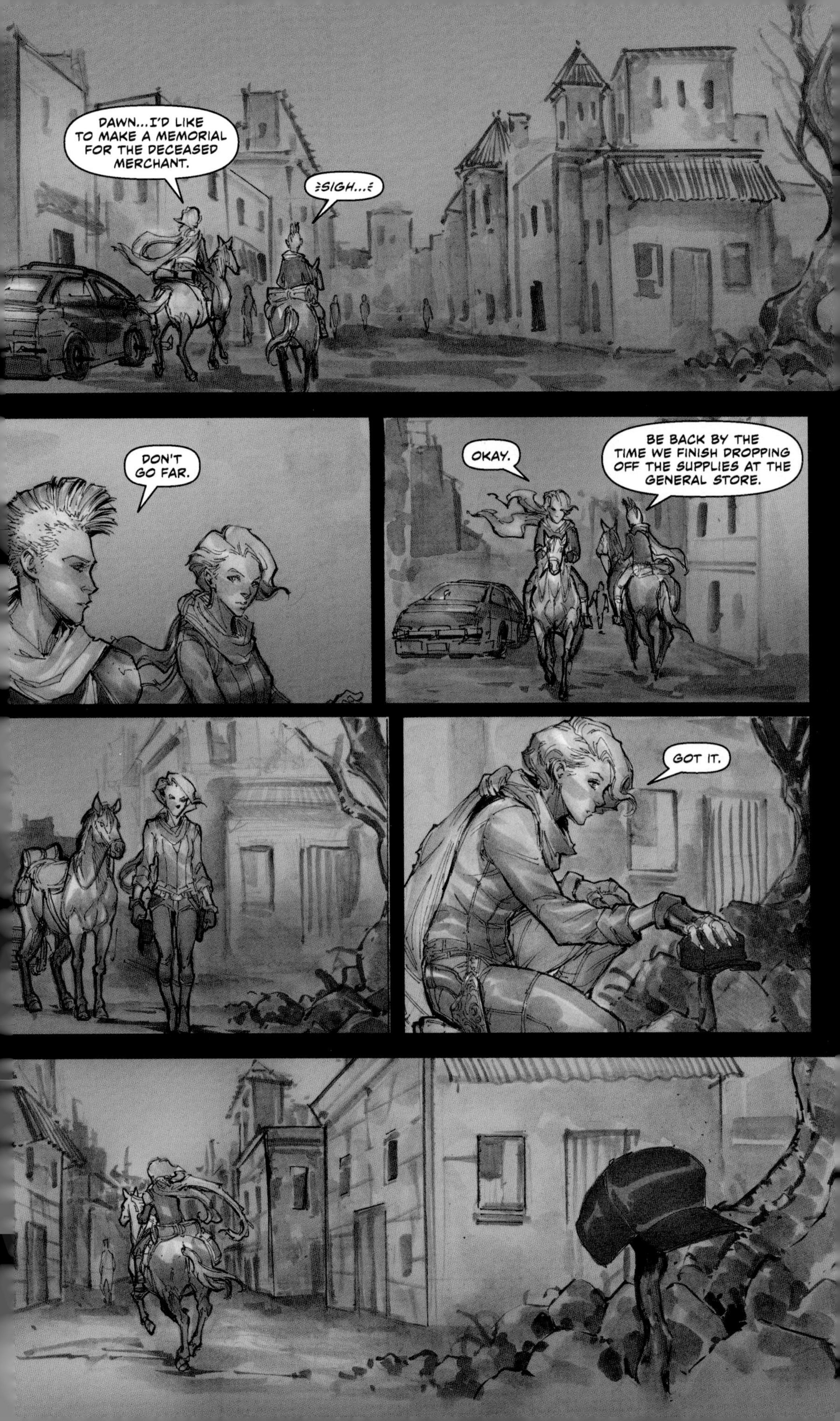
DAWN...I'D LIKE TO MAKE A MEMORIAL FOR THE DECEASED MERCHANT.
SIGH...
DON'T GO FAR.
OKAY.
BE BACK BY THE TIME WE FINISH DROPPING OFF THE SUPPLIES AT THE GENERAL STORE.
GOT IT.

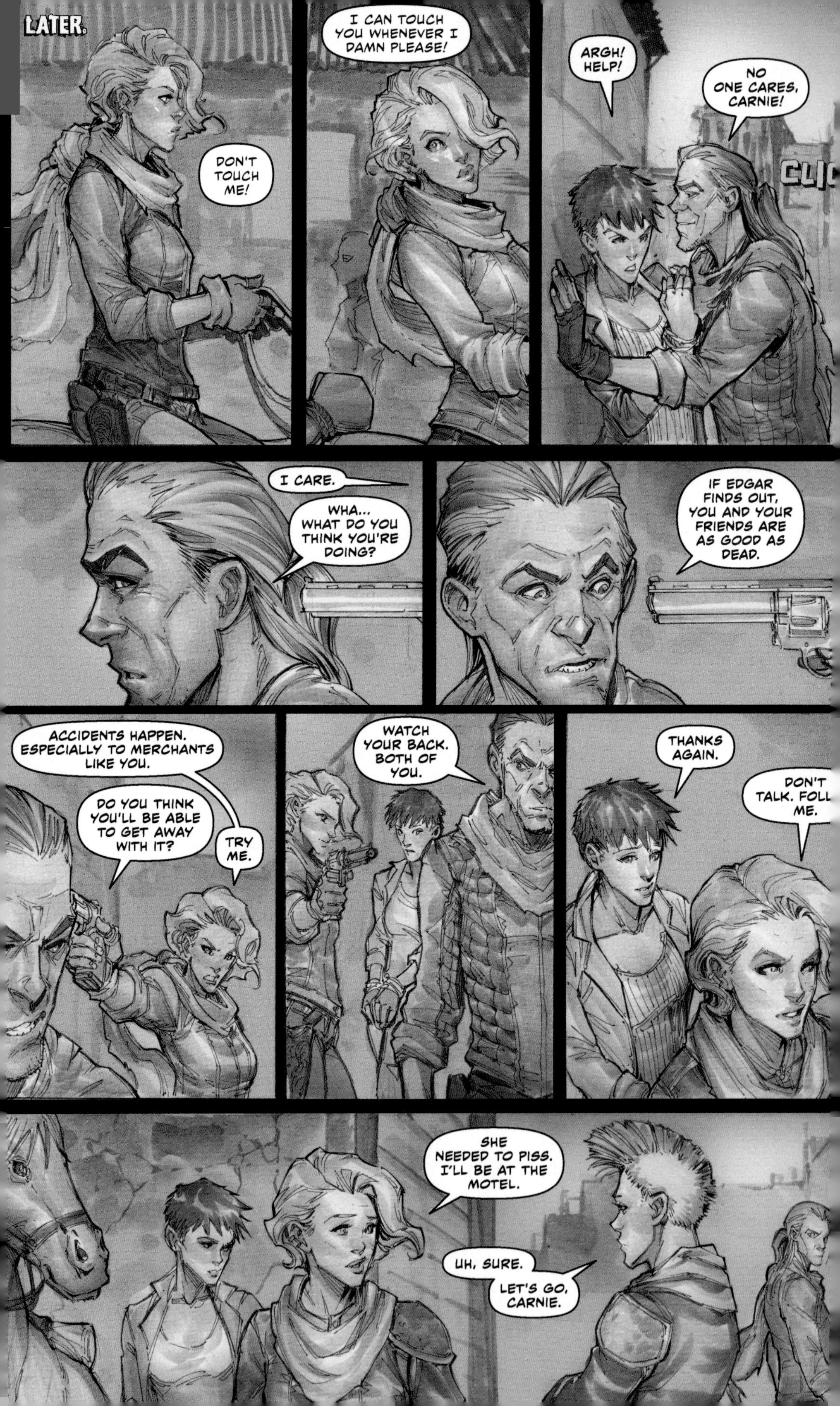
LATER.
DON'T TOUCH ME!
I CAN TOUCH YOU WHENEVER I DAMN PLEASE!
ARGH! HELP!
NO ONE CARES, CARNIE!
CLIC
I CARE.
WHA... WHAT DO YOU THINK YOU'RE DOING?
IF EDGAR FINDS OUT, YOU AND YOUR FRIENDS ARE AS GOOD AS DEAD.
ACCIDENTS HAPPEN. ESPECIALLY TO MERCHANTS LIKE YOU.
DO YOU THINK YOU'LL BE ABLE TO GET AWAY WITH IT?
TRY ME.
WATCH YOUR BACK. BOTH OF YOU.
THANKS AGAIN.
DON'T TALK. FOLL ME.
SHE NEEDED TO PISS. I'LL BE AT THE MOTEL.
UH, SURE.
LET'S GO, CARNIE.

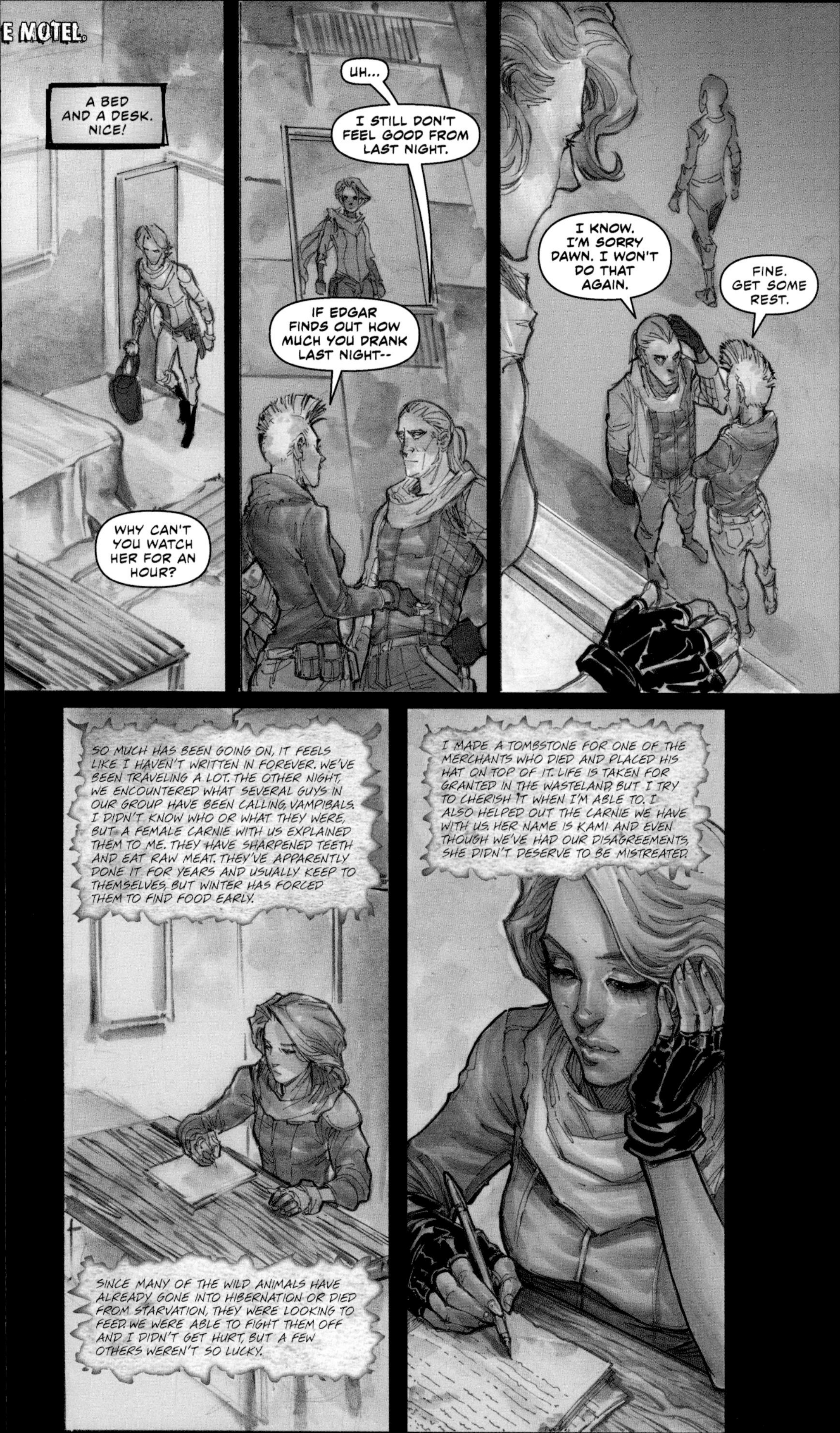
E MOTEL.
A BED AND A DESK. NICE!
WHY CAN'T YOU WATCH HER FOR AN HOUR?
UH...
I STILL DON'T FEEL GOOD FROM LAST NIGHT.
IF EDGAR FINDS OUT HOW MUCH YOU DRANK LAST NIGHT--
I KNOW. I'M SORRY DAWN. I WON'T DO THAT AGAIN.
FINE. GET SOME REST.
SO MUCH HAS BEEN GOING ON, IT FEELS LIKE I HAVEN'T WRITTEN IN FOREVER. WE'VE BEEN TRAVELING A LOT. THE OTHER NIGHT, WE ENCOUNTERED WHAT SEVERAL GUYS IN OUR GROUP HAVE BEEN CALLING VAMPIBALS. I DIDN'T KNOW WHO OR WHAT THEY WERE, BUT A FEMALE CARNIE WITH US EXPLAINED THEM TO ME. THEY HAVE SHARPENED TEETH AND EAT RAW MEAT. THEY'VE APPARENTLY DONE IT FOR YEARS AND USUALLY KEEP TO THEMSELVES, BUT WINTER HAS FORCED THEM TO FIND FOOD EARLY.
SINCE MANY OF THE WILD ANIMALS HAVE ALREADY GONE INTO HIBERNATION OR DIED FROM STARVATION, THEY WERE LOOKING TO FEED. WE WERE ABLE TO FIGHT THEM OFF AND I DIDN'T GET HURT, BUT A FEW OTHERS WEREN'T SO LUCKY.
I MADE A TOMBSTONE FOR ONE OF THE MERCHANTS WHO DIED AND PLACED HIS HAT ON TOP OF IT. LIFE IS TAKEN FOR GRANTED IN THE WASTELAND, BUT I TRY TO CHERISH IT WHEN I'M ABLE TO. I ALSO HELPED OUT THE CARNIE WE HAVE WITH US. HER NAME IS KAMI AND EVEN THOUGH WE'VE HAD OUR DISAGREEMENTS, SHE DIDN'T DESERVE TO BE MISTREATED.

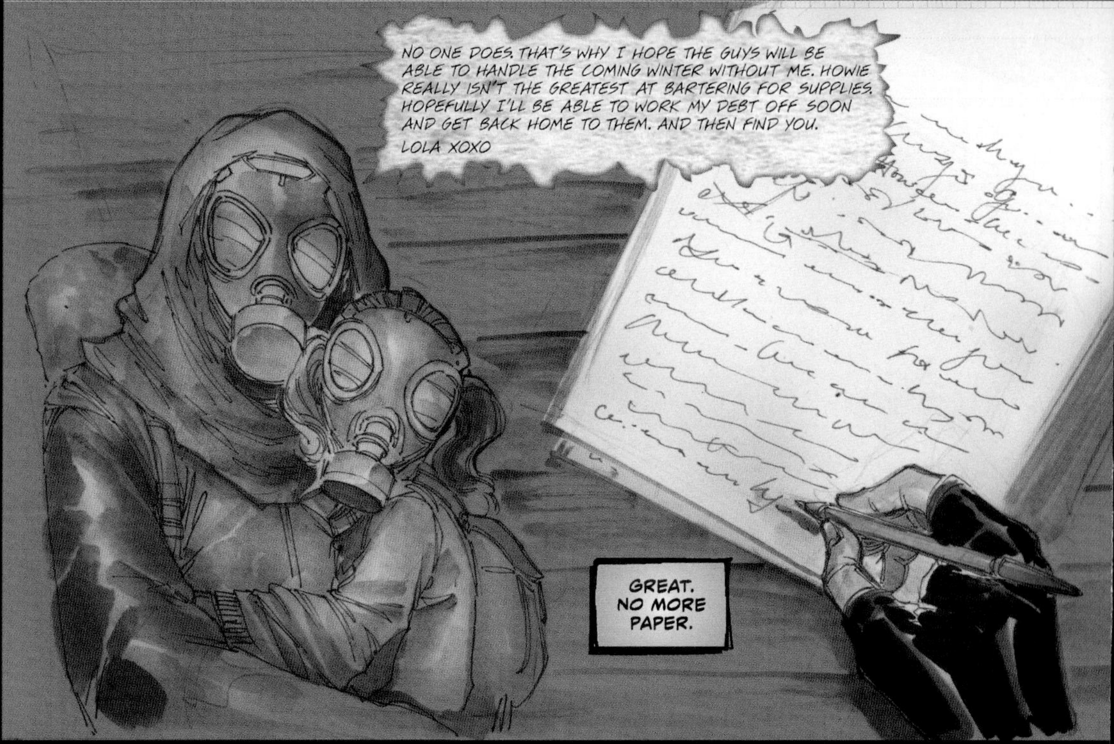
NO ONE DOES. THAT'S WHY I HOPE THE GUYS WILL BE ABLE TO HANDLE THE COMING WINTER WITHOUT ME. HOWIE REALLY ISN'T THE GREATEST AT BARTERING FOR SUPPLIES. HOPEFULLY I'LL BE ABLE TO WORK MY DEBT OFF SOON AND GET BACK HOME TO THEM. AND THEN FIND YOU.
LOLA XOXO
GREAT. NO MORE PAPER.

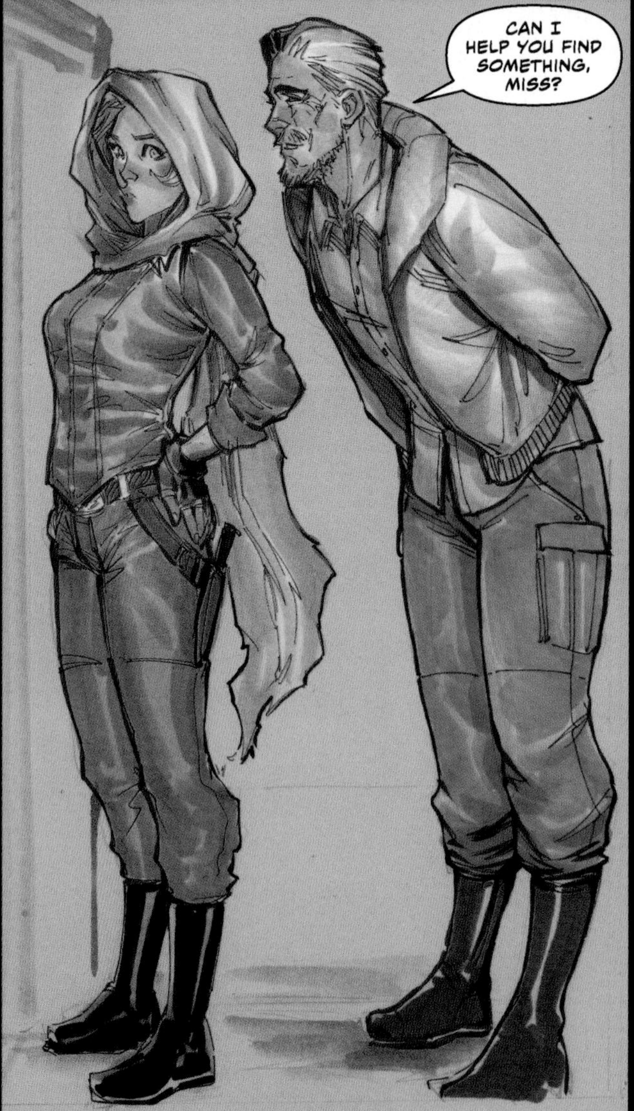
CAN I HELP YOU FIND SOMETHING, MISS?

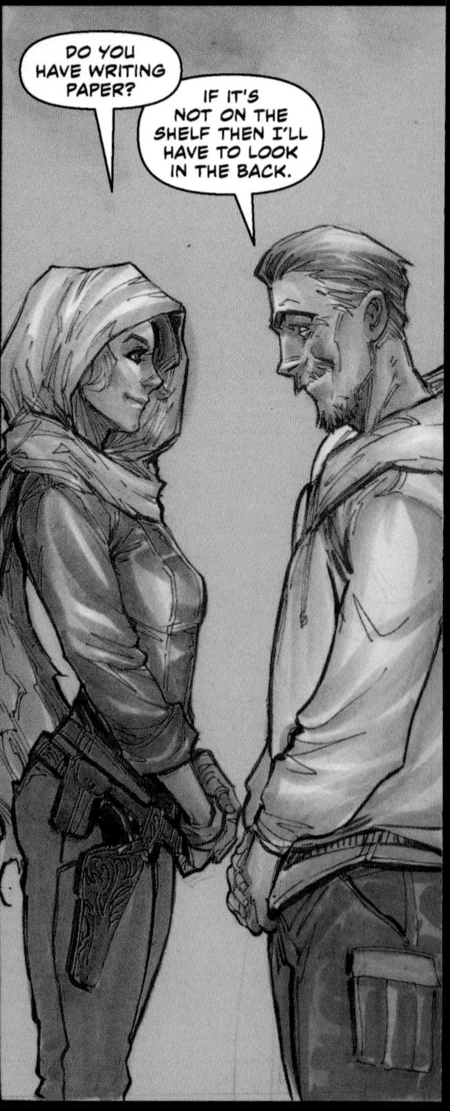
DO YOU HAVE WRITING PAPER?
IF IT'S NOT ON THE SHELF THEN I'LL HAVE TO LOOK IN THE BACK.

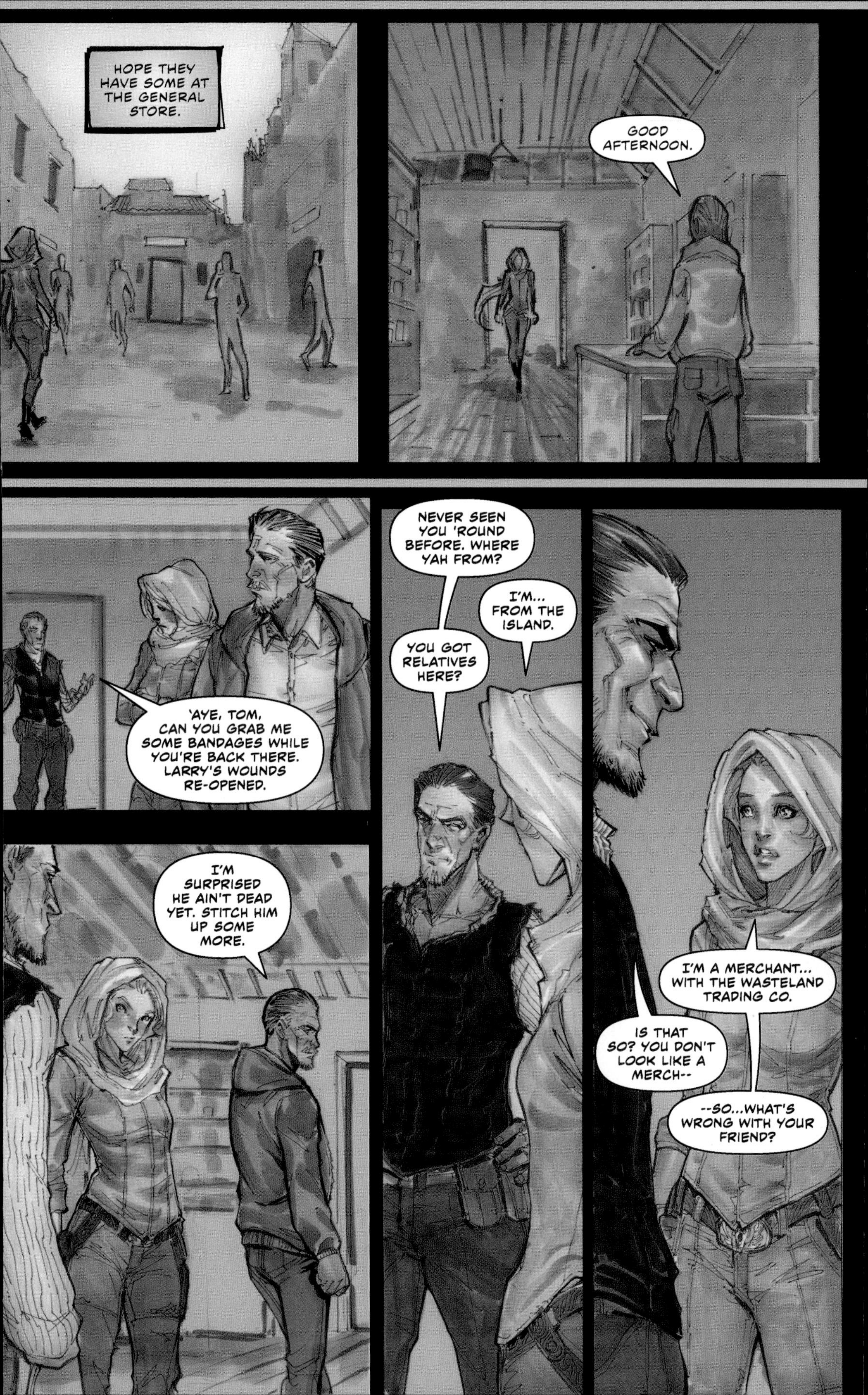
HOPE THEY HAVE SOME AT THE GENERAL STORE.
GOOD AFTERNOON.
'AYE, TOM, CAN YOU GRAB ME SOME BANDAGES WHILE YOU'RE BACK THERE. LARRY'S WOUNDS RE-OPENED.
I'M SURPRISED HE AIN'T DEAD YET. STITCH HIM UP SOME MORE.
NEVER SEEN YOU 'ROUND BEFORE. WHERE YAH FROM?
I'M... FROM THE ISLAND.
YOU GOT RELATIVES HERE?
I'M A MERCHANT... WITH THE WASTELAND TRADING CO.
IS THAT SO? YOU DON'T LOOK LIKE A MERCH--
--SO...WHAT'S WRONG WITH YOUR FRIEND?

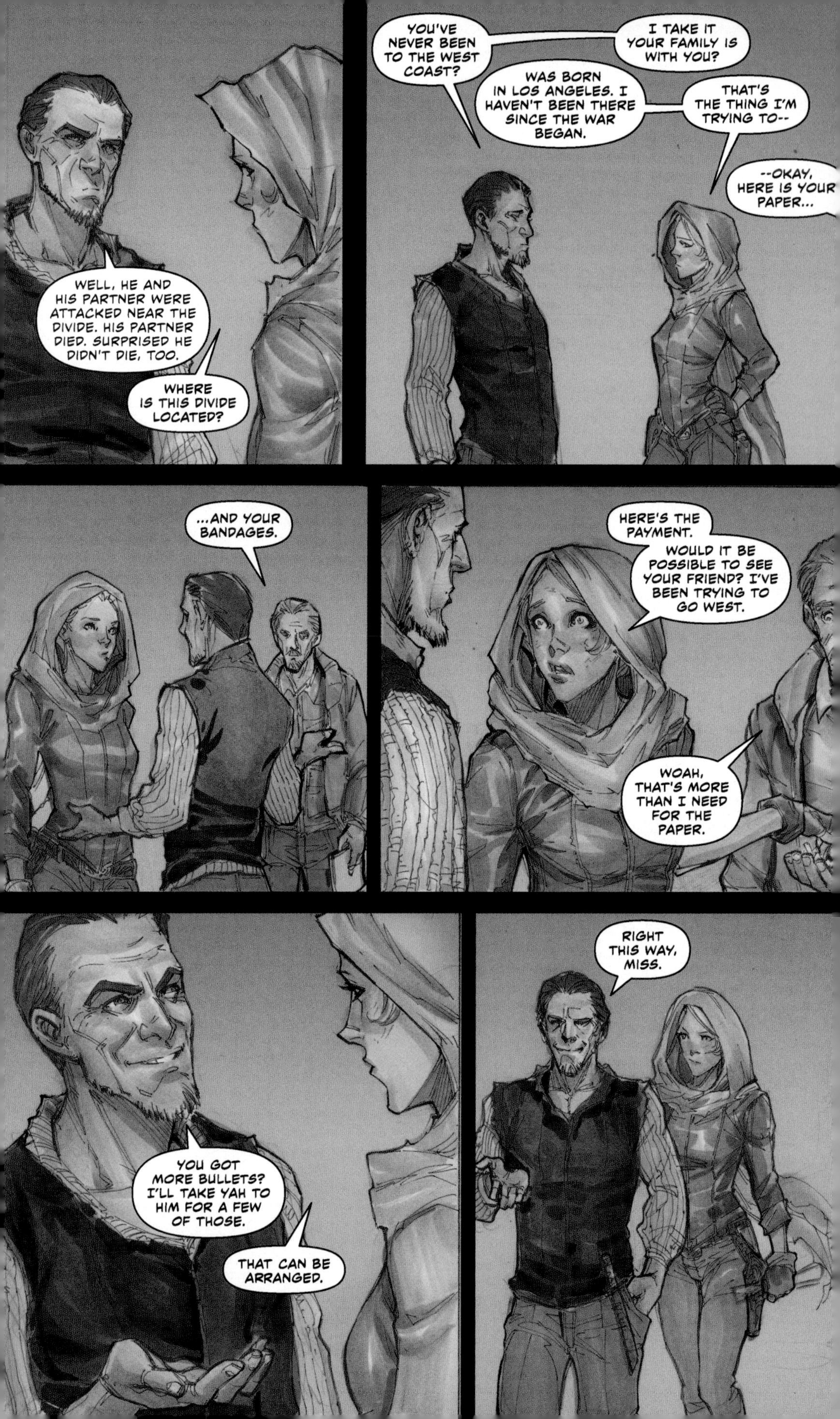
WELL, HE AND HIS PARTNER WERE ATTACKED NEAR THE DIVIDE. HIS PARTNER DIED. SURPRISED HE DIDN'T DIE, TOO.
WHERE IS THIS DIVIDE LOCATED?
YOU'VE NEVER BEEN TO THE WEST COAST?
I TAKE IT YOUR FAMILY IS WITH YOU?
WAS BORN IN LOS ANGELES. I HAVEN'T BEEN THERE SINCE THE WAR BEGAN.
THAT'S THE THING I'M TRYING TO--
--OKAY, HERE IS YOUR PAPER...
...AND YOUR BANDAGES.
HERE'S THE PAYMENT.
WOULD IT BE POSSIBLE TO SEE YOUR FRIEND? I'VE BEEN TRYING TO GO WEST.
WOAH, THAT'S MORE THAN I NEED FOR THE PAPER.
YOU GOT MORE BULLETS? I'LL TAKE YAH TO HIM FOR A FEW OF THOSE.
THAT CAN BE ARRANGED.
RIGHT THIS WAY, MISS.

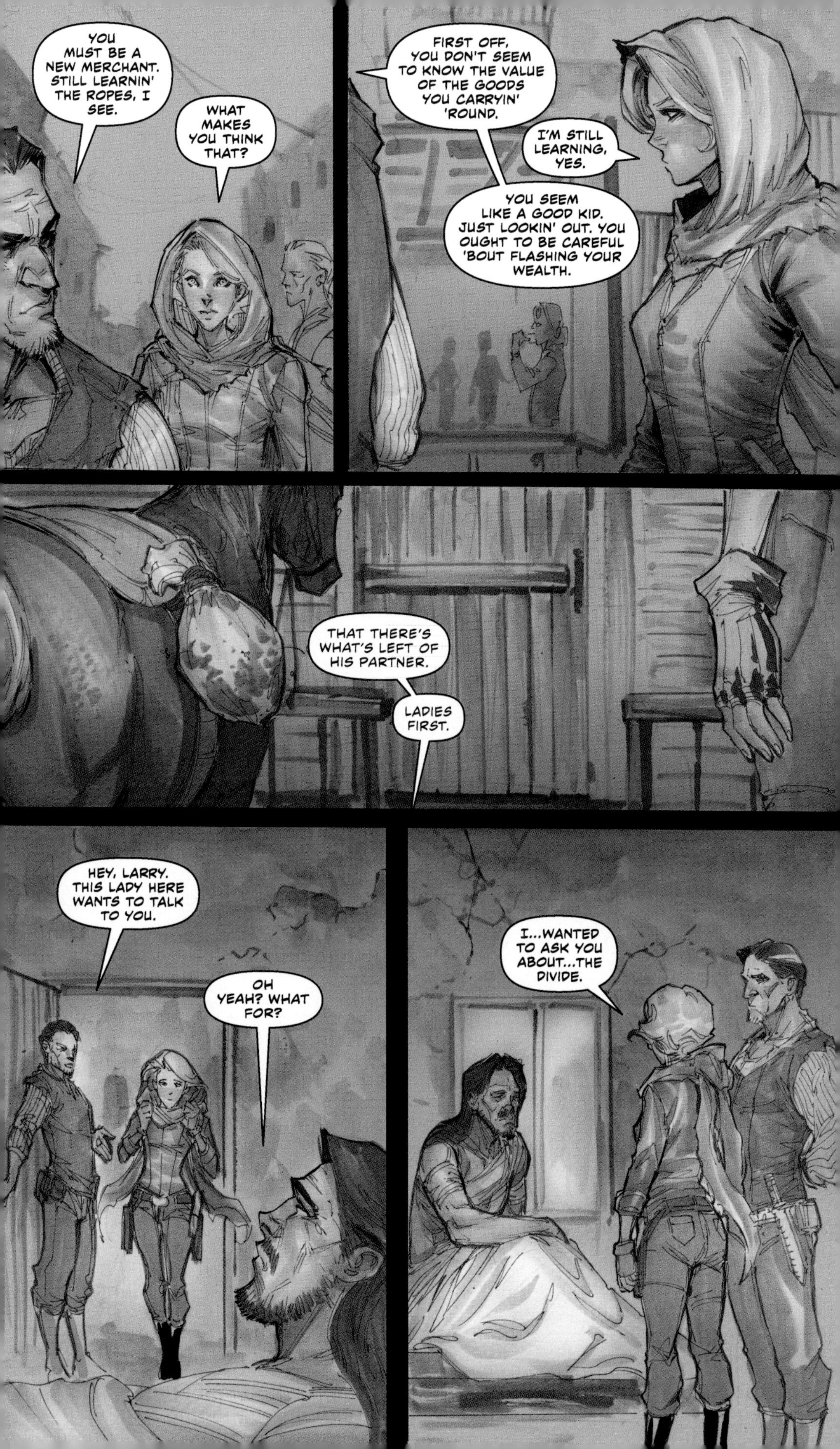
YOU MUST BE A NEW MERCHANT. STILL LEARNIN' THE ROPES, I SEE.
WHAT MAKES YOU THINK THAT?
FIRST OFF, YOU DON'T SEEM TO KNOW THE VALUE OF THE GOODS YOU CARRYIN' 'ROUND.
I'M STILL LEARNING, YES.
YOU SEEM LIKE A GOOD KID. JUST LOOKIN' OUT. YOU OUGHT TO BE CAREFUL 'BOUT FLASHING YOUR WEALTH.
THAT THERE'S WHAT'S LEFT OF HIS PARTNER.
LADIES FIRST.
HEY, LARRY. THIS LADY HERE WANTS TO TALK TO YOU.
OH YEAH? WHAT FOR?
I...WANTED TO ASK YOU ABOUT...THE DIVIDE.

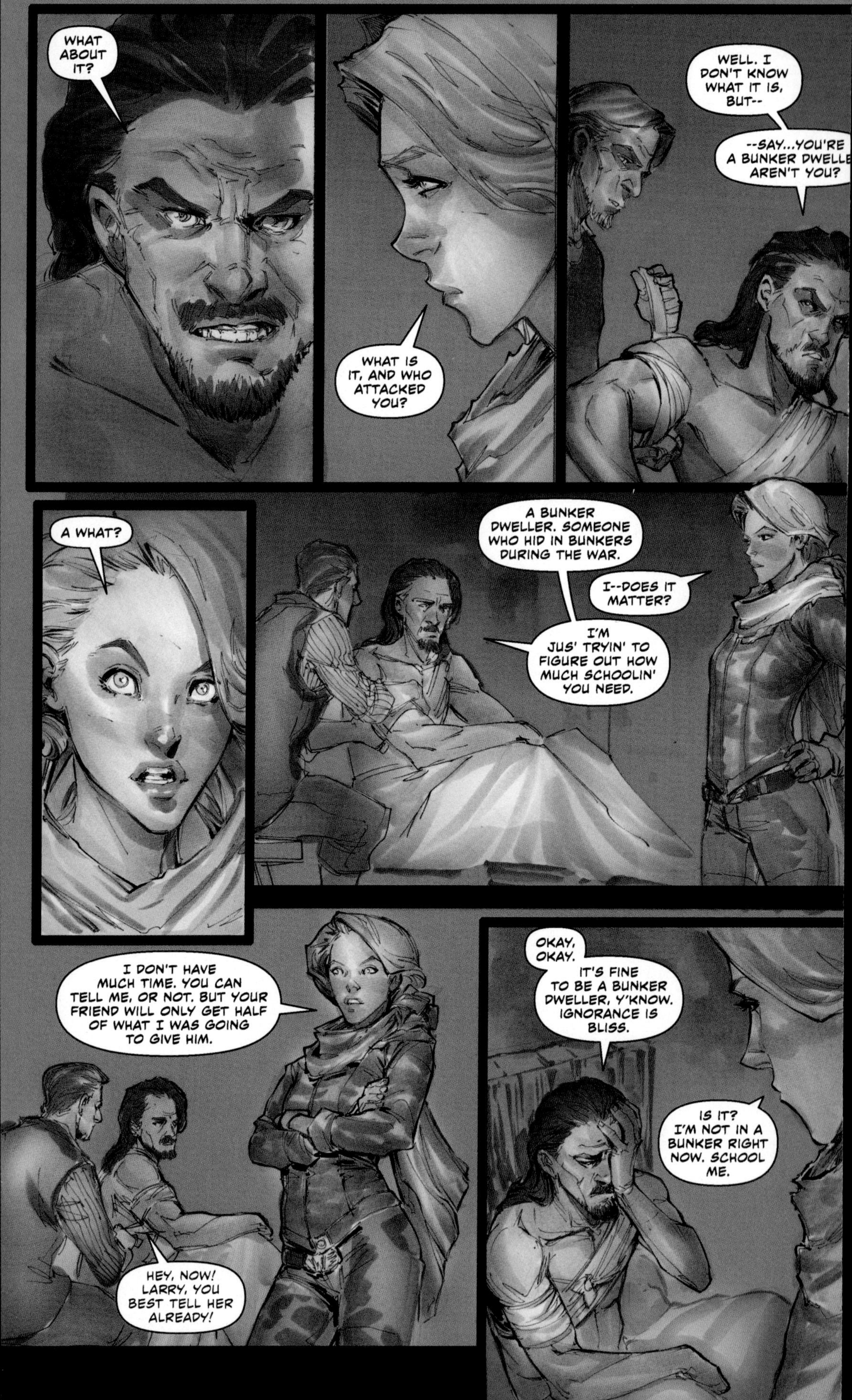
WHAT ABOUT IT?
WHAT IS IT, AND WHO ATTACKED YOU?
WELL. I DON'T KNOW WHAT IT IS, BUT--
--SAY...YOU'RE A BUNKER DWELLE AREN'T YOU?
A WHAT?
A BUNKER DWELLER. SOMEONE WHO HID IN BUNKERS DURING THE WAR.
I--DOES IT MATTER?
I'M JUS' TRYIN' TO FIGURE OUT HOW MUCH SCHOOLIN' YOU NEED.
I DON'T HAVE MUCH TIME. YOU CAN TELL ME, OR NOT. BUT YOUR FRIEND WILL ONLY GET HALF OF WHAT I WAS GOING TO GIVE HIM.
HEY, NOW! LARRY, YOU BEST TELL HER ALREADY!
OKAY, OKAY.
IT'S FINE TO BE A BUNKER DWELLER, Y'KNOW. IGNORANCE IS BLISS.
IS IT? I'M NOT IN A BUNKER RIGHT NOW. SCHOOL ME.

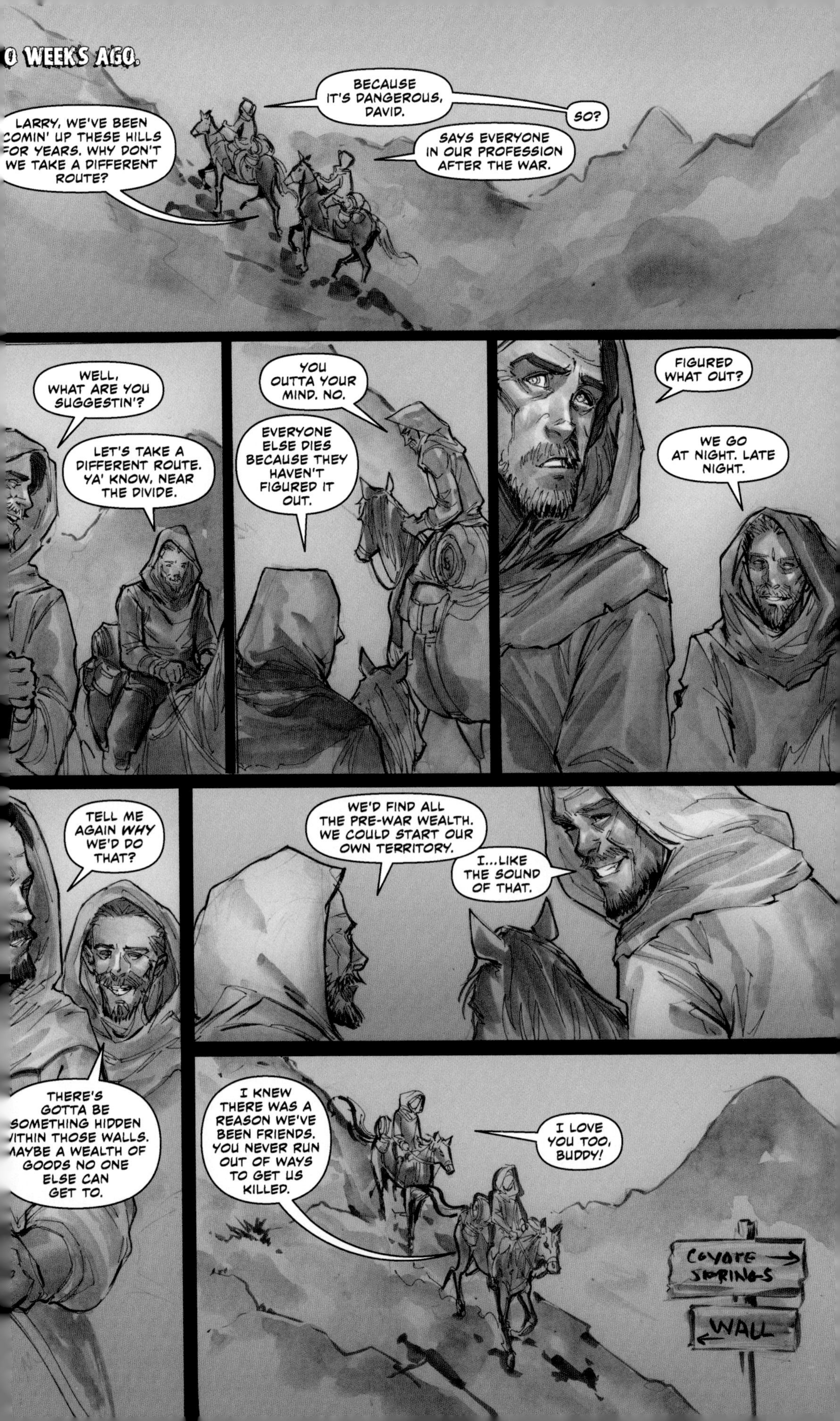

O WEEKS AGO.
LARRY, WE'VE BEEN COMIN' UP THESE HILLS FOR YEARS. WHY DON'T WE TAKE A DIFFERENT ROUTE?
BECAUSE IT'S DANGEROUS, DAVID.
SO?
SAYS EVERYONE IN OUR PROFESSION AFTER THE WAR.
WELL, WHAT ARE YOU SUGGESTIN'?
LET'S TAKE A DIFFERENT ROUTE. YA' KNOW, NEAR THE DIVIDE.
YOU OUTTA YOUR MIND. NO.
EVERYONE ELSE DIES BECAUSE THEY HAVEN'T FIGURED IT OUT.
FIGURED WHAT OUT?
WE GO AT NIGHT. LATE NIGHT.
TELL ME AGAIN WHY WE'D DO THAT?
THERE'S GOTTA BE SOMETHING HIDDEN WITHIN THOSE WALLS. MAYBE A WEALTH OF GOODS NO ONE ELSE CAN GET TO.
WE'D FIND ALL THE PRE-WAR WEALTH. WE COULD START OUR OWN TERRITORY.
I...LIKE THE SOUND OF THAT.
I KNEW THERE WAS A REASON WE'VE BEEN FRIENDS. YOU NEVER RUN OUT OF WAYS TO GET US KILLED.
I LOVE YOU TOO, BUDDY!
COYOTE SPRINGS
WALL

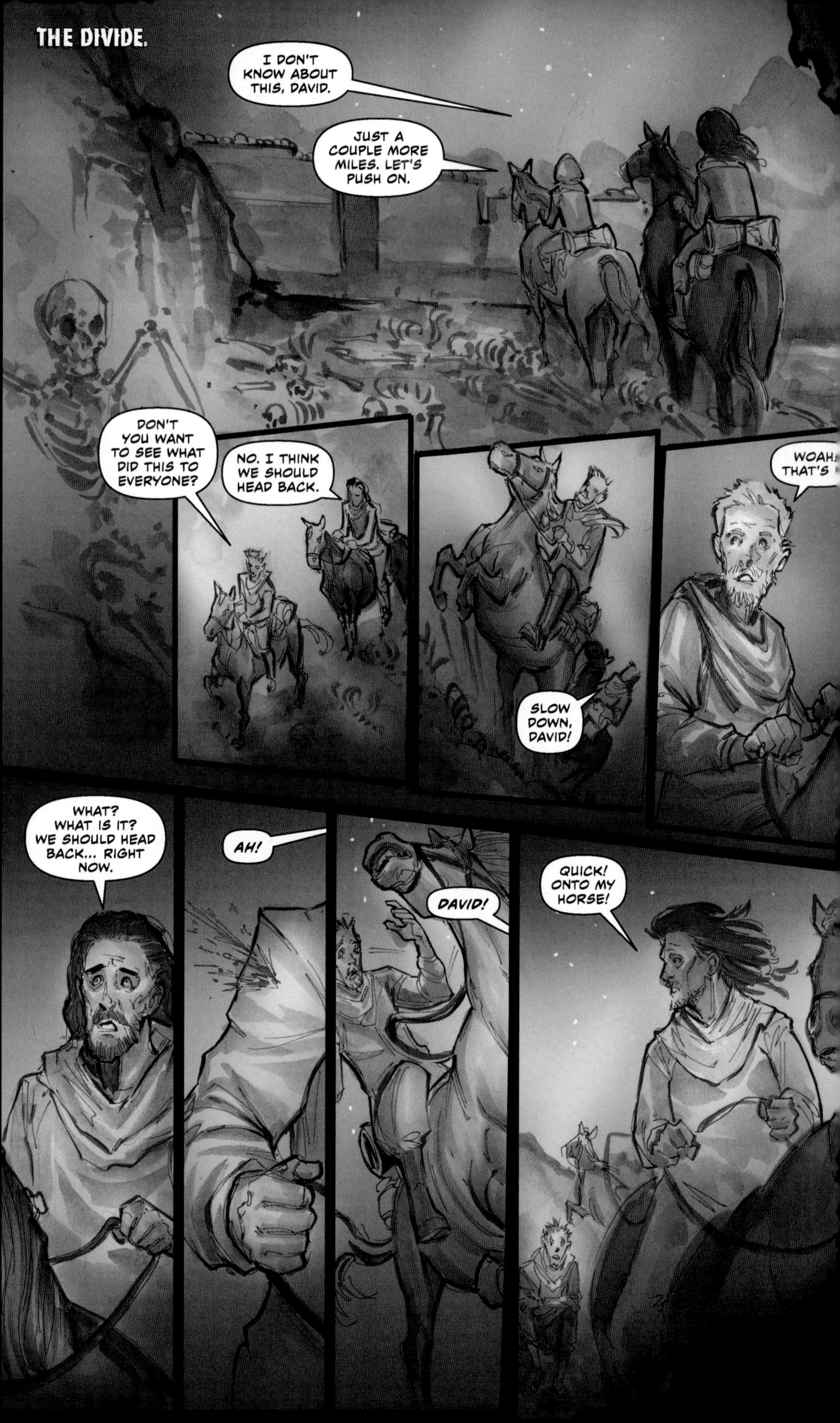
I DON'T KNOW ABOUT THIS, DAVID.
JUST A COUPLE MORE MILES. LET'S PUSH ON.
DON'T YOU WANT TO SEE WHAT DID THIS TO EVERYONE?
NO. I THINK WE SHOULD HEAD BACK.
SLOW DOWN, DAVID!
WOAH! THAT'S
WHAT? WHAT IS IT? WE SHOULD HEAD BACK... RIGHT NOW.
AH!
DAVID!
QUICK! ONTO MY HORSE!

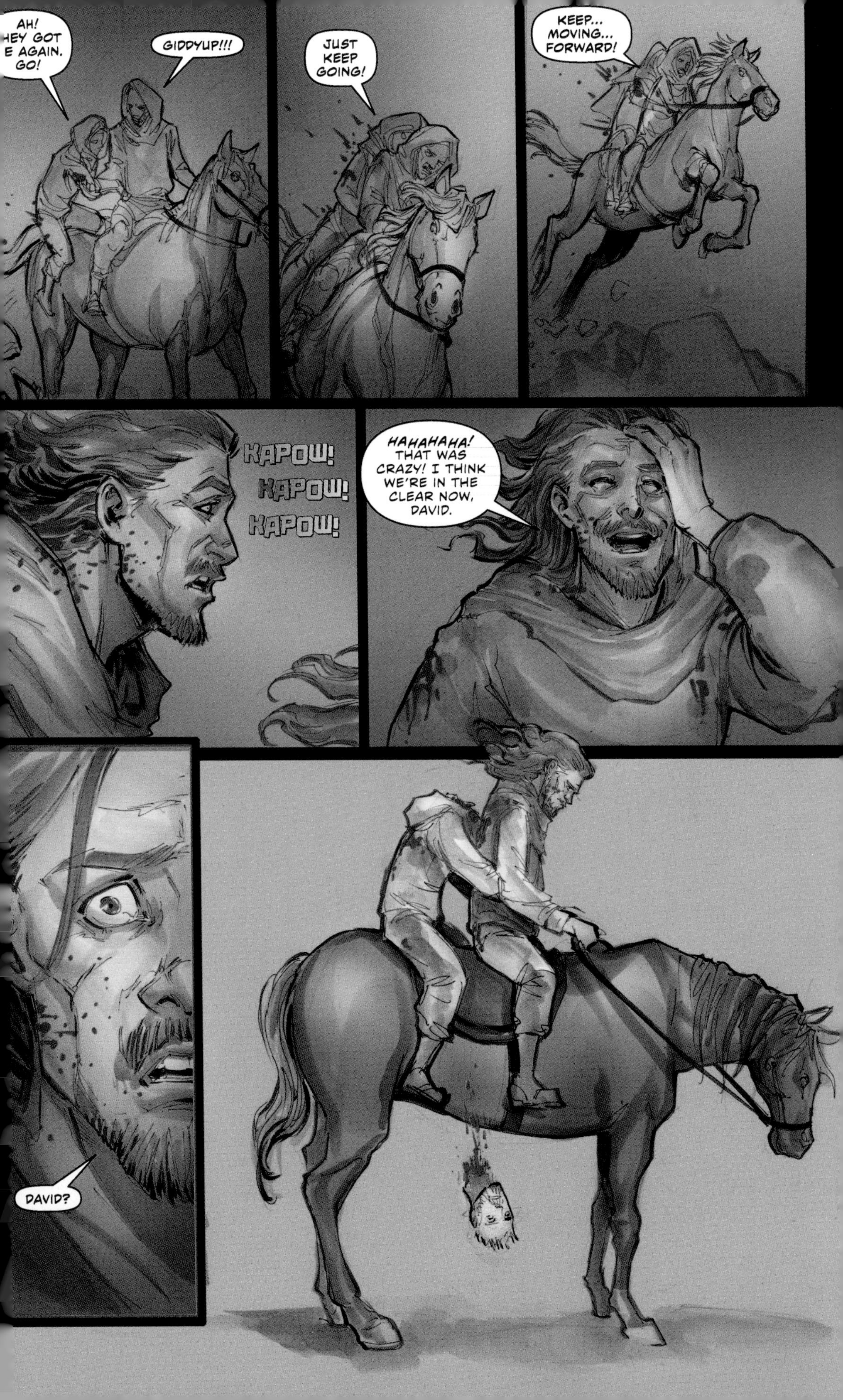
AH!
HEY GOT
E AGAIN.
GO!
GIDDYUP!!!
JUST KEEP GOING!
KEEP... MOVING... FORWARD!
KAPOW!
KAPOW!
KAPOW!
HAHAHAHA! THAT WAS CRAZY! I THINK WE'RE IN THE CLEAR NOW, DAVID.
DAVID?

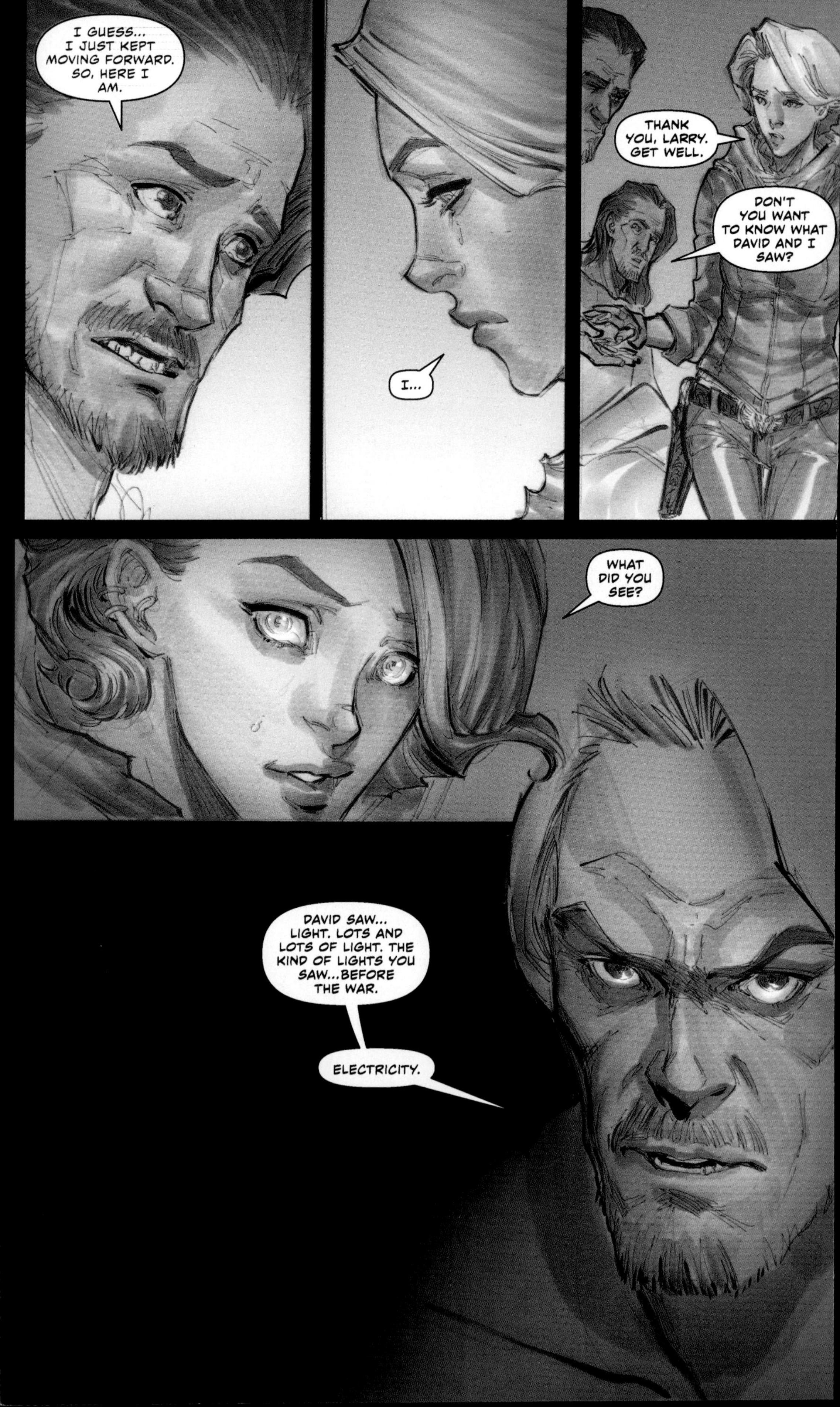
I GUESS...
I JUST KEPT MOVING FORWARD. SO, HERE I AM.
I...
THANK YOU, LARRY. GET WELL.
DON'T YOU WANT TO KNOW WHAT DAVID AND I SAW?
WHAT DID YOU SEE?
DAVID SAW... LIGHT. LOTS AND LOTS OF LIGHT. THE KIND OF LIGHTS YOU SAW...BEFORE THE WAR.
ELECTRICITY.

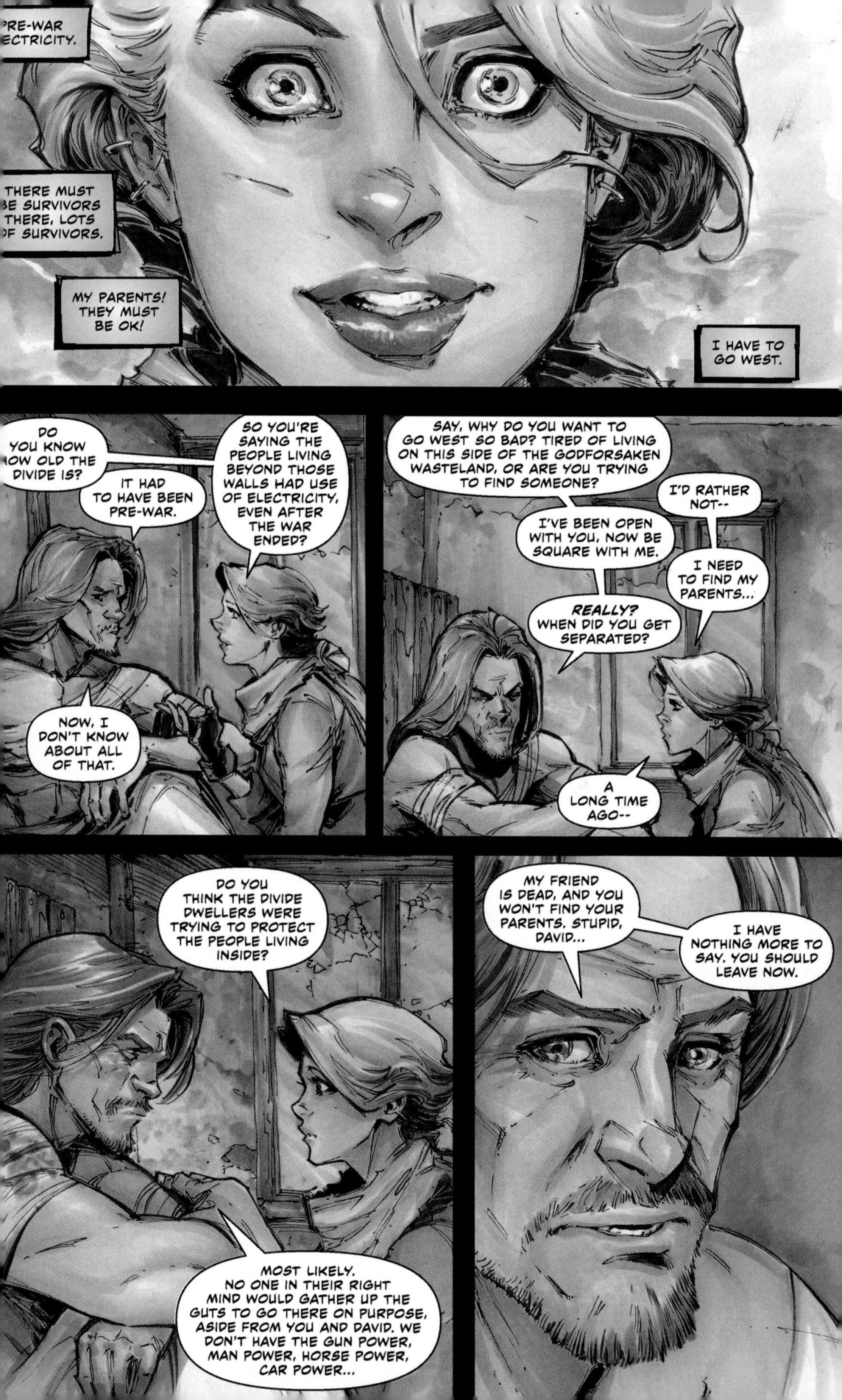
PRE-WAR ELECTRICITY.
THERE MUST BE SURVIVORS THERE, LOTS OF SURVIVORS.
MY PARENTS! THEY MUST BE OK!
I HAVE TO GO WEST.
DO YOU KNOW HOW OLD THE DIVIDE IS?
IT HAD TO HAVE BEEN PRE-WAR.
SO YOU'RE SAYING THE PEOPLE LIVING BEYOND THOSE WALLS HAD USE OF ELECTRICITY, EVEN AFTER THE WAR ENDED?
NOW, I DON'T KNOW ABOUT ALL OF THAT.
SAY, WHY DO YOU WANT TO GO WEST SO BAD? TIRED OF LIVING ON THIS SIDE OF THE GODFORSAKEN WASTELAND, OR ARE YOU TRYING TO FIND SOMEONE?
I'D RATHER NOT--
I'VE BEEN OPEN WITH YOU, NOW BE SQUARE WITH ME.
I NEED TO FIND MY PARENTS...
REALLY? WHEN DID YOU GET SEPARATED?
A LONG TIME AGO--
DO YOU THINK THE DIVIDE DWELLERS WERE TRYING TO PROTECT THE PEOPLE LIVING INSIDE?
MOST LIKELY. NO ONE IN THEIR RIGHT MIND WOULD GATHER UP THE GUTS TO GO THERE ON PURPOSE, ASIDE FROM YOU AND DAVID. WE DON'T HAVE THE GUN POWER, MAN POWER, HORSE POWER, CAR POWER...
MY FRIEND IS DEAD, AND YOU WON'T FIND YOUR PARENTS. STUPID, DAVID...
I HAVE NOTHING MORE TO SAY. YOU SHOULD LEAVE NOW.

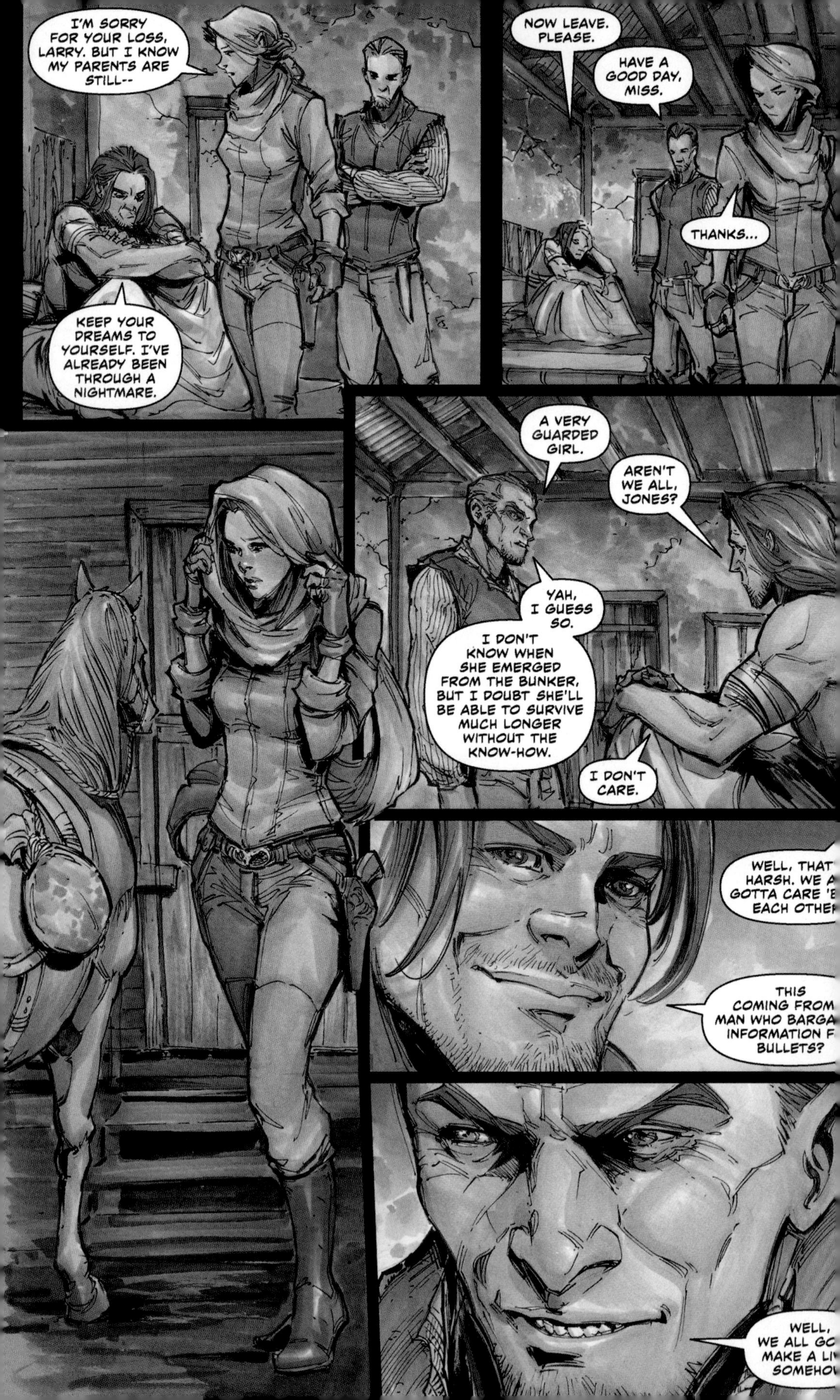
I'M SORRY FOR YOUR LOSS, LARRY. BUT I KNOW MY PARENTS ARE STILL--
KEEP YOUR DREAMS TO YOURSELF. I'VE ALREADY BEEN THROUGH A NIGHTMARE.
NOW LEAVE. PLEASE.
HAVE A GOOD DAY, MISS.
THANKS...
A VERY GUARDED GIRL.
AREN'T WE ALL, JONES?
YAH, I GUESS SO.
I DON'T KNOW WHEN SHE EMERGED FROM THE BUNKER, BUT I DOUBT SHE'LL BE ABLE TO SURVIVE MUCH LONGER WITHOUT THE KNOW-HOW.
I DON'T CARE.
THIS COMING FROM MAN WHO BARGA INFORMATION F BULLETS?

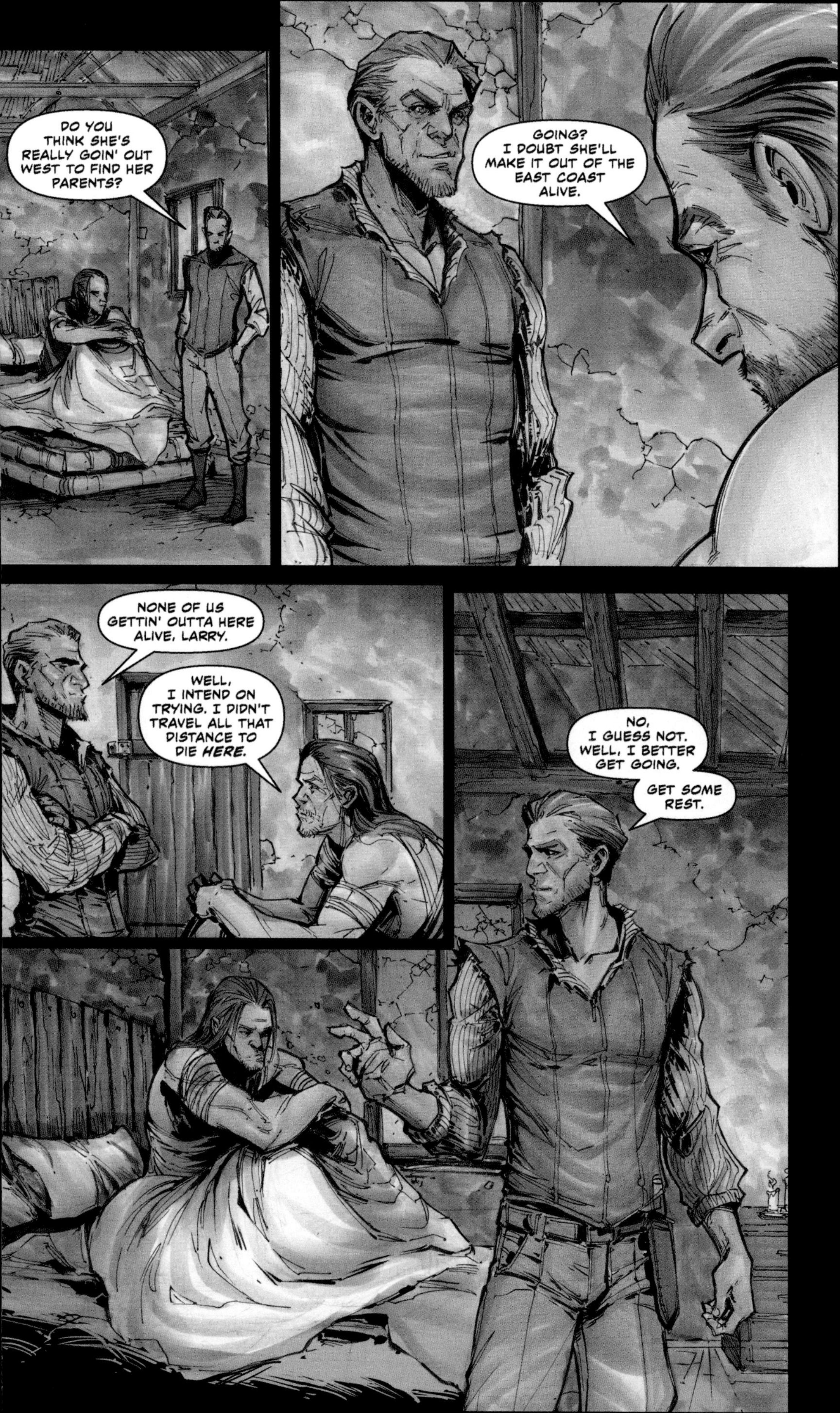
DO YOU THINK SHE'S REALLY GOIN' OUT WEST TO FIND HER PARENTS?
GOING? I DOUBT SHE'LL MAKE IT OUT OF THE EAST COAST ALIVE.
NONE OF US GETTIN' OUTTA HERE ALIVE, LARRY.
WELL, I INTEND ON TRYING. I DIDN'T TRAVEL ALL THAT DISTANCE TO DIE *HERE*.
NO, I GUESS NOT. WELL, I BETTER GET GOING.
GET SOME REST.

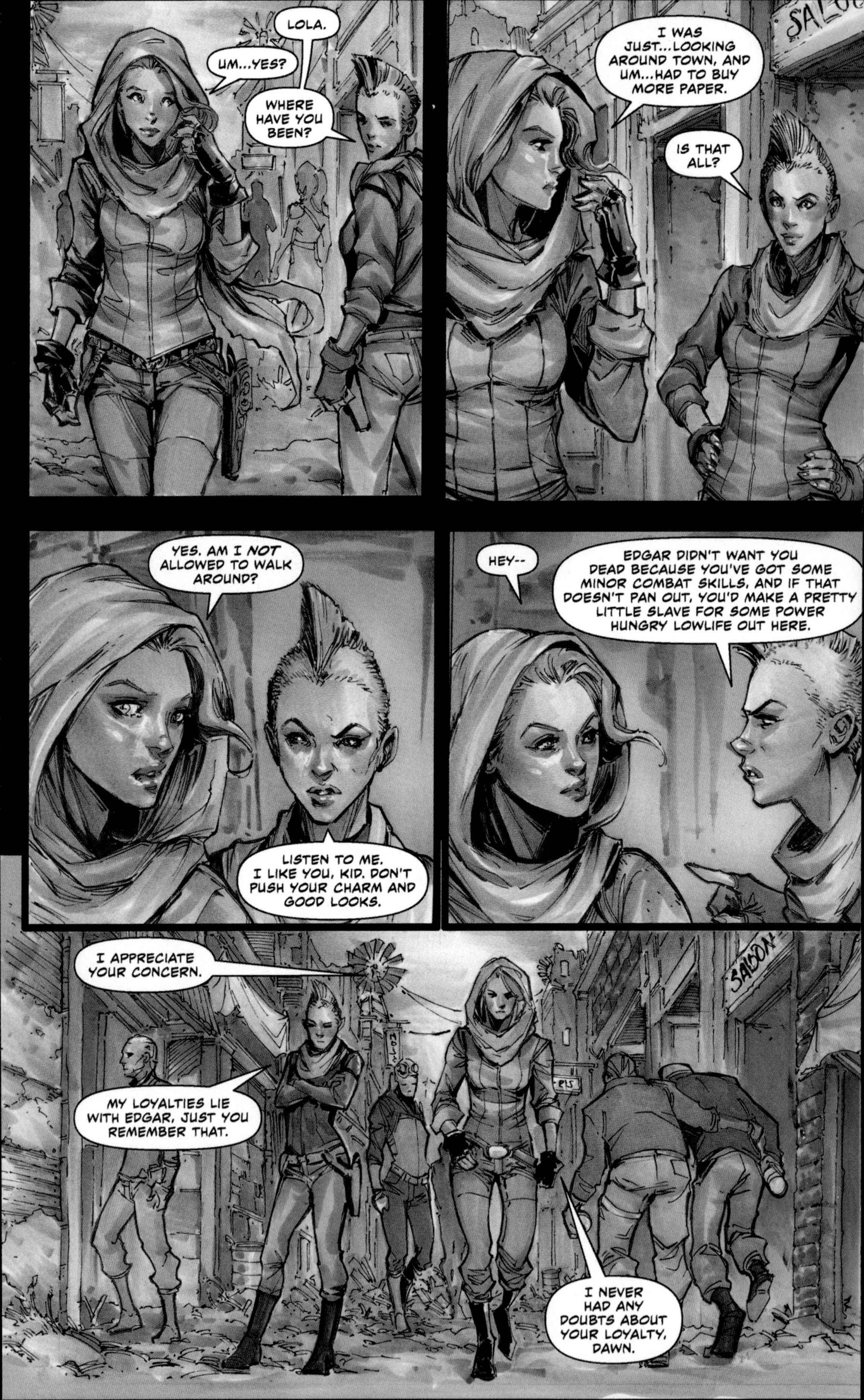
LOLA.
UM...YES?
WHERE HAVE YOU BEEN?
I WAS JUST...LOOKING AROUND TOWN, AND UM...HAD TO BUY MORE PAPER.
IS THAT ALL?
YES. AM I *NOT* ALLOWED TO WALK AROUND?
LISTEN TO ME. I LIKE YOU, KID. DON'T PUSH YOUR CHARM AND GOOD LOOKS.
HEY--
EDGAR DIDN'T WANT YOU DEAD BECAUSE YOU'VE GOT SOME MINOR COMBAT SKILLS, AND IF THAT DOESN'T PAN OUT, YOU'D MAKE A PRETTY LITTLE SLAVE FOR SOME POWER HUNGRY LOWLIFE OUT HERE.
I APPRECIATE YOUR CONCERN.
MY LOYALTIES LIE WITH EDGAR, JUST YOU REMEMBER THAT.
I NEVER HAD ANY DOUBTS ABOUT YOUR LOYALTY, DAWN.
SALOON

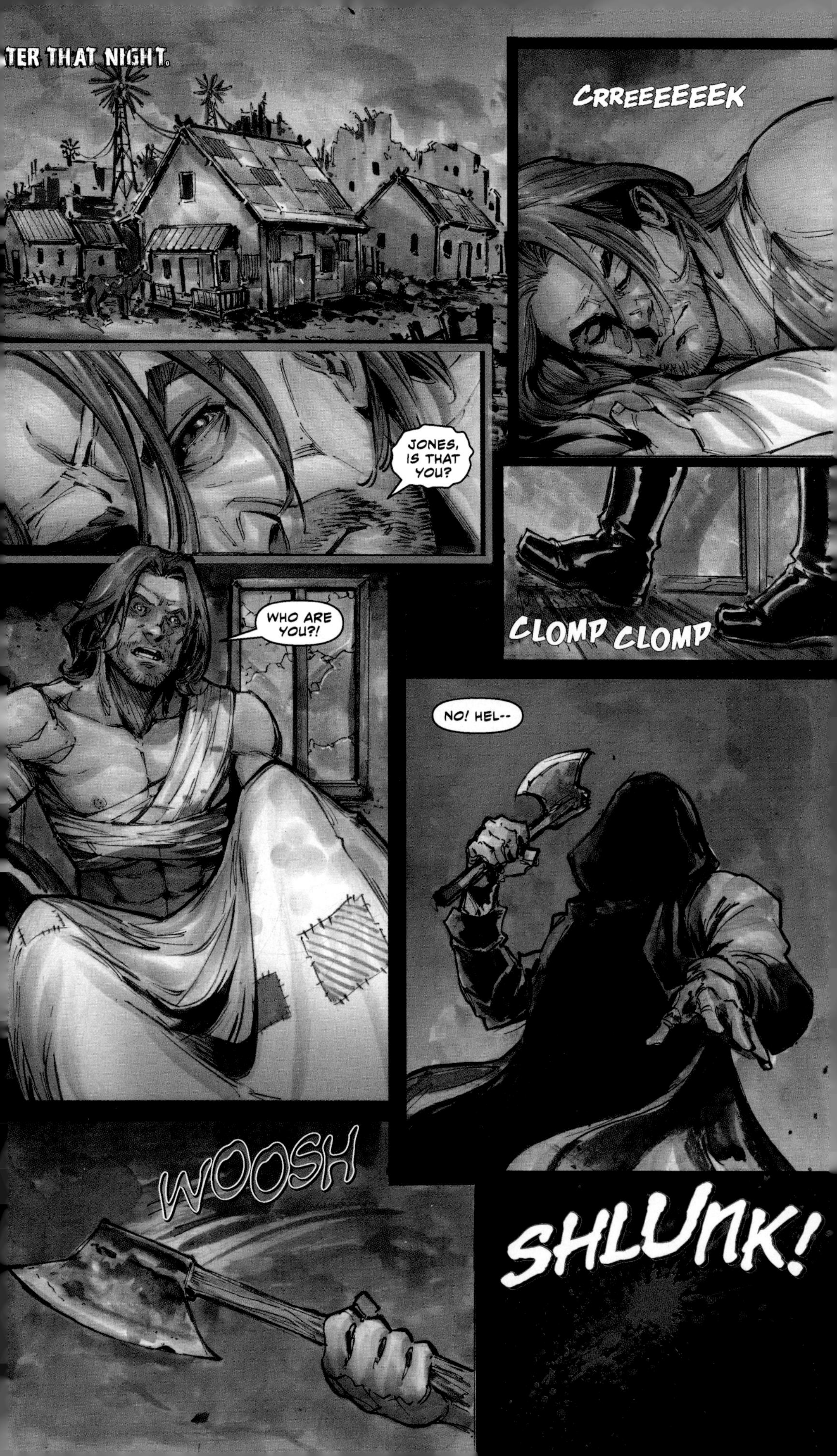
TER THAT NIGHT.
CRREEEEEEK
JONES, IS THAT YOU?
CLOMP CLOMP
WHO ARE YOU?!
NO! HEL--
WOOSH
SHLUNK!

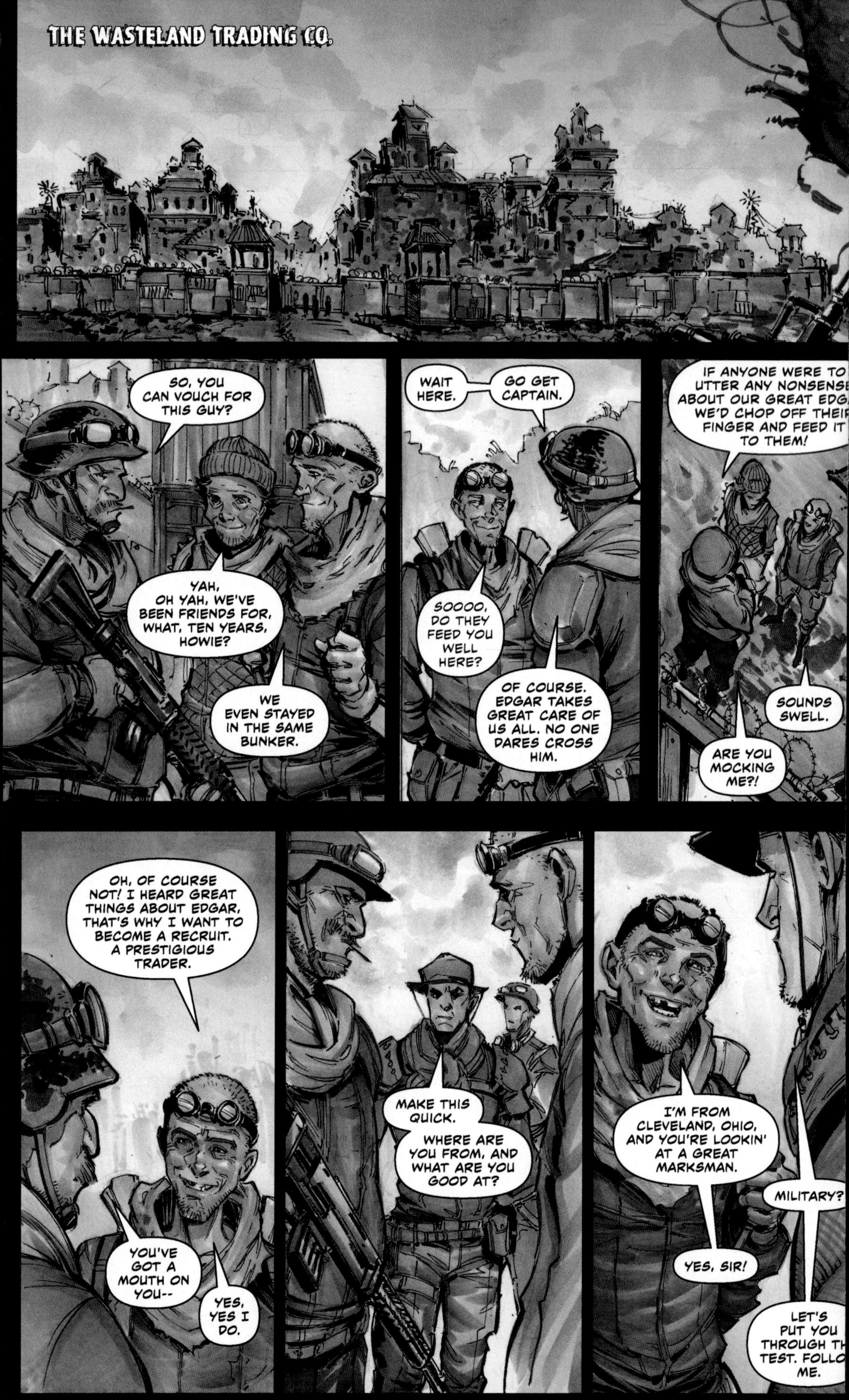
THE WASTELAND TRADING CO.
SO, YOU CAN VOUCH FOR THIS GUY?
YAH, OH YAH, WE'VE BEEN FRIENDS FOR, WHAT, TEN YEARS, HOWIE?
WE EVEN STAYED IN THE SAME BUNKER.
WAIT HERE.
GO GET CAPTAIN.
SOOOO, DO THEY FEED YOU WELL HERE?
OF COURSE. EDGAR TAKES GREAT CARE OF US ALL. NO ONE DARES CROSS HIM.
IF ANYONE WERE TO UTTER ANY NONSENSE ABOUT OUR GREAT EDGAR WE'D CHOP OFF THEIR FINGER AND FEED IT TO THEM!
SOUNDS SWELL.
ARE YOU MOCKING ME?!
OH, OF COURSE NOT! I HEARD GREAT THINGS ABOUT EDGAR, THAT'S WHY I WANT TO BECOME A RECRUIT. A PRESTIGIOUS TRADER.
YOU'VE GOT A MOUTH ON YOU--
YES, YES I DO.
MAKE THIS QUICK.
WHERE ARE YOU FROM, AND WHAT ARE YOU GOOD AT?
I'M FROM CLEVELAND, OHIO, AND YOU'RE LOOKIN' AT A GREAT MARKSMAN.
MILITARY?
YES, SIR!
LET'S PUT YOU THROUGH TH TEST. FOLLO ME.

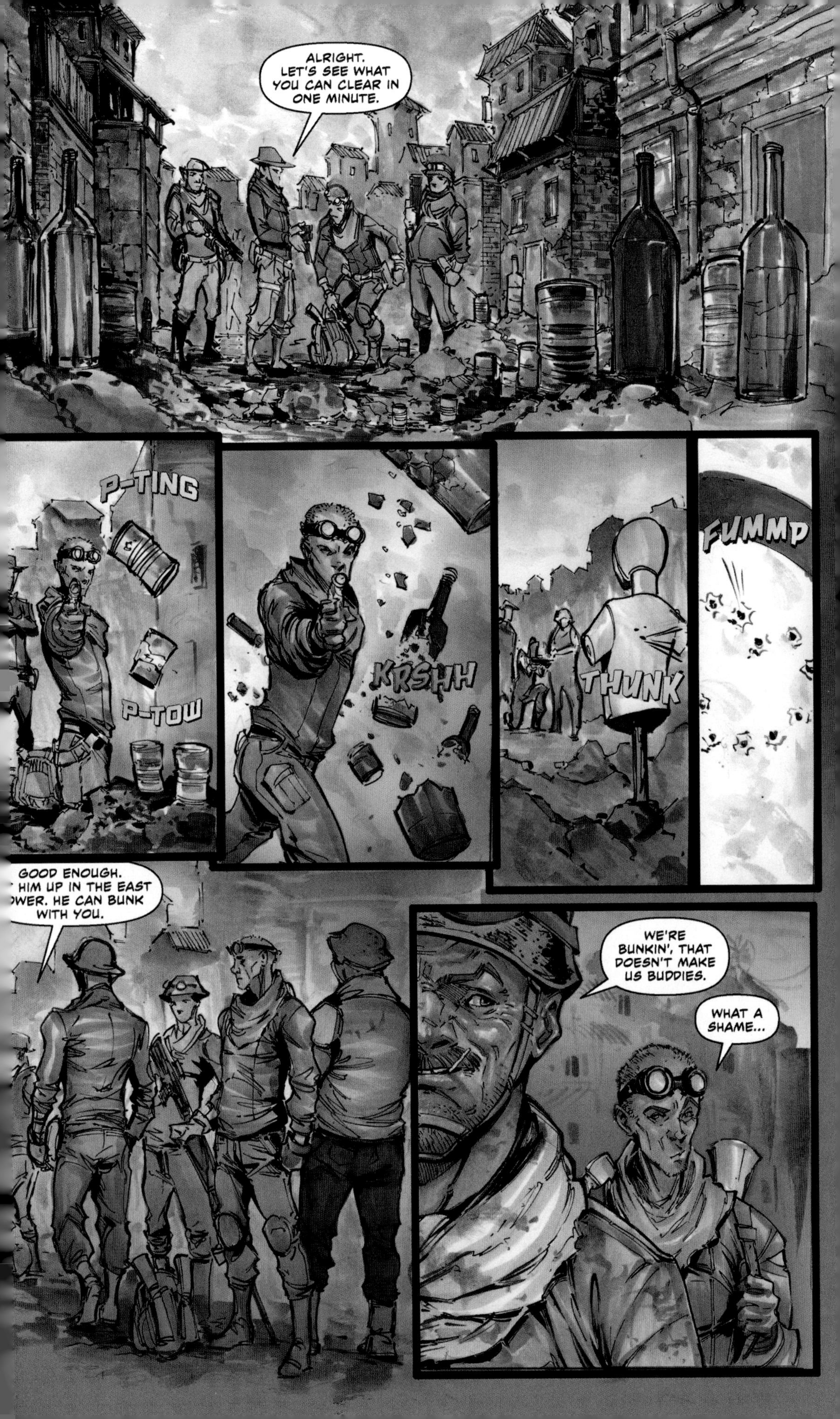
ALRIGHT. LET'S SEE WHAT YOU CAN CLEAR IN ONE MINUTE.
P-TING
P-TOW
KRSHH
THUNK
FUMMP
GOOD ENOUGH. HIM UP IN THE EAST OWER. HE CAN BUNK WITH YOU.
WE'RE BUNKIN', THAT DOESN'T MAKE US BUDDIES.
WHAT A SHAME...

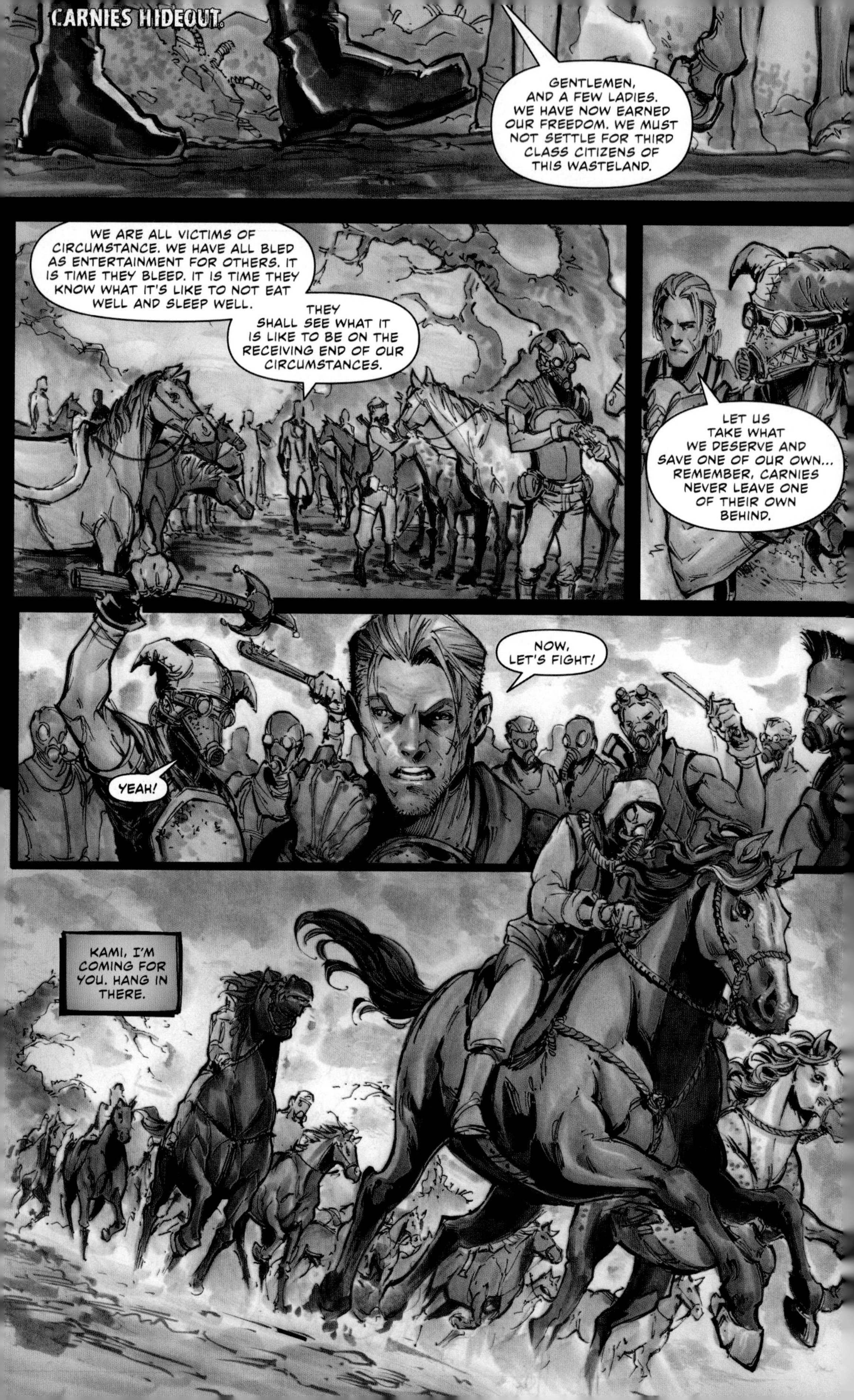
CARNIES HIDEOUT.
GENTLEMEN, AND A FEW LADIES. WE HAVE NOW EARNED OUR FREEDOM. WE MUST NOT SETTLE FOR THIRD CLASS CITIZENS OF THIS WASTELAND.
WE ARE ALL VICTIMS OF CIRCUMSTANCE. WE HAVE ALL BLED AS ENTERTAINMENT FOR OTHERS. IT IS TIME THEY BLEED. IT IS TIME THEY KNOW WHAT IT'S LIKE TO NOT EAT WELL AND SLEEP WELL.
THEY SHALL SEE WHAT IT IS LIKE TO BE ON THE RECEIVING END OF OUR CIRCUMSTANCES.
LET US TAKE WHAT WE DESERVE AND SAVE ONE OF OUR OWN... REMEMBER, CARNIES NEVER LEAVE ONE OF THEIR OWN BEHIND.
NOW, LET'S FIGHT!
YEAH!
KAMI, I'M COMING FOR YOU. HANG IN THERE.

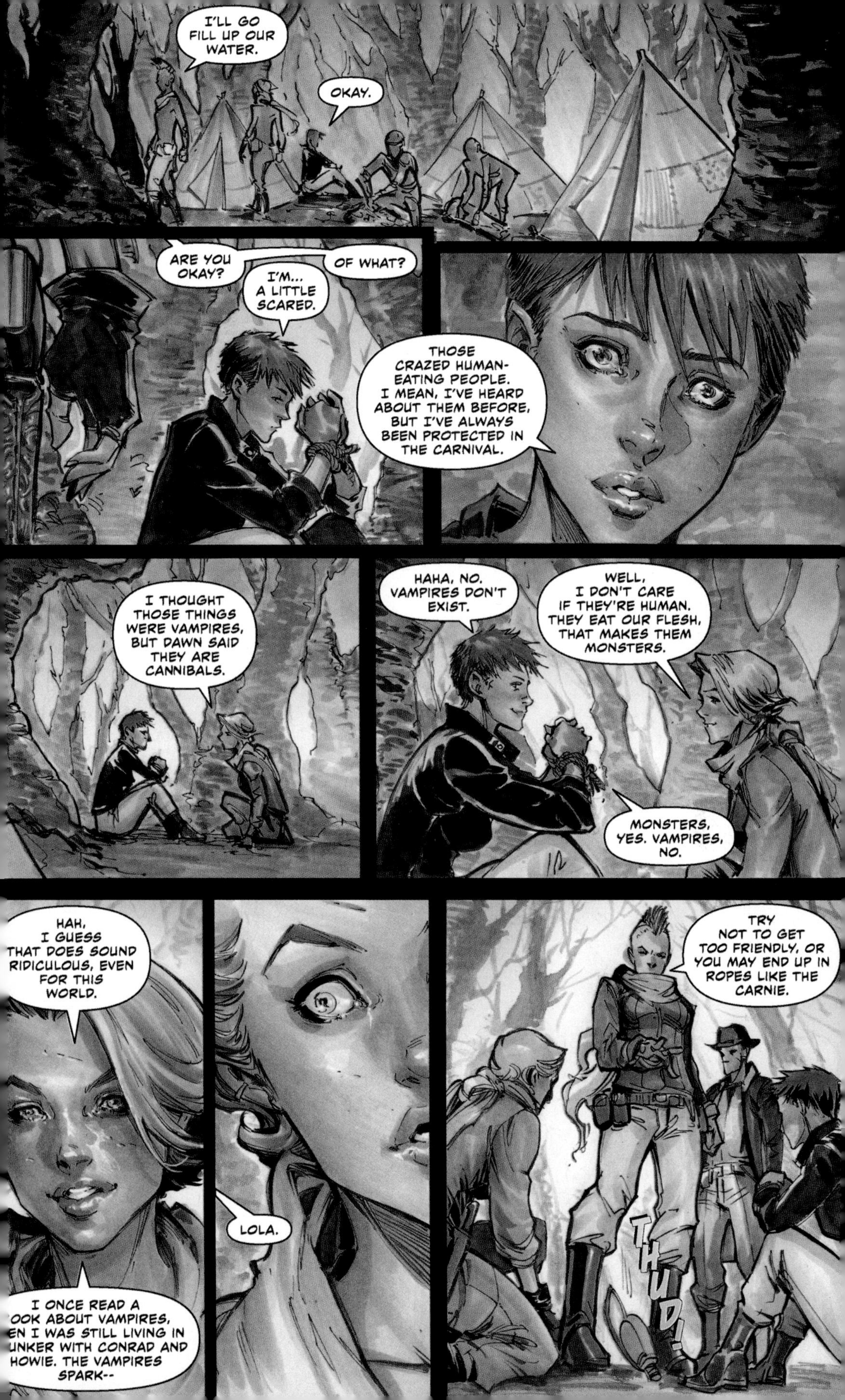
I'LL GO FILL UP OUR WATER.
OKAY.
ARE YOU OKAY?
I'M... A LITTLE SCARED.
OF WHAT?
THOSE CRAZED HUMAN-EATING PEOPLE. I MEAN, I'VE HEARD ABOUT THEM BEFORE, BUT I'VE ALWAYS BEEN PROTECTED IN THE CARNIVAL.
I THOUGHT THOSE THINGS WERE VAMPIRES, BUT DAWN SAID THEY ARE CANNIBALS.
HAHA, NO. VAMPIRES DON'T EXIST.
WELL, I DON'T CARE IF THEY'RE HUMAN. THEY EAT OUR FLESH, THAT MAKES THEM MONSTERS.
MONSTERS, YES. VAMPIRES, NO.
HAH, I GUESS THAT DOES SOUND RIDICULOUS, EVEN FOR THIS WORLD.
I ONCE READ A OOK ABOUT VAMPIRES, EN I WAS STILL LIVING IN UNKER WITH CONRAD AND HOWIE. THE VAMPIRES SPARK--
LOLA.
TRY NOT TO GET TOO FRIENDLY, OR YOU MAY END UP IN ROPES LIKE THE CARNIE.
THUD!

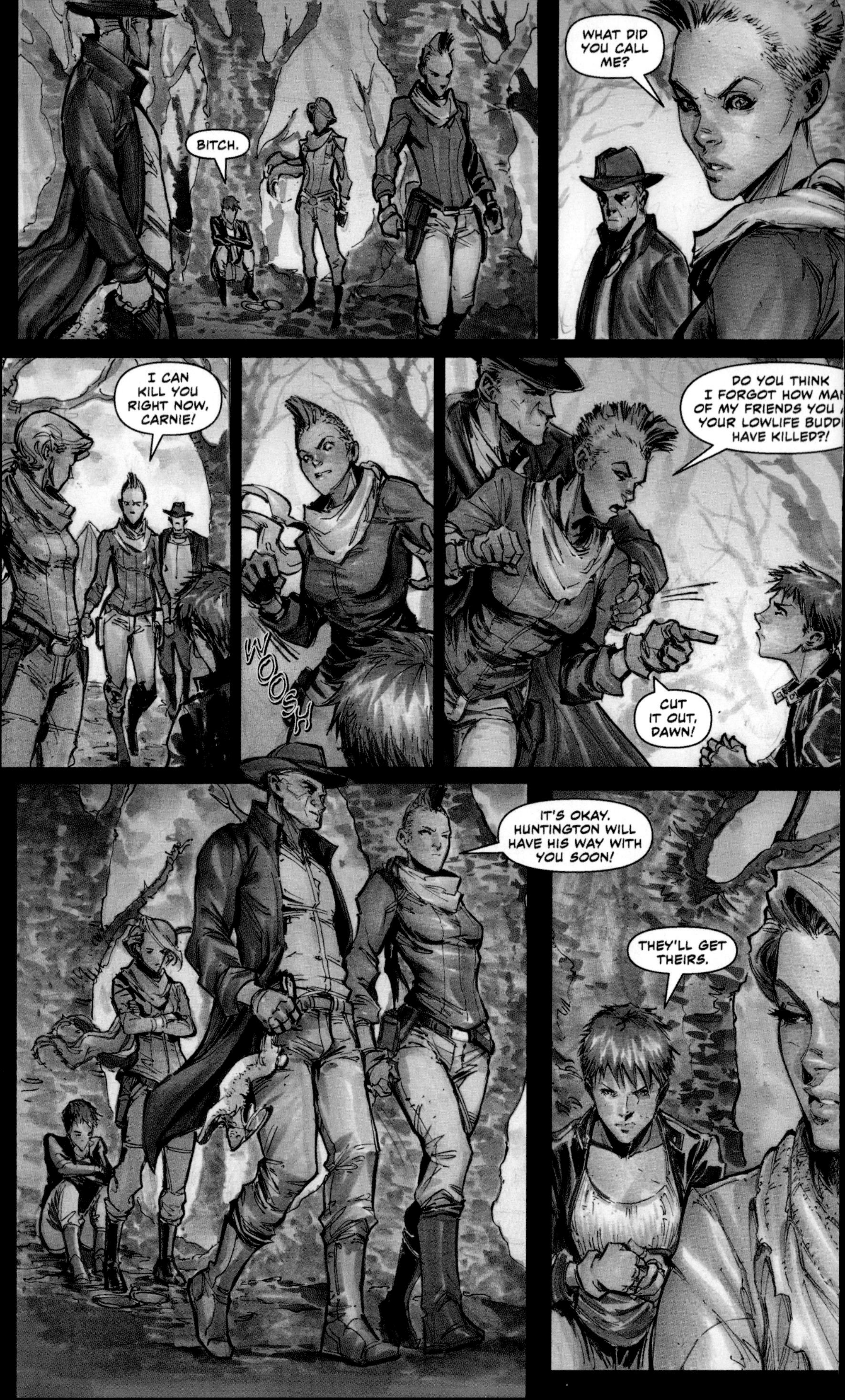
BITCH.
WHAT DID YOU CALL ME?
I CAN KILL YOU RIGHT NOW, CARNIE!
WOOSH
DO YOU THINK I FORGOT HOW MAN OF MY FRIENDS YOU A YOUR LOWLIFE BUDDI HAVE KILLED?!
CUT IT OUT, DAWN!
IT'S OKAY. HUNTINGTON WILL HAVE HIS WAY WITH YOU SOON!
THEY'LL GET THEIRS.

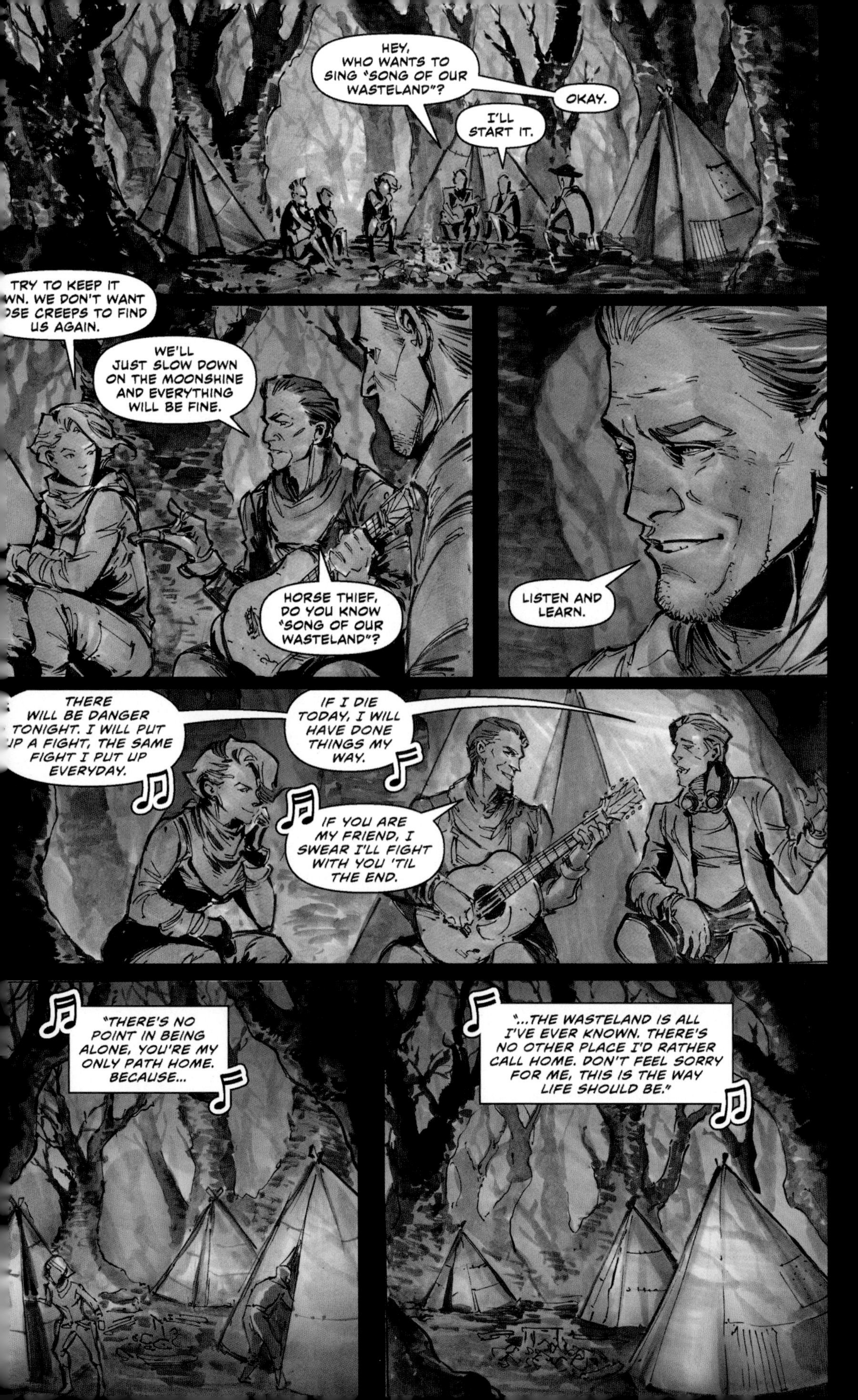
HEY, WHO WANTS TO SING "SONG OF OUR WASTELAND"?
OKAY.
I'LL START IT.
TRY TO KEEP IT WN. WE DON'T WANT OSE CREEPS TO FIND US AGAIN.
WE'LL JUST SLOW DOWN ON THE MOONSHINE AND EVERYTHING WILL BE FINE.
HORSE THIEF, DO YOU KNOW "SONG OF OUR WASTELAND"?
LISTEN AND LEARN.
THERE WILL BE DANGER TONIGHT. I WILL PUT UP A FIGHT, THE SAME FIGHT I PUT UP EVERYDAY.
IF I DIE TODAY, I WILL HAVE DONE THINGS MY WAY.
IF YOU ARE MY FRIEND, I SWEAR I'LL FIGHT WITH YOU 'TIL THE END.
"THERE'S NO POINT IN BEING ALONE, YOU'RE MY ONLY PATH HOME. BECAUSE...
"...THE WASTELAND IS ALL I'VE EVER KNOWN. THERE'S NO OTHER PLACE I'D RATHER CALL HOME. DON'T FEEL SORRY FOR ME, THIS IS THE WAY LIFE SHOULD BE."

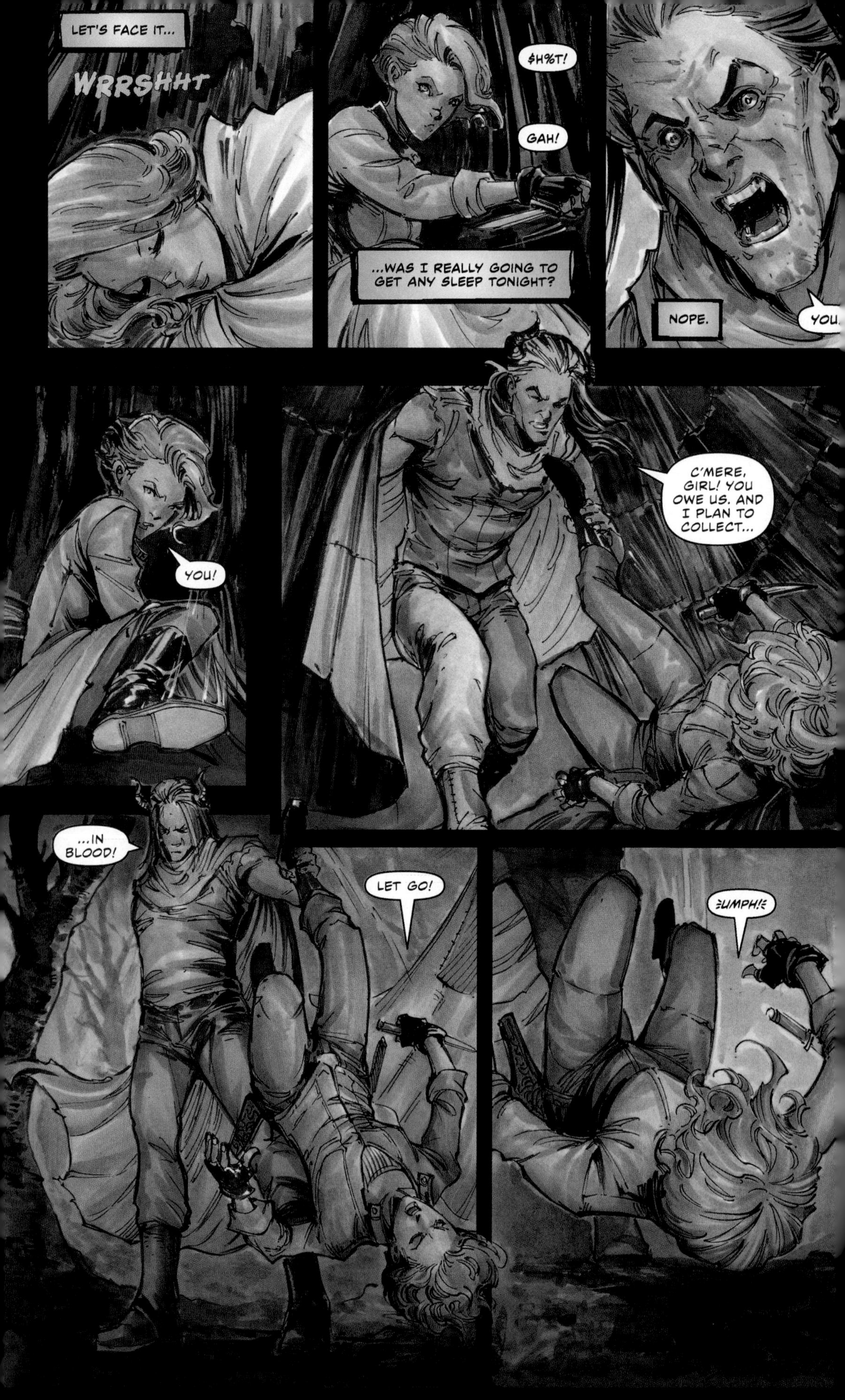
LET'S FACE IT...
WRRSHHT
$H%T!
GAH!
...WAS I REALLY GOING TO GET ANY SLEEP TONIGHT?
NOPE.
YOU.
YOU!
C'MERE, GIRL! YOU OWE US. AND I PLAN TO COLLECT...
...IN BLOOD!
LET GO!
UMPH!

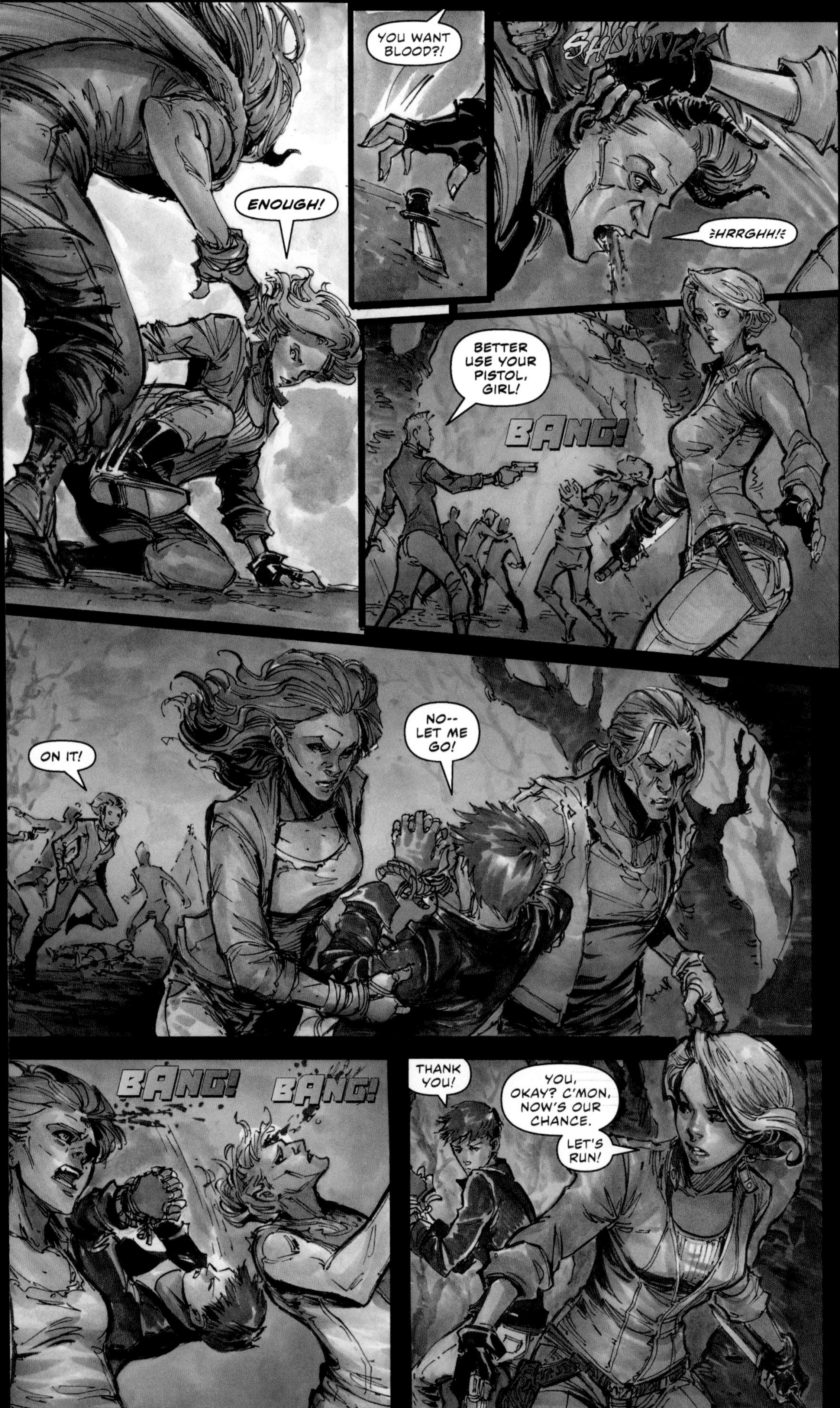
ENOUGH!
YOU WANT BLOOD?!
SHUNNK
HRRGHH!
BETTER USE YOUR PISTOL, GIRL!
BANG!
ON IT!
NO-- LET ME GO!
BANG!
BANG!
THANK YOU!
YOU, OKAY? C'MON, NOW'S OUR CHANCE.
LET'S RUN!

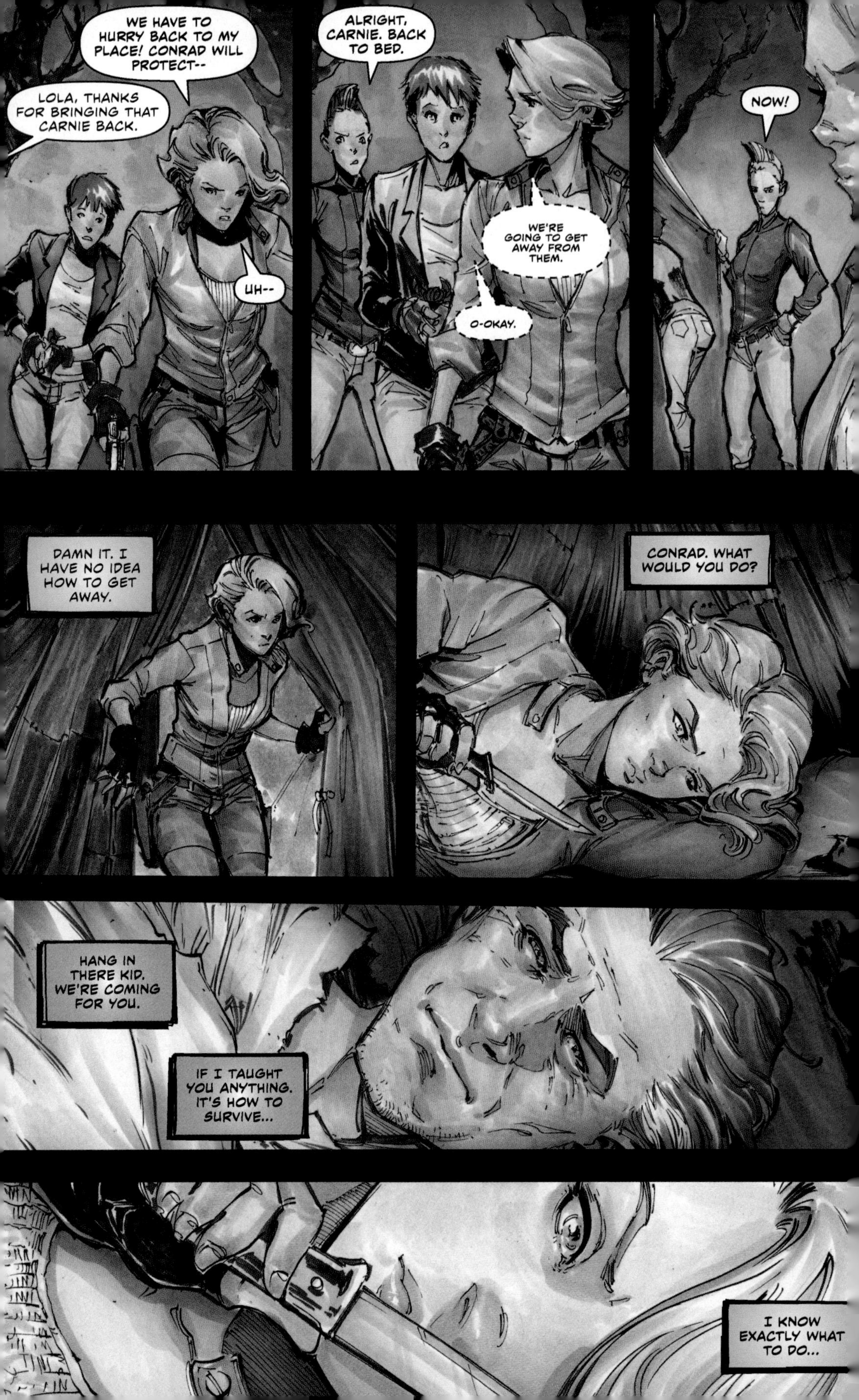
LOLA, THANKS FOR BRINGING THAT CARNIE BACK.
WE HAVE TO HURRY BACK TO MY PLACE! CONRAD WILL PROTECT--
UH--
ALRIGHT, CARNIE. BACK TO BED.
WE'RE GOING TO GET AWAY FROM THEM.
O-OKAY.
NOW!
DAMN IT. I HAVE NO IDEA HOW TO GET AWAY.
CONRAD. WHAT WOULD YOU DO?
HANG IN THERE KID. WE'RE COMING FOR YOU.
IF I TAUGHT YOU ANYTHING. IT'S HOW TO SURVIVE...
I KNOW EXACTLY WHAT TO DO...

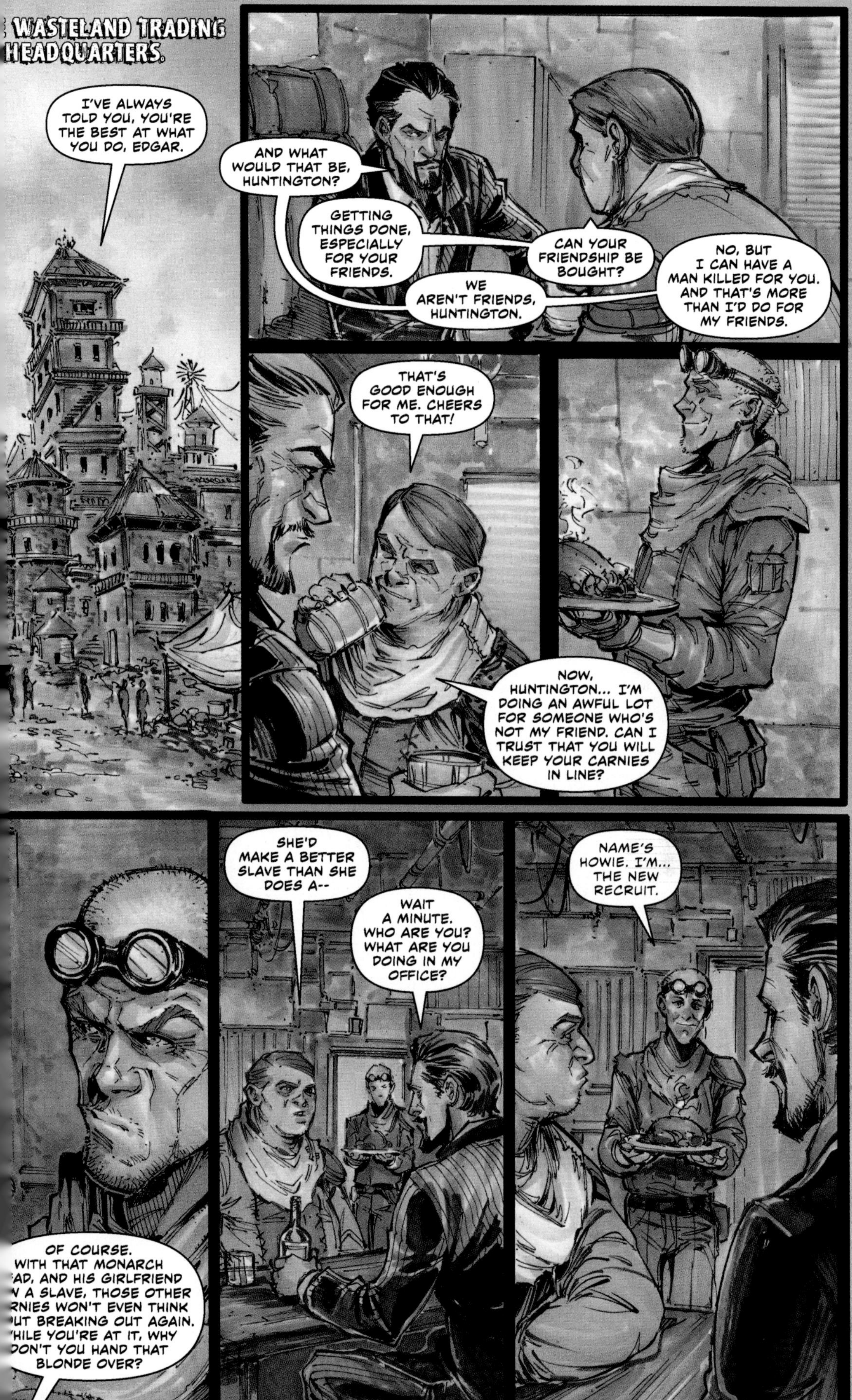

WASTELAND TRADING HEADQUARTERS.
I'VE ALWAYS TOLD YOU, YOU'RE THE BEST AT WHAT YOU DO, EDGAR.
AND WHAT WOULD THAT BE, HUNTINGTON?
GETTING THINGS DONE, ESPECIALLY FOR YOUR FRIENDS.
CAN YOUR FRIENDSHIP BE BOUGHT?
WE AREN'T FRIENDS, HUNTINGTON.
NO, BUT I CAN HAVE A MAN KILLED FOR YOU. AND THAT'S MORE THAN I'D DO FOR MY FRIENDS.
THAT'S GOOD ENOUGH FOR ME. CHEERS TO THAT!
NOW, HUNTINGTON... I'M DOING AN AWFUL LOT FOR SOMEONE WHO'S NOT MY FRIEND. CAN I TRUST THAT YOU WILL KEEP YOUR CARNIES IN LINE?
OF COURSE. WITH THAT MONARCH
AD, AND HIS GIRLFRIEND
A SLAVE, THOSE OTHER
RNIES WON'T EVEN THINK
UT BREAKING OUT AGAIN.
HILE YOU'RE AT IT, WHY
DON'T YOU HAND THAT BLONDE OVER?
SHE'D MAKE A BETTER SLAVE THAN SHE DOES A--
WAIT A MINUTE. WHO ARE YOU? WHAT ARE YOU DOING IN MY OFFICE?
NAME'S HOWIE. I'M... THE NEW RECRUIT.

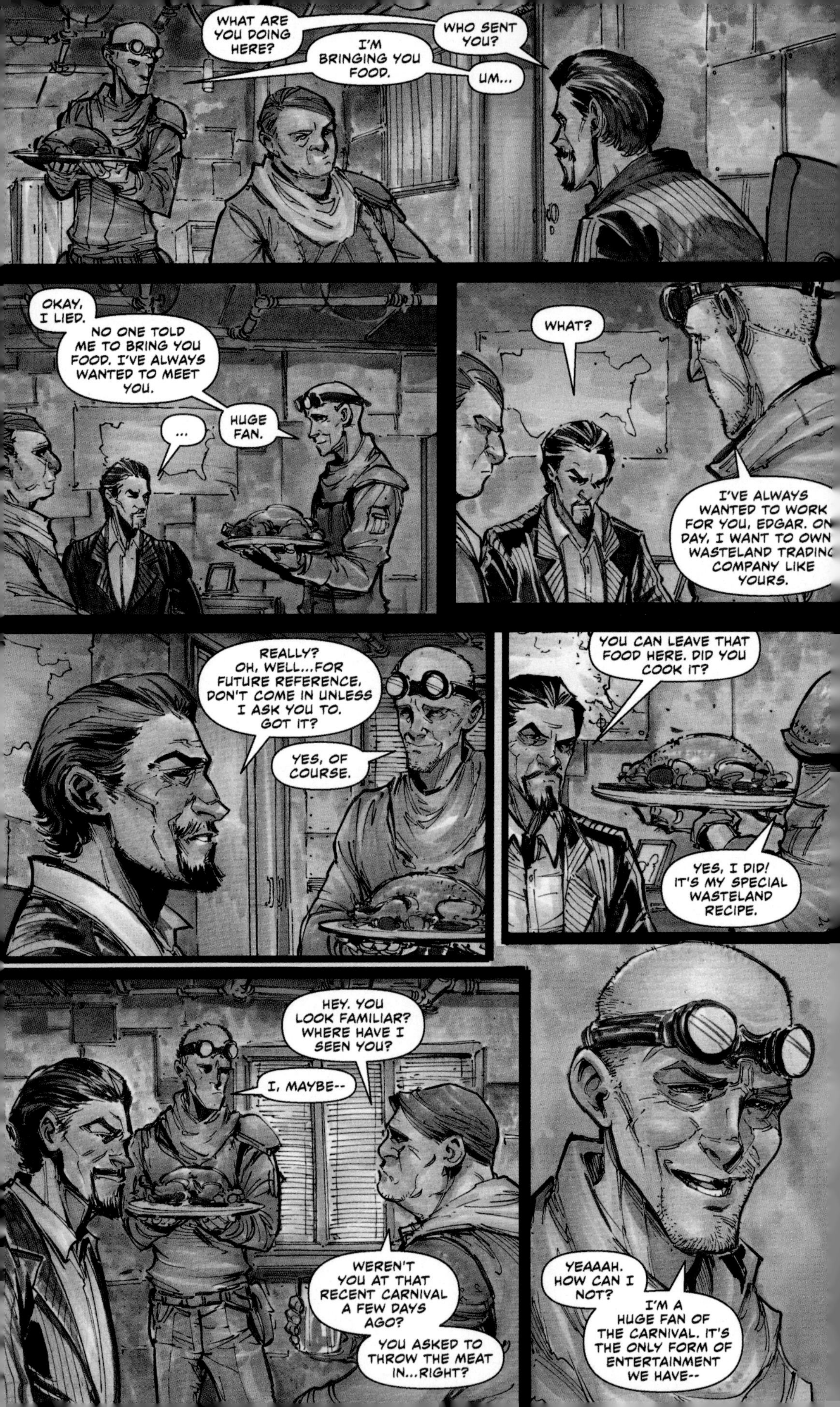
WHAT ARE YOU DOING HERE?
WHO SENT YOU?
I'M BRINGING YOU FOOD.
UM...
OKAY, I LIED.
NO ONE TOLD ME TO BRING YOU FOOD. I'VE ALWAYS WANTED TO MEET YOU.
...
HUGE FAN.
WHAT?
I'VE ALWAYS WANTED TO WORK FOR YOU, EDGAR. ON DAY, I WANT TO OWN WASTELAND TRADING COMPANY LIKE YOURS.
REALLY? OH, WELL...FOR FUTURE REFERENCE, DON'T COME IN UNLESS I ASK YOU TO. GOT IT?
YES, OF COURSE.
YOU CAN LEAVE THAT FOOD HERE. DID YOU COOK IT?
YES, I DID! IT'S MY SPECIAL WASTELAND RECIPE.
HEY. YOU LOOK FAMILIAR? WHERE HAVE I SEEN YOU?
I, MAYBE--
WEREN'T YOU AT THAT RECENT CARNIVAL A FEW DAYS AGO?
YOU ASKED TO THROW THE MEAT IN...RIGHT?
YEAAAH. HOW CAN I NOT?
I'M A HUGE FAN OF THE CARNIVAL. IT'S THE ONLY FORM OF ENTERTAINMENT WE HAVE--

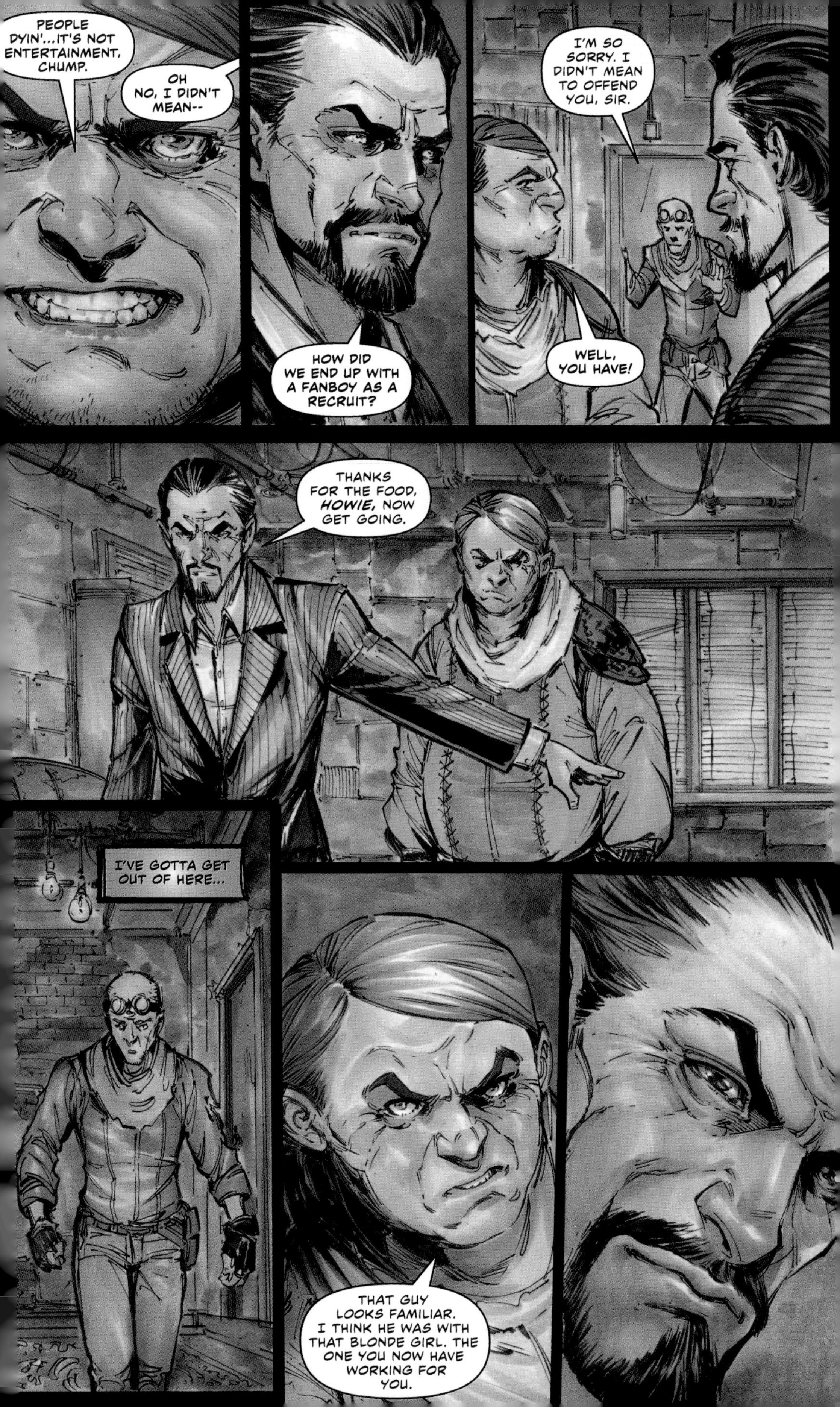
PEOPLE DYIN'...IT'S NOT ENTERTAINMENT, CHUMP.
OH NO, I DIDN'T MEAN--
HOW DID WE END UP WITH A FANBOY AS A RECRUIT?
I'M SO SORRY. I DIDN'T MEAN TO OFFEND YOU, SIR.
WELL, YOU HAVE!
THANKS FOR THE FOOD, HOWIE, NOW GET GOING.
I'VE GOTTA GET OUT OF HERE...
THAT GUY LOOKS FAMILIAR. I THINK HE WAS WITH THAT BLONDE GIRL. THE ONE YOU NOW HAVE WORKING FOR YOU.

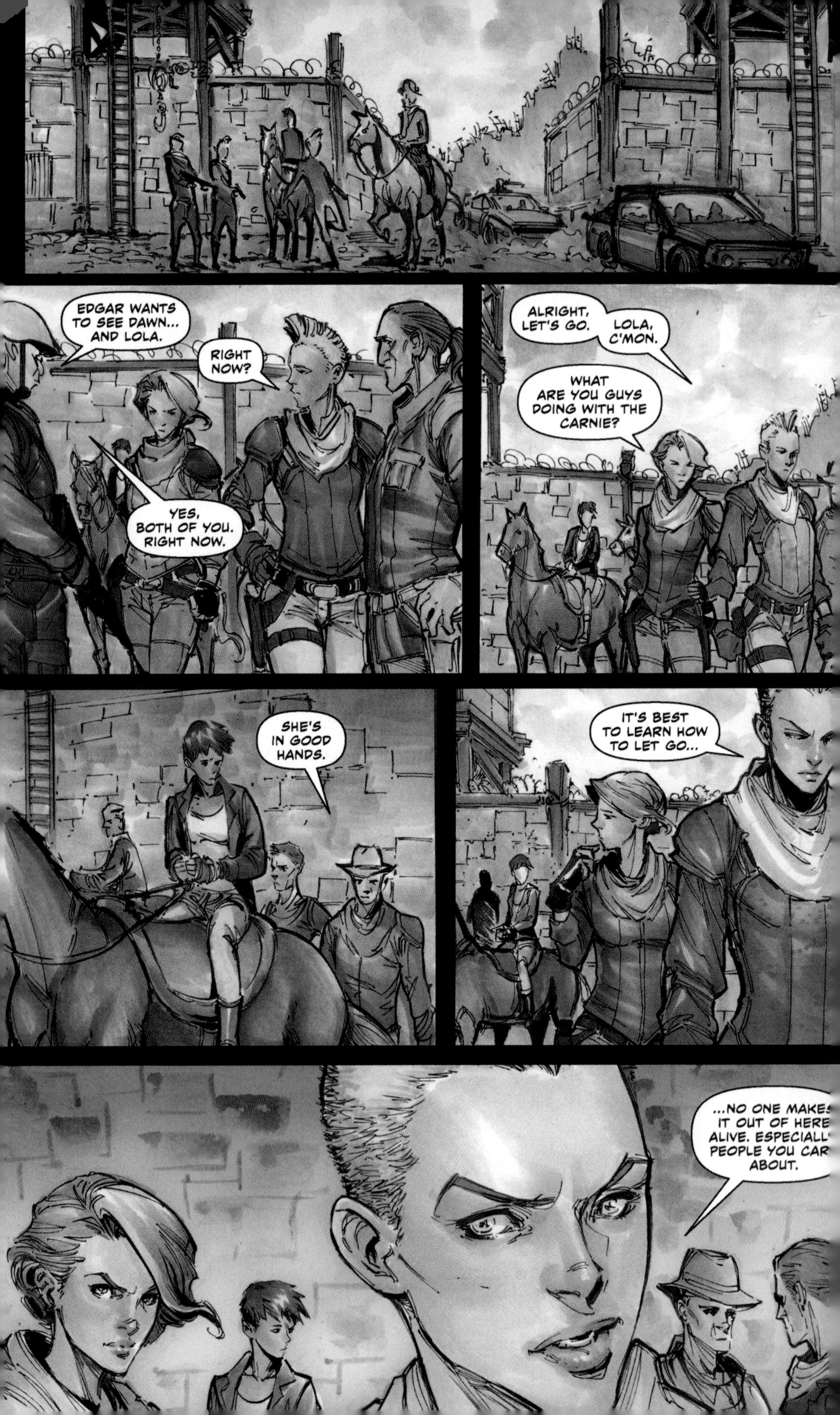
EDGAR WANTS TO SEE DAWN... AND LOLA.
RIGHT NOW?
YES, BOTH OF YOU. RIGHT NOW.
ALRIGHT, LET'S GO.
LOLA, C'MON.
WHAT ARE YOU GUYS DOING WITH THE CARNIE?
SHE'S IN GOOD HANDS.
IT'S BEST TO LEARN HOW TO LET GO...
...NO ONE MAKES IT OUT OF HERE ALIVE. ESPECIALL PEOPLE YOU CAR ABOUT.

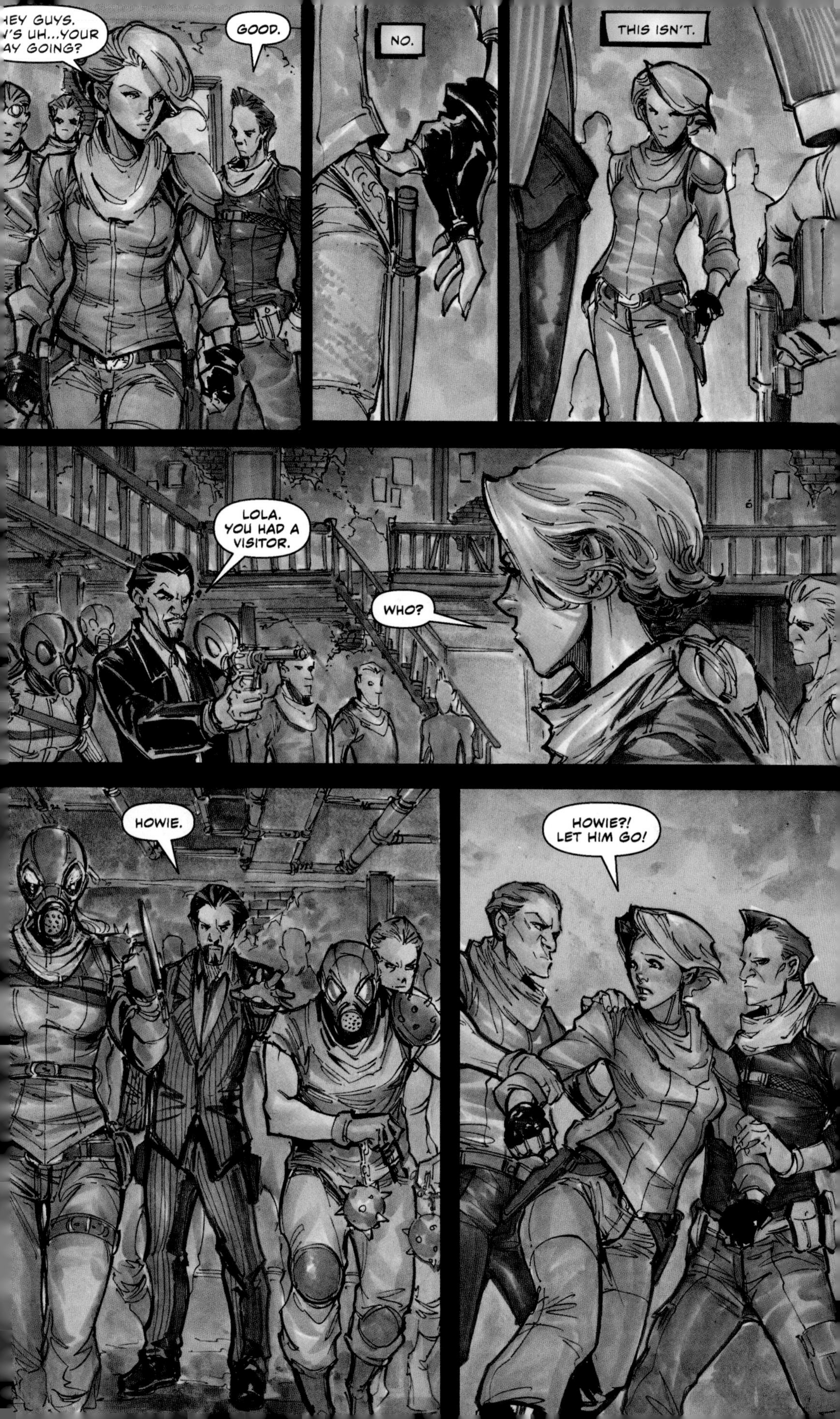
HEY GUYS.
'S UH...YOUR
AY GOING?
GOOD.
NO.
THIS ISN'T.
LOLA.
YOU HAD A
VISITOR.
WHO?
HOWIE.
HOWIE?!
LET HIM GO!

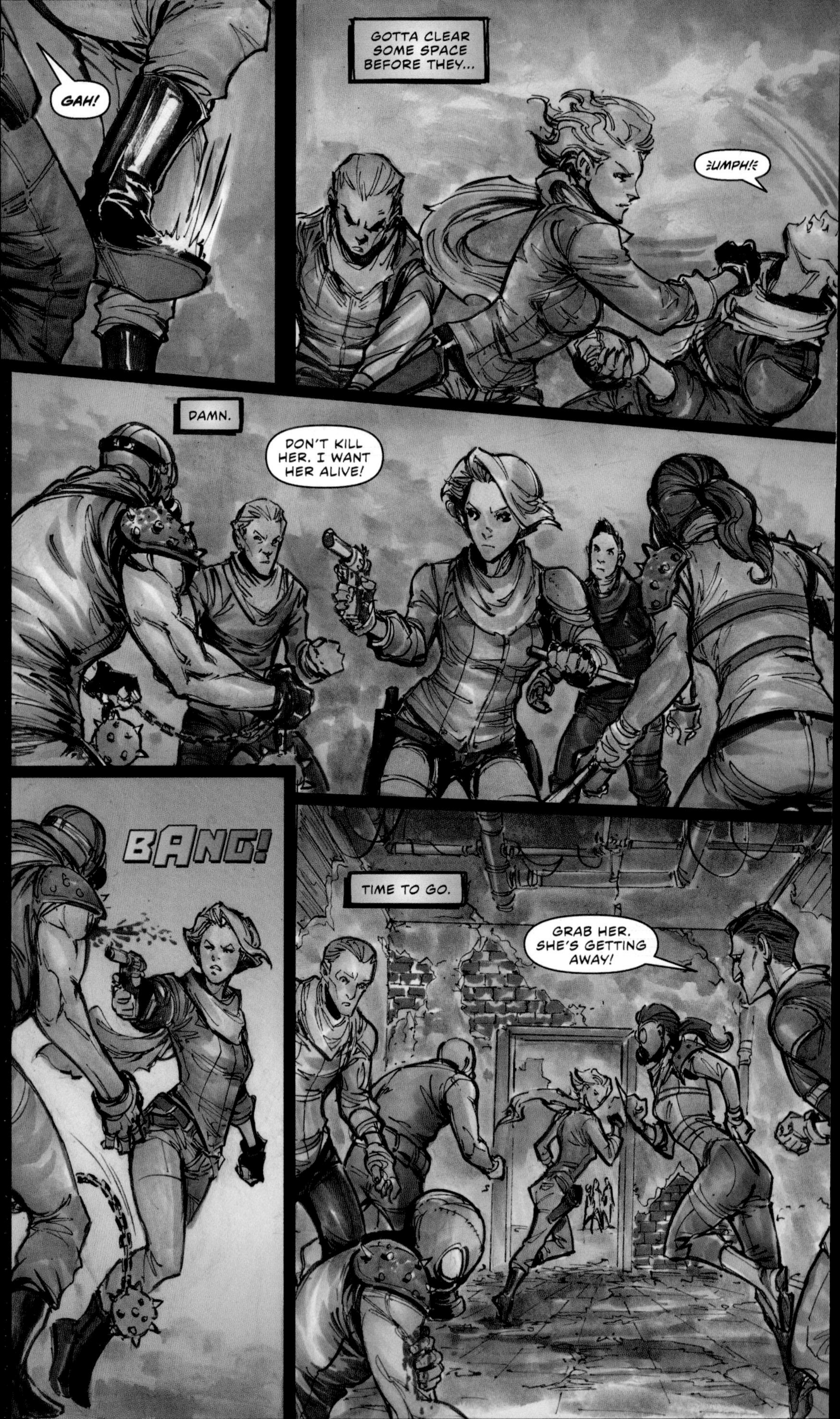
GAH!
GOTTA CLEAR SOME SPACE BEFORE THEY...
UMPH!
DAMN.
DON'T KILL HER. I WANT HER ALIVE!
BANG!
TIME TO GO.
GRAB HER. SHE'S GETTING AWAY!

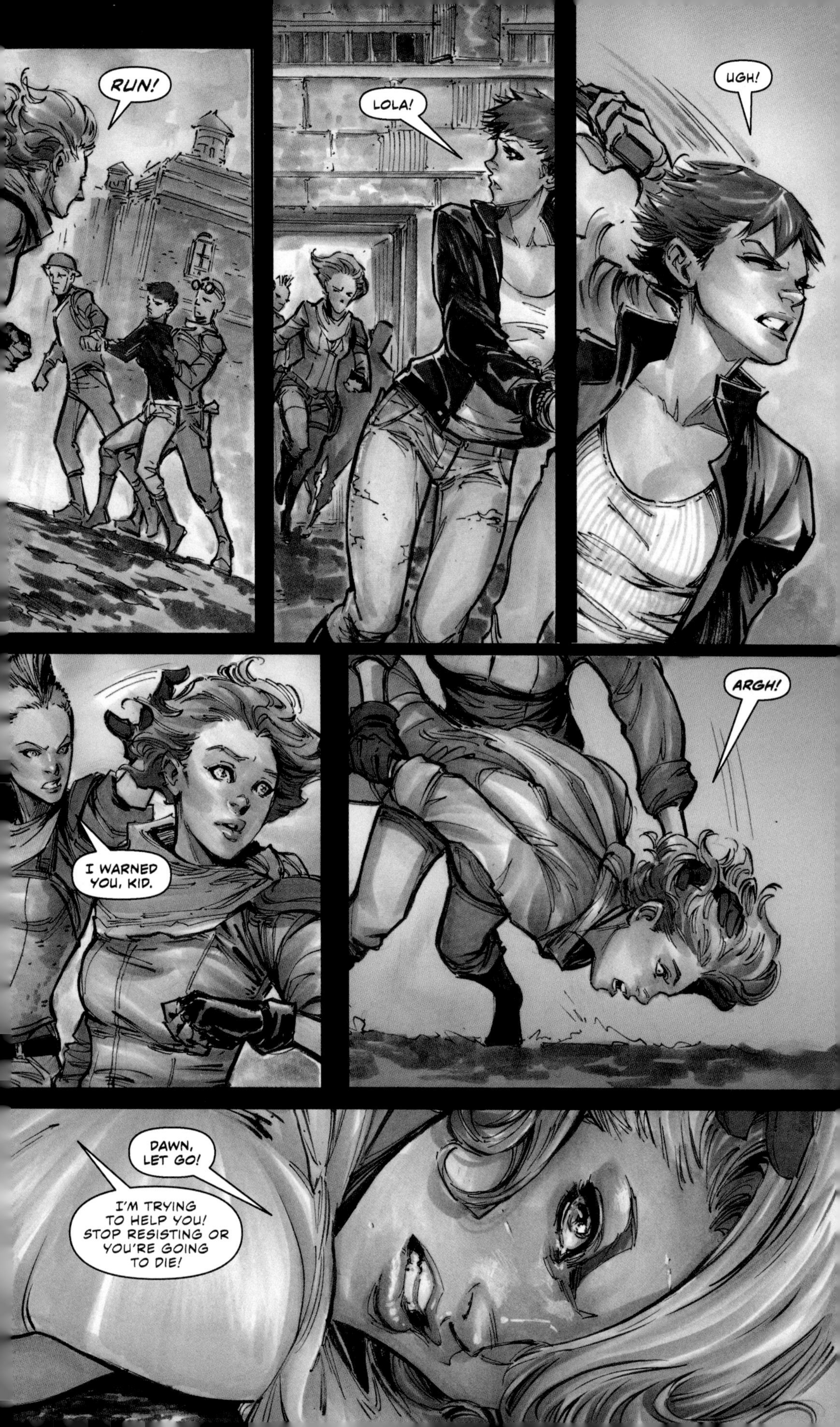
RUN!
LOLA!
UGH!
I WARNED YOU, KID.
ARGH!
DAWN, LET GO!
I'M TRYING TO HELP YOU! STOP RESISTING OR YOU'RE GOING TO DIE!

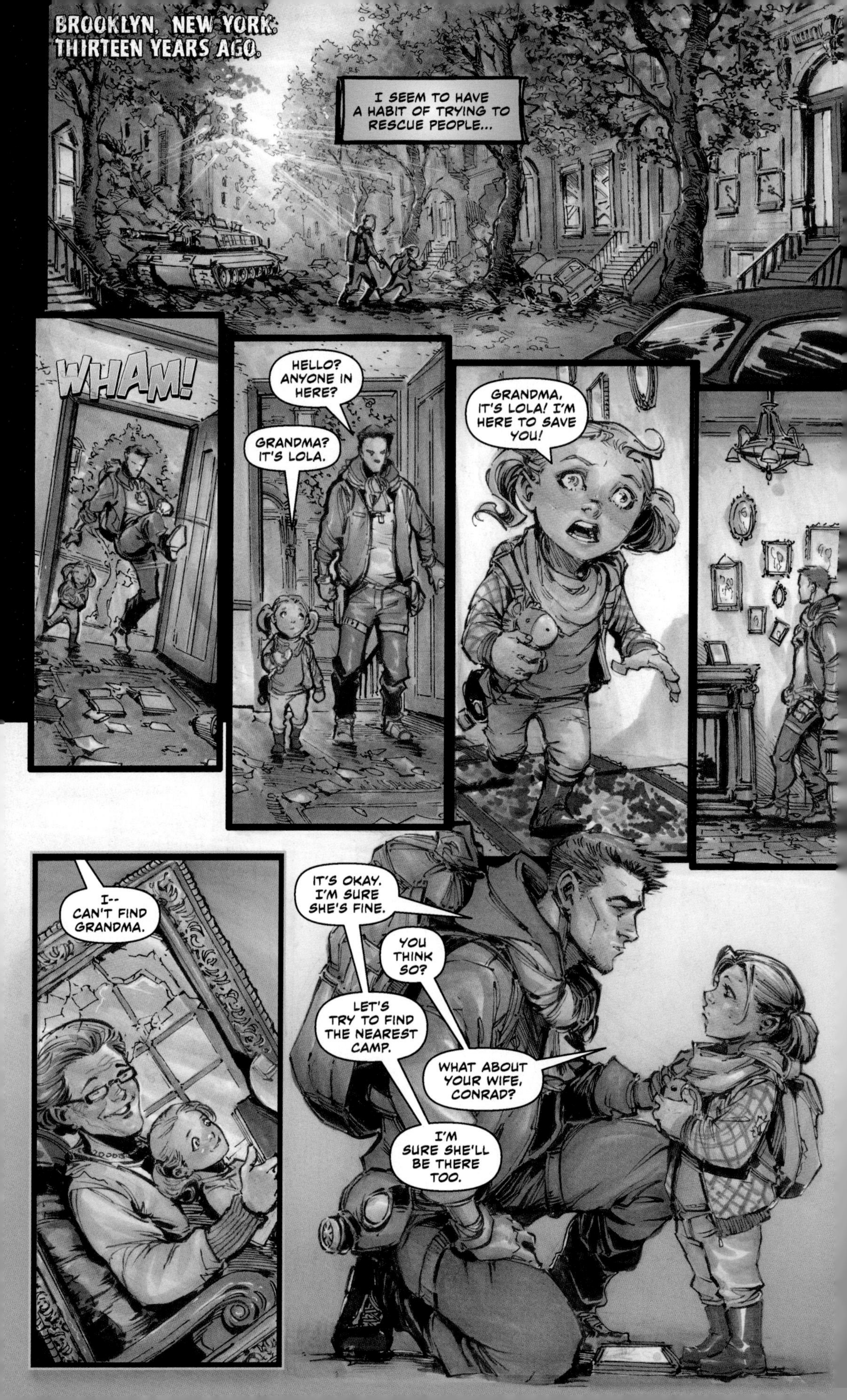
BROOKLYN, NEW YORK. THIRTEEN YEARS AGO.
I SEEM TO HAVE A HABIT OF TRYING TO RESCUE PEOPLE...
WHAM!
HELLO? ANYONE IN HERE?
GRANDMA? IT'S LOLA.
GRANDMA, IT'S LOLA! I'M HERE TO SAVE YOU!
I-- CAN'T FIND GRANDMA.
IT'S OKAY. I'M SURE SHE'S FINE.
YOU THINK SO?
LET'S TRY TO FIND THE NEAREST CAMP.
WHAT ABOUT YOUR WIFE, CONRAD?
I'M SURE SHE'LL BE THERE TOO.

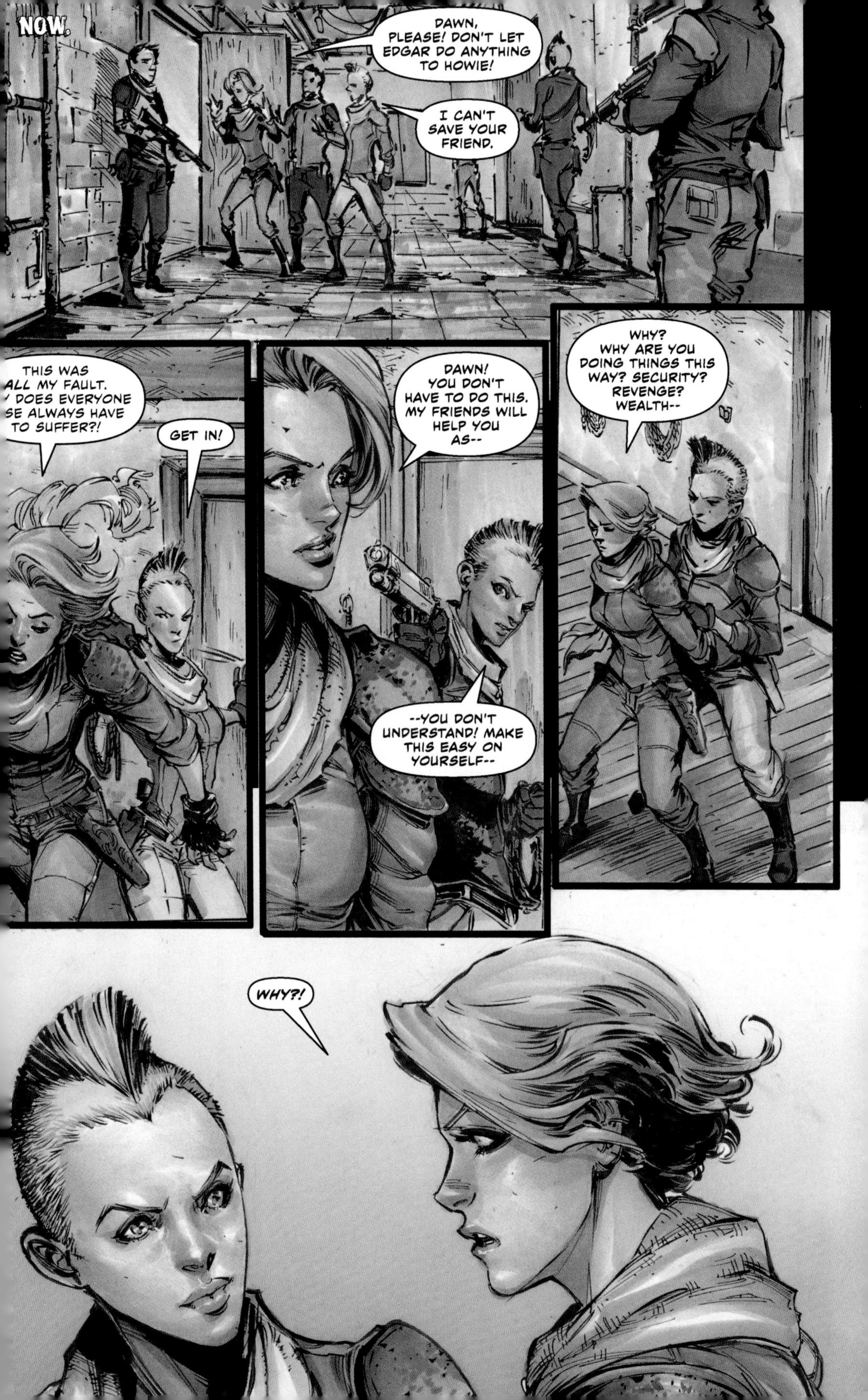
NOW.
DAWN, PLEASE! DON'T LET EDGAR DO ANYTHING TO HOWIE!
I CAN'T SAVE YOUR FRIEND.
THIS WAS ALL MY FAULT. DOES EVERYONE ALWAYS HAVE TO SUFFER?!
GET IN!
DAWN! YOU DON'T HAVE TO DO THIS. MY FRIENDS WILL HELP YOU AS--
--YOU DON'T UNDERSTAND! MAKE THIS EASY ON YOURSELF--
WHY? WHY ARE YOU DOING THINGS THIS WAY? SECURITY? REVENGE? WEALTH--
WHY?!

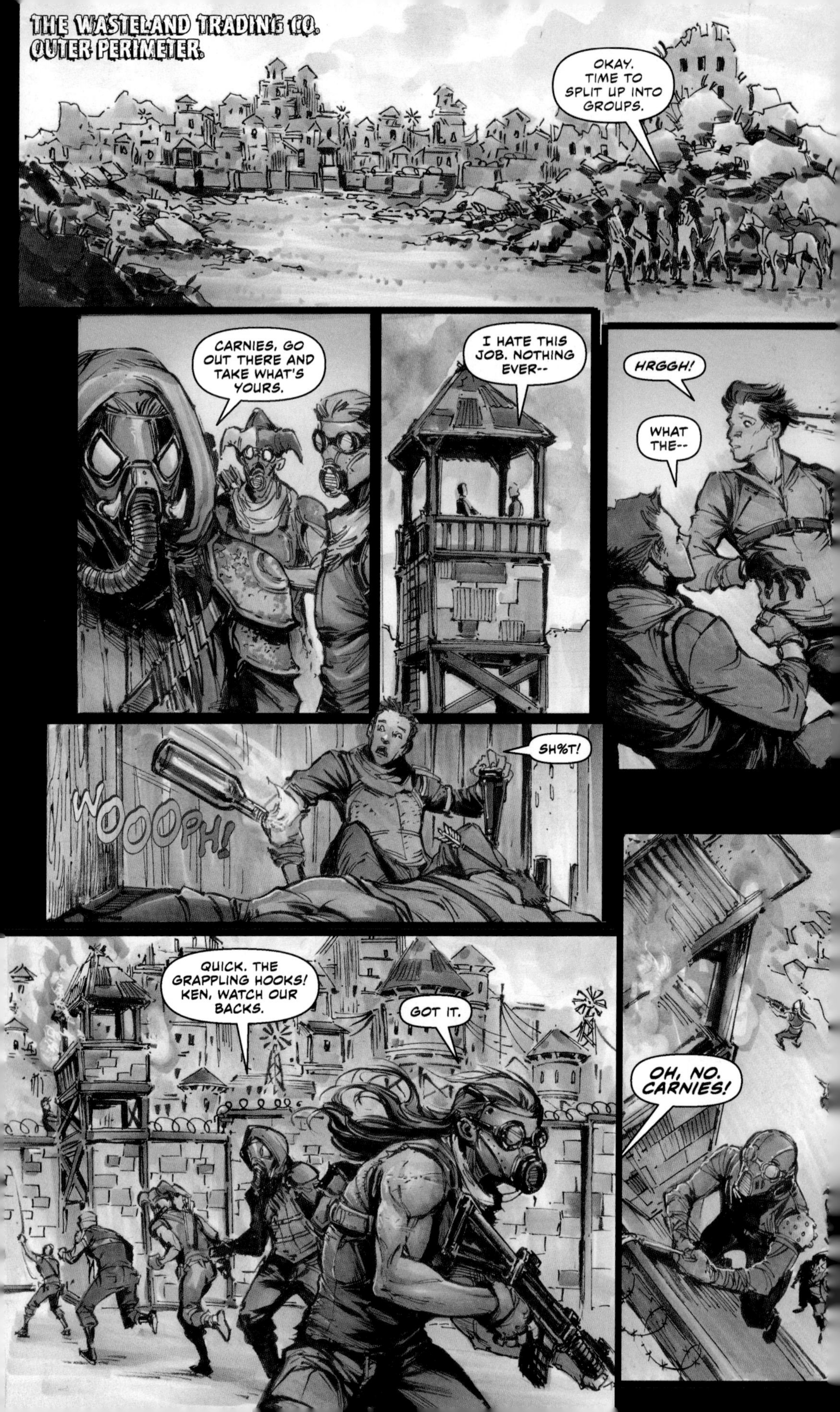
THE WASTELAND TRADING CO. OUTER PERIMETER.
OKAY. TIME TO SPLIT UP INTO GROUPS.
CARNIES, GO OUT THERE AND TAKE WHAT'S YOURS.
I HATE THIS JOB. NOTHING EVER--
HRGGH!
WHAT THE--
WOOOPH!
SH%T!
QUICK. THE GRAPPLING HOOKS! KEN, WATCH OUR BACKS.
GOT IT.
OH, NO. CARNIES!

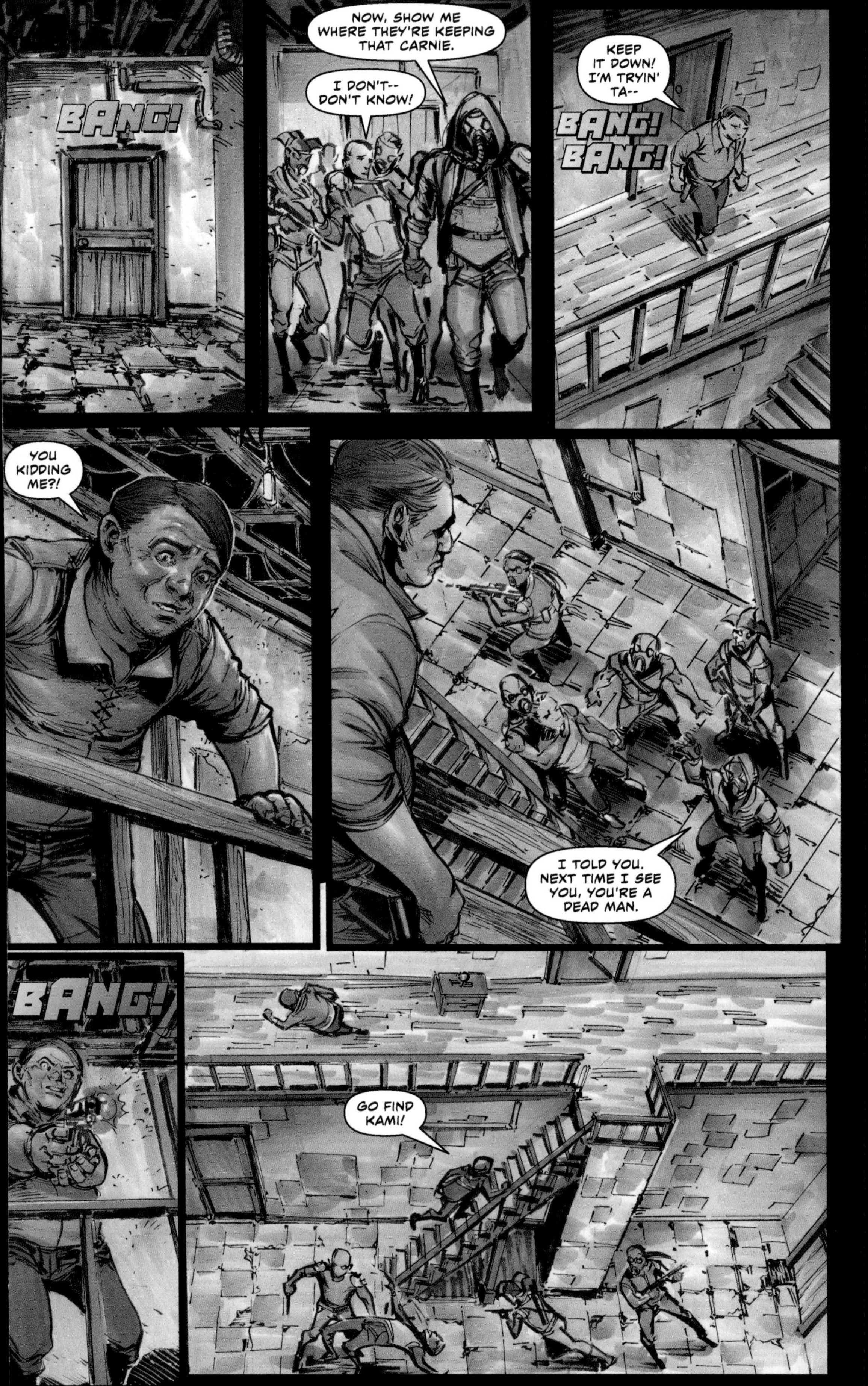
BANG!
NOW, SHOW ME WHERE THEY'RE KEEPING THAT CARNIE.
I DON'T-- DON'T KNOW!
KEEP IT DOWN! I'M TRYIN' TA--
BANG! BANG!
YOU KIDDING ME?!
I TOLD YOU. NEXT TIME I SEE YOU, YOU'RE A DEAD MAN.
BANG!
GO FIND KAMI!

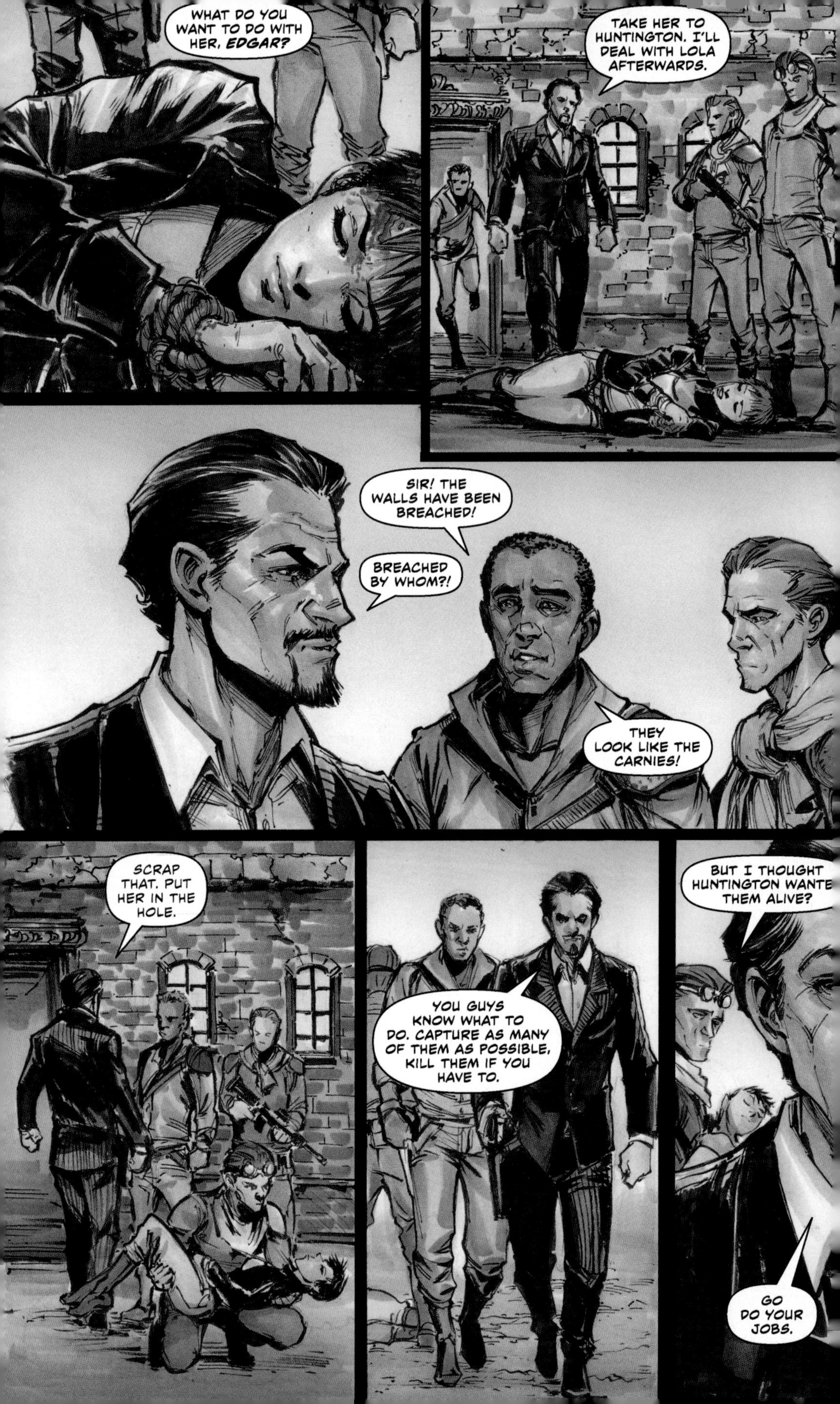
WHAT DO YOU WANT TO DO WITH HER, EDGAR?
TAKE HER TO HUNTINGTON. I'LL DEAL WITH LOLA AFTERWARDS.
SIR! THE WALLS HAVE BEEN BREACHED!
BREACHED BY WHOM?!
THEY LOOK LIKE THE CARNIES!
SCRAP THAT. PUT HER IN THE HOLE.
YOU GUYS KNOW WHAT TO DO. CAPTURE AS MANY OF THEM AS POSSIBLE, KILL THEM IF YOU HAVE TO.
BUT I THOUGHT HUNTINGTON WANTE THEM ALIVE?
GO DO YOUR JOBS.

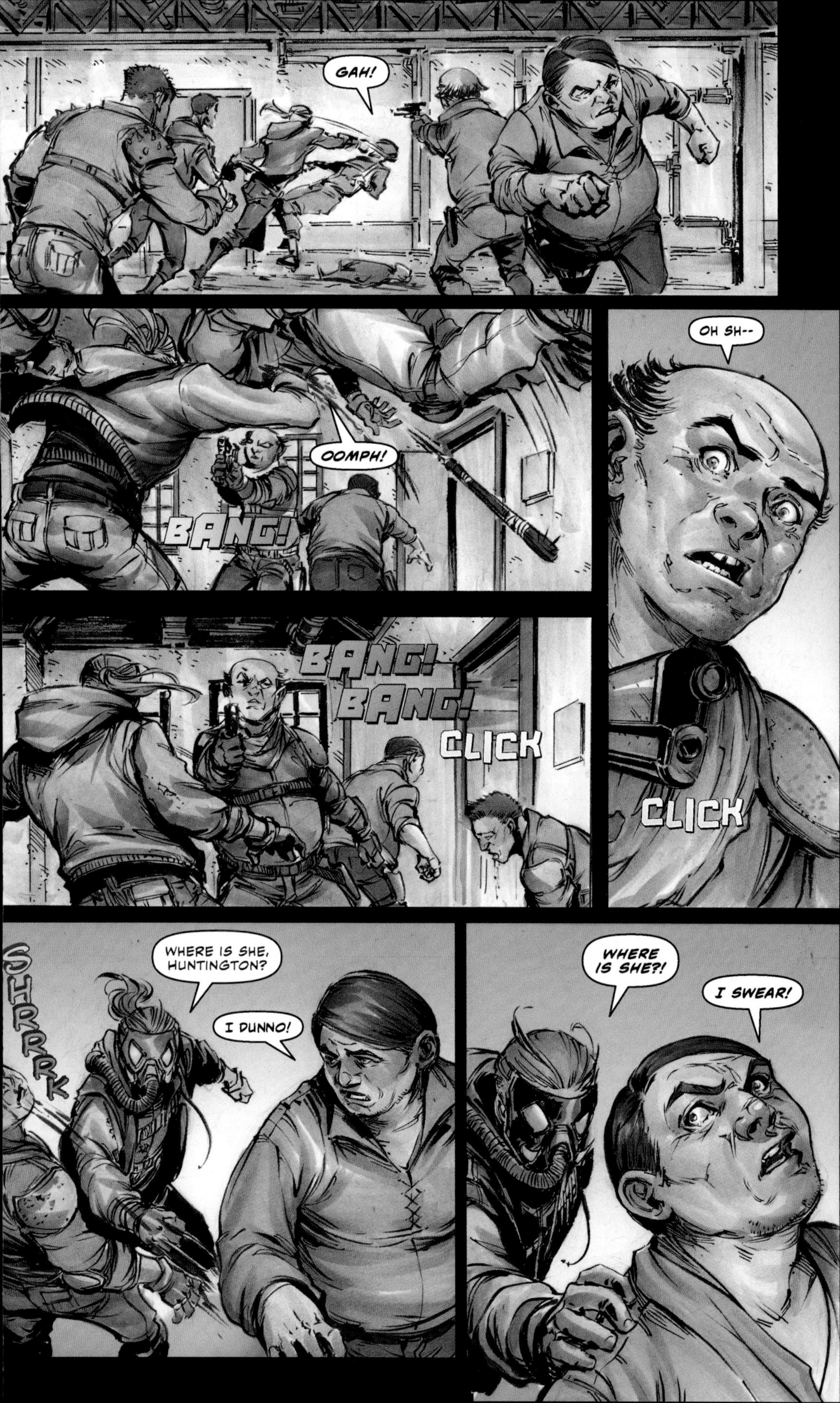
GAH!
OOMPH!
BANG!
OH SH--
BANG!
BANG!
CLICK
CLICK
SHRRRK
WHERE IS SHE, HUNTINGTON?
I DUNNO!
WHERE IS SHE?!
I SWEAR!

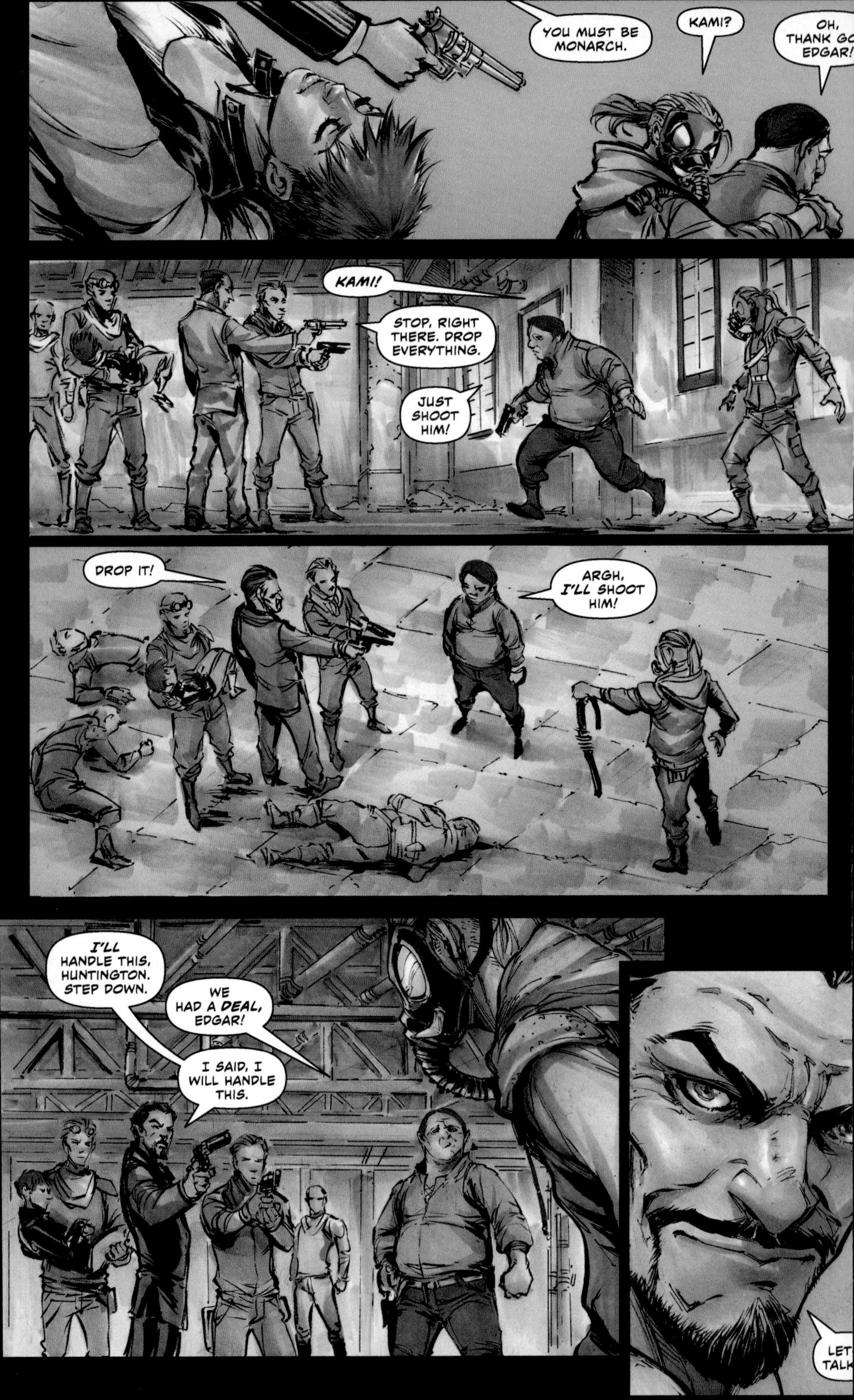
YOU MUST BE MONARCH.
KAMI?
OH, THANK GO EDGAR!
KAMI!
STOP, RIGHT THERE. DROP EVERYTHING.
JUST SHOOT HIM!
DROP IT!
ARGH, I'LL SHOOT HIM!
I'LL HANDLE THIS, HUNTINGTON. STEP DOWN.
WE HAD A DEAL, EDGAR!
I SAID, I WILL HANDLE THIS.
LET TALK

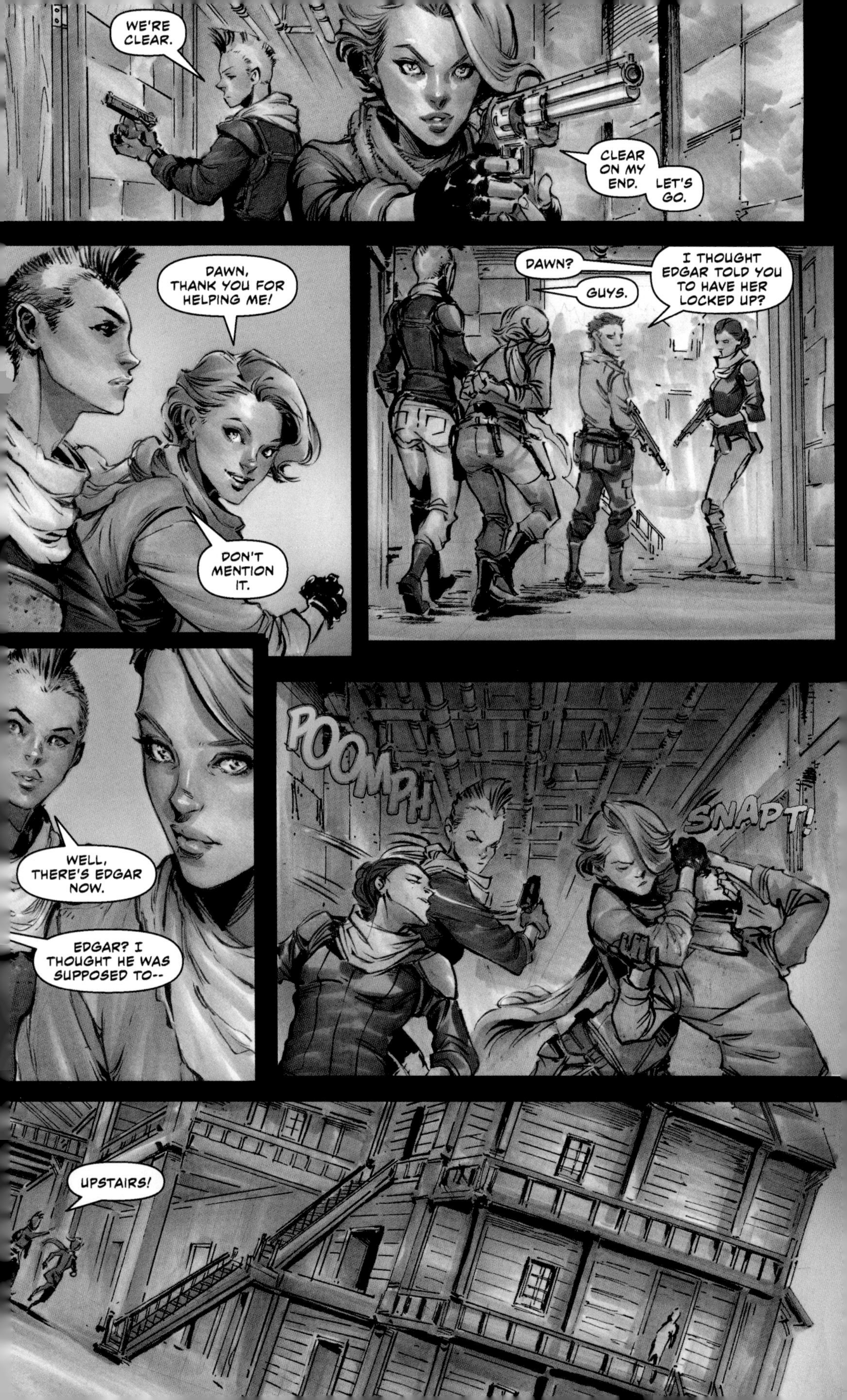
WE'RE CLEAR.
CLEAR ON MY END.
LET'S GO.
DAWN, THANK YOU FOR HELPING ME!
DON'T MENTION IT.
DAWN?
GUYS.
I THOUGHT EDGAR TOLD YOU TO HAVE HER LOCKED UP?
WELL, THERE'S EDGAR NOW.
EDGAR? I THOUGHT HE WAS SUPPOSED TO--
POOMPH
SNAPT!
UPSTAIRS!

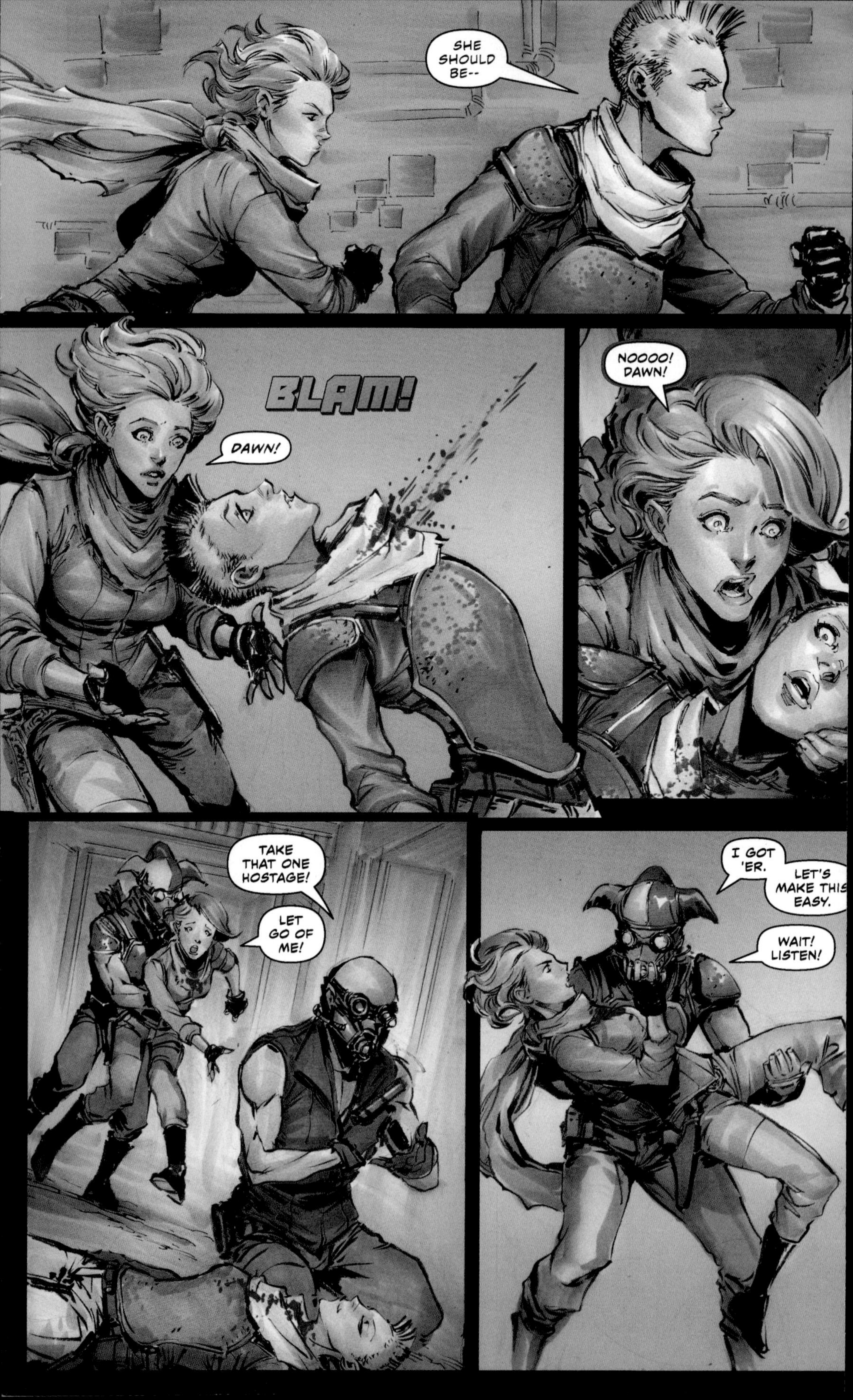
SHE SHOULD BE--
BLAM!
DAWN!
NOOOO! DAWN!
TAKE THAT ONE HOSTAGE!
LET GO OF ME!
I GOT 'ER.
LET'S MAKE THIS EASY.
WAIT! LISTEN!

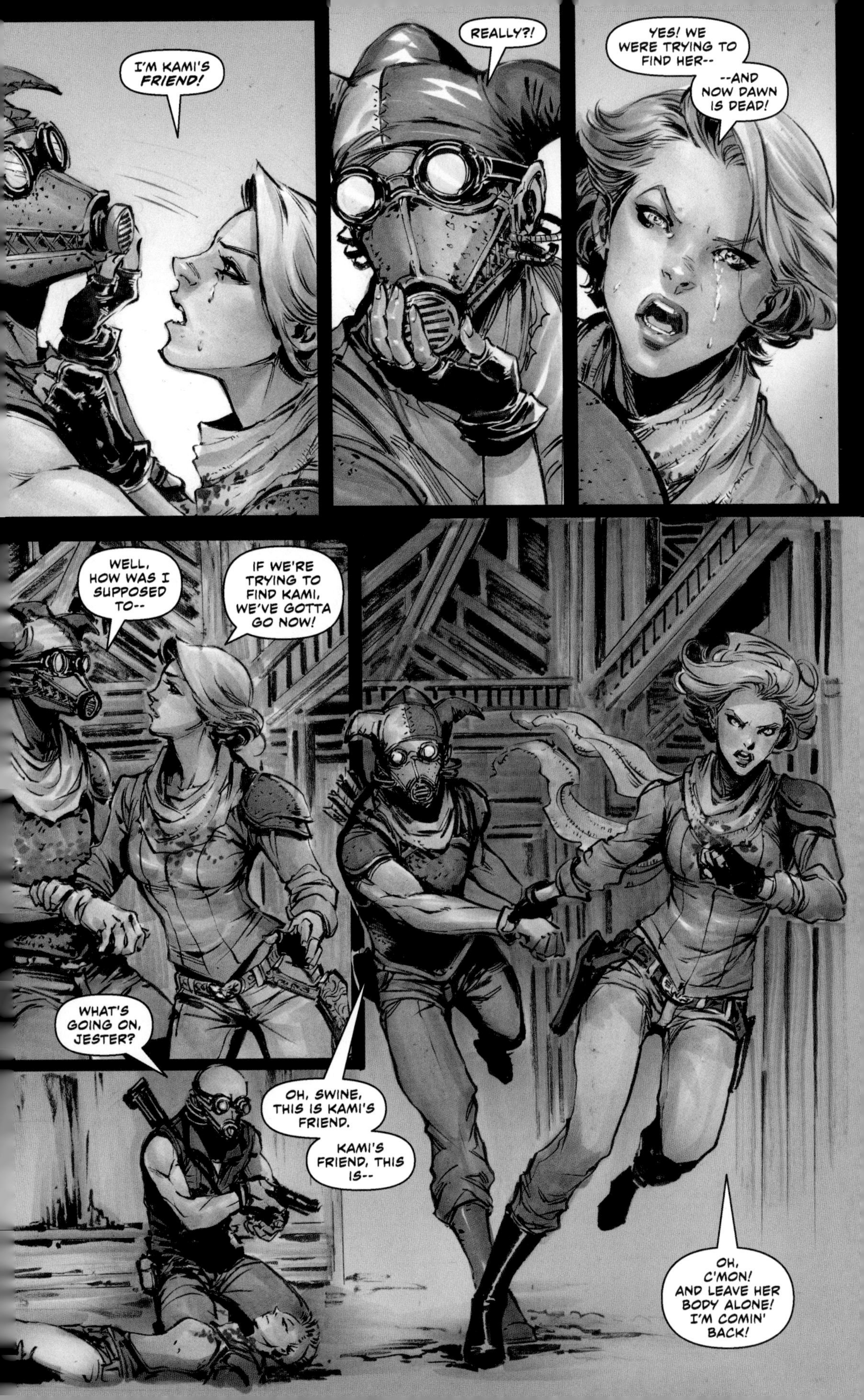
I'M KAMI'S *FRIEND!*
REALLY?!
YES! WE WERE TRYING TO FIND HER--
--AND NOW DAWN IS DEAD!
WELL, HOW WAS I SUPPOSED TO--
IF WE'RE TRYING TO FIND KAMI, WE'VE GOTTA GO NOW!
WHAT'S GOING ON, JESTER?
OH, SWINE, THIS IS KAMI'S FRIEND.
KAMI'S FRIEND, THIS IS--
OH, C'MON! AND LEAVE HER BODY ALONE! I'M COMIN' BACK!

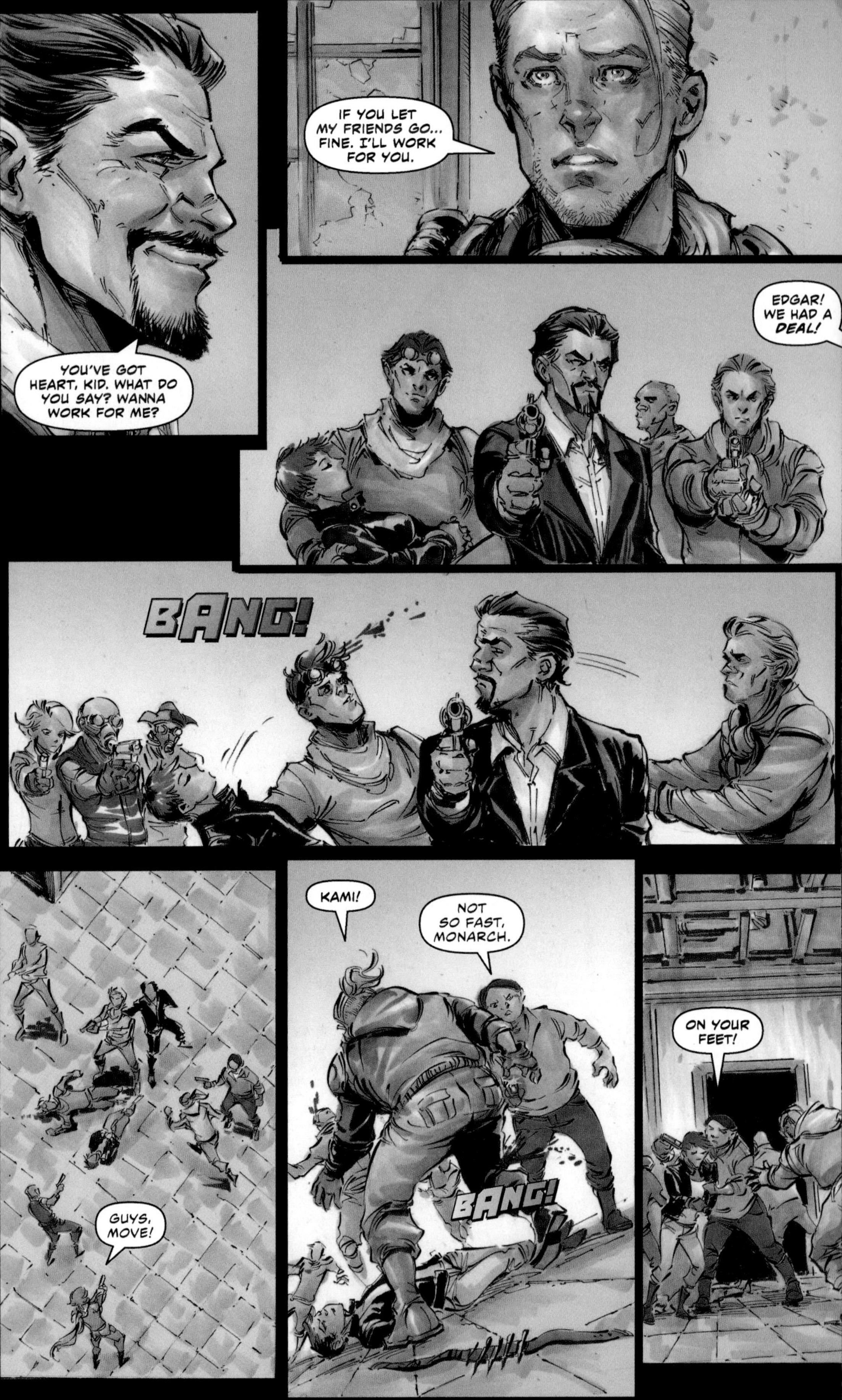
IF YOU LET MY FRIENDS GO... FINE. I'LL WORK FOR YOU.
YOU'VE GOT HEART, KID. WHAT DO YOU SAY? WANNA WORK FOR ME?
EDGAR! WE HAD A DEAL!
BANG!
GUYS, MOVE!
KAMI!
NOT SO FAST, MONARCH.
BANG!
ON YOUR FEET!

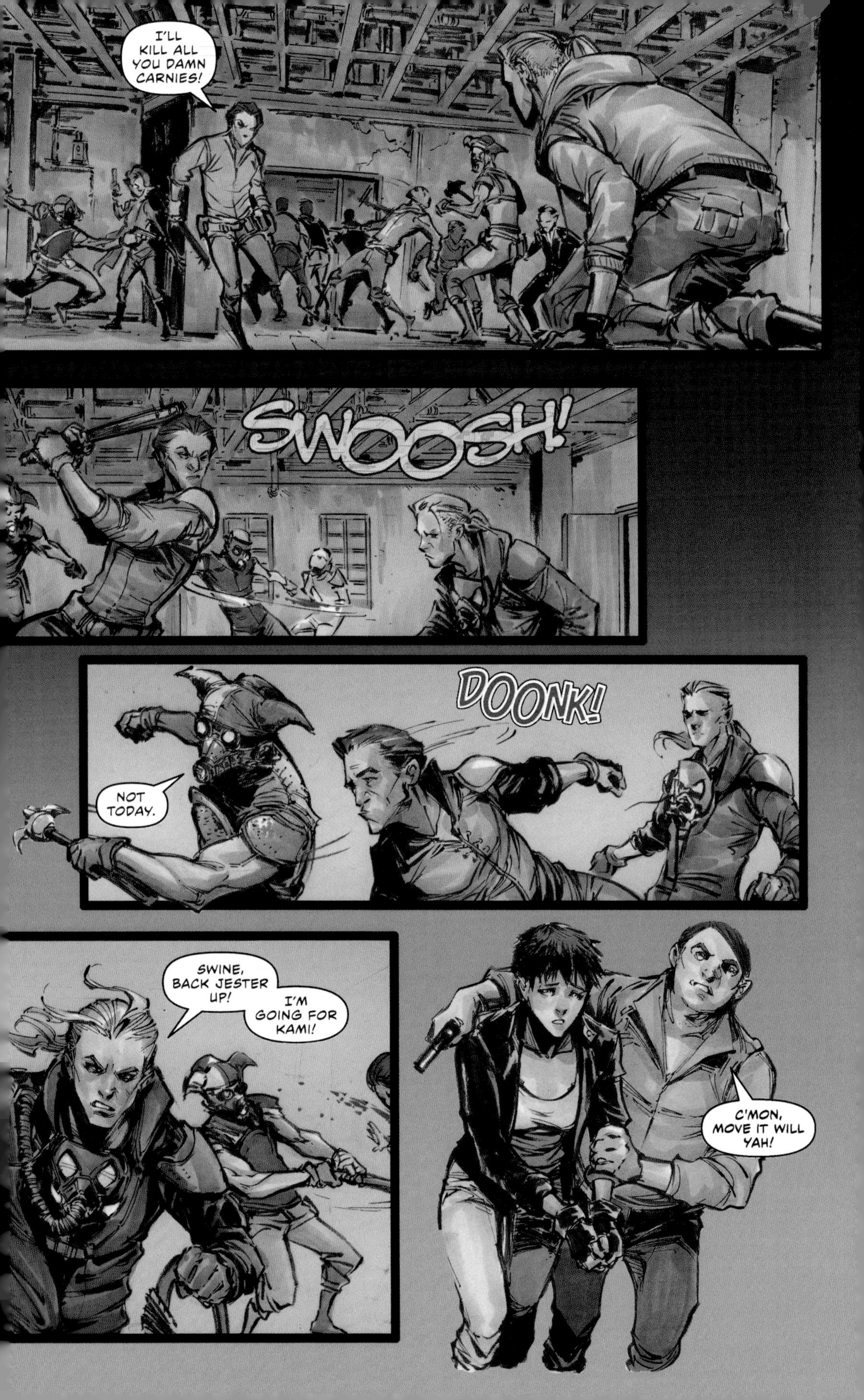
I'LL KILL ALL YOU DAMN CARNIES!
SWOOSH!
DOONK!
NOT TODAY.
SWINE, BACK JESTER UP!
I'M GOING FOR KAMI!
C'MON, MOVE IT WILL YAH!

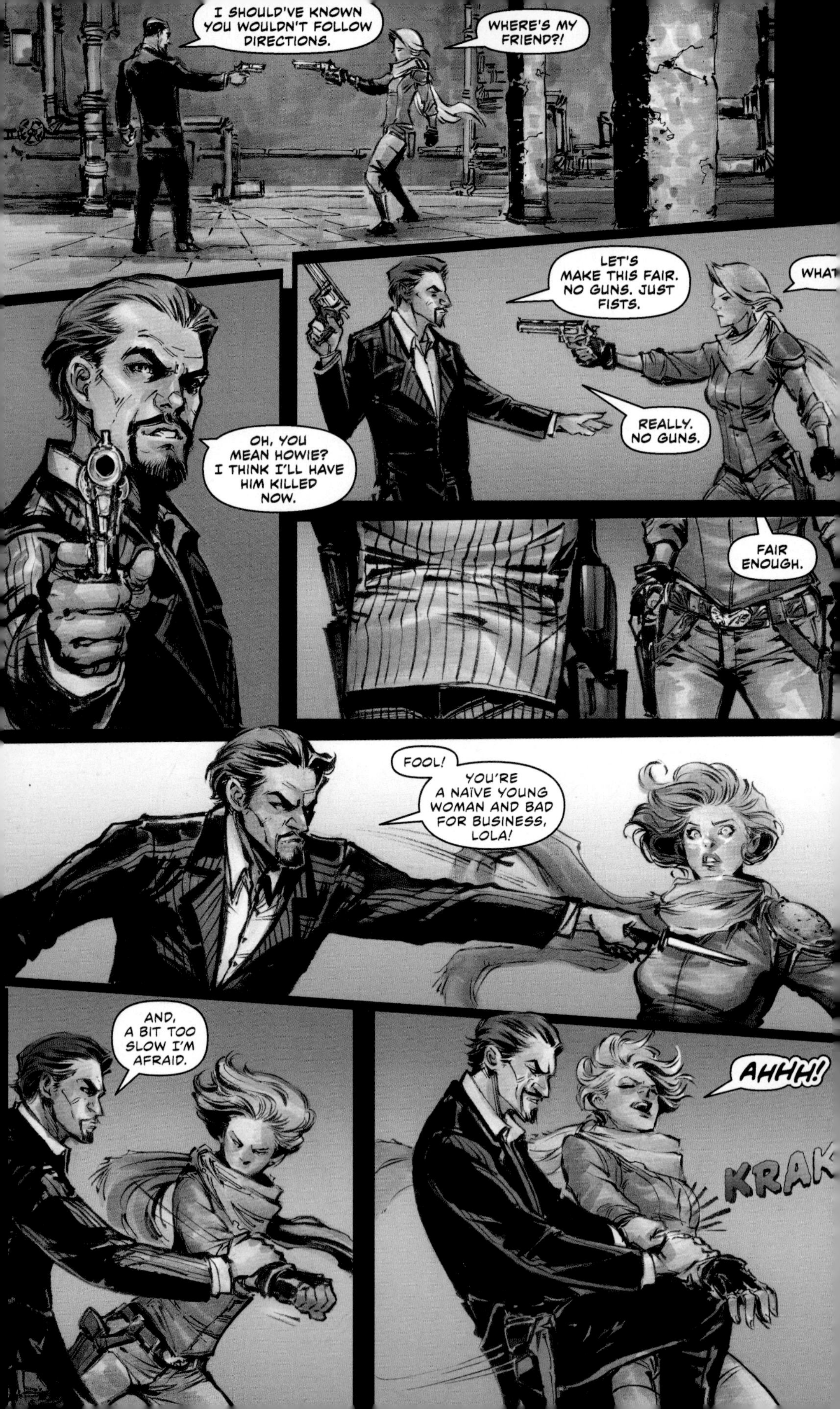
I SHOULD'VE KNOWN YOU WOULDN'T FOLLOW DIRECTIONS.
WHERE'S MY FRIEND?!
OH, YOU MEAN HOWIE? I THINK I'LL HAVE HIM KILLED NOW.
LET'S MAKE THIS FAIR. NO GUNS. JUST FISTS.
WHAT
REALLY. NO GUNS.
FAIR ENOUGH.
FOOL!
YOU'RE A NAÏVE YOUNG WOMAN AND BAD FOR BUSINESS, LOLA!
AND, A BIT TOO SLOW I'M AFRAID.
AHHH!
KRAK

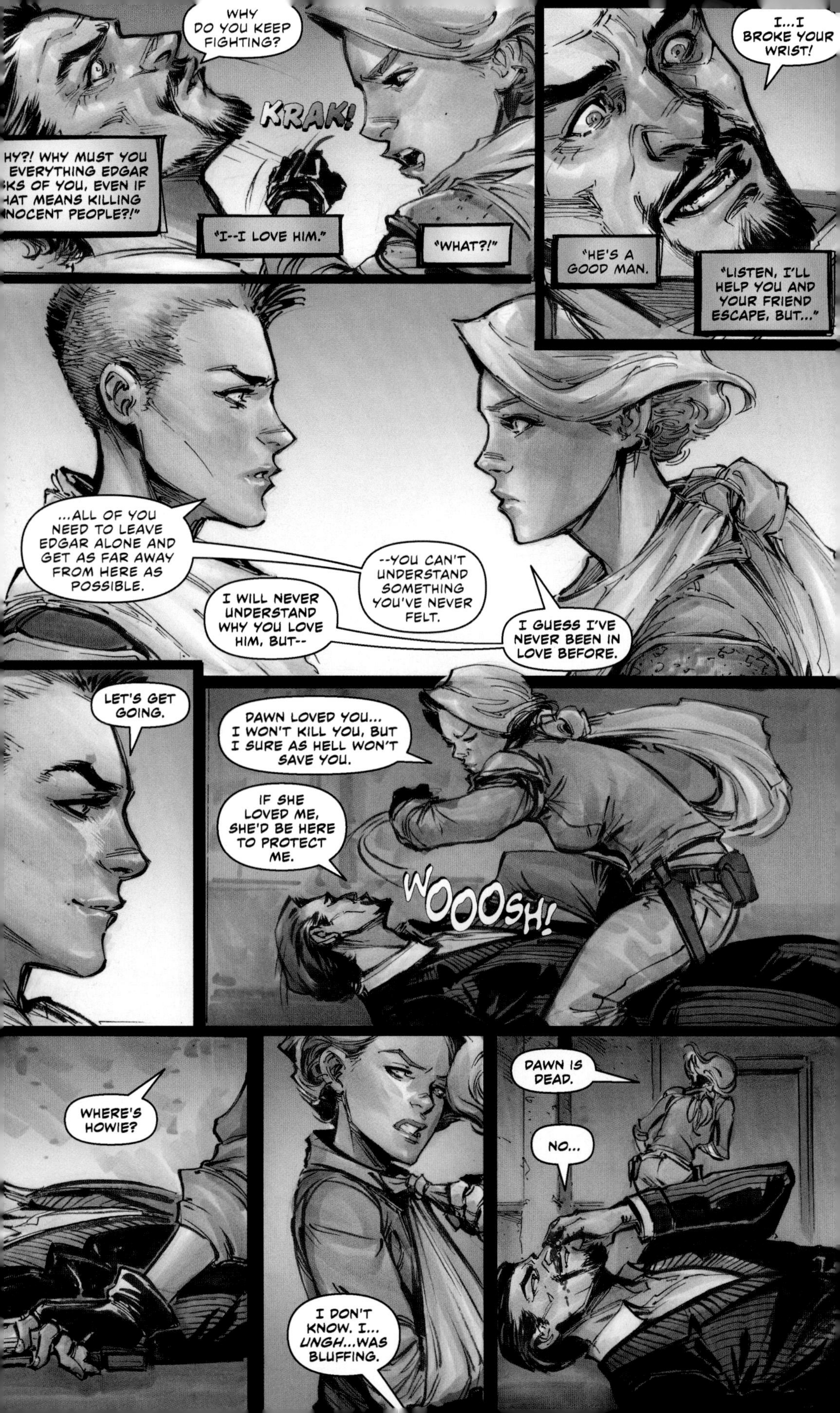
WHY DO YOU KEEP FIGHTING?
KRAK!
HY?! WHY MUST YOU EVERYTHING EDGAR KS OF YOU, EVEN IF HAT MEANS KILLING NOCENT PEOPLE?!"
"I--I LOVE HIM."
"WHAT?!"
I...I BROKE YOUR WRIST!
"HE'S A GOOD MAN.
"LISTEN, I'LL HELP YOU AND YOUR FRIEND ESCAPE, BUT..."
...ALL OF YOU NEED TO LEAVE EDGAR ALONE AND GET AS FAR AWAY FROM HERE AS POSSIBLE.
I WILL NEVER UNDERSTAND WHY YOU LOVE HIM, BUT--
--YOU CAN'T UNDERSTAND SOMETHING YOU'VE NEVER FELT.
I GUESS I'VE NEVER BEEN IN LOVE BEFORE.
LET'S GET GOING.
DAWN LOVED YOU... I WON'T KILL YOU, BUT I SURE AS HELL WON'T SAVE YOU.
IF SHE LOVED ME, SHE'D BE HERE TO PROTECT ME.
WOOOSH!
WHERE'S HOWIE?
I DON'T KNOW. I... UNGH...WAS BLUFFING.
DAWN IS DEAD.
NO...

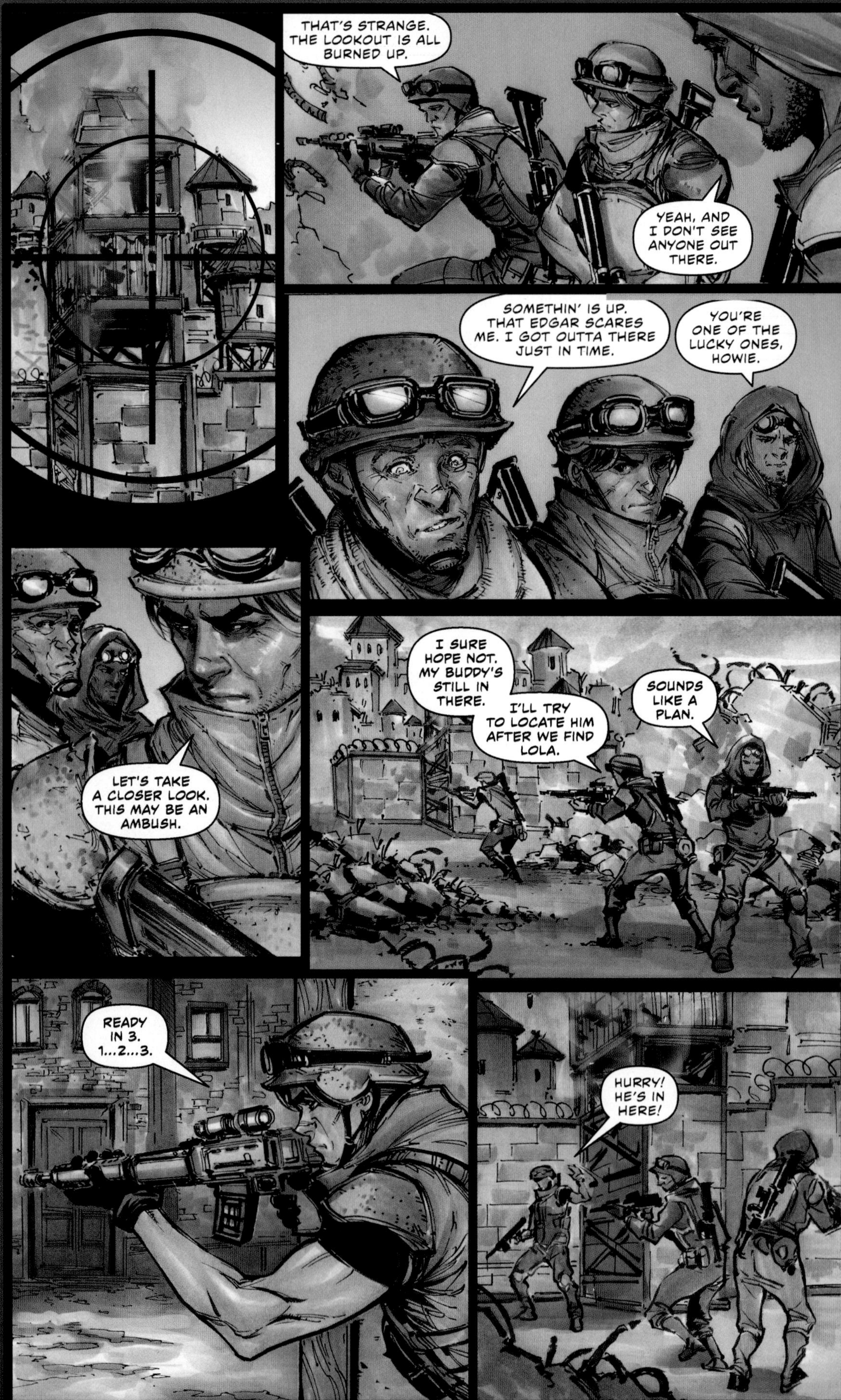
THAT'S STRANGE. THE LOOKOUT IS ALL BURNED UP.
YEAH, AND I DON'T SEE ANYONE OUT THERE.
SOMETHIN' IS UP. THAT EDGAR SCARES ME. I GOT OUTTA THERE JUST IN TIME.
YOU'RE ONE OF THE LUCKY ONES, HOWIE.
LET'S TAKE A CLOSER LOOK. THIS MAY BE AN AMBUSH.
I SURE HOPE NOT. MY BUDDY'S STILL IN THERE.
I'LL TRY TO LOCATE HIM AFTER WE FIND LOLA.
SOUNDS LIKE A PLAN.
READY IN 3. 1...2...3.
HURRY! HE'S IN HERE!

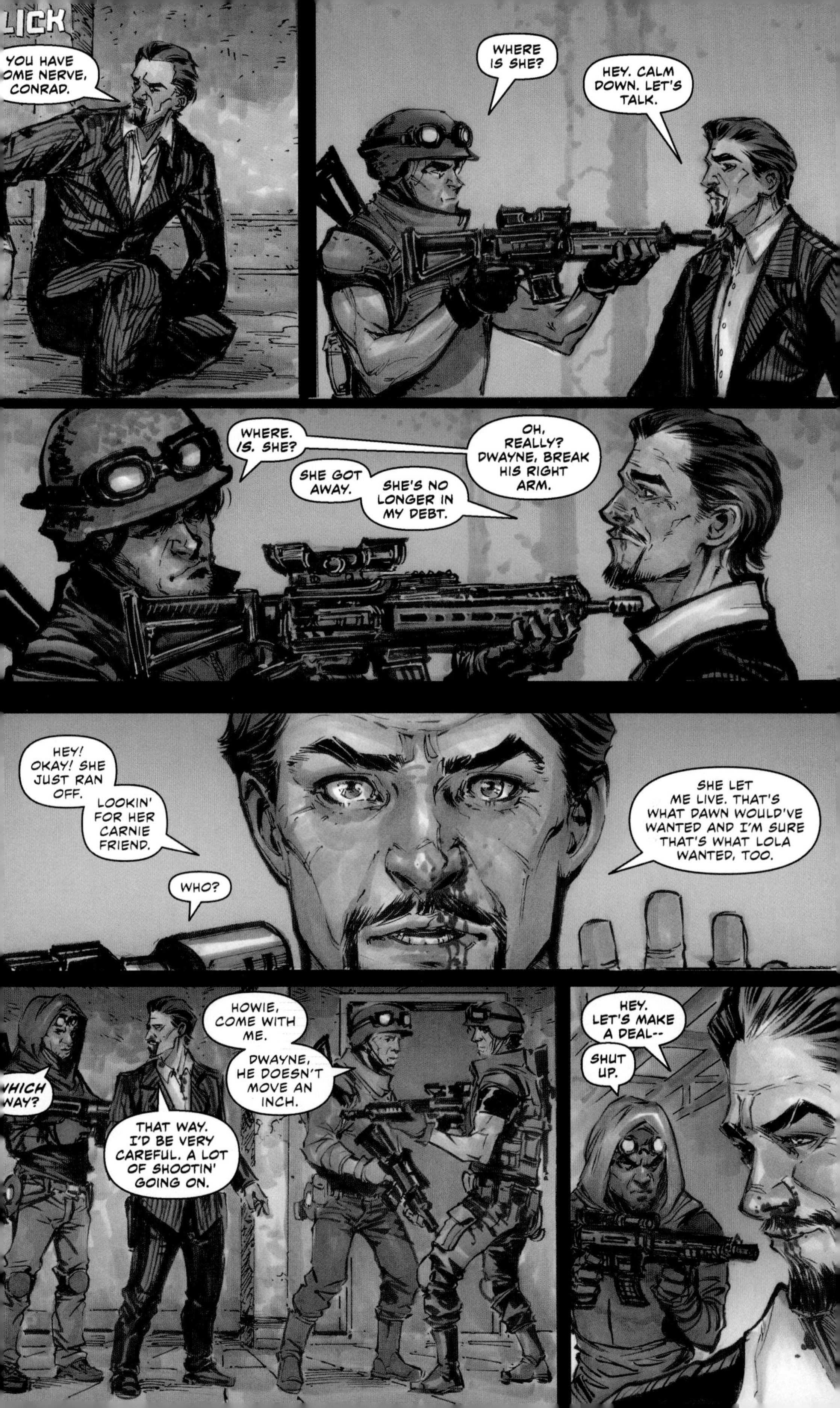
LICK
YOU HAVE
OME NERVE,
CONRAD.
WHERE IS SHE?
HEY. CALM DOWN. LET'S TALK.
WHERE. *IS.* SHE?
SHE GOT AWAY.
SHE'S NO LONGER IN MY DEBT.
OH, REALLY? DWAYNE, BREAK HIS RIGHT ARM.
HEY! OKAY! SHE JUST RAN OFF.
LOOKIN' FOR HER CARNIE FRIEND.
WHO?
SHE LET ME LIVE. THAT'S WHAT DAWN WOULD'VE WANTED AND I'M SURE THAT'S WHAT LOLA WANTED, TOO.
HICH
AY?
THAT WAY. I'D BE VERY CAREFUL. A LOT OF SHOOTIN' GOING ON.
HOWIE, COME WITH ME.
DWAYNE, HE DOESN'T MOVE AN INCH.
HEY. LET'S MAKE A DEAL--
SHUT UP.

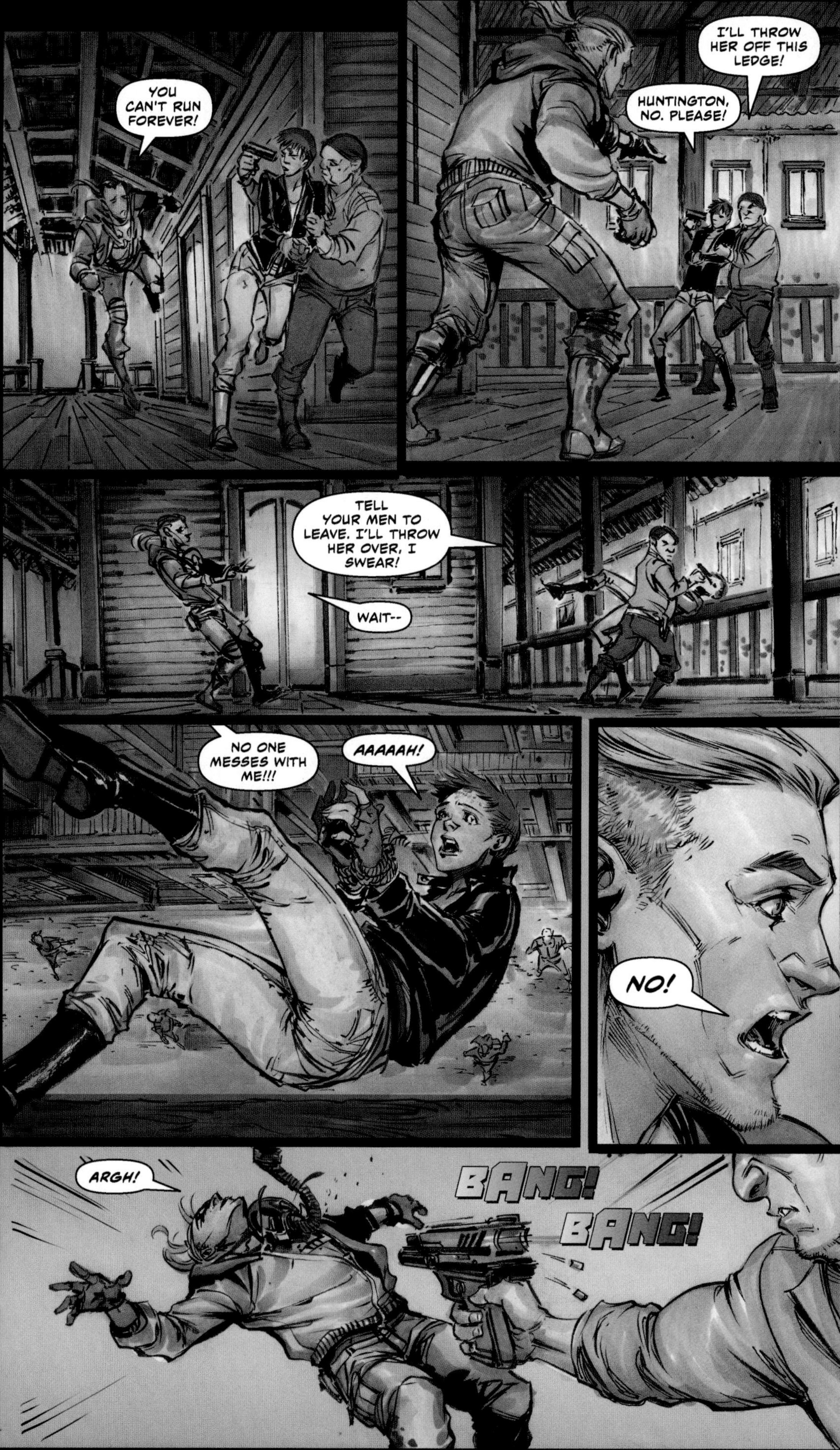
YOU CAN'T RUN FOREVER!
I'LL THROW HER OFF THIS LEDGE!
HUNTINGTON, NO. PLEASE!
TELL YOUR MEN TO LEAVE. I'LL THROW HER OVER, I SWEAR!
WAIT--
NO ONE MESSES WITH ME!!!
AAAAAH!
NO!
ARGH!
BANG!
BANG!

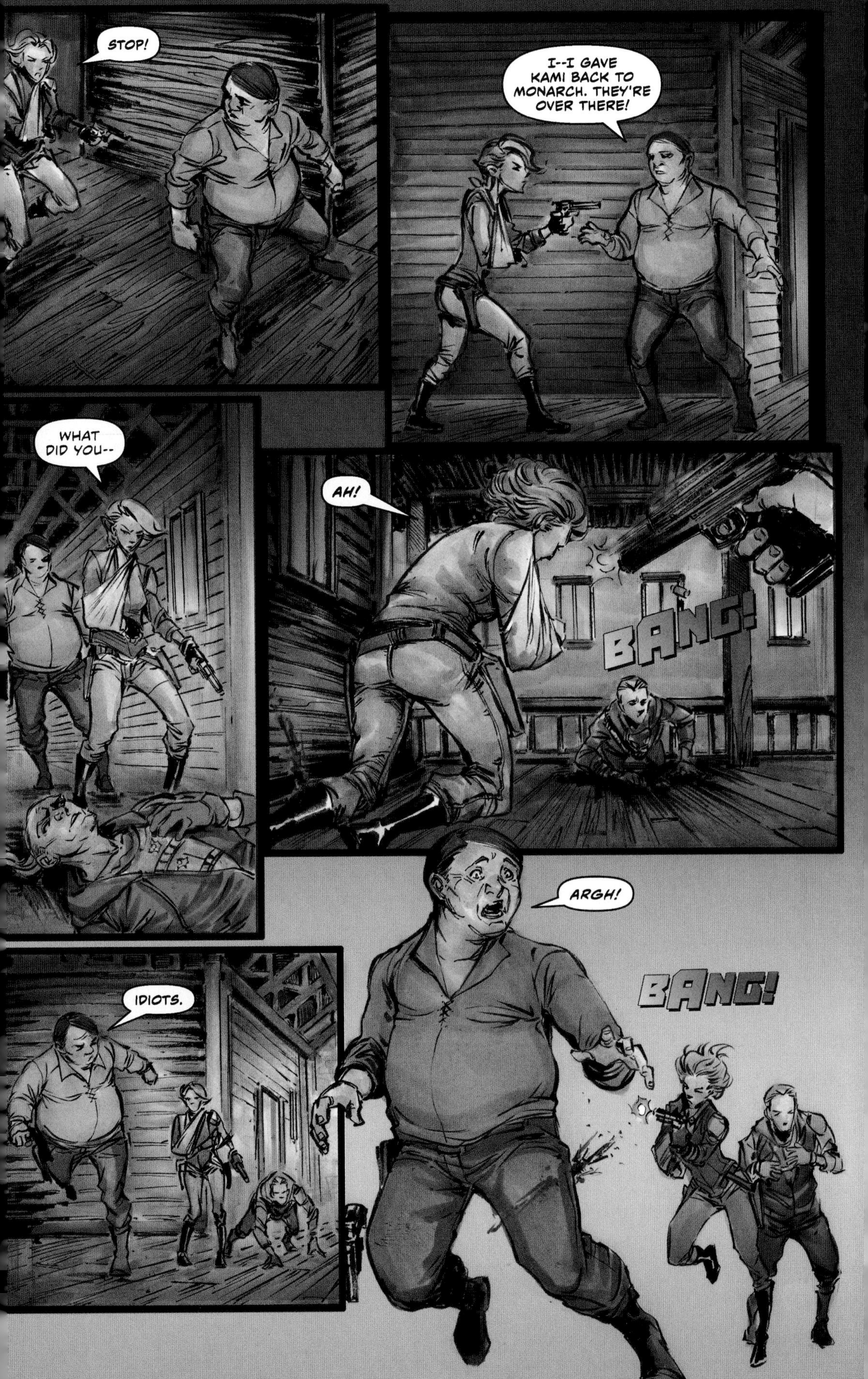
STOP!
I--I GAVE KAMI BACK TO MONARCH. THEY'RE OVER THERE!
WHAT DID YOU--
AH!
BANG!
ARGH!
IDIOTS.
BANG!

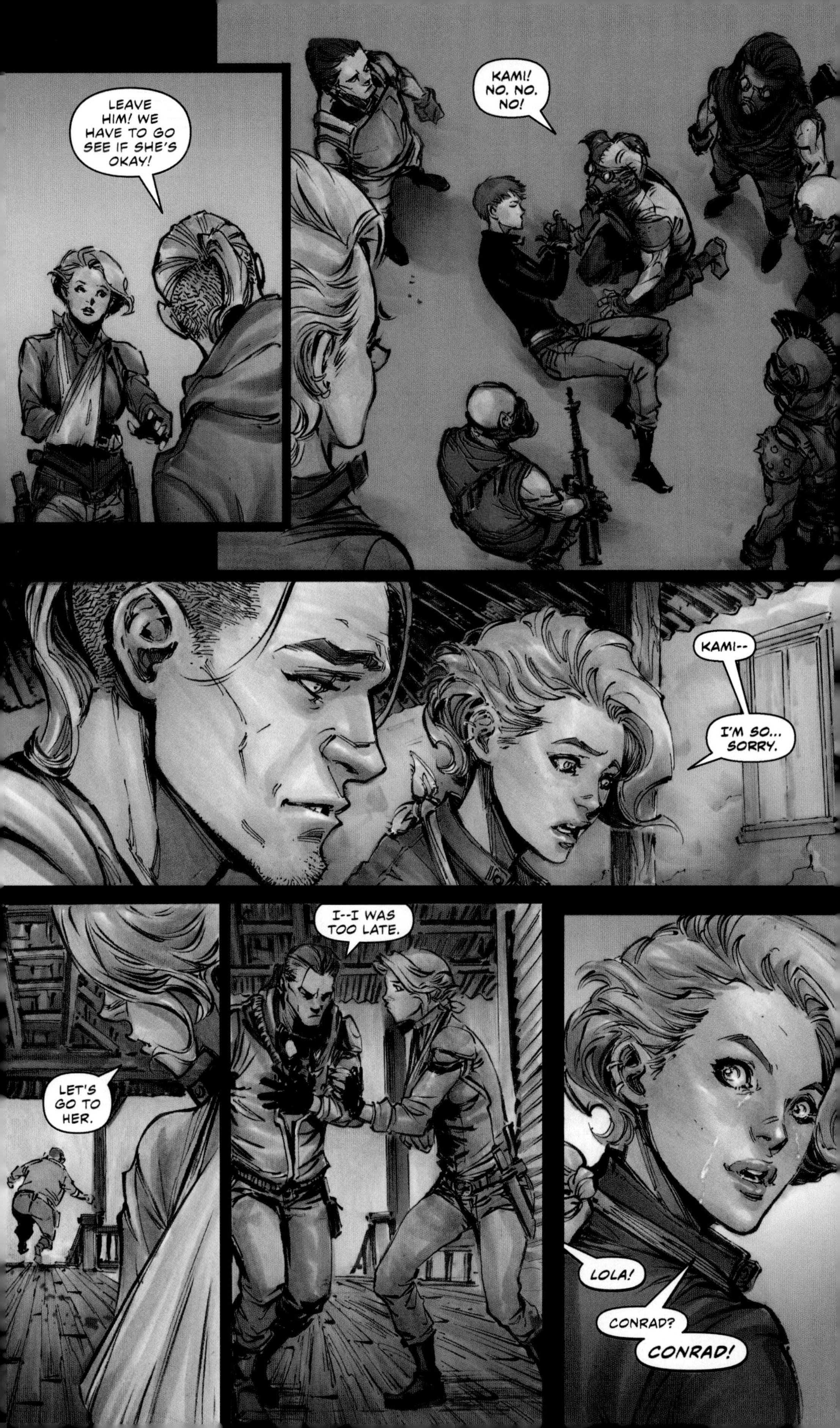
LEAVE HIM! WE HAVE TO GO SEE IF SHE'S OKAY!
KAMI! NO. NO. NO!
KAMI--
I'M SO... SORRY.
LET'S GO TO HER.
I--I WAS TOO LATE.
LOLA!
CONRAD?
CONRAD!

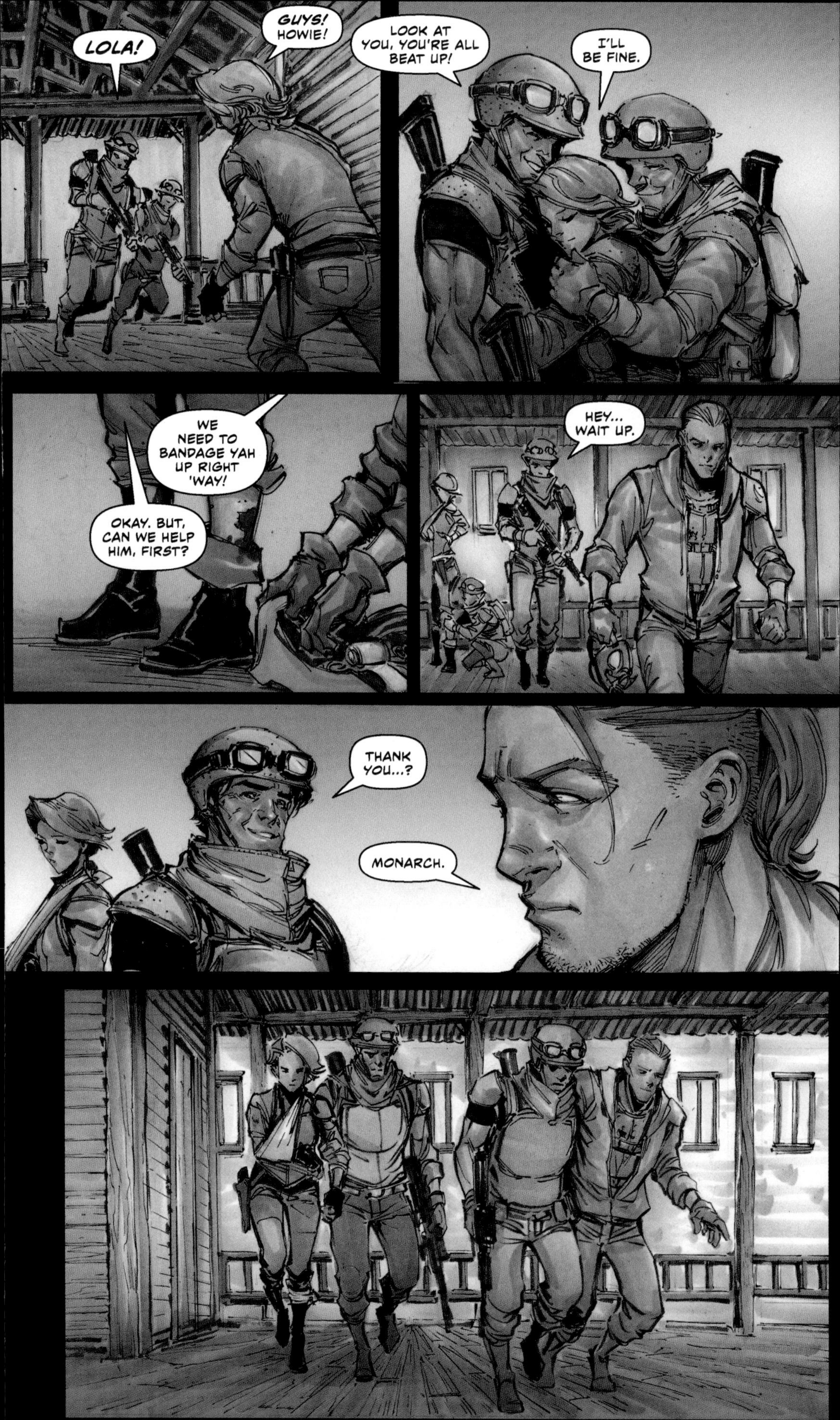
LOLA!
GUYS! HOWIE!
LOOK AT YOU, YOU'RE ALL BEAT UP!
I'LL BE FINE.
WE NEED TO BANDAGE YAH UP RIGHT 'WAY!
OKAY. BUT, CAN WE HELP HIM, FIRST?
HEY... WAIT UP.
THANK YOU...?
MONARCH.

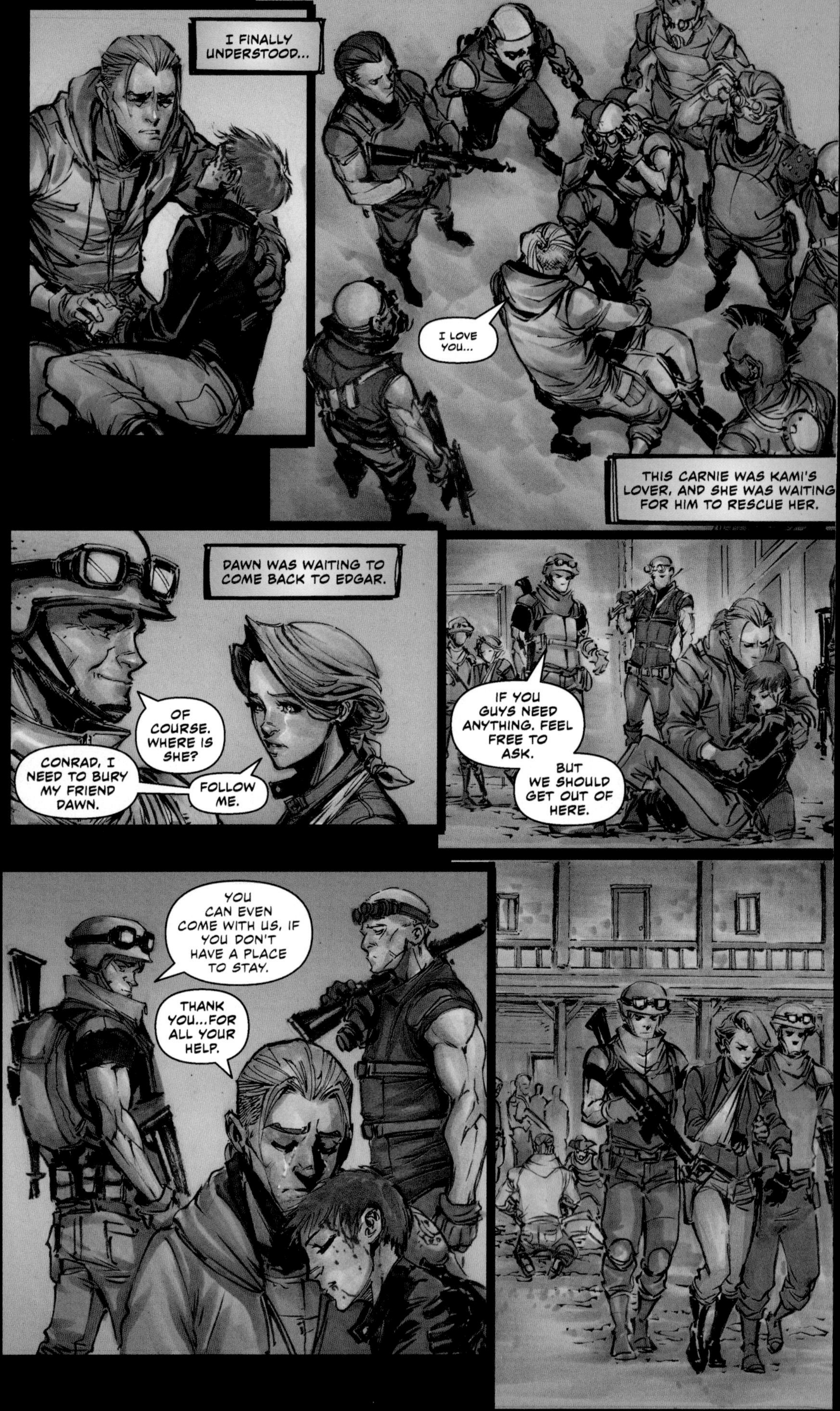
I FINALLY UNDERSTOOD...
I LOVE YOU...
THIS CARNIE WAS KAMI'S LOVER, AND SHE WAS WAITING FOR HIM TO RESCUE HER.
DAWN WAS WAITING TO COME BACK TO EDGAR.
CONRAD, I NEED TO BURY MY FRIEND DAWN.
OF COURSE. WHERE IS SHE?
FOLLOW ME.
IF YOU GUYS NEED ANYTHING, FEEL FREE TO ASK.
BUT WE SHOULD GET OUT OF HERE.
YOU CAN EVEN COME WITH US, IF YOU DON'T HAVE A PLACE TO STAY.
THANK YOU...FOR ALL YOUR HELP.

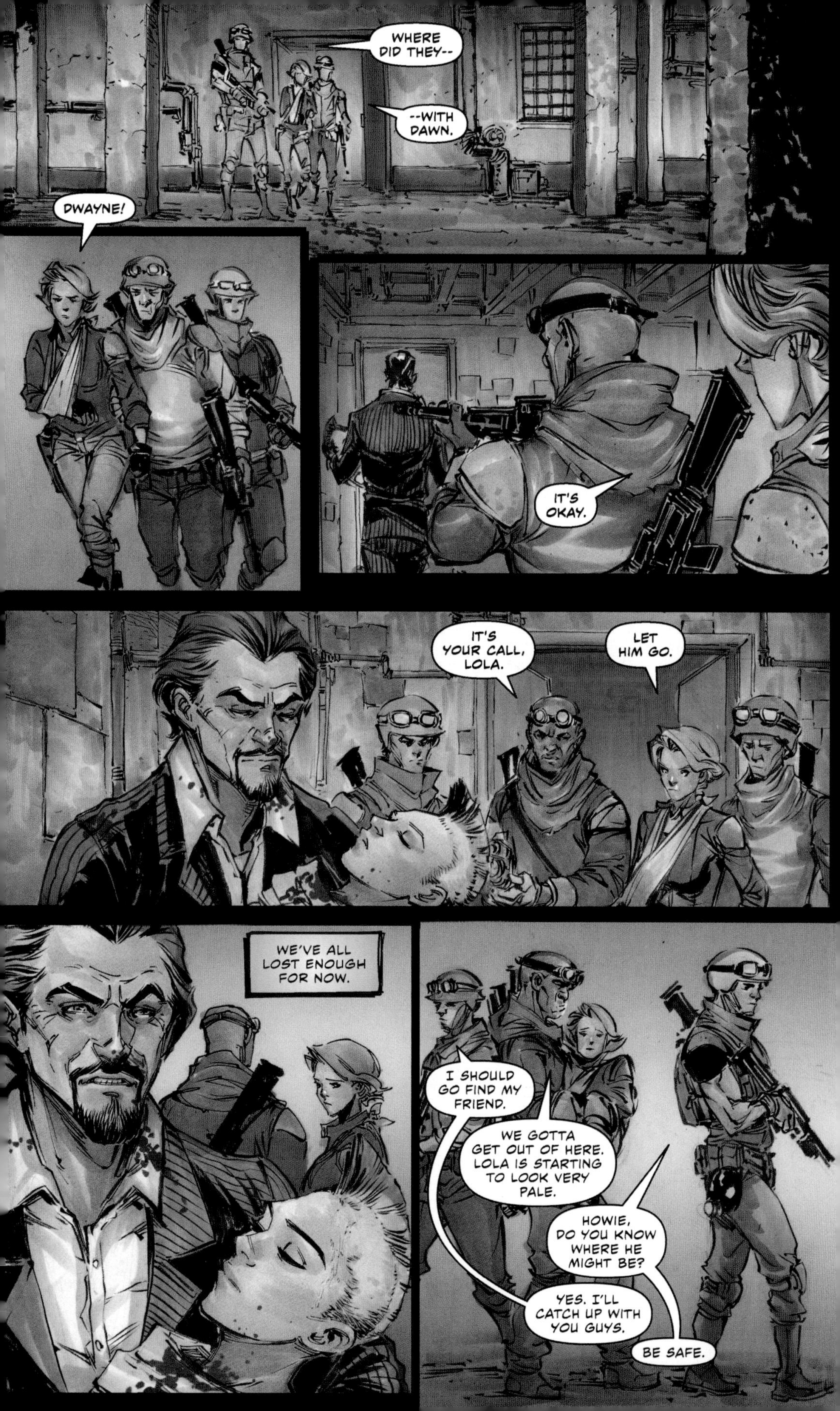
WHERE DID THEY--
--WITH DAWN.
DWAYNE!
IT'S OKAY.
IT'S YOUR CALL, LOLA.
LET HIM GO.
WE'VE ALL LOST ENOUGH FOR NOW.
I SHOULD GO FIND MY FRIEND.
WE GOTTA GET OUT OF HERE. LOLA IS STARTING TO LOOK VERY PALE.
HOWIE, DO YOU KNOW WHERE HE MIGHT BE?
YES. I'LL CATCH UP WITH YOU GUYS.
BE SAFE.

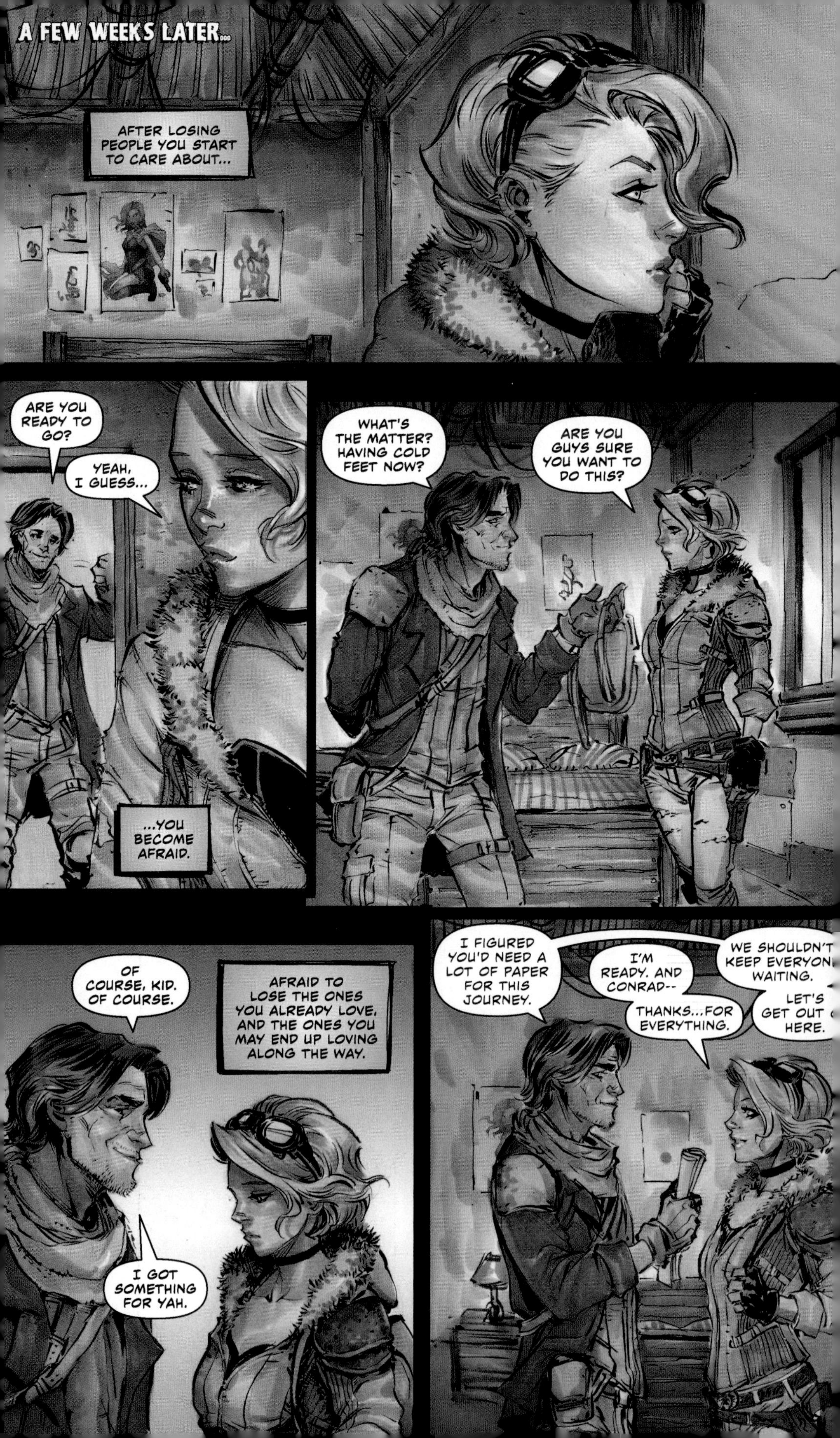

A FEW WEEKS LATER...
AFTER LOSING PEOPLE YOU START TO CARE ABOUT...
ARE YOU READY TO GO?
YEAH, I GUESS...
...YOU BECOME AFRAID.
WHAT'S THE MATTER? HAVING COLD FEET NOW?
ARE YOU GUYS SURE YOU WANT TO DO THIS?
OF COURSE, KID. OF COURSE.
AFRAID TO LOSE THE ONES YOU ALREADY LOVE, AND THE ONES YOU MAY END UP LOVING ALONG THE WAY.
I GOT SOMETHING FOR YAH.
I FIGURED YOU'D NEED A LOT OF PAPER FOR THIS JOURNEY.
I'M READY. AND CONRAD--
THANKS...FOR EVERYTHING.
WE SHOULDN'T KEEP EVERYON WAITING.
LET'S GET OUT HERE.

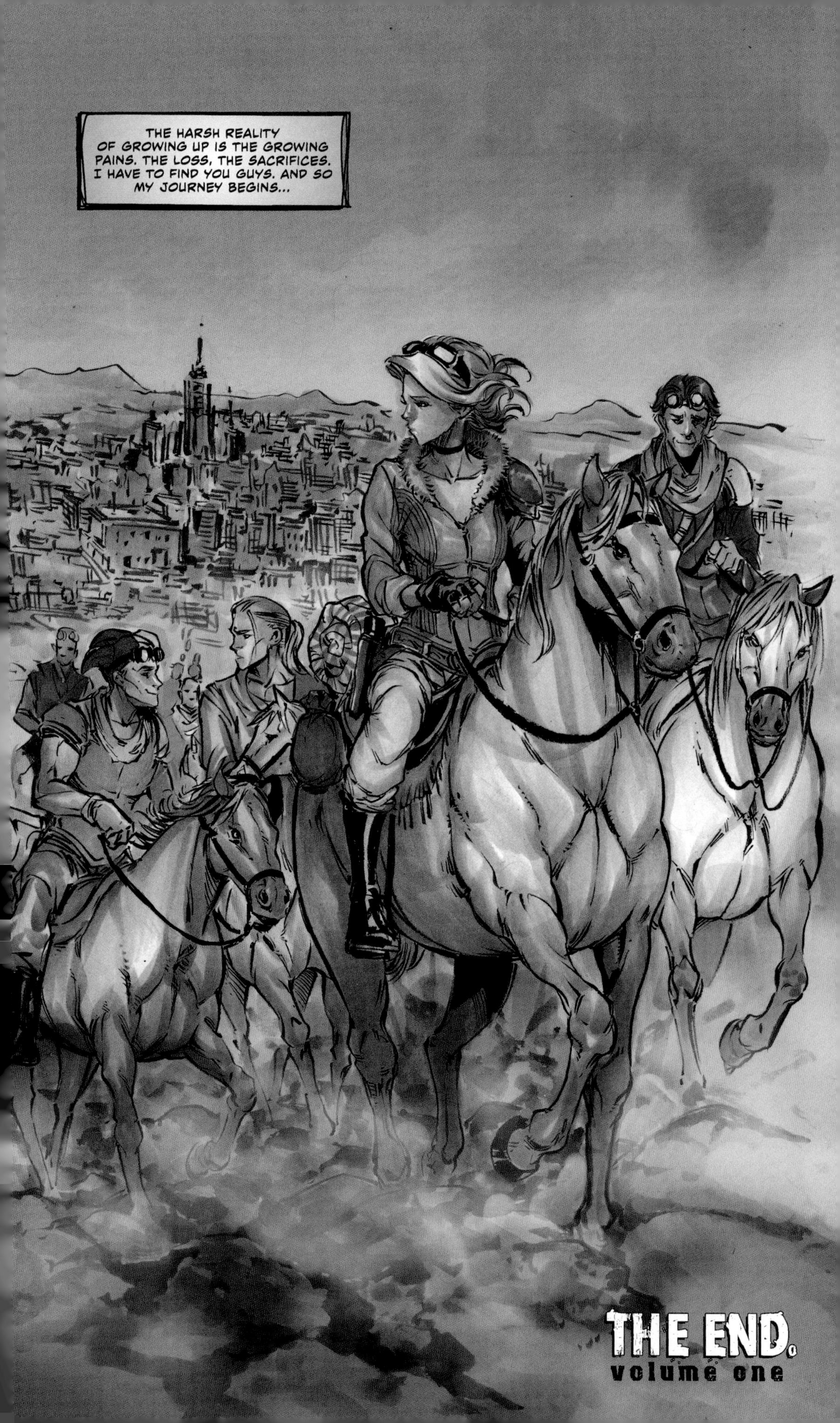
THE HARSH REALITY OF GROWING UP IS THE GROWING PAINS. THE LOSS, THE SACRIFICES. I HAVE TO FIND YOU GUYS. AND SO MY JOURNEY BEGINS...
THE END.
volume one

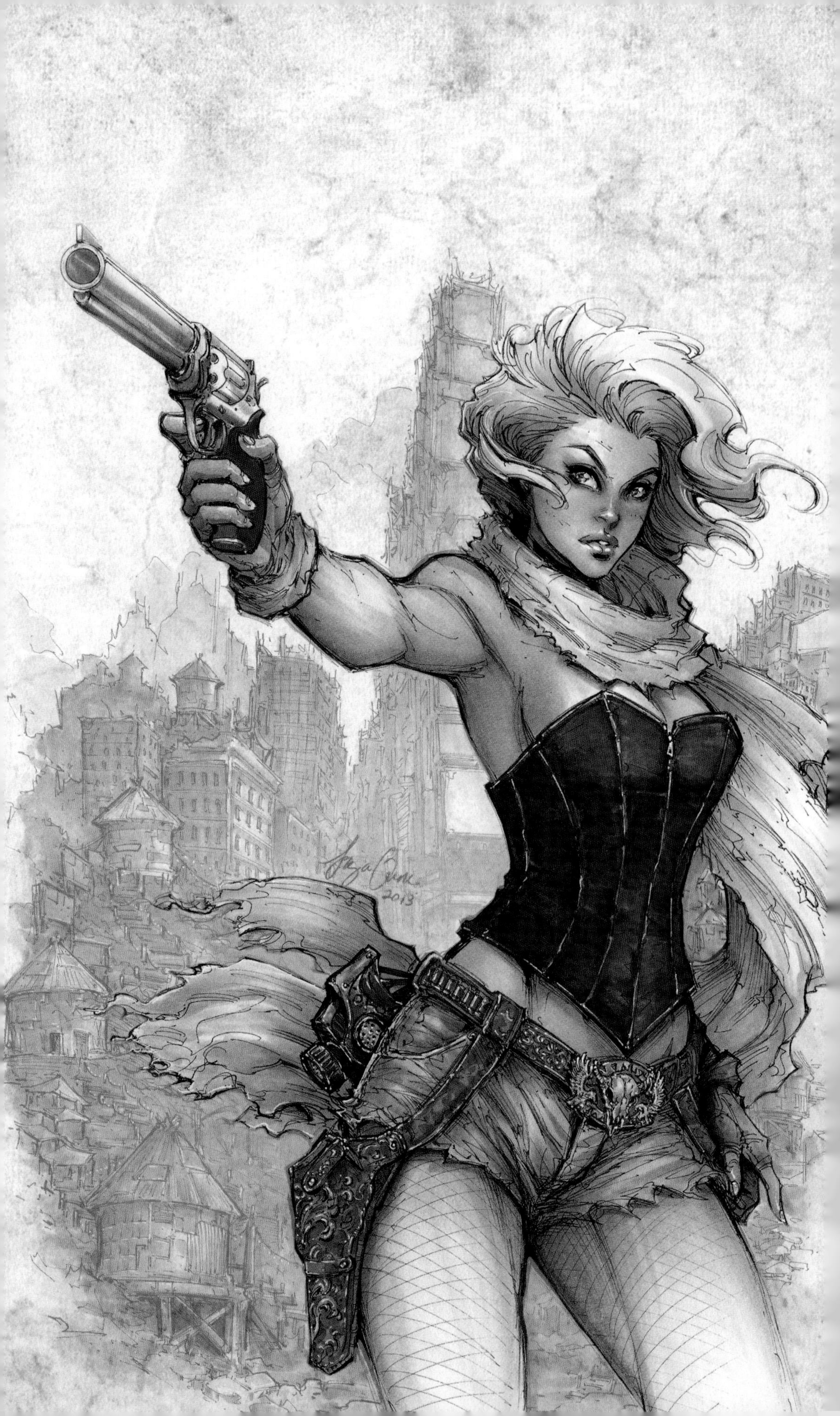

siya oum's

LOLA XoXo

™

COVER GALLERY

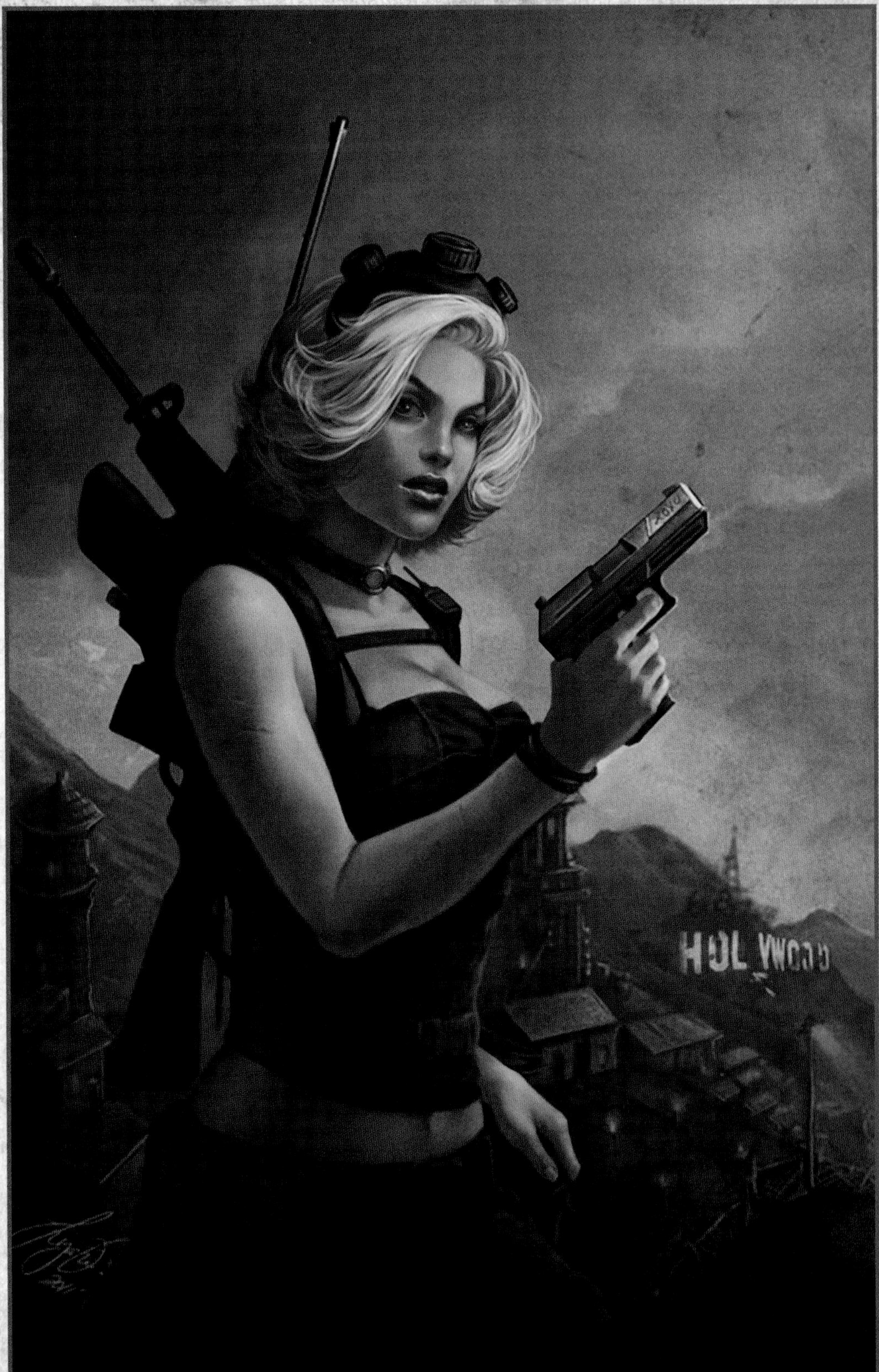
HOL YWOOD

Direct Edition Cover
LOLA XOXO NO. 1
BY
Siya Oum

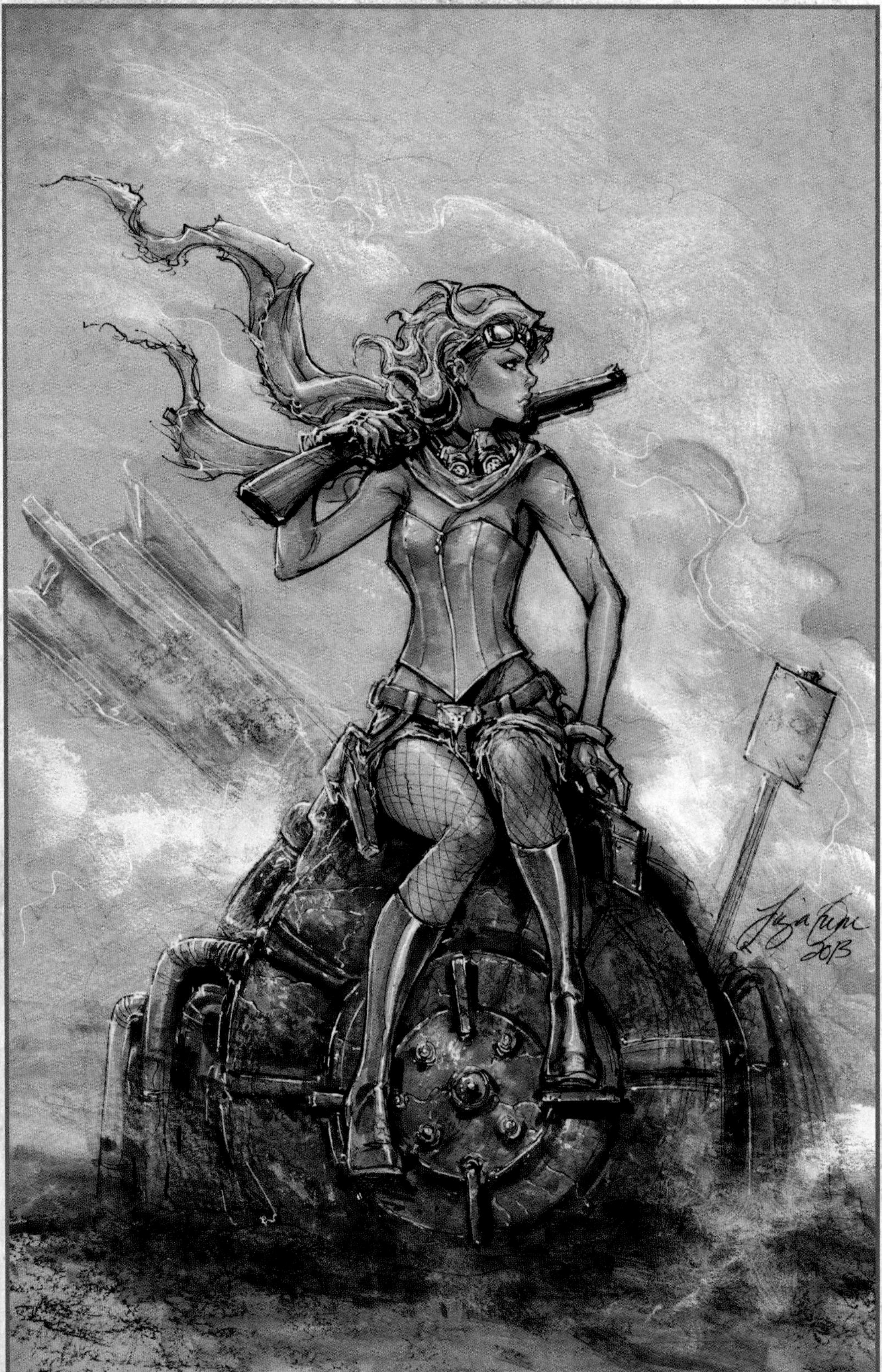

Retailer Incentive Edition Cover
LOLA XOXO NO. 1
BY
Siya Oum

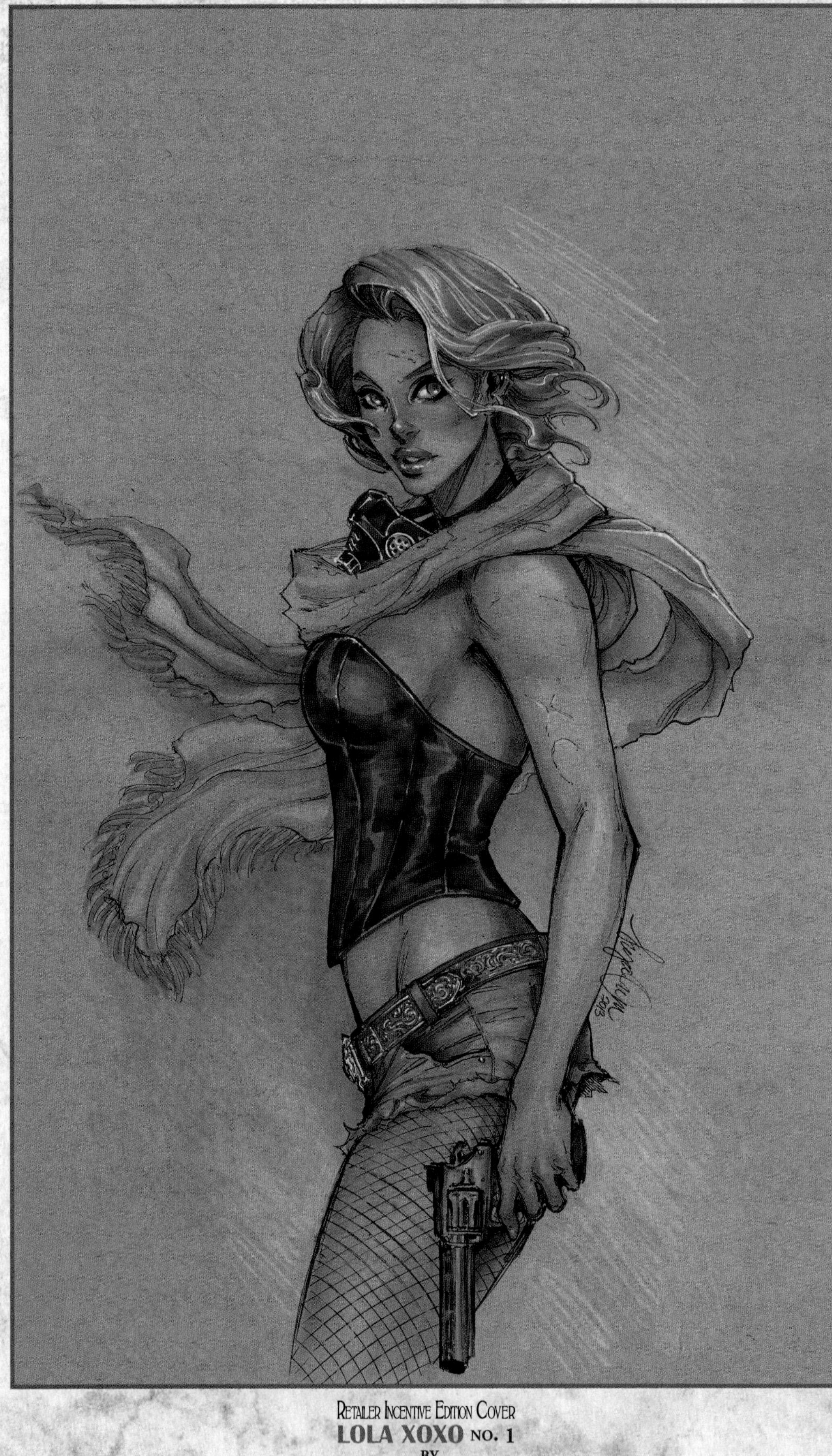

Retailer Incentive Edition Cover
LOLA XOXO NO. 1
BY
Siya Oum

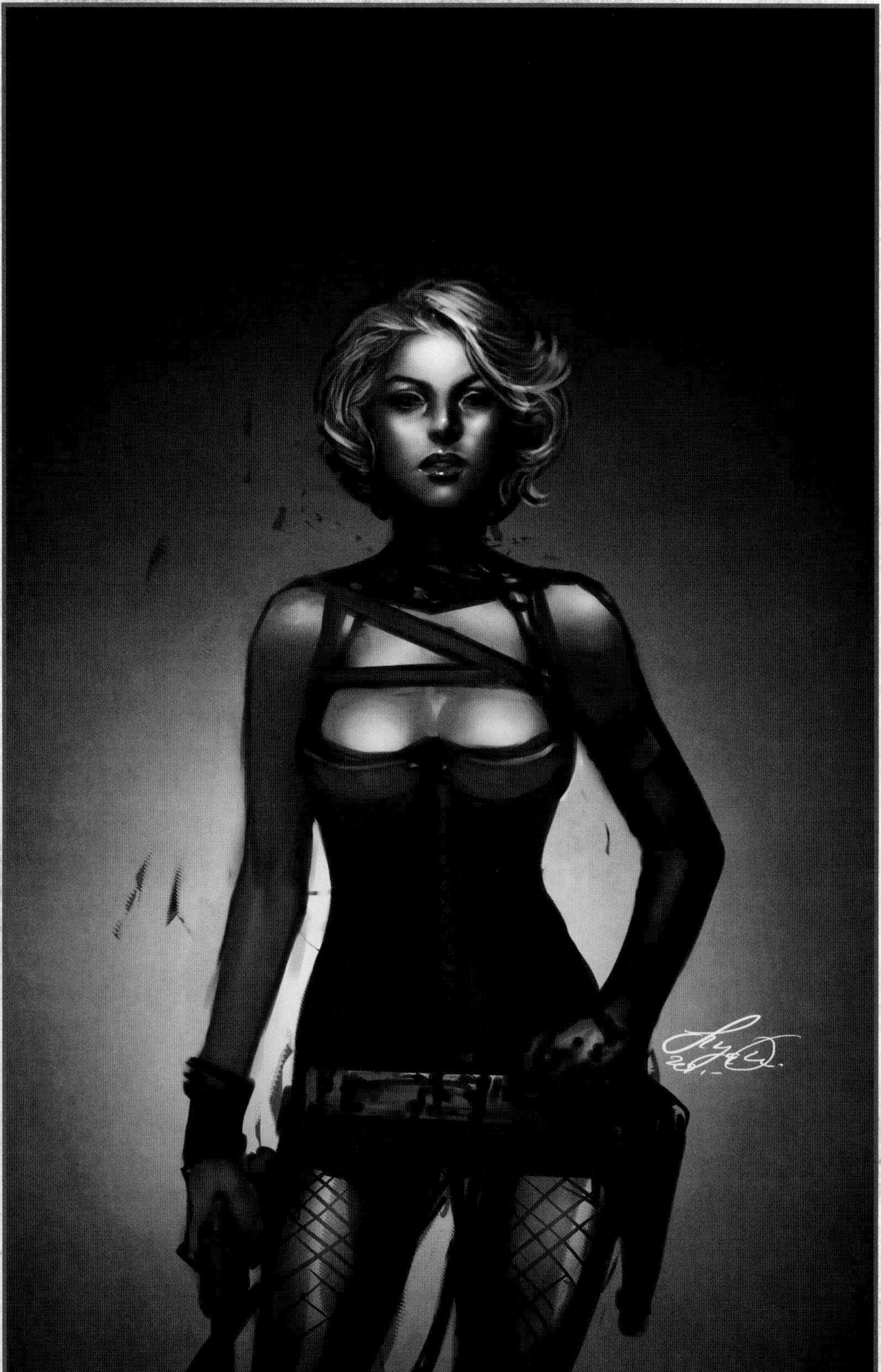

WonderCon Anaheim 2014 Limited Edition Cover
LOLA XOXO NO. 1
BY
Siya Oum

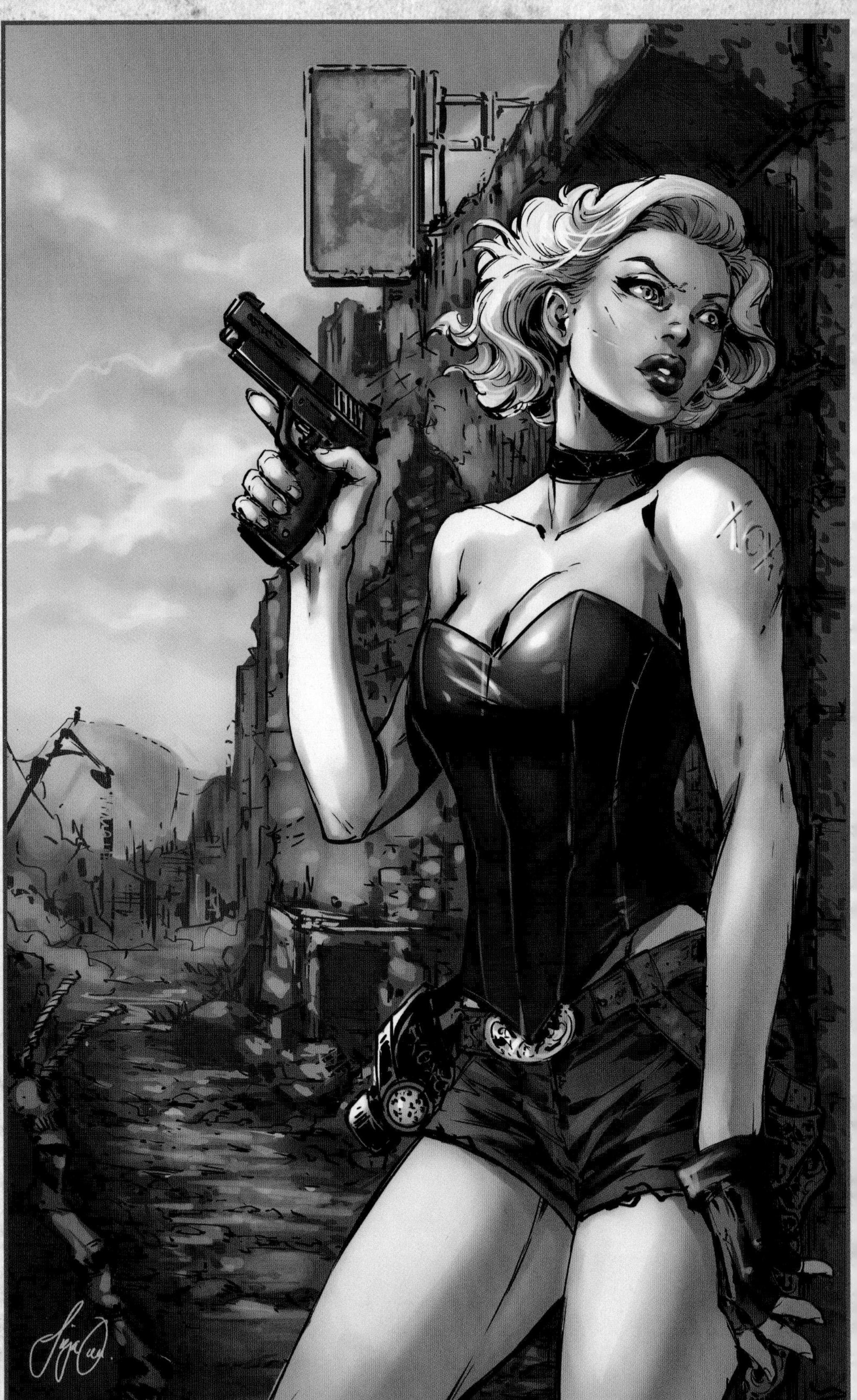
XOXO

Calgary Expo 2014 Limited Edition Cover
LOLA XOXO No. 1
By
Siya Oum

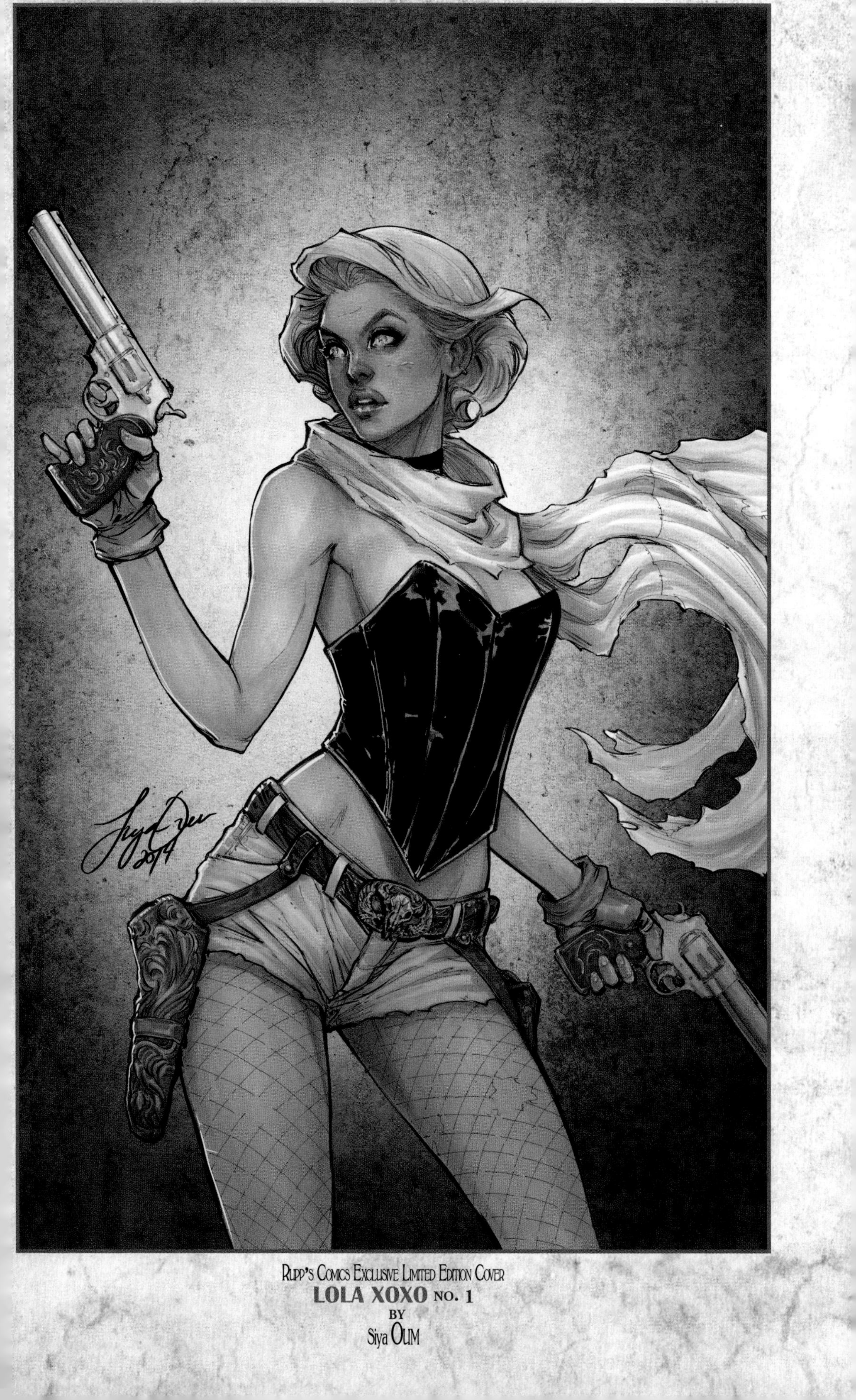

Rupp's Comics Exclusive Limited Edition Cover
LOLA XOXO NO. 1
BY
Siya Oum

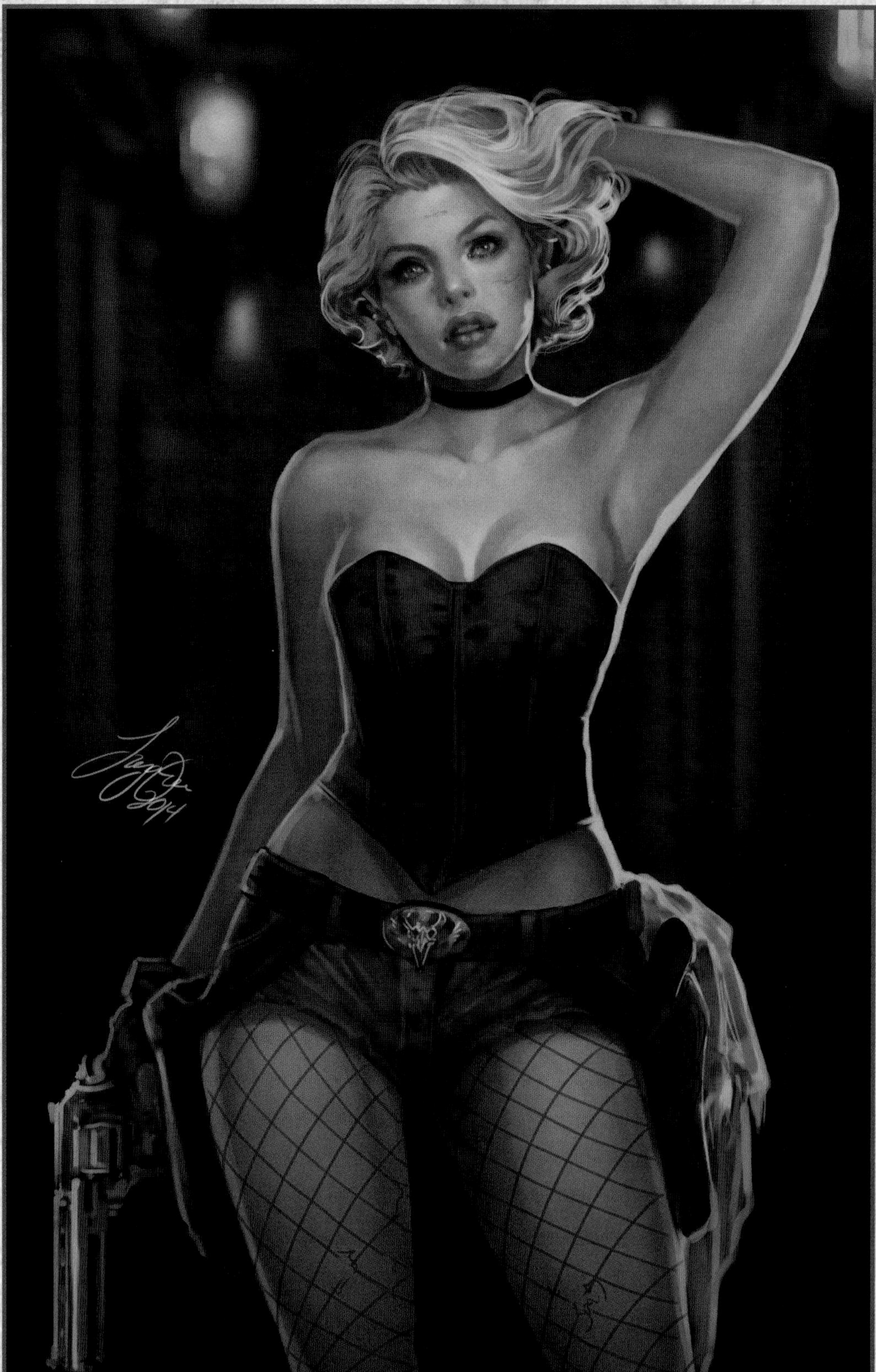

BlueRainbow Online Exclusive Limited Edition Cover
LOLA XOXO no. 1
by
Siya Oum

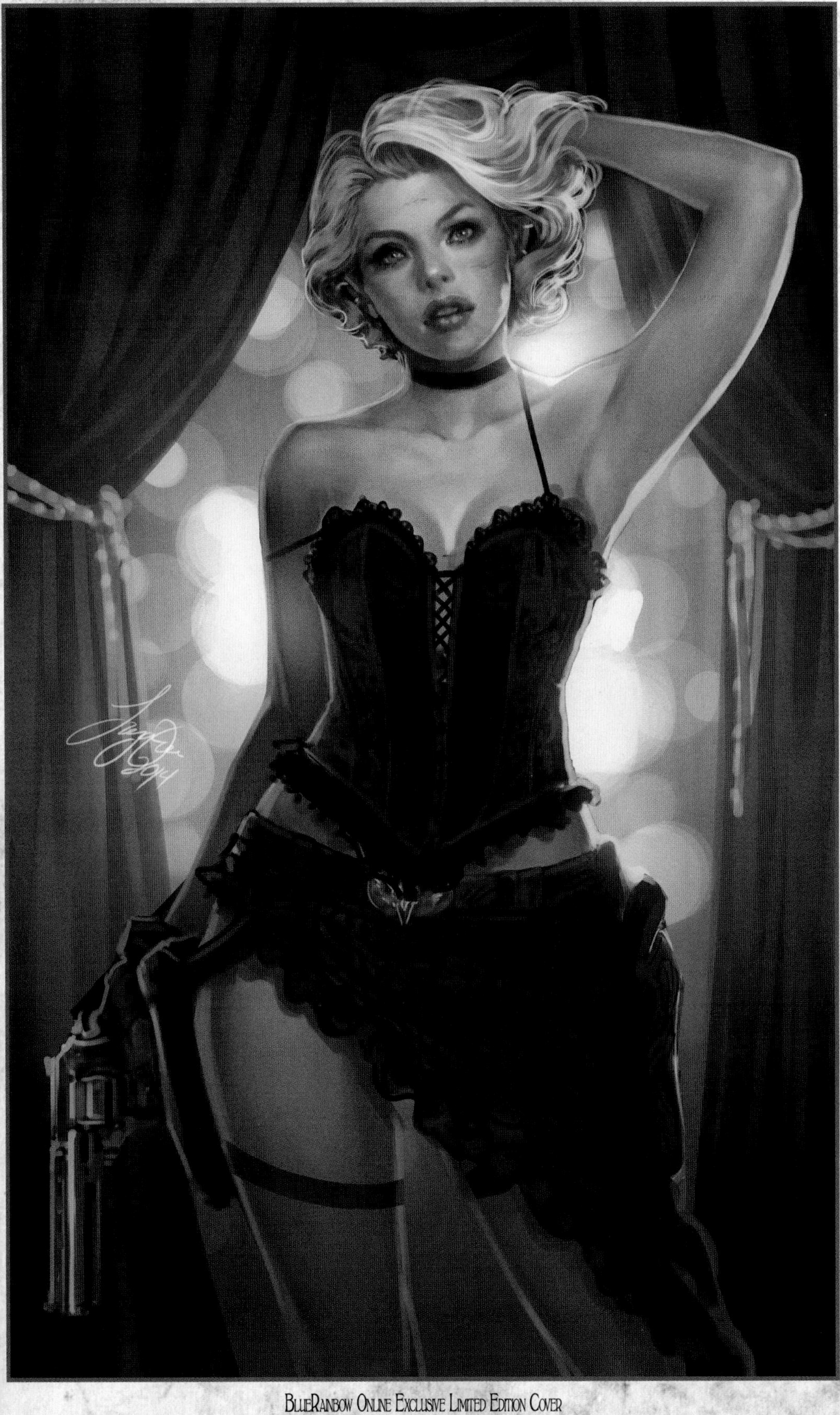

BlueRainbow Online Exclusive Limited Edition Cover
LOLA XOXO NO. 1
BY
Siya Oum

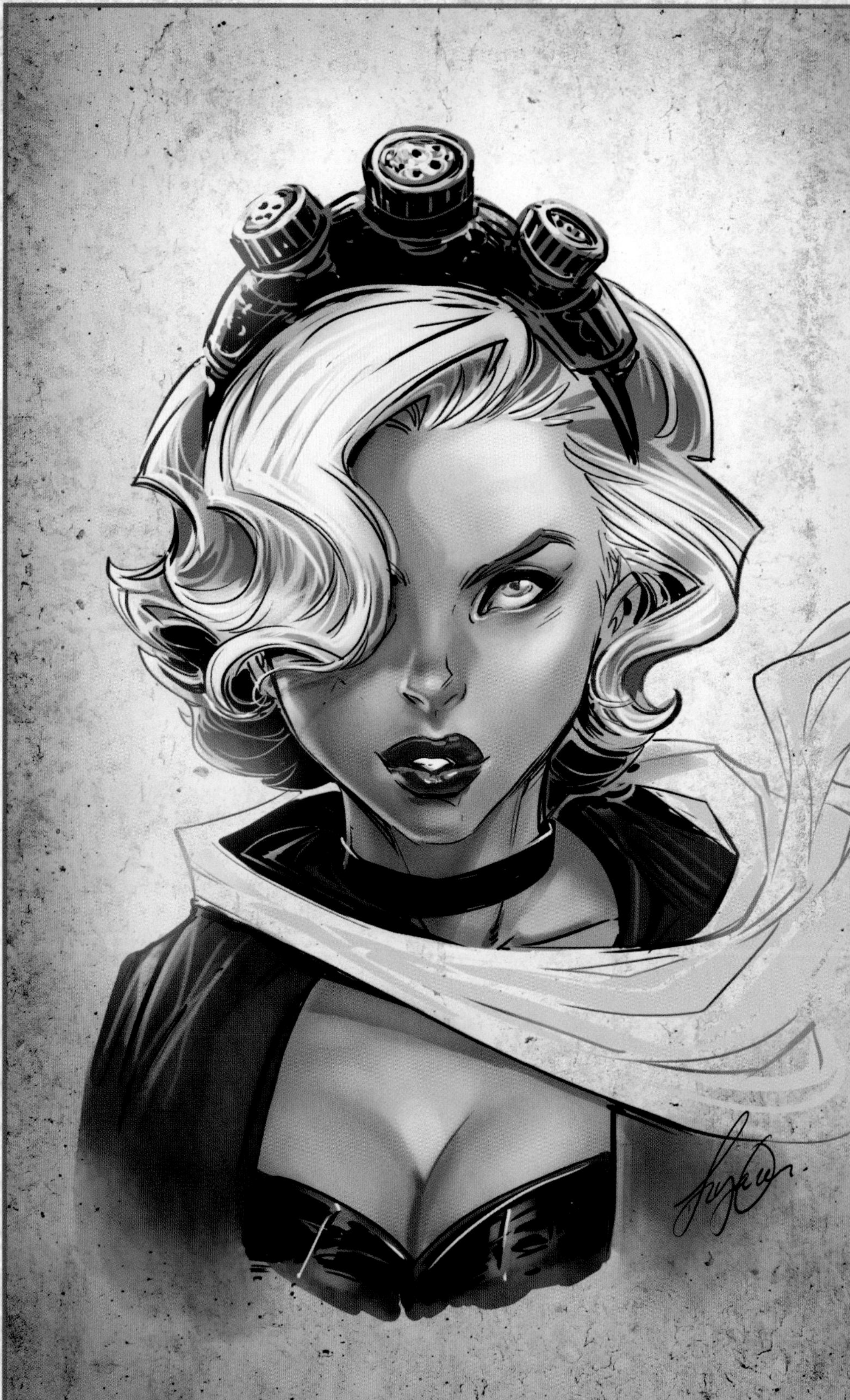

Gotham Central Comics Exclusive Limited Edition Cover
LOLA XOXO NO. 1
BY
Siya Oum

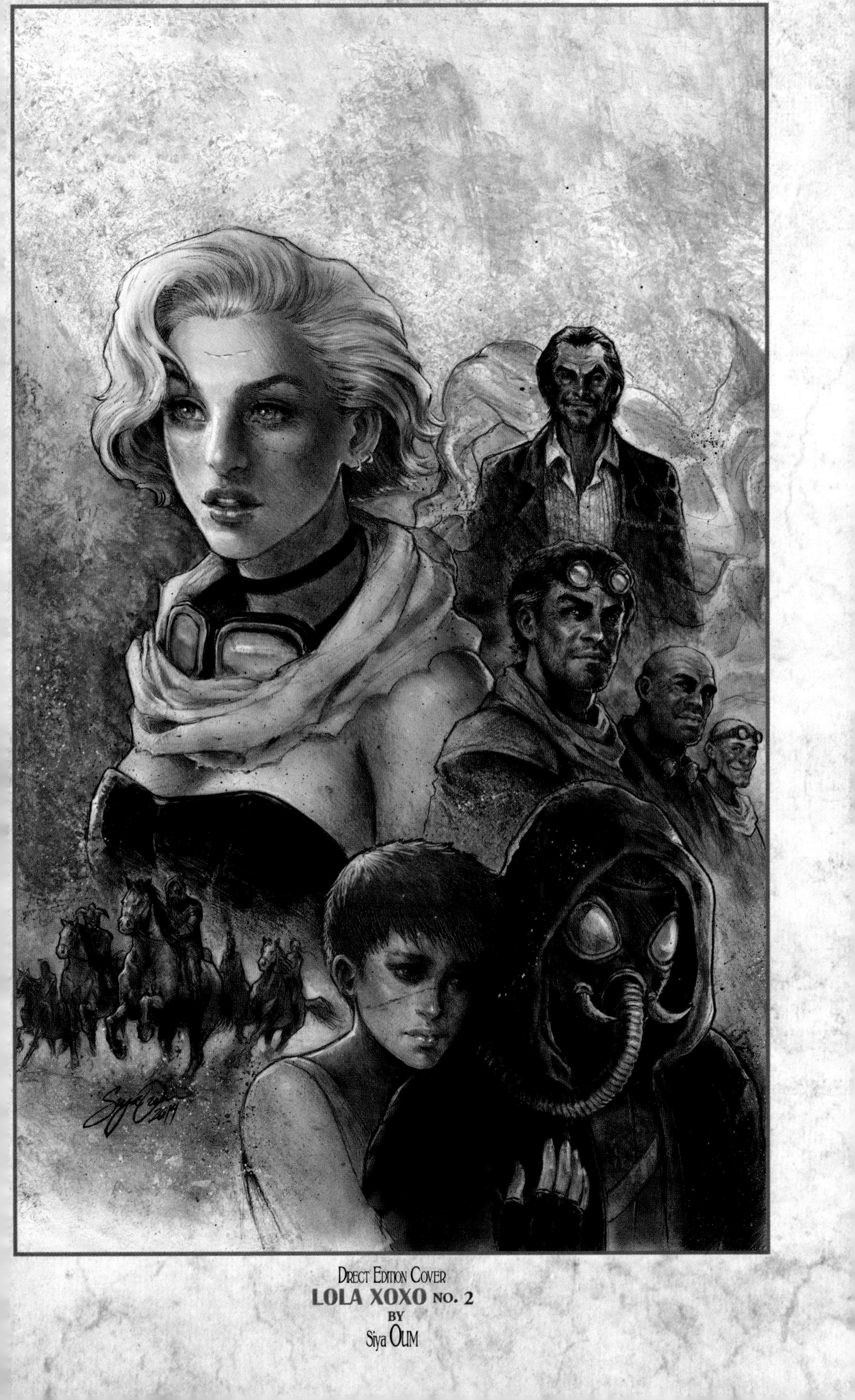

Direct Edition Cover
LOLA XOXO no. 2
by
Siya Oum

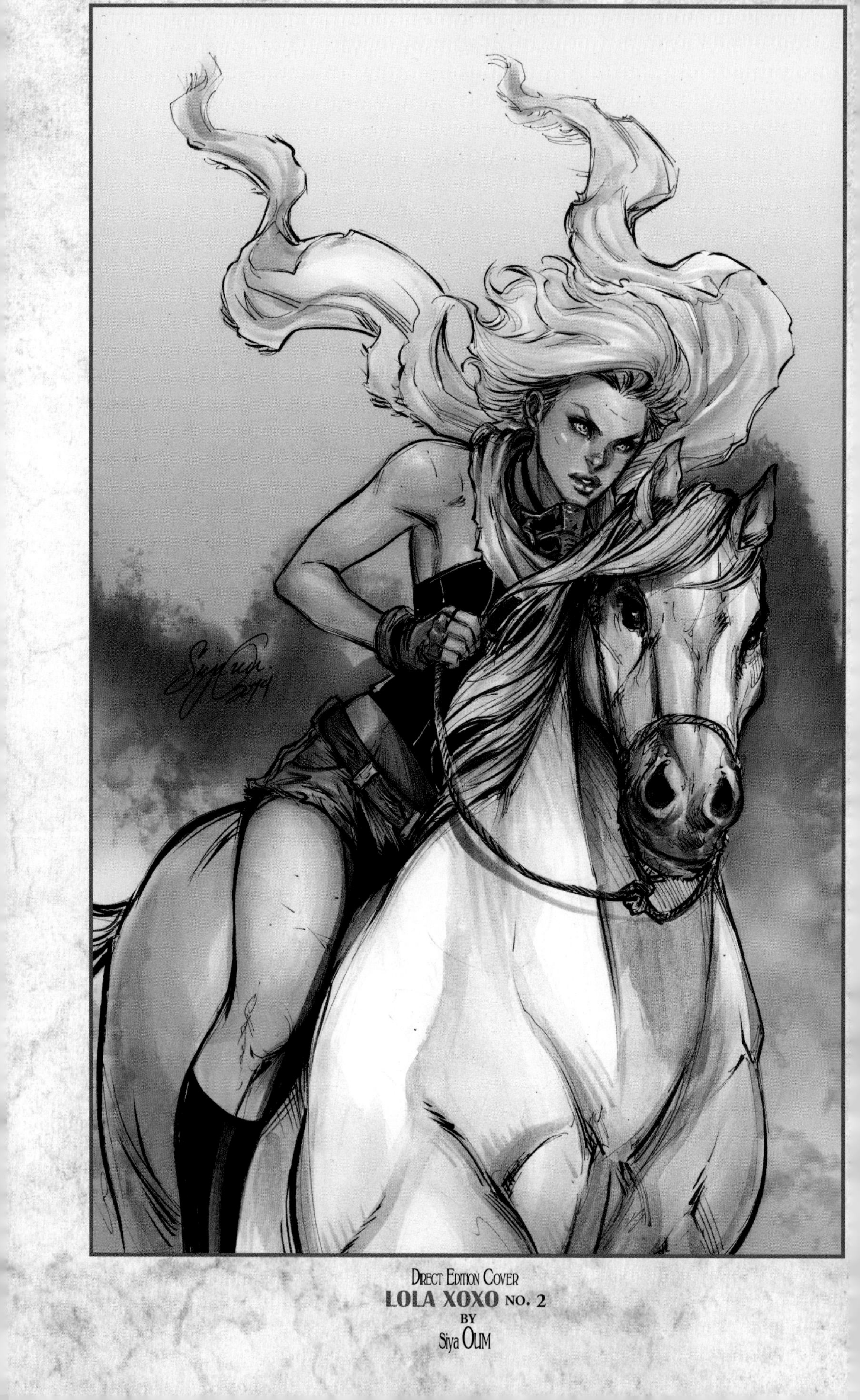

Direct Edition Cover
LOLA XOXO No. 2
by
Siya Oum

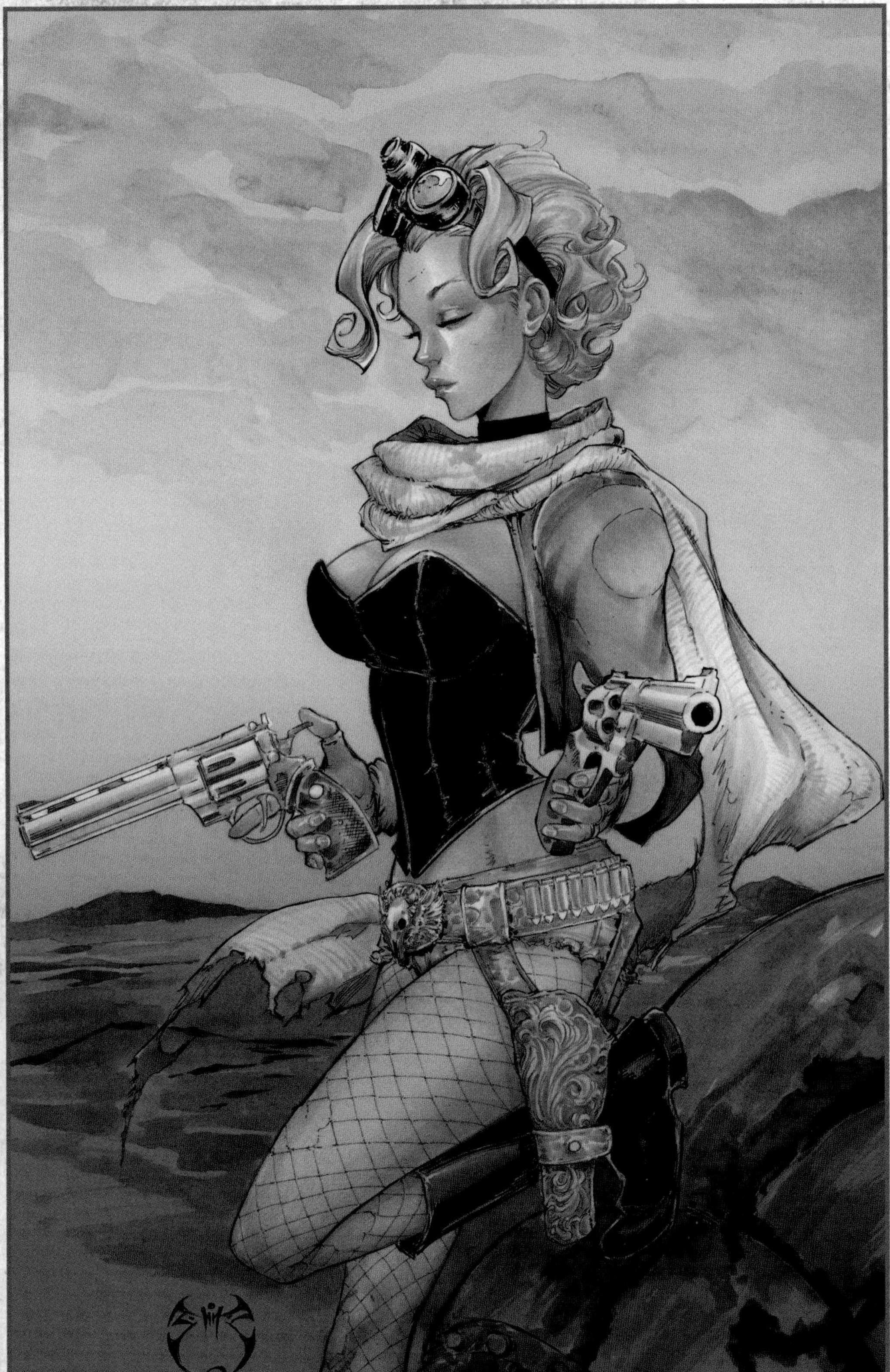

Retailer Incentive Edition Cover
LOLA XOXO NO. 2
BY
Joe Benitez & Siya Oum

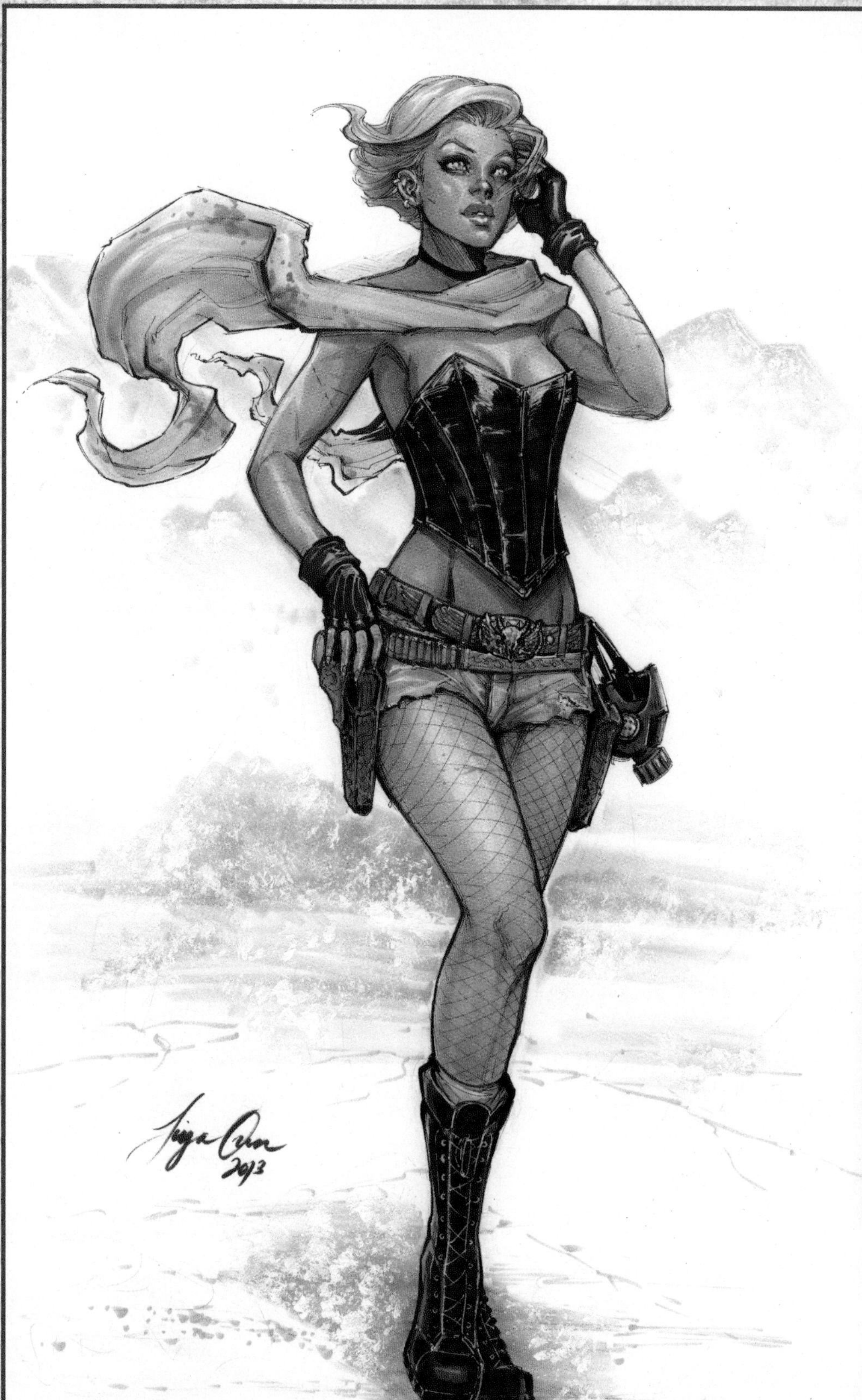

AspenStore.com 2014 Customer Appreciation Limited Edition Cover
LOLA XOXO no. 2
by
Siya Oum

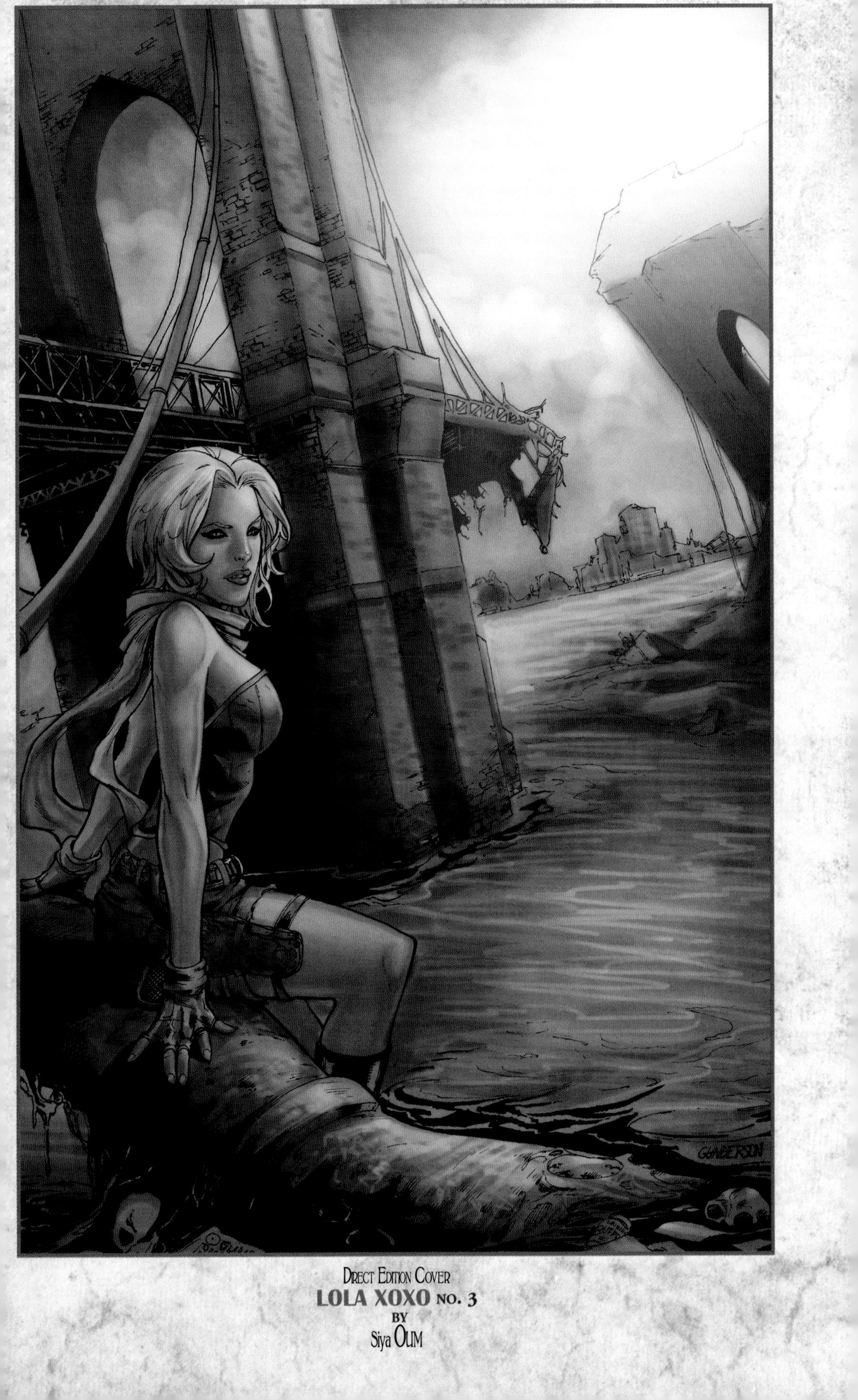
GUNBERSON

Direct Edition Cover
LOLA XOXO NO. 3
BY
Siya Oum

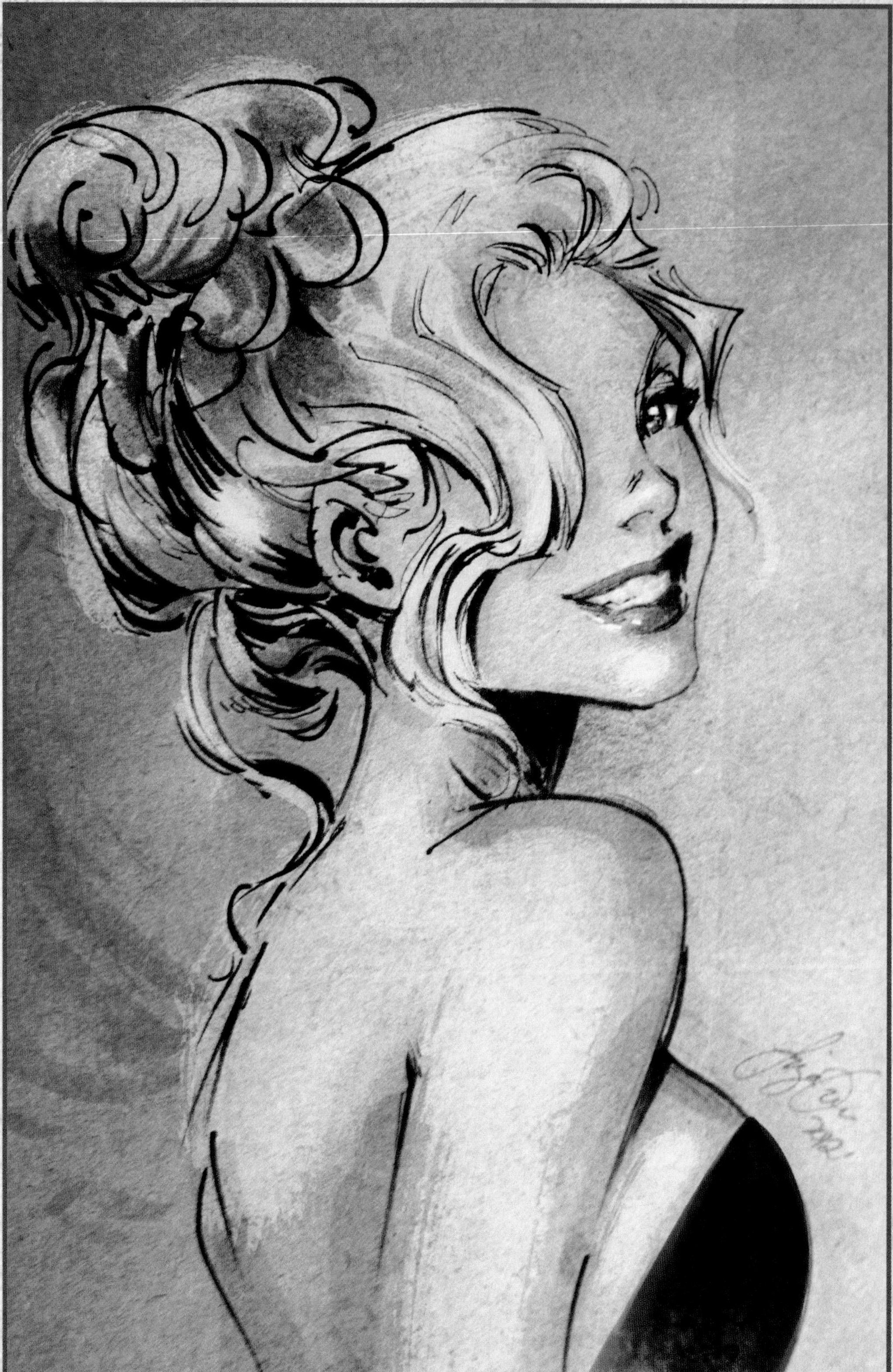

Retailer Incentive Edition Cover
LOLA XOXO no. 3
by
Siya Oum

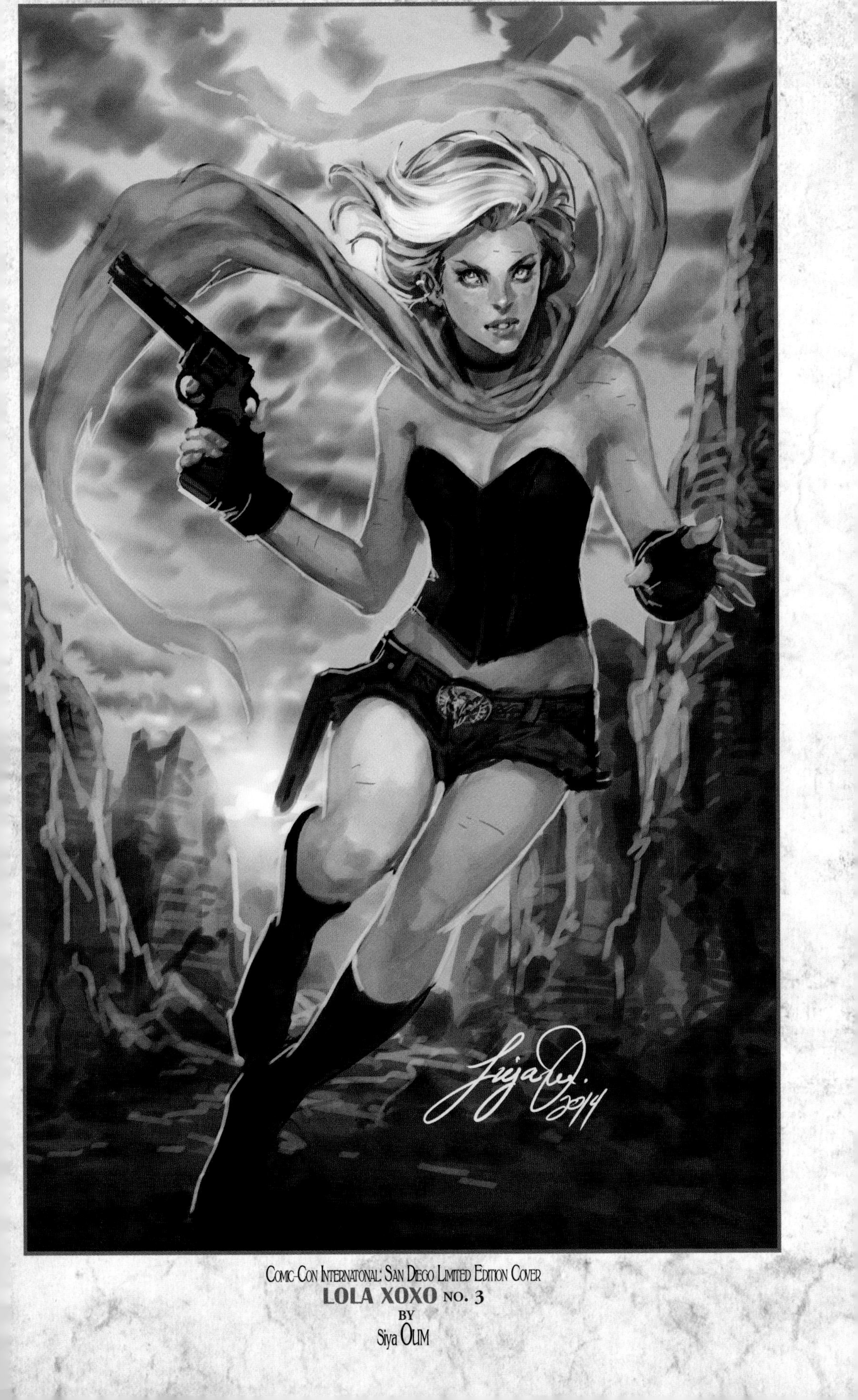

Comic-Con Internatonal: San Diego Limited Edition Cover
LOLA XOXO no. 3
by
Siya Oum

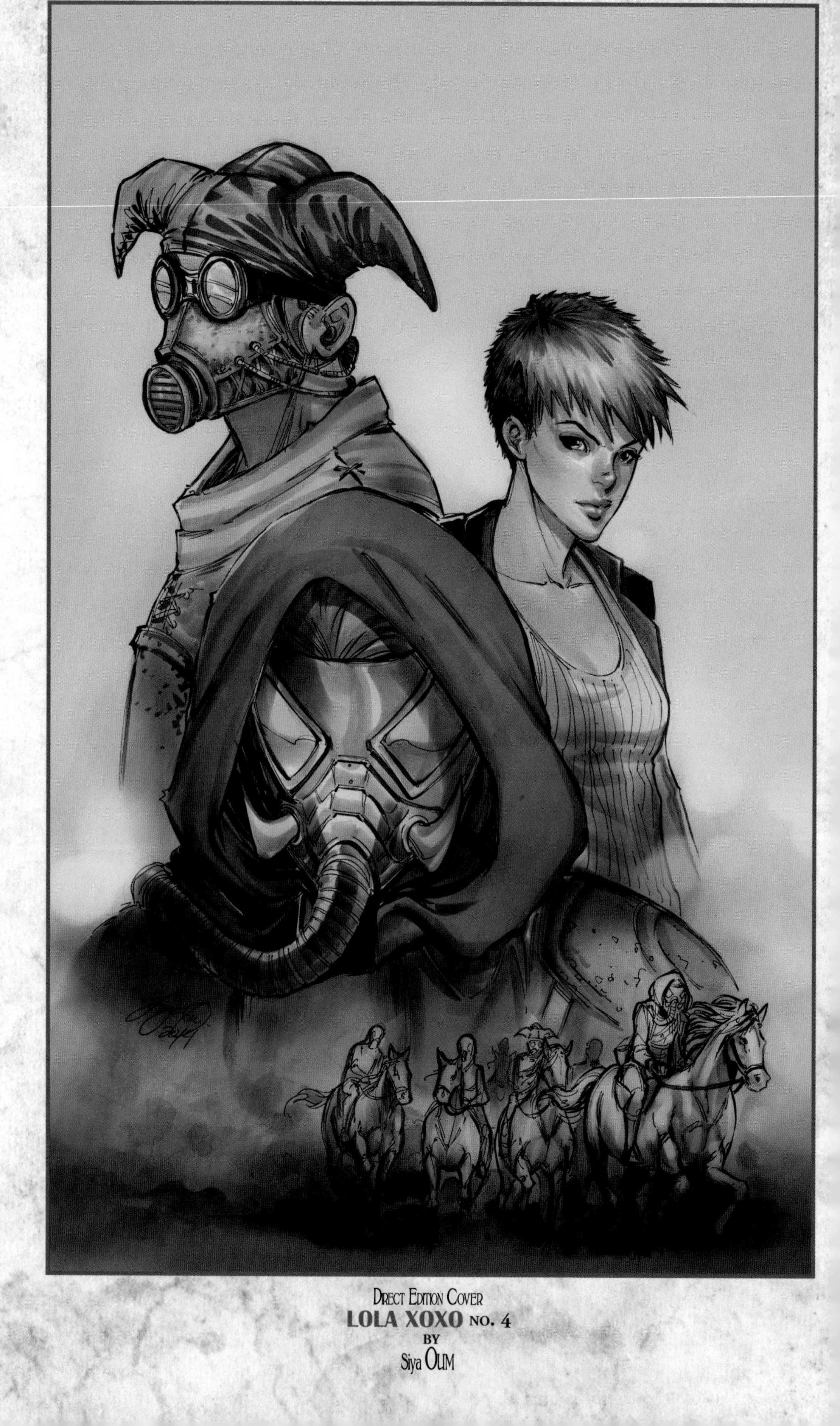

Direct Edition Cover
LOLA XOXO no. 4
by
Siya Oum

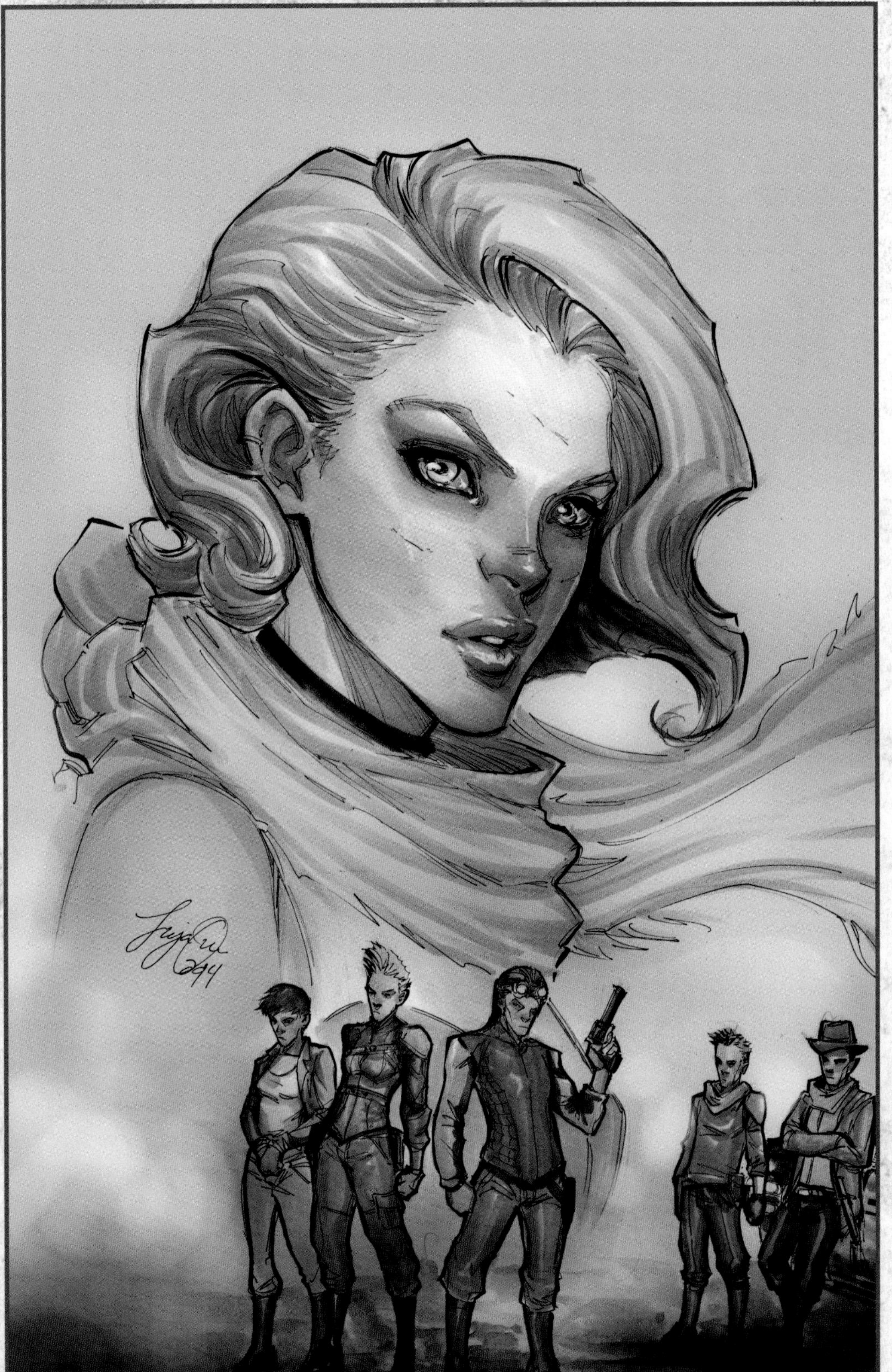

Direct Edition Cover
LOLA XOXO no. 4
by
Siya Oum

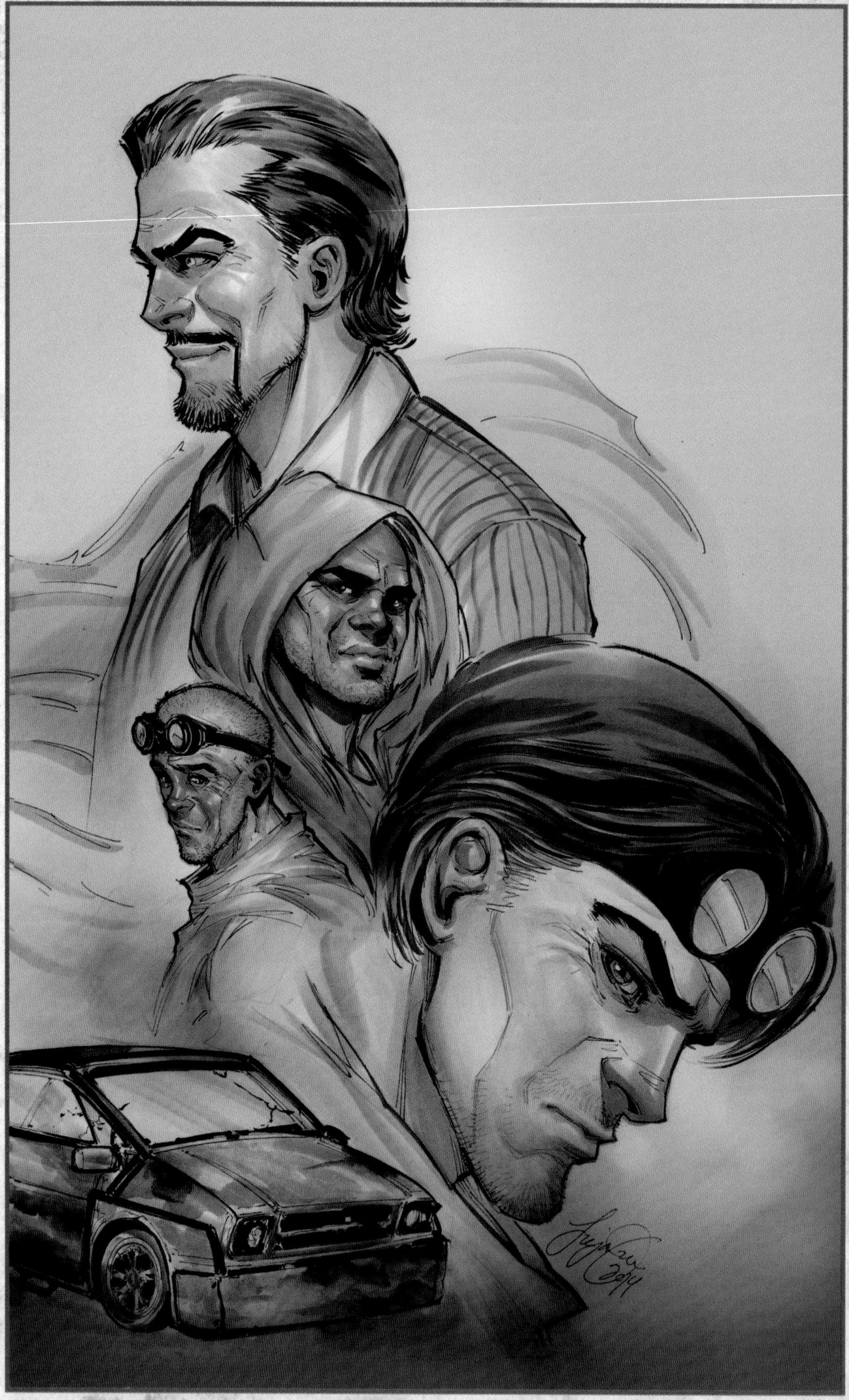

Direct Edition Cover
LOLA XOXO NO. 4
BY
Siya Oum

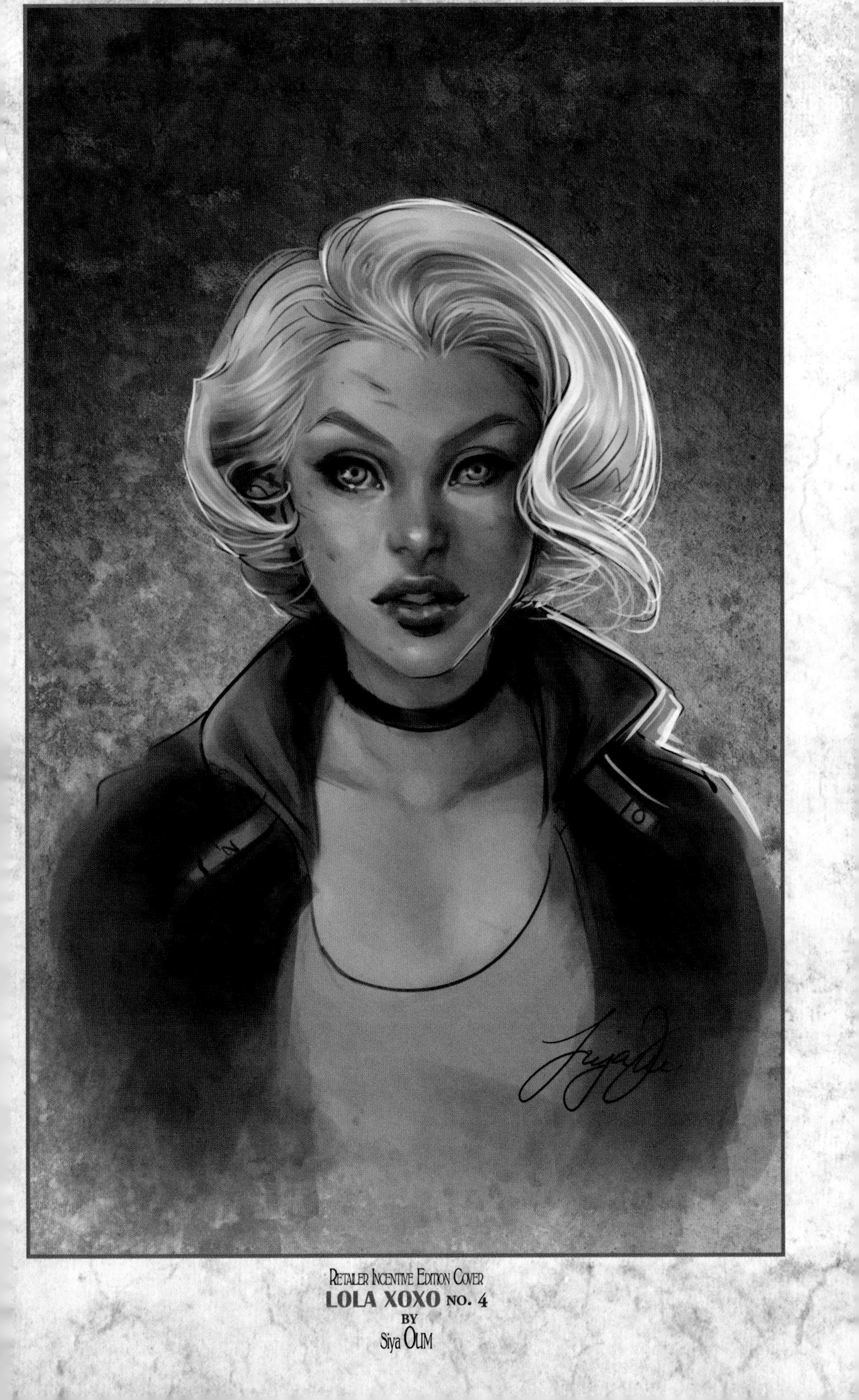

Retailer Incentive Edition Cover
LOLA XOXO NO. 4
BY
Siya Oum

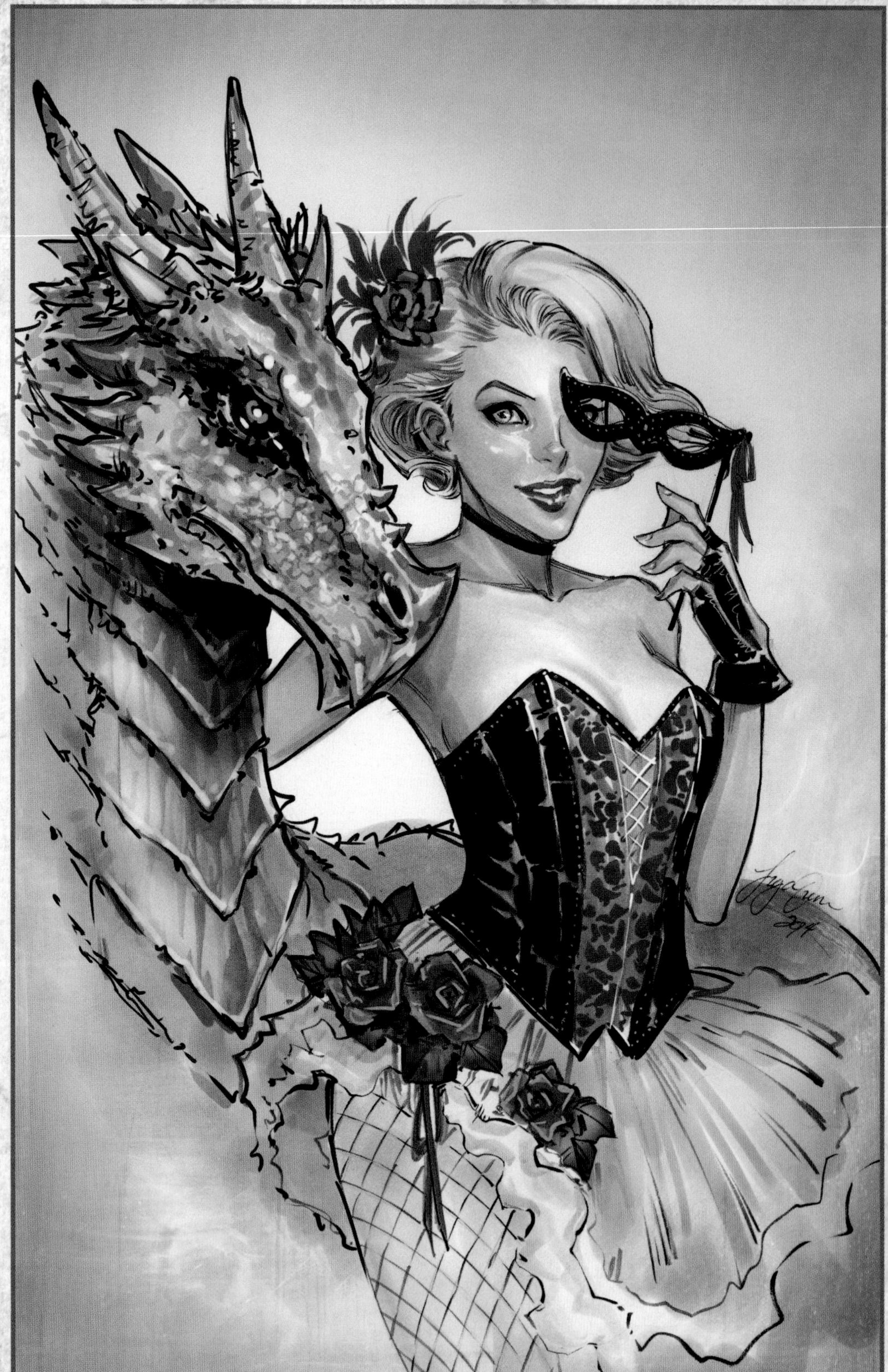

Dragon Con 2014 Limited Edition Cover
LOLA XOXO No. 4
by
Siya Oum

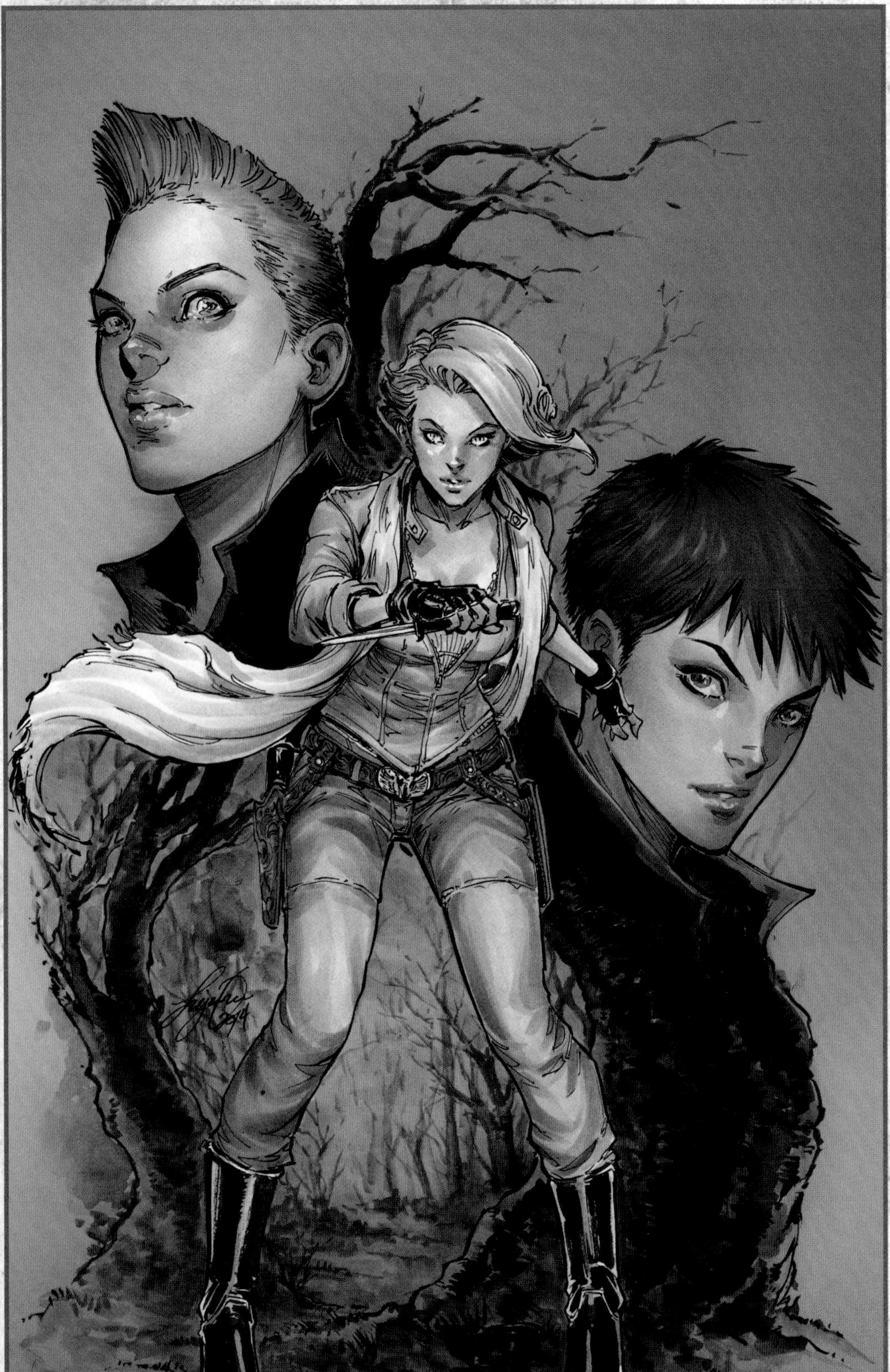

Direct Edition Cover
LOLA XOXO NO. 5
BY
Siya Oum

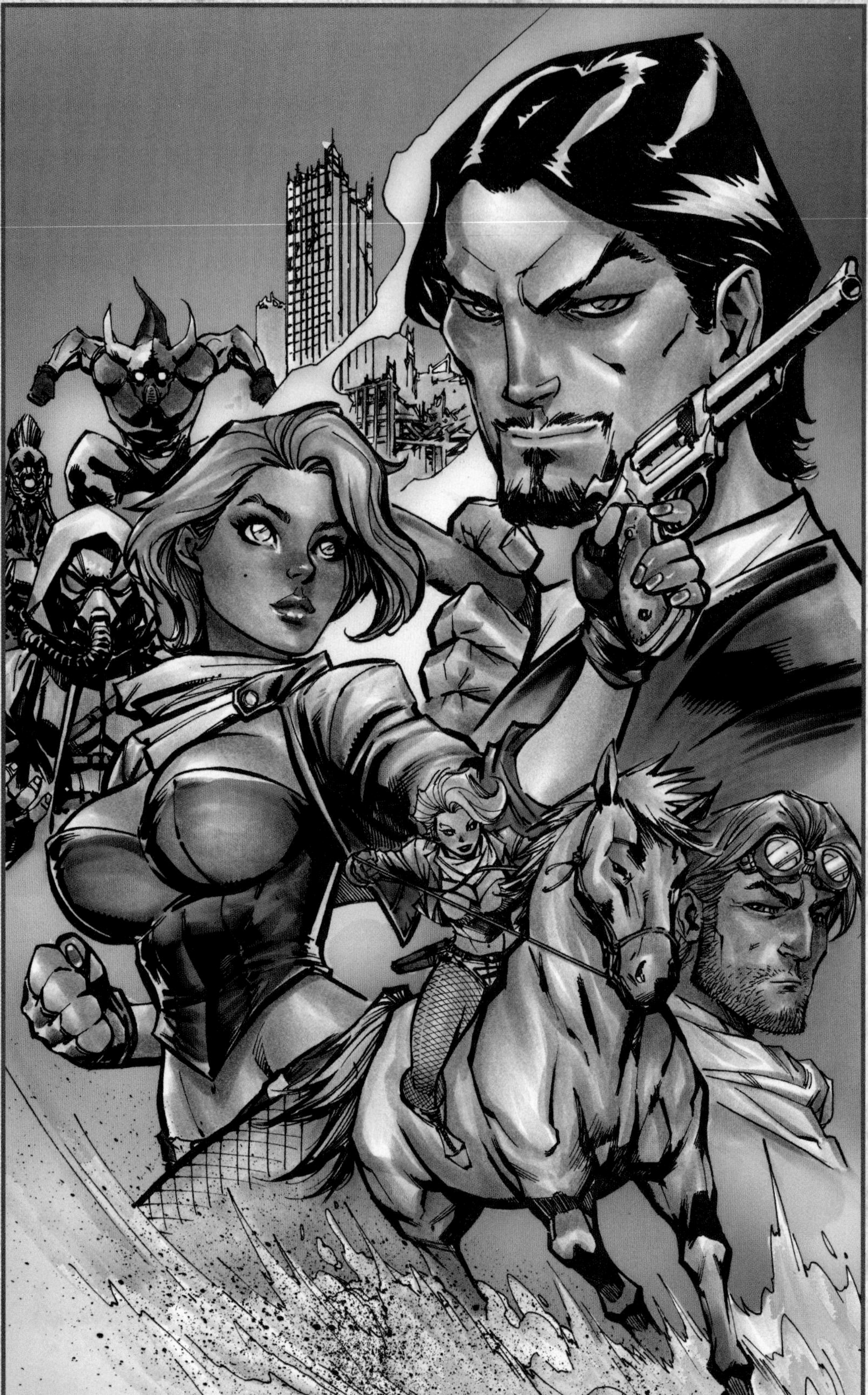

Direct Edition Cover
LOLA XOXO no. 5
by
Alé Garza & Siya Oum

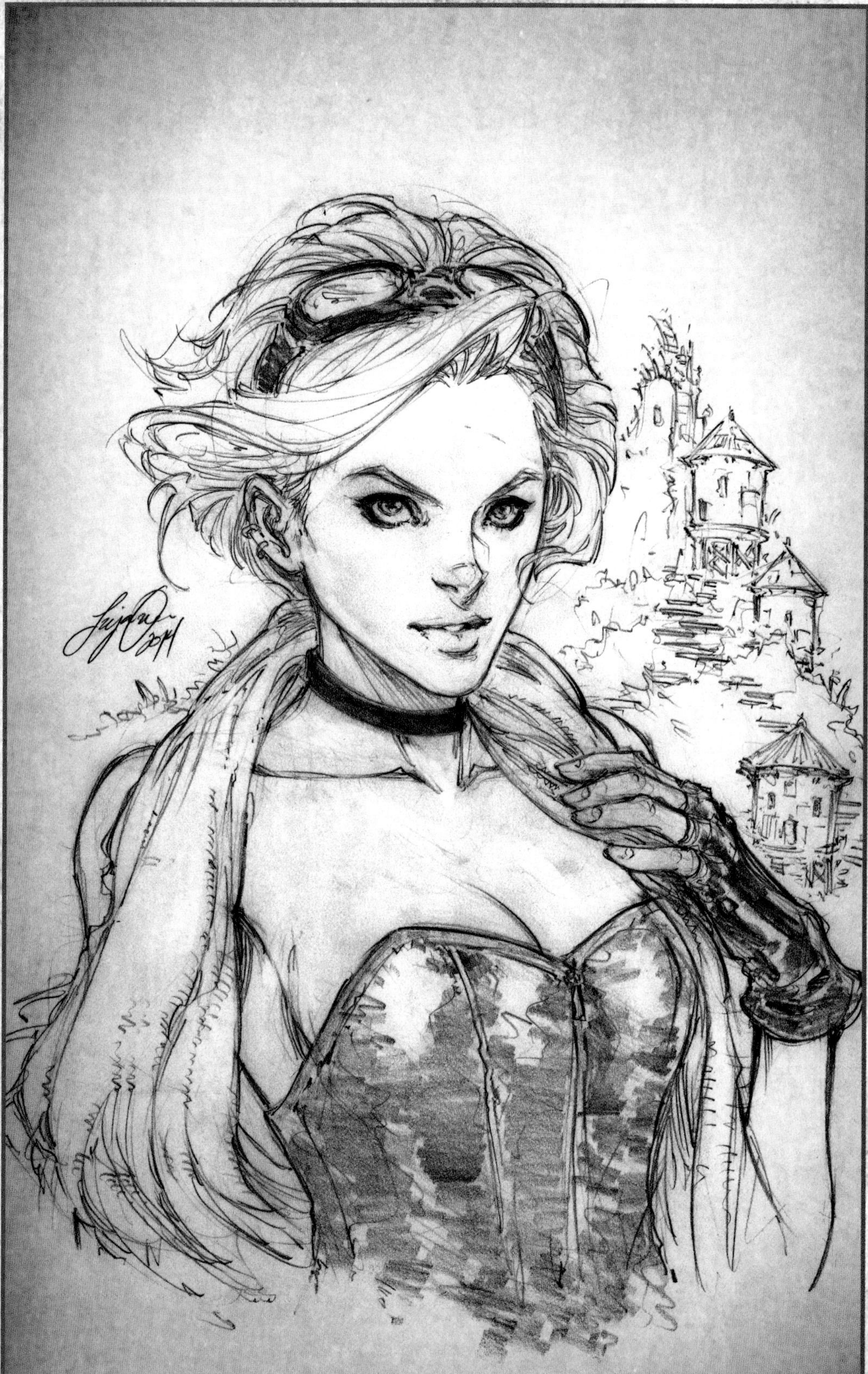

RETAILER INCENTIVE EDITION COVER
LOLA XOXO NO. 5
BY
Siya OUM

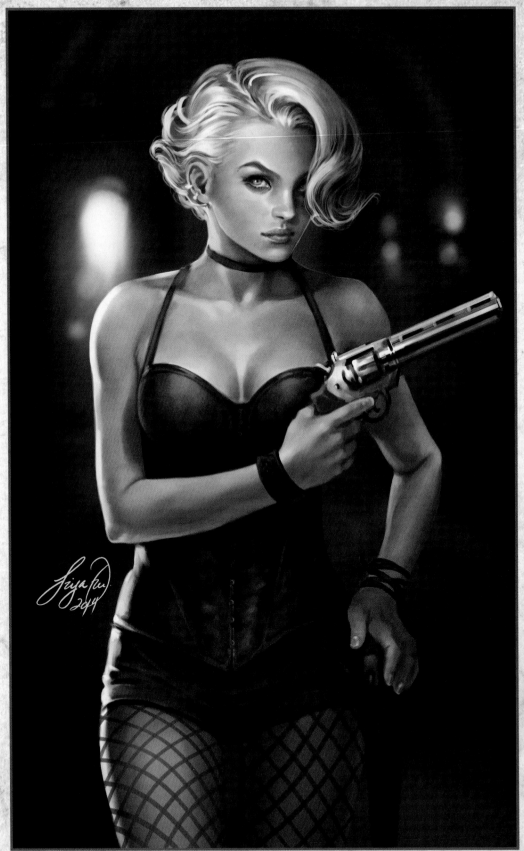

AspenStore.com Black Friday Limited Edition Cover
LOLA XOXO no. 5
BY
Siya Oum

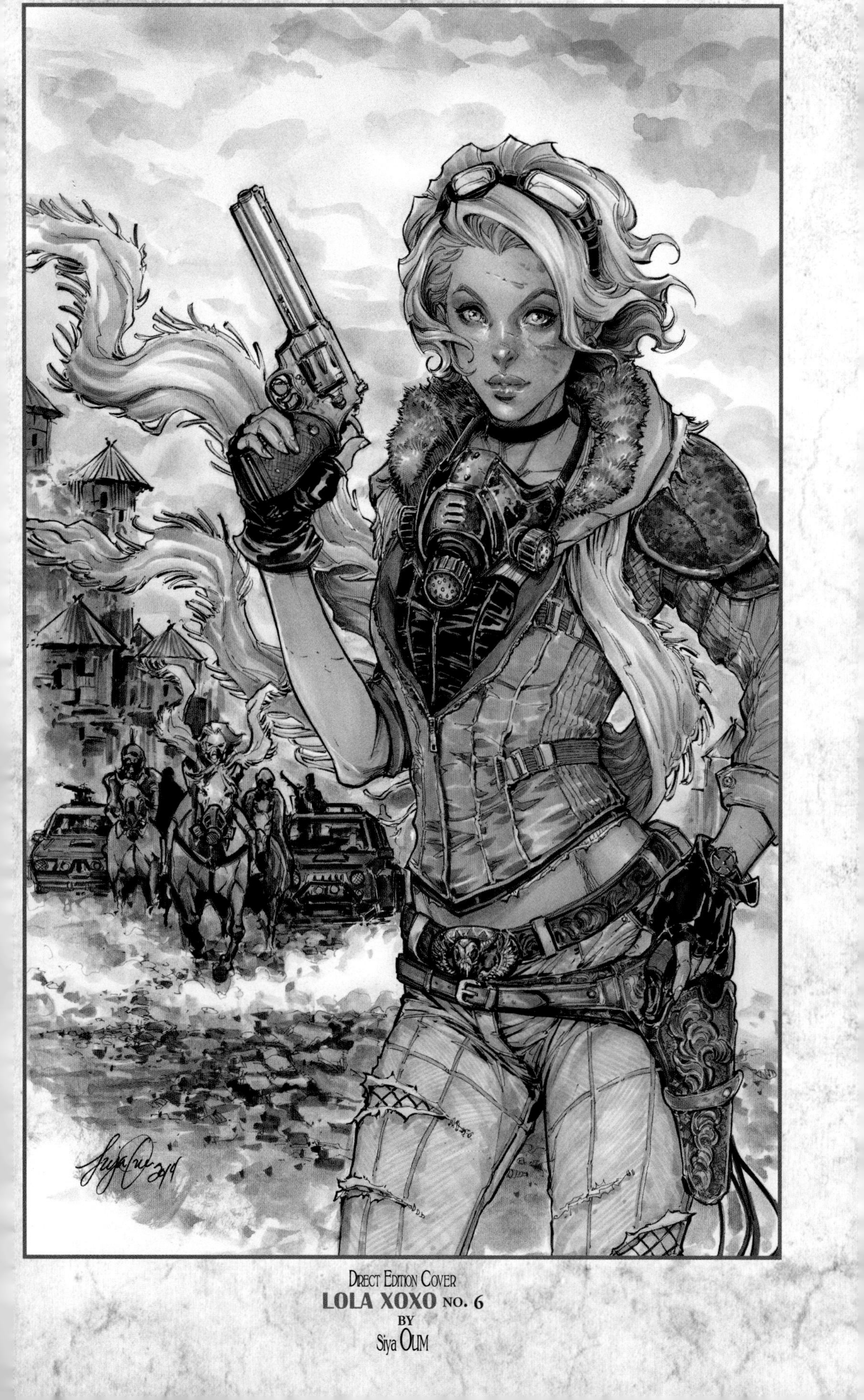

Direct Edition Cover
LOLA XOXO no. 6
by
Siya Oum

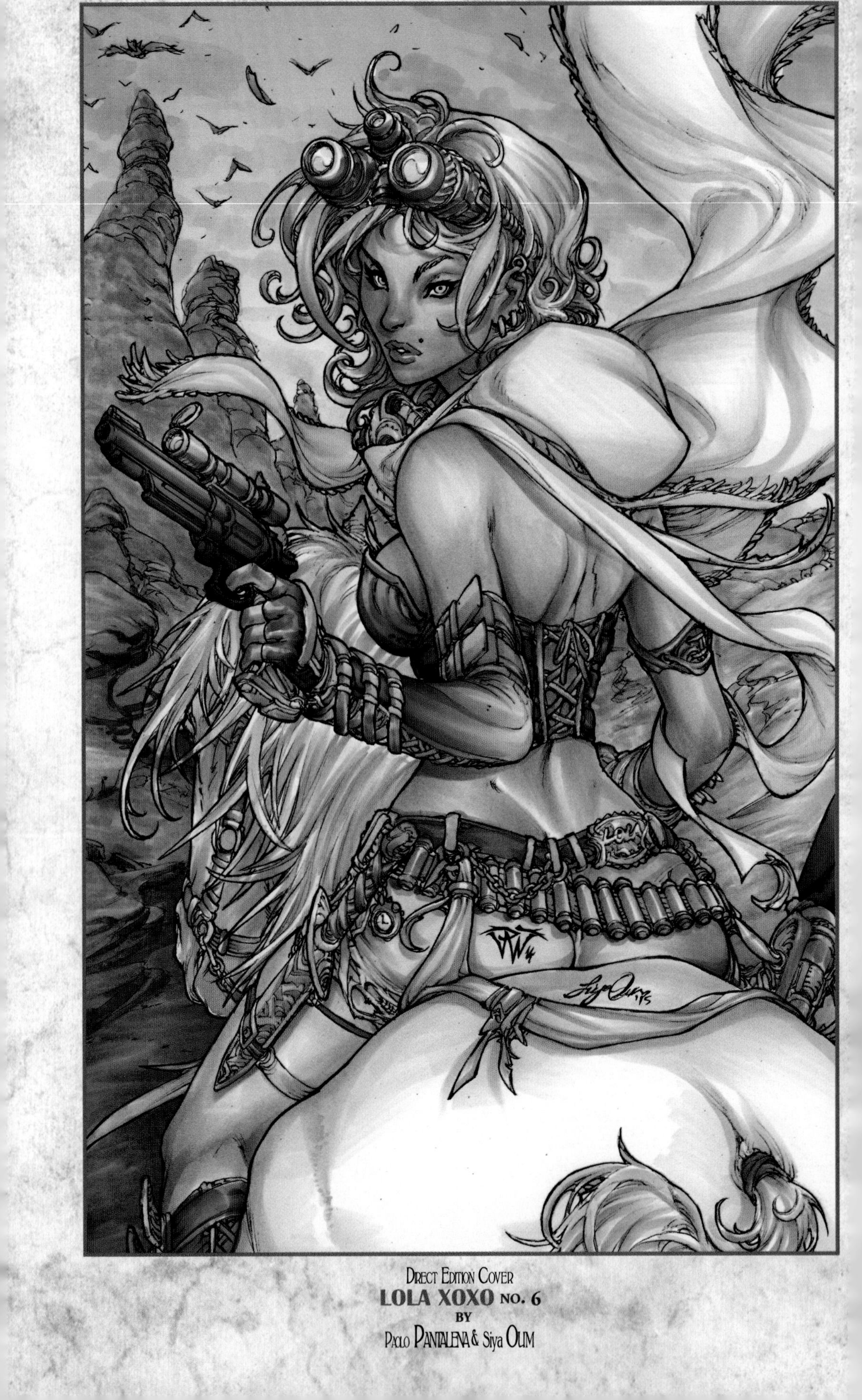

Direct Edition Cover
LOLA XOXO no. 6
by
Paolo Pantalena & Siya Oum

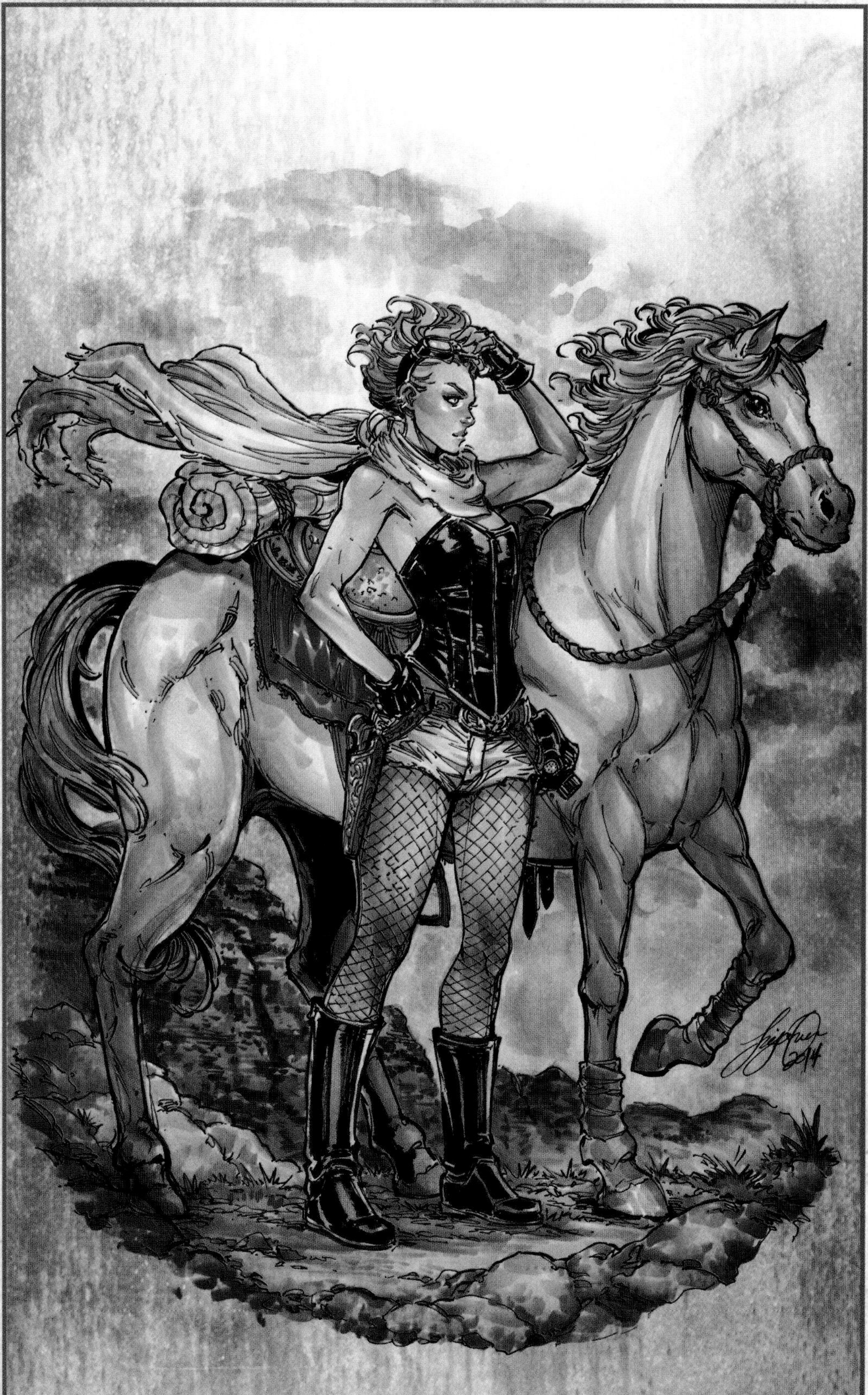

Retailer Incentive Edition Cover
LOLA XOXO no. 6
by
Siya Oum

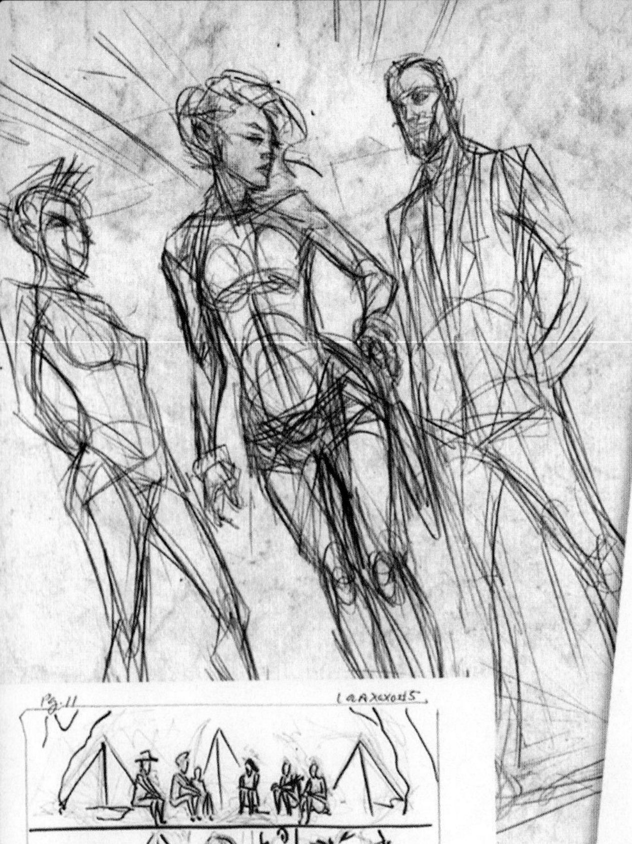

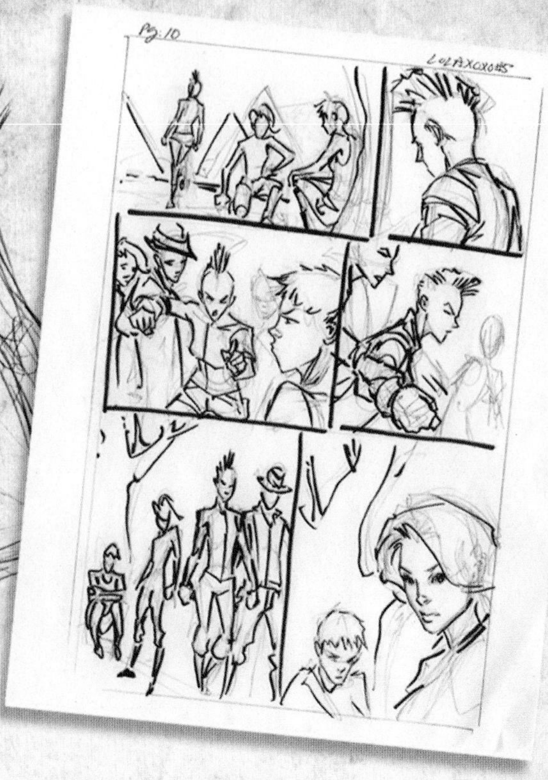
Pg. 10

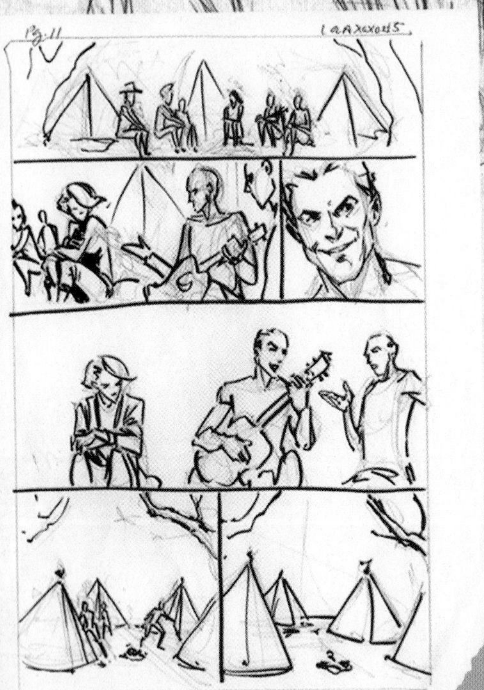
Pg. 11

LAYOUTS & SKETCHE

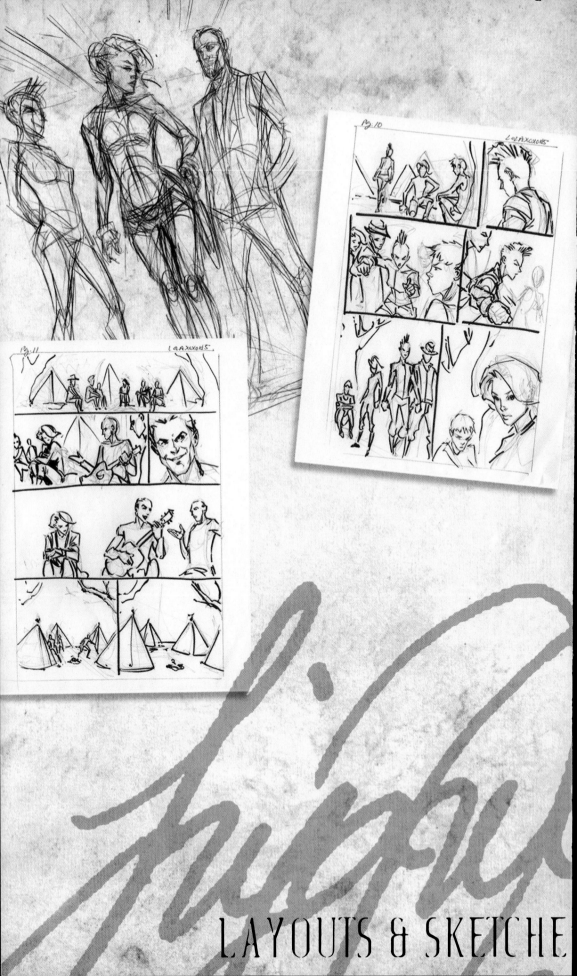

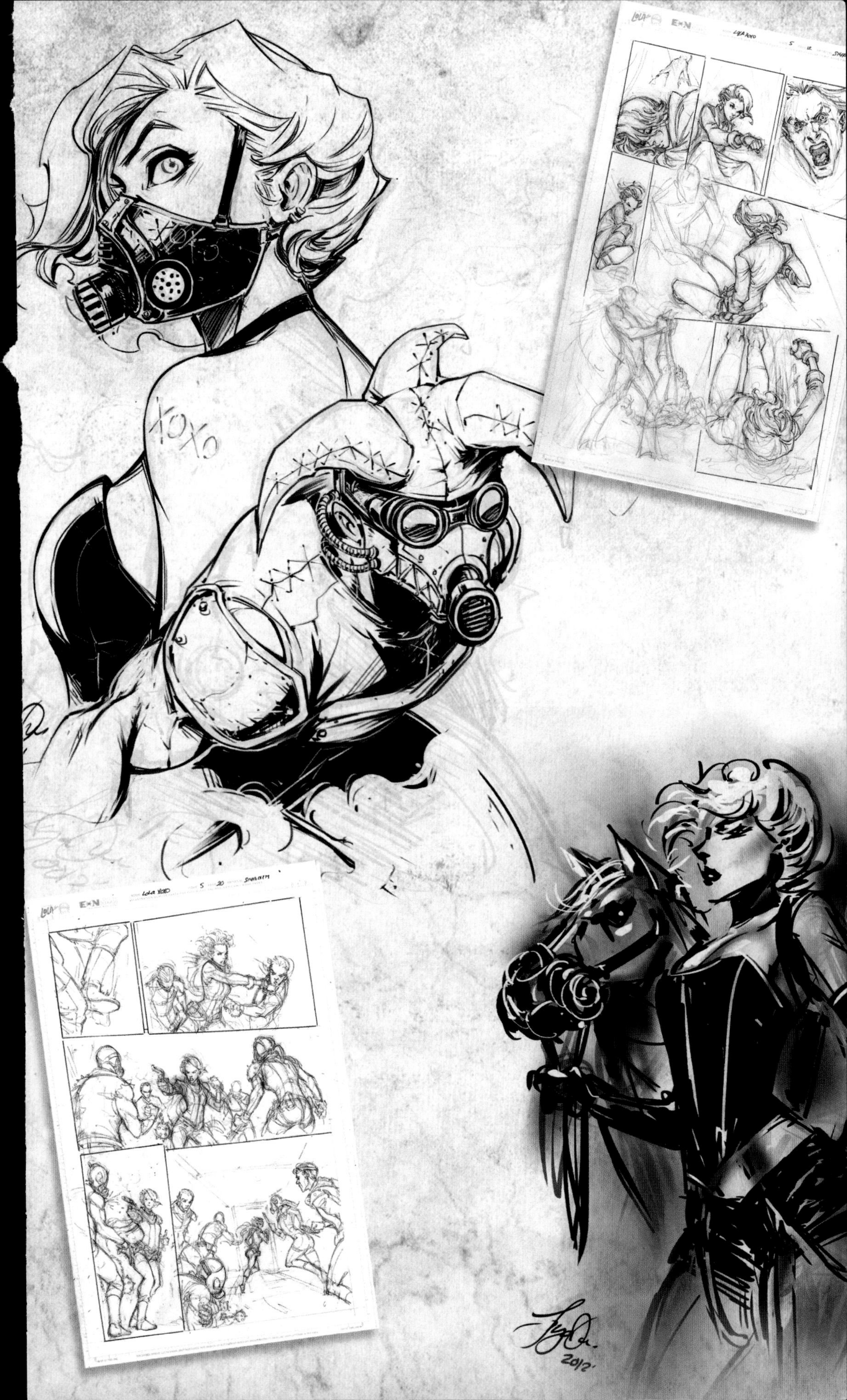
XOXO
2012

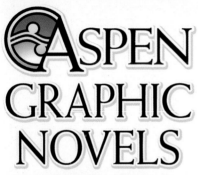